It does have a hang-on-to-your-seat twist in the end. I found all the characters to be quite believable and fascinating. Thank you for giving me the opportunity to read your novel! It really was a pleasure!"

--Beth Gillespie, Professional Technical Writer and Copy Editor.

Ron Stotyn

This book is a work of fiction. All of the characters, organizations, locations and events portrayed in this novel are either figments of the author's imagination or are used entirely in a fictitious manner.

Published by Ronald Irwin Stotyn at
North of Forty Nine Publications
(dba of Marron Holdings LLC)

For information: northoffortynine@gmail.com
Subject=The Chechen's Revenge

Cover Graphics by Shaun F. Stotyn

ISBN: 978-0-692-33721-9

Printed by CreateSpace, An Amazon.com Company
Available from Amazon.com and other online stores
Available on Kindle and other devices

For my sons, their mother, daughter-in-law, and granddaughter.

Ron Stotyn

Table of Contents

(Author's Note: I have used standard government style abbreviations throughout this novel. To aid the reader I have constructed a Glossary following my notes at the end.)

The Chechen's Revenge

A Novel
by
Ron Stotyn, PhD

{Preface}

Vol. 140, No. 13 — March 28, 2002

The Anti-terrorism Act

Order Accepting the Recommendation of the Minister of Defense that The Canadian Anti-Terrorism Agency be established as a branch of the Department of Defense with its Director reporting directly to the Minister.

Whereas, in accordance with R.S., c. F-7 1992, c. 51, s. 102(1) of the National Defense Act His Excellency the Governor General in Council accepted written notification from the Minister of Defense of the Government of Canada pursuant to Article 3 of The Anti-Terrorism Act; recommending establishment of an agency directly responsible to the Minister of Defense for the purpose of developing information about the conduct of Terrorism against the Dominion of Canada, investigation of evidence of such activities, pursuit and bringing to justice perpetrators of such activities. The Canadian Anti-Terrorism Agency shall be subject to all laws of Canada in its conduct and mandate. The Minister shall appoint the Director and agents of the Canadian Anti-Terrorism Agency according to determined need. Any agent of the agency having prior military enrollment shall be reinstated and given a brevet rank commensurate with the level of appointment to the agency. Each member of the agency shall further be subject to the requirements and stipulations of the Official Secrets Act, Security of Information Act, Canada Evidence Act, Canadian Security Intelligence Service Act, National Defense Act, and other rule of law as determined by the Supreme Court of Canada

Therefore, His Excellency the Governor General in Council, on the recommendation of the Minister of Defense, pursuant to subsection 102(1) of the National Defense Act, chapter 10 of the Statutes of Canada, 2001, hereby fixes March 15, 2002 as the day on which The Canadian Anti-Terrorism Agency comes into force.

(Author Note: The above is entirely fictitious.)

Ron Stotyn

{1}

Health Wisdom Integrity (Motto of Stanstead College, Stanstead QC)

Saturday, the first day of April, very early morning: Ottawa, ON

It was an odd time to be in the downtown business section, unless perhaps one was homeless. So early in fact, that the public transportation system had not yet begun its daily runs. There was no activity on O'Conner Street, seen from the dark shadows of an alleyway where a very tall, lithe, dark haired man had already been standing for nearly half an hour on April Fool's Day. The time was approaching 5 AM, fairly early even for him, especially on a weekend day, despite the fact he preferred to run before dawn most days. With no schedule calling for his immediate attention; he was no fool. This man was deliberate and not homeless.

Though very early in the spring, this particular Ottawa day was mild. There had been a thaw and the street was bare of snow. Ottawa had a reputation for being a clean and tidy city and this street was no exception. Most buildings in the Parliamentary District were old, federal architecture in style which meant uninspired to his mind, mainly of granite construction, probably Stanstead granite, but of good repair. He had walked with resolute stride to this spot across 11 blocks of darkened, empty streets from the Lisgar Extended Stay Suites. That was a somewhat tired residential hotel at Lisgar and Cartier, on the edge of the Parliament Hill district of downtown Ottawa. He'd checked in just a couple of days earlier, having left his apartment in Montreal for a change of locale occasioned by a new job. This morning he had dressed in a charcoal and deep red jogging suit for the cross town walk, the better for fading into the shadows. Anyone who saw him in such garb so early in the morning would take little notice of a man out for exercise. His athletic shoes made no sound on the pavement. The dark outfits had served him well many times when he needed others to disregard his presence.

He had walked at a steady efficient pace, though not overly brisk, taking about twenty minutes to his destination, as he considered that he was being loaned to a relatively new agency within the Department of National Defense. *Or was it a loan,* he wondered, as he thought that maybe there was a message in the action that he should move on to new things. *It is an incontrovertible fact that my style annoys my superiors.*

He had been posted in Ottawa before; following his 1984 graduation with a BA (Hon) in Political Science and Economics from the Royal Military College (RMC) in Kingston, ON. That event had followed a battery of academic coursework and four summers of military training as an Officer Cadet, beginning with basic officer training from July to August prior to his first year. His experience as a 17-year-old cadet was rough, despite having considerable athletic ability; he had been stretched almost beyond endurance. *Certainly there were times I thought I could not survive the rigorous daily physical routines.* His second summer prior to second year was spent at Canadian Forces Leadership and Recruit School, Saint-Jean-sur-Richelieu, Quebec in the BMOQ program. *Again, I had to endure physically and psychologically demanding courses with considerable mental stress during the training. Had I not been successful, and I nearly was not, I certainly would not be here today. My most basic mistake had been a failure to control an academic arrogance; a mistake quickly disciplined by the RSM.*

He mentally corrected himself as he recalled that fearsome soldier was actually a Master Warrant Officer. Regimental Sergeant Major was an appointed position rather than a rank in the Canadian Forces. The experience was a lesson relearned several times since. *My academic achievements, excellent, were matters of fact, nothing more, but my expression of that was often perceived differently than intended. At least once I am sure that had meant a delayed promotion that I had earned.* His third and fourth summers involved Canadian Army Environmental and trade specific training courses without much incident. *Well, without significant discipline and also without notable excellence.* That still frustrated him and enforced the focus of his attention to details.

Ron Stotyn

Upon graduation, he'd been commissioned only as Second
Lieutenant, despite his Honors level BA. He knew that his classmates,
for the most part, had received the rank of Lieutenant and he knew, to
his regret, it was because they had learned better than him to be team
players. Still, because of his academic excellence, he got his preferred
assignment to the Canadian Forces Security Branch, but then was
seconded immediately to the 5e Régiment d'artillerie légère du
Canada, a unit of the Royal Canadian Horse Artillery. It was meant to
be a year of on-the- job training in Quebec City, a learning experience
in leading others. That had also been a mental struggle, for his heart
was far away from artillery command. His record showed he was
adequate, but just barely. Excellence once again eluded him, part of his
continuing frustration. After a year he was returned to his priority
assignment. It now was to the Intelligence Branch which had split off
from the Security Branch earlier in 1985.

The posting was Ottawa. His promotion to Lieutenant finally
came a year after that, leaving him two years behind his classmates.
He never caught up. He left army service in 1998, having completed
the five years required service and then some. This came after a unit
command Major suggested privately that his single-minded focus on
completing two criminology degrees persuaded the Commandant that
he would never be suitable senior officer material. Criminology was
still a passion, often driving his deep need to catch the perpetrator of
whatever transgression as his obligation to resolve. He remembered
the branch Motto: Out of Darkness, Light. *Have I ever seen the light?*

With no army career no longer possible, but an MA and a
Ph.D. in Criminology in hand, he chose an unconventional approach to
his future. He had decided to become a policeman and so applied to
the Sûreté du Quebec. To his surprise, he was accepted as a novice
detective and assigned to the district of Abitibi-Témiscamingue-Nord-
du-Québec. He was first required to attend an intensive 15 weeks of
police training at the Institute de police du Quebec, now named École
nationale de police du Quebec. He had railed privately at the repetition
of many of the same things endured during his RMC summers. But he
could not permit himself to flunk out so he endured. He graduated with
the Diploma and the rank of sergeant, which made him superior to all

lesser ranks, but with no authority or responsibility over a team. Undoubtedly, the appointment was an acknowledgement of his criminology studies. *My training supervisor was not convinced I would ever be a standout officer. Sergeant I remain to the present day. My superiors, previous and current, continue to judge me insufficient as a team player.* Nevertheless, his crime-solving accomplishments moved him through several districts and ultimately to headquarters in Montreal for the past two years. Partners came and went, none of them resistant to the idea of moving on to other partners or transfers. *There was, by most of my fellow officers, only some grudging respect for my independent dogged focus on concluding difficult cases.*

Undoubtedly, the recent award of the Croix de Bravouredes Policiers, presented in January by the Quebec Minister of Public Security for an act of heroism in exceptionally dangerous circumstances precipitated the latest career move. He was fully recovered from two bullets to his shoulder, the result of a gun fight with a motorcycle gang in Montreal. His action had prevented the death of two of the squad as they tried to arrest the leaders in a murder-for-hire scheme. He had defied procedure, left safe cover and dragged the two men out of the line of fire. Only then had he realized he was in excruciating pain from gunshot wounds to his right shoulder.

His Deputy Director, with the approval of the Director General of the QPP/Suréte du Quebec, recommended his appointment as Chief Investigator of the Canadian Anti-terrorist Service. The Canadian Minister of National Defense, Paul Mackey had agreed and so here he was, much to his surprise. *Still, I understand that the fact remained I am not seen as a good team player. My habit of independence, however, is ingrained and possibly unchangeable.*

Arriving finally at the alley, he had refocused on his goal of the moment; to observe the building directly across the street. This was not his first visit. His practice was to take as many opportunities as possible to satisfy the need to know.

{1.1}
A dark alley across from CAS HQ: Ottawa ON

Ron Stotyn

The structure across the street from where he stood hidden in the alley, like most of the others in the immediate area showed no signs of life. Only the lobby had a single light on, which barely illuminated the entrance. After nearly half an hour watching, he was satisfied no one was in the building, except perhaps a sleepy sentry at the front desk. That was of little concern as he had no intention of entering by the front door. As he left his solitary observation post, he carefully looked up and down the street before moving off to the right, crossing the street out of sight of the building's façade. Coming back toward the building on its side of the street, he entered the alley opposite where he had been watching. He moved quickly to a service door that he had fixed to stand the slightest bit ajar the day before; satisfied that it would go unnoticed. There had been a lack of movement at that side of the building during the time he spent roaming the building. Most of the building was unoccupied. Office suites, especially on the two mid level floors, appeared not to be rented. That was a curiosity.

He entered and climbed the stairs to the top floor. Waiting for a moment in the vestibule of the emergency stairwell, he listened carefully in the dark. He was nothing if not an unusually cautious man, a significant way to avoid serious harm to one's body. Hearing nothing, he went to the sole office entrance and let himself in with a bit of sleight of hand on the surprisingly insubstantial lock. He stood alone in a new office space, new to him at least. The offices were empty. No lights on, but now enough dawn daylight from a few tall narrow windows, in the wall he faced, to see several desks grouped in the center of the room. He could also make out several small offices along the windowed wall and a larger one in the corner. He supposed that would be the space reserved for the directeur, his new boss.

He amended his thought to 'director', since he was now in Ottawa, that bastion of primarily English speaking government. As he did so, he also wondered which of the smaller rooms, not much more than cubicles, would be his reserved cubby. He was, after all, the newly appointed chief investigator for the Canadian Anti-Terrorism Service, known simply as the CAS. *I was considered by my superiors to be well practiced for the position, though some might think I am much too exacting to be effective. I am not able to come to terms with that view, my attitude is that excellence demands an iron control of investigative skills.*

Precision and energetic self-confidence had been part of his lifestyle ever since his years as a day student at the renowned Stanstead College, that served junior and senior high school students from Canada and around the world, located in his hometown of Stanstead Plain, Quebec. Growing up in Stanstead Plain, one of the three villages that merged to become Stanstead QC, (the others were Beebe Plain and Rock Island), was a delight. He had thrived in the freedom small towns afford. Situated right against the border with Derby Line, VT, the region was economically vibrant. Granite cutting was a major industry, having brought the railroad in 1871. The educational opportunities were excellent as his experience had demonstrated. By the time he graduated with his grade 12 diploma in 1980, he had lettered in three sports: Hockey, Basketball and Track and had participated in others. *My athleticism contributes to my sense of excellence and the need to achieve whatever the cost.*

Most Quebecois students did not take grade 12 courses, but went after grade 11 to a College of General and Vocational Education (CEGEP) for college and university preparation. This was the typical Quebec process. His academic work had been superior, one of the reasons he'd been admitted in the first place as a day student when the school was mainly residential. *I still embrace the school's intent to have students understand the importance of respect, responsibility and self-discipline.* These dictates had molded him and had remained an integral part of his raison d'être. He respected his superiors even if they did not return it.

Putting his mind back on the scene before him, he considered that the fact that the office was empty did not entirely surprise him, it was after all Saturday and early in the day; but given the nature of the work conducted here, he thought some activity might have been possible. His new field of investigation into terrorism, after all, was not dictated by so called bankers' hours. Terrorists, he understood, certainly did not keep such hours. It seems a given that a terrorist would work devious plots whenever their furious mood struck.

Ron Stotyn

He was early arriving in the city and not expected until Monday. That was a characteristic, suddenly appearing on a scene before anyone knew he was coming. Ruefully he acknowledged *that that caused workmates to feel uncomfortable as they try and often fail to understand my motives. Motive was something criminology has taught about; my own is not always easy to discern. I am unwilling to change because the element of surprise helped to satisfy my curiosity,* another strong trait that he exercised vigorously. That also caused dismay, because his curiosity knew no bounds; which meant he often trod on the privacy of others. Still, he rationalized, first reactions by others as part of the scene often are instructive. Knowledge about others is indeed powerful.

But today, no others were present. He was alone, early so that he could assess what would become part of his physical circumstances and where he would undoubtedly spend too much time at hours not conducive to rest. At his age, now 46, rest was often much to be desired and often difficult to attain. There were too many individuals who wanted to do harm in the world to afford easy rest. Besides he thought *bringing a situation to a logical conclusion was rest in its own fashion.*

He was inside without official permission, not that that bothered him overmuch. He had persuaded the building security officer at the main lobby desk of his right to enter the building on the day before. Persuasion aided by a quick flash of his badge declaring him to be a Sergeant of the Sûrété du Quebec. A glimpse not long enough for the security officer to see the jurisdiction was not Ottawa. Still, it sufficed and now on Saturday with the building apparently empty, here he was moving toward the center of the room, stopping amidst the grouping of desks. He touched nothing, relying instead on the third of what he thought were his most important traits. He was by nature a man who took everything in, looking carefully and seeing small details which he stored for later contemplation. *I will remember everything, as I do always.*

As he stood at the center of the room, his initial thought was it was larger than seemed necessary, given the relatively few desks surrounding him. *Of course the office, as the central hub of several locations across the country, will probably expand and I understand as well that my work will put me on the road more often than I might prefer.* Terrorists did not always choose to establish themselves in smaller cities like Ottawa. *I will need to learn quickly the make-up of the staff in the other CAS locations.* For the moment he examined the desks around him for the little things that would indicate personalities. As expected, each desk had a computer screen, but they were larger than normal, flat screen monitors.

A good sign, he thought, for 28 inches would allow the display of much detail without overcrowding one's visual field. It was interesting that this modern computing equipment was placed on desks that had been part of government offices for decades. They were that old. *Typical that the newest agencies got the oldest castoffs. You have to prove yourself to get perks.* He moved thoughtfully from desk to desk, taking in details such as the state of the desktop. The way in which materials, flotsam and memorabilia were positioned could be indicative of personal habits and behaviors. *My desk will more than likely remain empty of such debris. My past is not always comfortable memory.*

Characteristically, the edges of monitors are often places for notes scrawled on bits of sticky backed paper. As he moved closer, he saw that several monitors displayed exactly that. He bent close, absorbing the information, still unconnected but nevertheless interesting, pointing to a variety of possibilities. On one desk he noted the name plaque of Betty-Anne Grabler. The desk was very ordered, everything seeming to be in a precisely determined place. A large well used calculating machine implied perhaps an accounting or statistical function. The separate machine, when the computer could do the same function suggested some traditional preferences in the user. There was nothing else in view to confirm such a notion.

On another desk bearing the placard for Everet Tailfeathers, that name probably signifying a First Nations member, he noted a large sketch pad and several soft lead pencils lined up. Curiously there was an eraser wedged into what looked like a .308 caliber shell case. That must indicate an artist, though why the shell casing he had no idea at the moment.

Ron Stotyn

He remembered what he saw for he had an eidetic memory, sometimes a curse; he never completely forgot anything. The amount of information he retained was sometimes distracting unless he was tightly focused. He expected to begin connecting the disparate observations when he met for the first time each desk's resident agent and received information of their credentials. His own academic studies, which had led to a Criminology Ph.D., suggested to him that even small details should never be overlooked. He tried not to overlook even the minutia. A detail missed could be a mistake costing lives lost. He was also glad to see that no desk had secure documents left out for anyone to see. Security is critical for success against terrorists.

Paying attention now to the empty reaches of the room he saw, as the morning daylight in-creased, that one wall opposite the cluster of desks was festooned with maps, whiteboards, and several 60-inch diagonal HDTV monitors. The mix of old and new technology was both an oddity and yet encouraging. It showed the government of Canada was serious about the problems faced by anti-terrorism squads, but also that resources were still lacking. Another good sign he saw was that each desk faced the wall with a clear line of sight. There was, in fact, a sort of informal semi-circle of desks in three rough lines. That suggested a singular connection with the wall. The maps on the wall were marked with pins of various colours, and several had ribbons leading to remarks written on the white boards. The orderly approach was very attractive. He liked order in his life.

As he moved closer, he saw clear indications of active investigations into suspected terrorist cells. He knew his work would immediately become complex. Inevitably, the suspect cells would need to be connected to each other, if possible, and to the controlling cell. *That exercise will be fraught with difficulty if information is scarce, which is a distinct probability. My lead as chief investigator will have to be without fault, otherwise disaster, will become imminent. Even then some detail, significant or not, might be missed and that detail could be the trigger for a severe situation.* He would not be stressed by such a thought but neither could he distance himself from that potential reality. He understood that somewhere there might well be an extremist on the verge of something momentous at this very moment. *I pray always that I will not fail.*

His time, as allotted by himself for this first examination, was expiring. He moved more quickly now to make a circuit of the perimeter of the room, taking a broader view of the physical space. He saw that the small office cubicles had no tops to them, no ceilings to make conversations more private. He wondered where confidential discussions were held. *If there were not any such designated spaces, that situation would need to be rectified. Certain conversations need to be kept contained until the time was appropriate for revelation.* His style was to be as certain as can be that the most important deliberations of the squad did not find their way prematurely into the world. *It will not do for terrorists to have any information that might help them hide.*

Moving toward the small offices, he noted an elderly architectural style reminiscent of venerable bank buildings that kept the tall narrow windows high above the floor. Indeed, his research indicated that this building had once been the headquarters for a major bank. The Dominion Bank founded in 1869, had long since been swallowed up, in 1955, by one of Canada's world class banks. That was TD Bank founded in 1855, now 6th largest in North America.

Only by standing tall could one hope to see any view. At six foot three inches, he would not experience any difficulty. Indeed as he entered one office, whose door stood ajar so that he did not have to touch the handle, he could see toward Canada's parliament buildings. Just at the corner of the view he realized, somewhat ironically, that the Peace Tower was visible. Peace is a most difficult thing to imagine in the modern world.

Stepping back outside into the main room he continued his walk along the row of offices. Two doors later, he came upon one with no name lettered on the glass. Instead, he found a small bit of sticky paper with one word scrawled upon it: La Rivierre. Seeing the misspelling and the incorrect capital R, O'Dwyer-Lariviere made a mental note to have that misinformation corrected upon his arrival on Monday morning. He noted to himself that it is not customary to have the prefix separated from the main part of a Quebecois last name, nor,

Ron Stotyn

to have the first letter of that second part capitalized. His own hyphenated last name conformed to Quebec Language Law and thus the leading letter L was capitalized. He had found his office and saw that he would have an unobstructed view of the wall of maps, whiteboards, and monitors. He also would have a similar view of the desks organized in the center of the main room. He would be able to notice and collect necessary information with relative ease. Inside the office, however, he saw nothing. That also would require some action as soon as possible so he wouldn't have to borrow a desk in the outside section of the office for any longer than necessary. His comfort level as Chief Investigator demanded his scheme of what his office should be.

My furnishing needs will be simple. A serviceable desk, a comfortable swivel chair, a few book cases, a filing cabinet, and an overstuffed chesterfield for nights when returning home was not an option would suffice. The chesterfield, or couch as he reminded himself of that name others preferred, would do also for any visitors to his office. Indeed there was hardly room enough to add extra chairs. In all, standard Government Issue pieces would do for most items needed. Besides government issue was likely all he could get.

Then, turning way from the office which was to be his, he allowed a contented thought: he was several offices away from that of the director situated in the corner. Was that a matter of protocol, he wondered, or just happenstance? He had seen no indications of officer ranks by any of the names on the other office doors so could not determine if any superiors occupied the three offices between his and that of the director. He had not yet been given information about the hierarchy, not surprising since the agency was of a sensitive nature. He did recognize the name on the director's door, Leif Isaksson, as a former commander of Canadian Special Forces Operations Command (CSOFC).

He knew Isaksson's identity from his own days as a Lieutenant in the Canadian Forces Intelligence Branch (CFIB), while posted in Ottawa. He had returned to Quebec in 1998 when he joined the Sûrété du Quebec as a novice detective in training in Montreal. With Isaksson in charge he would learn any necessary information on Monday. He was certain Isaksson was still inclined to be forthcoming with necessary and relevant information, rarely holding anything back. And the various superiors, whoever they were, would add information about him beginning on Monday, some of which, he thought wryly would be easily found in his thick dossier surely already on their desks. *My career has not always gone smoothly in the eyes of previous supervisors. I've never been able to prevent that.*

O'Dwyer-Lariviere was a complicated man. Now as he prepared to leave the CAS office space, he proved his complexity. Still without touching anything, he exited so his brief presence could not be noticed. The lock was not a problem; his gloved hands left no marks. Returning to the back staircase he descended the four flights by which he had risen, there being no elevator in the rear of the building. He would not have used it in any event, since that would draw attention to his furtive visit. He left the building by the same back exit, noting again how lax the security was, something that also needed fixing. As he returned to his nondescript hotel a few blocks away, he determined that there was much already to think about, and think he would about ways to ensure the CAS would do its work well without being compromised.

{1.2}
A few blocks from CAS HQ, about 6:30 AM: Ottawa ON

A few blocks south of the CAS office, he found Café Slater just opened for breakfast. He entered thinking how nice it would be to find Saskatoon Jelly for his toast. Alas, there was none, he had to make do with Blueberry. As he sat with a second cup of strong black coffee, he was not yet aware that in another city just about 300 miles away, another man was sitting quietly in half light contemplating a deadly scheme. Of course he could not be aware for he was still unconnected with certain facts that would change the immediate focus of his new job. That new information was a little over 24 hours into the future.

An hour or less later, following his light breakfast, just toast and coffee, for he rarely ate eggs and bacon before running, O'Dwyer-Lariviere went for his morning lope. He had first walked to loosen up,

Ron Stotyn

increasing his pace until ready to do a full out run. He chose
Confederation Park which bordered Slater Street and on the way back
to his hotel. It felt good to stretch and prepare for his morning workout
when he reached the park. As he ran with his long legs covering the
ground in long flowing strides, he was able to focus his mind on what
he had seen inside the office of CAS. Running was an exercise he
favored because it allowed a full mental flow simultaneously with the
athletic workout that he valued.

He reviewed first some of what he had seen on the various
desks, starting with that of Betty Anne Grabler. Aside from the large
well-used calculating machine which he had already considered
unconnected with other items on the desktop, he recalled two pictures.
Male and female, the photos showed teenagers, probably late teens,
their faces alive with the exuberance of youth. The logical assessment
was that they were the children of Grabler, though not knowing the age
of Grabler the possibility had to include grandchildren. The existence
of the photos implied a familial connection at the very least. Both
children bore a strong resemblance to each other and showed
considerable intelligence. That was shown in the eyes, he thought. He
would expect to see the same in the eyes of the mother, if that was
indeed who Betty Anne Grabler was.

On the desk had also been a daily calendar, open to the week
to come. Grabler, it was likely her handwriting, had noted a meeting
for Monday morning at 10 AM, marked with the single word
URGENT!, formed in precise upper case and underlined with a hard
stroke of the pen. He wondered briefly if that had anything to do with
his scheduled arrival to join the CAS organization. *I cannot yet think of
myself as part of a team because I do not really know how I will be
interacting with the other members of the Ottawa HQ of the new anti-
terrorism operation.*

He had expected to find sticky notes on some of the computer
monitors, and indeed there was one on Grabler's monitor. Like many
such notes, it was a bit cryptic, probably just a fragment of a sentence
intended to remind the owner of something that needed to be done or
needed to be remembered. In this case the note specified: "check
Toronto rumor." That certainly suggested that the Toronto office had

something they were concerned about. He made a mental note to find out more about that as soon as he could on Monday. *I don't much like rumors; they are much too fuzzy for factual assessment.*

One other thing had attracted his attention on that desk. It was a piece of fragmented metal, also not apparently connected to anything else on the desk. But, it looked as if it had been the result of an explosion. His mind veered slightly: *Explosions are violent; I have experienced a lot of violence. I wonder about what she has endured.*

Satisfied that he had considered everything seen on the desktop of Betty Anne Grabler, his mental processes moved on to the desk of Everett Tailfeathers. *That name is certainly of a First Nations individual, but I cannot place it to any particular band with which I am familiar.* Not surprising, because he had little occasion to even think about First Nations people outside of Ontario and Quebec. Most of his experience with aboriginals, as a member of the Sûreté du Quebec, had been in his home province. All too often his involvement as a detective had been to investigate suspicious death on one reserve or another, usually in cooperation with the Gendarmerie Royale du Canada, who of course had federal jurisdiction. Those First Nations Reserves members tended to just barely tolerate the federal oversight exercised in such cases by the RCMP (GRC). Maybe that was understandable, considering how they had been unjustly treated over the years. He had felt similar reactions as a Quebecois when posted in Ottawa with the CFIB.

He had already come to a reasonable conclusion that Tailfeathers was an artist of some importance to the CAS operation. Not only was there the sketch pad and a row of sharpened soft lead pencils on the desk, he had seen two penciled images of people, presumably persons of interest, attached to the white boards at the head end of the main office space. It was reasonable to understand that they had been produced by Tailfeathers. If so, that individual had considerable talent. The renderings were very lifelike. He understood completely that sketches were often the only images available during the early stages of an investigation. Terrorists did not generally pose willingly for the camera. An artist was needed to create a picture based on descriptions by witnesses and they were hard enough to find. He

Ron Stotyn

expected that Tailfeathers would turn out to be a valuable participant in his investigations, but it would take face to face meetings before his conclusions could be solidified.

Tailfeathers also had notes attached to his monitor. One was apparently a personal matter, probably an appointment with a dentist or physician, though it could be a professional person possessing a doctorate, for midweek coming up. A second note said BE READY, MONDAY 10 AM. That likely echoed the same note he'd seen in Grabler's calendar. His mental calendar entry put that day and time down as one to be prepared for. He looked forward to the event with his usual curiosity. He still pondered the meaning of the eraser impaled upon the bullet casing. That remained a bit of a mystery that he could not connect to his mental picture of an artist. *Although the eraser fit, the brass case did not. It is not practical to jump to any conclusions about the meaning.*

Now he addressed in his mind what he had seen in the office/cubicle he had stepped into briefly. The name on the door was Ryan McLeod. On the wall opposite the desk, he had noticed a picture of the RCMP mounted unit known as the Musical Ride. On the desk was a crop, typical of riders in such an organization. From this, O'Dwyer-Lariviere surmised with reasonable certainty that McLeod was connected with and likely was a member or former officer of the RCMP. There was enough evidence to allow for the probability of such a conclusion. The room was otherwise devoid of items that could prove the point. That McLeod occupied an office cubicle led to another reasonable conclusion that the man held a position of some authority or importance. That the office was next to the one he had identified as his own, led to a probable connection to his own position in the organization. There were no sticky notes attached to the monitor but on a cork board behind the desk he had seen several small pictures with notes attached. But he had not gone close enough to read them. He mentally chastised himself for that failure, as it meant he lacked what could be useful information. *Such shortsightedness is inexcusable under ordinary circumstances and even worse if allowed to occur during sensitive situations.*

He turned his attention now to what he had seen on the white boards. This was not in the order in which he had observed in his recon, but rather in the order his mind placed on items from seeming least to most important. He tended to organize his analysis in terms of details that built up to crucial importance. What he had seen at the head of the room had impressed upon him that the Ottawa CAS was considering a number of significant issues. There had been maps with pins and ribbons leading to notes.

One note that stuck out in his mind was attached to a pin stuck into Chechnya located in the Northern Caucasus Mountains of the former USSR. At the time he had not made a particular connection to anything in his own experiences. But now he recalled that he had once met a young Chechen in connection with his service on the Council of Trustees at Stanstead College. He had joined the council in 1999, the same year a scared, skinny Chechen boy named Malik Bisliev had come to the college for a year of ESL. He'd met the boy only as a matter of being introduced during a trip to the college and a foray into several classrooms. The boy had been about 13 or 14 but otherwise he'd not been the subject of his attention. That brief encounter didn't seem particularly important at that time, so he'd let the memory retreat. The note that he'd seen was not very explanatory, but given what he knew about Chechnya, that country certainly demanded attention, being a hotbed of terrorist activity within its political situation. Knowledge that the CAS was paying attention to something so far away, gave him increased confidence that he would be able to do his job well. *I am always interested in unconventional situations.*

His run now done, after completing a full circuit of Confederation Park, he paused to do some more stretches before a cool off walk back to the hotel. He estimated a run of about 3 miles altogether, a bit shorter than his normal forays, but enough for the moment. After refreshing himself he would get some lunch later and prepare for his afternoon appointment with a real estate agent. He needed to find an apartment so that he could get settled and focus more completely on his assignment with the CAS. *Having a place to live is never the most important thing in my life, but it does mean that attention will more easily be paid to whatever is primary on the job.*

Ron Stotyn

That reality, though, has proved to be a difficulty in my previous married life; both times.

His first marriage had produced one child, a girl, rarely seen after a divorce just a couple of years into the marriage. That he rarely saw the girl, was partly due to the lasting estrangement with his former wife, but probably more due to his focus on his work as an intelligence officer with the CFIB. Long hours at the office and at university had sealed that situation. There is no doubt I caused the break. The same could be said for my second marriage. His decision to leave the military and join the Sûrété du Quebec had not been the subject of consultation with his second wife. Her attitude was that he had not tried hard enough to advance in the military. Joining the police was to her a decision to accept failure. There had been no children this time; she left the marriage and soon after the divorce married a rising Major. He had not wanted to consider the possibility that she'd been seeing the man prior to their breakup.

In the meantime, a man who would become his primary opponent in the next few weeks was just finishing his contemplations about plans to bring some Monday morning madness to the city of Toronto. This man was about to act out of his very significant fury and absolute desire for revenge.

{2}

Our names and surnames will be changed and revenge will be sweet! Jihad will go on despite our enemies' efforts. We become stronger. Allah, who helps us, says to us: "O you who believe persevere in patience and constancy; vie in such perseverance; strengthen each other; and fear Allah; that you may prosper." (SURA - ÂLİ IMRÂN, 3:200)

Early morning, Saturday April 1: Toronto ON

A solitary man in a darkened apartment in the Little Poland district of Toronto sat remembering the atrocities he had experienced and endured for too long. He knew privation and days without sufficient food and water. His body, though wiry and fit, was still smaller than normal because of that. His homeland had suffered for generations. In his desolation he cried for his dead parents and destroyed extended family. His thoughts refreshed his utter anger. He believed with an unforgiving sense of certainty that Canada had failed to help. Instead it had sided with Russia, tacitly perhaps, but complicit nevertheless, because it had not condemned murderous actions taken against the Chechen. That was indeed the righteous argument of the revered Baseyev who had changed his name to Imir Addullah Shamil Abn Idris, a militant Chechen whose every thought was freedom for the country. Freedom was a desperate goal that the man shared with many. Fewer, like him, had made obtaining freedom the fuel that fired revenge.

The man's soul ached for revenge. It was the core of his fury. Revenge was in fact the center of his renewed belief in Islam over the past ten years or so. *Revenge is my obligation from centuries of Chechen tradition. Revenge is my right and responsibility. Revenge is mine to take now.* His teacher and mentor had told him that so often. He knew very well the history that showed, for at least 8,000 years, conflict with outsiders desiring to be the rulers of his nation and people, rulers who then brought much suffering. The suffering had never been as horrendous as it had been during his youth.

Ron Stotyn

From the graven memories of his younger years he recalled
the conflict that had been with Russia and before that the USSR.
Chechnya, situated as it was in the Northern Caucasus Mountains
within the Southern Federal District, had become a federal subject of
Russia. Part of the problem, perhaps a main factor, was that Chechens
were mostly Muslim, while the hated Russians were infidels of the
worst kind; a nation of widespread corruption and prone to the most
evil of abuses.

He was Muslim. Every fiber of his being evoked the principles
of Islam, as he was taught and as he understood them. He prayed
faithfully the required five times daily. After his ancestors had
converted to Islam, tension with the Turks had subsided, but conflict
with Christian neighbors intensified. Resistance to Russia had been
going on since the 18th century. He was convinced that he was
necessarily part of that resistance. Russia had forced that upon him.
Only after the fall of the USSR in 1991, and with the formation of the
Chechen Republic, had there been any hope of self-rule.

He recalled again that the struggle for independence began to
rise again in 1991. But the formation of the Chechen National
Congress under the leadership of President Dzhokhar Dudayev was
strongly opposed by Boris Yeltsin's Russian Federation. Yeltsin
argued that the Chechen's possessed no right to succeed. Then in 1994
began the first Chechen War. Russia was not able to overcome
Chechen guerilla raids. A ceasefire was negotiated in 1996 and a peace
treaty was signed the next year. There had been heavy losses on both
sides and especially to the civilian population. Thousands of traditional
Islamic families were forever disrupted by death. Such disruption was
a personal experience for the man from his earliest memories. At age
five, Marek's life had already been disrupted by war and death for most
of his tender years. The destruction had become part of his
development; it was certainly a contributing factor to his attitude of
fury. The promise of peace and that broken also contributed.

The year 1997 brought parliamentary and presidential
elections. The then new President, Aslan Maskhadev, began receiving
funding from Russia intended to help Chechnya rebuild, but
Maskhadev distributed most of the funds instead to highly favored

warlords who used it to cement their own control. Nearly 500,000 people, approximately 40 percent of the population, were displaced to refugee camps or overcrowded villages. As a result, some of the country's Muslims became attracted to a more extreme form of Islam known as Wahhabism, though proponents would say it was a more pure form.

Soon, in 1998, open clashes between the Chechen National Guard and Islamist militants provoked Grozny officials to declare a state of emergency. A year later in August 1999 the second Chechen War began. The IIPB rebels ran unsuccessful incursions into neighboring Dagestan, seeking independence for that state. This time, Russian counter-actions were much better organized than in the previous war. They established control over most Chechen regions using brutal force. Maskhadev was killed. Marek's parents were murdered by drunken out-of-control Russian soldiers that same year. Destruction was now an inescapable part of his psyche, this also contributing further to his fury.

Marek, not his real name, of ruddy tanned complexion like a man who had spent a lifetime outdoors in a severe climate, sat quietly just ten years later in his Little Poland half lit room in a rundown apartment located near Toronto's Dundas Street West. His apartment was close to the intersection of Dundas and Roncesvalles Avenue within a small triangular neighborhood bounded by Ritchie Avenue on the southeast. It was only a short walk to the bus line; transportation that he needed as he had no car. He didn't expect to live here long enough to need one. He had a mission to accomplish, that when finished would require that he disappear to surface elsewhere for a new task. *I am at ease with my attitude of fury. It suits my mission.*

Little Poland was a comfortable place for Marek. He didn't know the origin of the name Little Poland as a designation for the quarter, but that did not concern him. What was most important was that he could go around largely unnoticed, for the neighborhood was filled with mainly Russian and Eastern European residents along with many ethnic shops, bakeries, and café's. The food, culture and frequent special events brought tourists and people from other parts of the city, but they paid little attention to people like him. He blended fairly well,

Ron Stotyn

with his dark hair and short black beard, short slender build now in generally fit condition. His manner of dress was vaguely Eastern European rather than Chechen; most of his clothes were from Honest Ed's, an emporium in Mirvish Village along Bloor Street. He shopped there also for the few bits of kitchen and other apartment things he needed. His revolutionary training had inculcated avoidance of the trappings of wealth and the diseased accoutrements of western capitalists. His fury recognized that the decadence of the west was a cause of the troubles of his nation.

The presence of Russians was a difficulty because of his hatred of them. He could however pretend to put up with them, as he prepared to make a statement about their crimes against his people. His command of Russian was good and his accent did not given him away as a Chechen. It suited him in some ways to be reminded daily by the presence of Russians. It was a constant prompt that they had frustrated the right of Chechnya for generations to rule itself. Even though Russia had officially ended counter-terrorist activities against Chechens earlier in the year, Marek could not believe there was no ulterior motive. Sooner or later he believed they would again move against Chechen freedoms, hard won and usually short-lived. Marek was pleased to note that at home there was still some separatist movement activity and that there was still some regional tribal or clan control. The flame may have died down but the spark was still alive. He anticipated his own successful role in achieving the holy goals. That was why he had been sent to Canada. The spark needed to be fanned to a brighter flame. *My mission will be an abrupt reminder to the world of the unfeeling Russian acts.*

It was not his first visit to Canada. Nearly ten years earlier he had spent a term as an exchange student attending the ESL program at Stanstead College in Stanstead QC. It had been an extremely difficult time for the Muslim child to be in a Christian environment. There were no friends from that year; he had been frightened at the beginning, then as time passed keeping alone waiting to return to the Imam who had taken care of his needs so far, his acquisition of English had gone well. Some years later, he had been able to add to his fluency while a student at the University of Engineering and Technology in Peshawar,

Pakistan. Many of his professors in Chemical Engineering were English speakers and he had sought every opportunity to engage them in that language. He had also learned to converse comfortably in Urdu and Pashto. That latter language had proved to be useful here in Canada. He had Afghans on his team. *Their harsh experiences and shared fury with Russian oppression serve my purposes very well.*

He had wanted to attend the Chechen State University, destroyed by the Russians during the Second Chechen War between 1994 and 1996, but his mentor Imam Ali Ibn al-Hassan dissuaded him even though classes had resumed in April of 2000. His Wahhabist teacher was a forceful disciplinarian. Slowly he had realized the wisdom as he grew in understanding of the Wahhabist ideals for restoring Islam to purity. His Imam made perfect sense in his repeated discourse about the Qur'an's call for the oneness of Allah, to praise Allah constantly, for a jihad against those who practiced jahilayya, that is, were barbarous and ignorant. In time he had accepted completely that his perfect role in life was that of the terrorist, the only strategy that could correct the wrongs perpetrated against his people. The salafi jihad was his destiny entirely. He embraced terrorism and terrorism embraced him. *It is in fact a necessary fury.*

Now at age 23, his was a dire mission, but surely most necessary as he understood this completely; to plan an unmistakable statement that wealthy nations should not forsake the welfare of poorer brothers. *Brotherhood is the key; it calls true believers together to protect one another. It calls brothers to engage in a blood bond, to develop as needed a willingness to fight for each other to the death.* The two Chechen wars had certainly made it clear that a militant Islam was required to release the oppression of Chechnya. Indeed he recalled that it was President Dudayev, *blessed be his name*, who had declared that Russia had forced his people to take the Islamic jihadist path. He and his fellow warriors in this auspicious jihad would succeed. Indeed was not his own real name Malik, meaning possessor, indicative of Allah's blessing; he believed this with all his heart. Of course, no one would ever know that it was Malik Bisliev who would soon accomplish a great victory. His real name was merely a memory of a disturbed past. His mentor was responsible for Marek becoming an

Ron Stotyn

entirely dedicated individual separated from his past, though it continued to dictate his future and fury.

His birth name had disappeared into the distressing Chechen history just as soon as he had embarked on a journey of reawakening. Just turned age 12, the Imam had found him dirty, nearly starving, a wanderer of the streets of Shali, his home abandoned following a raging debauchery by drunken Russian soldiers; murderers of his parents. The sight of his mother being raped, his dead father nearby, still raged through his mind when he thought about his responsibility. Tradition dictated that he seek revenge. With no family left, he submitted to the apparent kindness of the foreign cleric. For no understandable reason he had not been punished for trying to steal food from the mosque.

The Imam had recently arrived from Saudi Arabia. The cleric gave him the option to be renewed by changing his name. Change had been good but it did not erase the trauma, suffering, humiliation and bereavement that he still felt. Only the fury fed by revenge and self-sacrifice can absolve those feelings. So he had accepted the name change, at the time not completely under-standing, as he did now, that change would set him on a path where only revenge would satisfy the jihadist he had become. Now, his closest compatriots in the immediate task did not know his real name. When the task was complete, it would not matter what name was associated, the message was only about retribution.

Only a chosen few even knew his assumed last name, Kafirov, and then only by necessity. He allowed himself a small smile as he thought how appropriate it was that he had taken the name used by Chechen mujahedeen to identify that most hated Russian puppet, the assassinated former Chechen president Ahmad Kadyrov. *Planning mayhem using that name has a kind of poetic justice about it.* Marek's plan, when successful, would be a complete act of reprisal on the Russians and their toadies. In the meanwhile most of those with whom he associated on the streets of Little Poland where he lived and worked called him Borz. It meant wolf and that suited him for he saw himself as a cunning stalker. Those casual acquaintances, of course, had no idea of his purpose. They were merely people with whom it was practical to be civil. He did need to seem an ordinary citizen going about normal business. He would soon close in on the target and satisfaction then would be most glorious indeed.

So Malik Bisliev/Marek Kafirov/Borz contemplated his assignment before getting himself ready for his daily task as a tea waiter in the Samovar House restaurant. He wore that skin of normalcy as easily as he thought about vengeance. His fury led him to thoughts of reprisal most of his waking hours. In some circumstances his steadfast focus in that regard might be regarded as an honorable thing. In Canada, a growing awareness of the dangers of terrorism would make kindly regard of vengeance a very iffy proposition.

{2.1}
Dawn, Little Poland, Saturday April 1: Toronto ON

Marek had established himself as a reliable server at the Samovar House over the past three months always arriving for his shift promptly, impeccably arrayed in the black trousers, white shirt, and formal waistcoat that was the uniform of the staff in the front of the house. He poured tea with considerable style, creating a long stream from the teapot to the glass, often achieving nearly three feet without a drop spilled. The fat indulgent customers never failed to be impressed, but few ever really paid attention to the man providing the service. That was just as well because after he triggered the scheme, he would shave his short black beard and become truly invisible among the crowds of Torontonians hurrying daily along the streets. It would be astonishing if anyone would be able to identify him as the unassuming waiter. He would move on to the next assignment. Lesser men would be the martyrs this time. His turn would come soon enough. Let there be madness in Canada before that occurred. He often entertained the idea of madness, but not about himself, that was a condition he ascribed to his enemies. His fury made that conclusion seem absolutely logical.

Still early on Saturday morning, it was just coming on seven AM, following his morning prayers kneeling toward the East in his threadbare bedroom. Marek did not attend a mosque. He had not found

Ron Stotyn

an Imam who proclaimed the pure form of Islam that he had learned
from Wahhabist teachers and leaders. He had explored a bit, going a
couple of times to the Bosnian Mosque on Dundas West, but the Imam
there was much too traditional and, in his mind, likely to corrupt his
desire toward an utter commitment of properly honoring Allah with
constant praise. The Bosnians who attended had abandoned any
concern about the troubles in their homeland. He despised them for
their apathy about the plight of oppressed Muslims. *Besides, a regular
attendance at a mosque would increase the chance that I might
become a suspect individual, especially if I cannot seem to be
complacent. I must be completely focused on my task. My planning
must be precise, if Canadians were to suffer appropriately for their
egregious attitude about Russia and its behavior in the world.*

Marek turned his attention to the map on the worn chrome
table in front of him. Once again he examined the routes of the Go
trains that brought thousands of commuters into the city from the
expansive suburbs. By their own publicity Go Transit carried more
than 51 million passengers every year. A large portion of these
travelled on the trains into the city mornings and returned evenings to
their homes. More than 5 million people lived in the service area
extending from Hamilton, Milton and Guelph in the west, Orangeville,
Barrie and Beaverton in the North, Stouffville, Uxbridge and Port
Perry to the northeast and Oshawa and Newcastle in the east. On a
Monday morning soon, commuters on seven train lines would
experience his plan for madness. They would meet a fiery end to their
complacent living. Marek did not expect that the event would satiate
his fury, but was sure it would be relieved for a moment.

The plan is nearly ready. Tomorrow Marek would meet as
usual with his cells' leaders, each committed to the vision of the Jihad's
leadership to bring a message to the world that complacency in the
face of Russia's cowardice would no longer be tolerated. The Sunday
meetings had gone on now for nearly three months, ever since Marek
had arrived from Chechnya. Marek smiled again as he thought of the
appropriateness of plotting mayhem on the day the world's Christians
held to be sacred. Soon they would see that Allah judged infidels
severely for their failure to join and hold to the true faith. His own

faith was focused entirely on the need to expunge the Russian control of his people so that Islamic righteousness would once again serve the people. He was a committed Wahhabist, along with his team leaders; he was certain as he could be, with all that portended for violence. *Vengeance for each of them is a deeply held sacred duty. Only in that way, I fully believe, is my fury justified.*

The cell leadership had been carefully chosen based on their loyalty to Wahhabism. They all had embraced those teachings following the disastrous Second Chechen War. Like Marek, they fully believed that Islamist reformer Mohamed Ibn Alid al-Wahhib had correctly understood a more pure form of Islam that asserted the oneness of Allah. They agreed that so-called sacred tombs and shrines should be destroyed, that there should even be wars on any badly informed Muslim who thought in terms of jahilayya. They each were committed to become suicide-terrorists in aid of the salafi jihad, recognizing in their hearts and minds that was the best way to reap revenge on the enemy. Theirs was a radical and militant faith.

Psychologically each was entirely comfortable with Wahhabist theory that any unrighteous civilian should be killed to achieve holy goals. There was no horror when contemplating such acts as the killing of 129 infidels at Moscow's Dubrovka Theater in 2002. There was in fact admiration for the bombings in Moscow's metros in 2004. That had produced a worldwide media attention, admired because it brought some awareness of the cause, itself deplored because the western influenced media had failed to show the full extent of Russian complicity in the Chechnya abuses. The youthfulness of his team would be their strength for they were full of conviction. They were in fact fanatic. Each had their own strong sense of fury.

Each leader and their teams of four were in Canada under assumed names just as was Marek. It was surprising how easy entry into Canada had been. It was as if the country had no concern about terror. That worked toward his purposes. The leaders had obtained jobs with the Go Train system using fraudulent documentation that complacent employer managers had only casually inspected if at all. The lesser cell members had various cover stories of which Marek was aware though he had not met any of these soldiers in the jihad. Some

Ron Stotyn

were enrolled as students at local universities and colleges, some worked in ethnic restaurants or other service businesses, while others had identities and documents that enabled them to obtain government subsistence allowances. Marek admired the skill with which the leadership of the movement had adeptly used al Qaeda strategies for infiltrating warriors into important positions and readying them for action at the right moment. Most importantly, the leaders were as dedicated as was Marek to the grand plan to teach the world a much needed lesson. Canada was merely the first student that would suffer a fascinating madness. Marek rejoiced with a steadfast mantra supported by his memories of destruction.

Only the leaders of the strike teams ever met with Marek. He never met with their hand-picked soldiers. Indeed, he only met with a few of the leaders at any one gathering in order to limit who knew who the others were. Of the seven cells there were three groups of leaders who knew only the few others of their own particular group. Never did they meet anywhere close to Marek's place of residence. It was always at a different and neutral location. To do otherwise would be to invite error. In case of any police inquiry, there could be no breakdown of the entire network. *My position will not be compromised.* It was improbable due to the expected utter loyalty of each leader who would die before revealing their real identity. The remaining cell leaders would be able to institute the plan, at least after tomorrow's round of meetings were completed. The whole plan would be presented at that time. Keys to transit-passenger lockers at designated commuter stations would soon be distributed; there the leaders would find and distribute packages of explosives to each team member for use at the specified time and place. That schedule was coming quickly.

Everyone, both leaders and team members he was assured, was ready to give up life for the great cause. They did not know, however, and did not need to know that he would not die with them in the glorious task. His future was already defined to create more revenge events elsewhere. Seven designated groups of bombers were ready to strike seven train lines at a coordinated time on a Monday morning soon. Each group would embark from an outlying station carrying explosive devices ready to detonate them according to a precise schedule at a specific location designed to create significant damage. Rehearsals would take place over the next two weeks, using disguised packages matching to what would be found in the lockers. At no point was there any risk of the explosive packets being exposed to the even casual scrutiny of an onlooker. The packages were of the sort of thing carried daily on the trains by the multitudes of passengers. When the time came, each dead passenger and bystander would be atonement for a dead Chechen ravaged by Russian troops. His deceased team members would relish their reward in paradise.

{2.2}
Mid Morning, Little Poland, Saturday April 1: Toronto ON

Marek paused in his study of the Go Train map to reflect on the more than 10 years, in his personal experience, of Russian state organized terror against the Chechens. *It was,* he thought, *a reality of criminal repression. Who could possibly blame his people for taking hard responses?* The war conducted by Russian troops and security forces had provoked his people in unimaginable ways. Yes, it was true that some of the retaliations had not always been well thought out. The hostage taking, for example, at the Beslan children's school, organized by Shamil Baseyev, was improbable and had failed entirely to measure any effective victory. But the Russian position against Chechnya had inevitably hardened the nature of the Chechen rebellion, increasing the resolve of its fighters, and solidifying the necessary extreme position of Islam among the country's rebel leaders. Marek was a full supporter of the separatist aspirations of his countrymen, an attitude that had persisted well back into Tsarist history. *Freedom is always the point; Freedom by any necessary means. Revenge demands no less.*

Marek then turned his attention to the Go Train schedules he had picked up at Union Station just the day before. These were the latest editions showing revised arrival times for all the outlying stations. Marek always went to Union Station to collect schedules. He could have gone on-line but even though that was a generally innocuous thing, he felt that the anonymity of a supposed passenger taking schedules from a rack would go more unnoticed. He was a bit

Ron Stotyn

paranoid about the Internet, knowing that certain kinds of navigations could be tracked. Even when it was necessary to send emails to his team leaders, he went to a cyber café and never the same one twice in a row. He considered that his tradecraft was impeccable as a result.

One thing, though, that he had discovered by browsing the Go Train website at a recent cyber-café visit, was a schedule of construction at some of the outlying Go Train stations. This information was very useful for his planning. The elevated level of construction confusion should allow his teams to enter trains with less scrutiny from any train security that might be around the platforms. Based on information published on the Go Train website he determined that the stations at Agincourt, Oakville, Oriole and Union Station could be useful for adding horrendous confusion to the already upset movement patterns caused by construction in those locations. Union Station was especially important as the main hub in the system. The explosive devices scheduled for this location would be made as strong as possible without being unwieldy; the suicide bombers would locate themselves strategically within the building upon arrival to create the largest possible damage. He had chosen York University station as a bombing site for the volume of young people that would be present. Similarly Bloor Street station was an active transfer point for business people going to work in the downtown area. Erindale was chosen mainly because it was distant from the other planned explosion points. At Erindale, the train should be mostly full because that was just three stops before the destination in the city center. In each planned disbursement of explosive packages, it was critical that at least one be deployed inside the train to disable the system. Packets deployed for platforms would render many deaths. Before a final decision to launch the scheme, he would check schedules a last time to ensure arrival times at key stations were unchanged, and he would review each chosen location for its viability. His plan demanded a certain synchronicity for maximum confusion.

The arrival times at each chosen site were important for the required close coordination for all the teams. Coordination of the detonations would cause considerable confusion for the authorities such that the damage and death would be escalated before any hope of finding survivors could occur. Distance between the selected stations was important. It would mean first responders would be divided in their attempts to deal with the devastation he would cause. He did not want all the rescue agencies rushing to a single location. Marek was certain that simultaneous detonation sites scattered across the metropolitan area would be more effective. The detonation sites would be chosen according to the greatest number of passengers embarking at the chosen times. Go Train publicity was a great help in that regard; the published train volume and patterns ensured a massive destruction.

In all this planning, Marek had received no specific direction from his own leaders. None of them were in the country. Marek was well aware that he had received his key instructions before leaving home and was now completely on his own. *I am secure in the knowledge that I am trusted to plan, organize and carry out a flawless plan.*

{2.3}
Saturday April 1, later that day, about 3 PM: Toronto ON

Marek, now dressed in the uniform of the servers at Samovar House, topped with an old wool overcoat against the chill wind, was on his way to work. On the way he stopped at an Internet café that he had not used now for several weeks. He judged it would be safe to send three emails to team lead captains to set tomorrow's meetings. They would similarly pass the message to the remainder of their subgroup's cell leaders. His own day would be a long one because he would need to travel considerable distances on the Go Transit and TTC bus line systems to three locations well away from his own residence. He would go first to Oakville on the Lakeshore West line. He wanted to see the extent of construction there, and then meet his team leaders in a nearby restaurant. That meeting would need to be early in the morning, so he would take his breakfast as if with a few good friends meeting for that reason. Normal activity was good subterfuge.

His next stop would be back along the Lakeshore West Line and then north to Aurora, where his cell team unit captain was stationed, using Go and TTC buses because the Barrie line did not

Ron Stotyn

operate on the weekends. On the way he would see the Yorkdale Go Bus Terminal. He thought it might be valuable to change the deployment of explosives on that line slightly to explode one or two devices among the buses. It would be early afternoon just around 1 PM by the time he arrived for his second meeting, scheduled for a chess club meeting room. Cell leaders stationed at Bramalea and Meadowvale on the Georgetown and Milton Go Train Lines would take Go Bus lines connecting to north bound buses east of Rutherford and York Mills. That would be appropriate because they would not have to pretend indifference if they saw each other, as they would likely arrive at their transfer points at different times. The team leaders would huddle around a chess board as if avidly fraternizing and kibitzing the chess play. He would have to pick up a sandwich for his noon meal while passing through Union Station. It would give him a chance to see progress on the stairway construction that would link platforms 3-9 from the new Bay West Teamway entrances to the Go Concourse. Use of construction debris could help in distracting from the locations of the explosive devices planned for the event.

His final meeting of the day was located in Oshawa, back through Union Station and onto the Lakeshore East corridor. He was a bit concerned that the leaders responsible for the Richmond Hill and Stouffville lines would be late, but they did have bus schedules that could connect them directly to the Whitby station, so they should be able to manage a timely arrival. They all should arrive around 5 PM, so for this meeting, a restaurant was again arranged. He had found one with a table in a sort of a cul-de sac at the rear of the restaurant's main room, somewhat removed from most patrons, and had reserved it. That should give sufficient privacy. By the time he got back home it would be quite late. He'd also miss the dictated times for prayers, but that could not be helped. Allah would surely understand the need to glorify him by means of the planned retribution. There would be much praise for Allah on that day.

Sunday's meetings with his leaders would be important. They would receive his instructions for putting finishing touches on what would be an inspired Monday morning of madness. With that thought he arrived at the Samovar House ready to begin his shift, thinking of the certainty of the changes due in his future, but completely unaware that things would change in ways not yet foreseen.

Ron Stotyn

{<u>3</u>}

"You are what you repeatedly do. Excellence is not an event - it is a habit." Aristotle

Paroisse Notre-Dame-De-L'Isle, about 6:30 AM, Sunday April 2: Gatineau-Hull QC

Jean Pierre René Girau, Major (ret), early on Sunday morning April 2nd, the optional liturgical day for Saint Francis of Paola, was discomfited. He was sitting alone, in the confessional at Paroisse Notre-Dame-De-L'Isle, trying to come to terms with his circumstances. He was not there to make confession but to hear them; waiting for parishioners that he knew would not come to confession so early, even though a few would come to the mass that would start shortly.

Girau was a priest, the parish pastor in fact, and that was part of his problem. Too few of the flock practiced the proper steps to confession these days; there was rarely any serious contrition, certainly inadequate self-examination, an unwillingness to tell a priest about the darkness of the soul, and rarely a true keenness to practice a penance. Those that did come tended to be repetitive; they confessed minor peccadilloes that were the same ones week after week. He was frankly tired of that. That was another part of his problem. He didn't feel at all priestly or forgiving. Several decades in the priesthood and a recently abrupt change in his specific vocational assignment had left him weary and frustrated.

Pere Girau was appointed pastor of the parish ever since leaving army life just over two years previously. Girau tried to take comfort from some knowledge of Saint Francis, not the one known as Assisi but a compatriot who had founded the Hermits of Assisi, later known as the Minim Friars. They were called 'the least of all the faithful'. Their distinguishing feature was humility. But Girau did not feel humble at the moment. *In truth I do not feel qualified to be a pastor, or even adequate for that matter. I'm not skilled in the pulpit. I'm very aware that my homilies are too stern. I understand that is because of my military training where homilies were needed to prop up the military goals and commitments of the servicemen and women. I am not at all comfortable making house calls on the sick and infirm. I don't really know how to react to people who are suffering from the ailments of old age, despite my background in cultural and social psychology. I am so much more comfortable handling the spiritual needs of soldiers who have been wounded or injured in military skirmishes or incidents.*

He was lost in his duties, uncertain about what he should be doing or for that matter how to do it. He felt a lack of direction. That certainly described his circumstances at 52 years old. His superior at the Archdiocese of Edmonton had believed he needed to find a renewed vocation and had transferred him to this diocesan post of pastor in Hull. Surely there had been an error of judgment, either his deciding to retire from the army, or perhaps the decision to accept the proffered pastoral position. He did not allow himself more than a fleeting consideration that the problem was the decision of his Archbishop in making the arrangement happen. That thought was unkind at the very least, even if possibly true. He was, after all, a priest and one trained to respect higher authority, both religious and military.

Father Girau appreciated the basic reason for the pastoral posting. He had been a priest for nearly 30 years, so he understood it was somewhat a matter of his seniority. The Archbishop of Edmonton, in the city where Girau had mustered out of the 1st Battalion PPCLI at CFB Edmonton, had known of the opening in Hull's parish church Our Lady of the Island and had proposed the transfer. The previous pastor, having served this congregation for more than 40 years had died, thus the vacancy. Girau went, partly because one did not often successfully argue with the Archbishop about assignments. He also thought he did need to move away from Edmonton and his life as a Chaplain/Psychologist in the military, even though he was particularly pleased about his association with 1st Bat. PPCLI, the second in precedence of the CF Infantry and one of the most decorated regiments in the entire Canadian Forces. *A clean break had been needed, at least so I had thought at the time. Surely that also had been an error of judgment.*

Ron Stotyn

The bishop in Hull, however, was new to the archdiocese and did not really know him. *Certainly it was clear this bishop had not considered my psychology training and specialty in personality analysis. My records should have shown two advanced degrees in that field of study. The records should also have clearly revealed that I had no prior pastoral experience outside the chaplaincy, which really was a rather different scenario for any priest. It would have been better if my talents have been recognized as a logical fit with Catholic Social Services or Catholic Charities. In such organizations my doctoral work in social and cultural psychology could be brought to bear on the troubles ordinary Catholic families were experiencing, especially in the hard economic times that Canadians were suffering at the moment. None of that seemed to have been considered. I could make a real difference in that kind of work. Now I minister mainly to the once a week variant of the devout.* That was frustrating.

Pere René Girau, MA (Psych), Ph.D. realized increasingly that he missed the tension and even the stress of serving in the military. That was where he enjoyed his unit practice using his psychological training and work to help souls in turmoil returned from battle zones, sometimes with serious mental trauma. He was skilled in treating personality disorders such as PTSD. Girau understood the problems; he felt and thought like a warrior. He had taken basic training like any ordinary soldier. He had worked out with them in the gym, rode with them on convoys, marched with them in drills. He could climb barriers, crawl under barbed wire courses, and even fire their weapons alongside them. That latter had been at his insistence to the company commanders. He argued a need to know their maneuvers in order to understand the soldier mentality; thus to serve them well when they experienced mental and spiritual needs at home and on foreign deployments. He truly was a warrior-priest. And now he was cut off from his fellow soldiers. He had served 25 years and at the time had believed his army service was truly done. Now he wasn't so sure. Perhaps he had made a mistake. *I can't speak about it to my bishop, who would just tut-tut and send me back to the parish telling me I should pray.*

Officially, he had been a chaplain, which gave him a certain cachet with the soldiers. Even though most Canadian soldiers were not Roman Catholic, they seemed to trust chaplains regardless of the denominational background. Unlike many chaplains, due to his unique perspective and clarity of understanding of the human psyche, his role had almost always been more than just spiritual counselor. His part was also as a mender of the human spirit, to get to know a soldier's mental state, to draw conclusions about personality and motivations. Then, he worked to try and help the soldier heal and return to functionality in the reality of position as a protector of the country. Over the years he believed he had been effective. *As a priest I've learned to avoid pride, but I am certainly more comfortable as warrior/healer/comforter.*

Heaving a sigh, almost bitter about his indecision, Girau left the confessional to prepare for the first Mass of the Sunday morning schedule. As he generally did, he went outside for a stroll around the parish grounds. It helped him to feel calmer as he readied himself to provide holy service for the parishioners. He whispered a prayer that begged strength. He would celebrate the Mass three times today, by standing permission of the bishop, because the parish was sufficiently large. Girau intended only a low mass this early in the morning and would save the liturgy for Saint Francis of Paola for 10 o'clock when the majority of the parish would show up for their weekly obligation. With his head down, still thinking of his quandary, he turned the corner of the chapel and looking ahead for a moment, made a surprising encounter. It would change his take on life in unexpected ways.

{3.1}

Outside Notre-Dame-De-L'Isle Sunday April 2 about 7 AM: Gatineau-Hull, QC.

Sunday was another spring-like day despite being early April. O'Dwyer-Lariviere was enjoying it, but pessimistically was ready for another week or two of cold and snow. That would be typical of Ottawa weather at this time of year. It was early in the morning, nearly

Ron Stotyn

seven A.M., and he was dressed again in a warm jogging outfit, ready this time to actually go running. Today, he planned to run in Parc Dupuis just a few blocks away adjacent to Rue St-Etienne. But first, he had arrived in front of Paroisse Notre-Dame-De-L'Isle on Boulevard Sacré-Coeur in Hull across the river from Ottawa, ready to take in morning Mass. That was his weekly habit, deep-rooted since childhood. Habits are often hard to discard, especially those insisted upon by Maman, a mortal saint if ever there was one. *My mother remains a great influence in my life. Like most mothers she is concerned about my lifestyle, my being divorced twice and my current single status. My divorces especially make my relationship to the church difficult, if not nearly impossible. I wonder if I should abandon the church altogether... can I even think it as long as Maman lives?*

He had driven from his hotel in his own car, a retired Crown Victoria Police Interceptor unmarked cruiser that he'd purchased from the Sûreté de Quebec, to revisit the church he had frequented during his days in Ottawa with CF Intelligence Branch. He had enjoyed the parish and its elderly but mentally very sharp pastor who'd served many years there. It was warm and friendly with a comfortable fellowship. He hoped that had not changed. Indeed, he would welcome the opportunity to find an apartment nearby within the parish, and soon he hoped, as he probably could not afford to stay in the Lisgar Extended Stay Suites very long. He'd started that search the previous afternoon and had seen two good possibilities. He would see several more, later today, with the leasing agent he had contacted before arriving in Ottawa. He hoped to finalize an apartment in the next day or two.

O'Dwyer-Lariviere could remember few times in his adult life when he did not attend a weekly service, usually the first Mass of the day. There was something about the routine that seemed to put a good start on the week. Truth to tell though, he could not be described as particularly devout in the faith. Perhaps there was some element of faith left in his life, but mostly he paid little attention to that. His work had given him a rather severely diminished appreciative view of people who had chosen to be involved with criminal activity. *That lack of faith has spilled over into my regard for the church. Still, church-*

going is not a habit easily broken, nor do I think I could as long as my parents are still alive. That would create disappointment.

His parents, both Roman Catholics, were Maeve Bridgett O'Dwyer-Lariviere and Jean Girard Lariviere. His mother could certainly be described as devout, having gone to morning Mass nearly every day, and still, of her life. That was definitely from her Irish heritage, where the parish church was central to the small Irish communities like Carney, the village of her birth in County Sligo. His father, less so, but was certainly a greater participant in church life than his own practice. Girard was a member of the Knights of Columbus and regularly participated in fundraising efforts for Presbytere Sacré-Coeur De Stanstead, the parish of his own childhood and where his father had been born. But his father's practice was not quite a daily attendance, being more like Saturday and Sunday Mass and, of course, holidays and holy days. But, it was true that their example had contributed to his outlook toward the church, at least until the moment he entered Royal Military College. From that point to the present, his work dictated his life pursuits; church became less often a primary focus. Most of the time, in fact, church was rarely even a secondary position.

His faith had been subjected to a liberalizing influence. He ascribed that to his studies of political science and to realizations that church of any kind really had little significant influence in the lives of so many people in the country. *Church has become less of a stabilizing influence and more a symbolic comfort at times when my life is not so well organized.* His failed marriages and his failures as a team player meant those times occurred more often than he might prefer. He realized he had made it something to fall back on as needed instead of a mainstay. He understood in the moment that habits are indeed hard to break; just as he heard a remembered voice call out.

"Sean-Guy, is that you?" Father Girau was certain he knew the man; the height of more than six feet and the muscular lithe build was unmistakable in his mind. "What a surprise to see you after so many years. It is a delight. You have been delinquent, my son, in keeping in touch with me." O'Dwyer-Lariviere turned in surprise to see Pere René Girau, short and stocky with a French peasant's face as he had

Ron Stotyn

remembered, hurrying toward him. The priest called, "What are you doing here in Hull? I thought you were still toiling away in Montreal trying to crack unsolvable crimes."

"Pere René, I am equally surprised to see you," replied Sean-Guy. "I have just come to attend Mass. Are you serving here then? I thought you were still a chaplain with the 5e Régiment d'artillerie légère du Canada. That was the last time we were together I think, do you agree? I am delighted to see you. We have much to catch up on. Perhaps a café-au-lait after the Mass is completed?" Sean-Guy recalled his friendship and had to agree he was remiss in not keeping up. His work with the Sûrété had made him an even more solitary man than he had been in the military. Innumerable nights on stake-out made friendships difficult to establish or maintain. *Indeed I have rarely even had the opportunity to form a close relationship with a partner; most of my partnerships have been temporary at best.*

"Sean-Guy, regrettably I am not available until noon. I have a full schedule of Mass this morning, but I suggest we meet for lunch at Bosco Patates on Boulevard Saint-Joseph. I have a weakness for Poutine, you might remember," said the priest, who looked a good deal older than Sean-Guy remembered. The hair was grayer and there was a tired expression on the face. The exuberance Sean-Guy recalled was no longer evident.

O'Dwyer-Lariviere replied, "Of course, and I do remember your penchant for Poutine, which I share with you. I can meet you after your schedule is done this morning, about 12:30 or 1 o'clock I think. Yes?"

"D'accord" replied the priest. "It is settled," as he turned and hurried toward the chapel. Looking back over his shoulder, he called out laughing, "Try not to be late," knowing full well the cop was rarely late unless he could not control the situation. Whatever else was among Sean-Guy's faults, the priest knew there were some, but tardiness was not one.

Sean-Guy proceeded toward the entrance of the chapel, ready to attend Mass, amused and bemused by the priest's demeanor and delighted to meet up with him again. His day had begun on a happy note. After the mass he would still have time to run, return to the hotel for a shower and meet his friend on time.

Elsewhere was a man similarly pleased but for singularly different reasons.

{3.2}
Union Station, about 7 AM Sunday April 2: Toronto ON

Marek Kafirov was inside Toronto's Union Station, having taken a bus from Dundas Street West near his apartment in Little Poland. He could have connected to the Lakeshore West line at a station closer to his district and in the direction of his first meeting site, but had wanted the chance to check up on the new Union Station staircase construction to see if it would be a useful detonation site. It would do just that, he discovered, due to available hiding spots amongst the construction equipment and rubble. Explosions there would create considerable confusion and death from debris shrapnel effect resulting from the detonations. Satisfied about the possibilities, he went to the platform to wait for the train to Oakville where he would conduct the first leader's meeting of the day. On the way he picked up a lamb gyro sandwich, which would likely satisfy his Halal needs, at a food court kiosk near the main hall. Even if the lamb were not properly slaughtered, the rule permitted the eating of certain non-Halal foods.

The train arrived promptly; he had calculated his arrival carefully according to the schedule, also a test he would expect his teams to perform several times in the next two weeks. He found a seat in the first car next to the engine, sitting as close to the adjoining end of the car as he could. The plan called for this position to be a designated location for the team member assigned to detonate an explosive charge on the planned Monday morning. His cell leader, employed in the Go Train yards would also place a shaped charge under the floor just above the trucks. That should cause an accordion reaction of the following cars with considerable loss of life. Throwing the power unit off the tracks would mean a disruption in service for days, a welcome addition to the madness being planned. His

Ron Stotyn

imagination was stimulated by the seating spot as he looked forward to the opportunity to further inspire his team leaders with thoughts of their approach to paradise.

His first meeting was with two captains, a pair of dedicated leader-warriors devoted to the cause, entirely accepting of the prospect of entering paradise by taking revenge on the friends of their enemies. These jihadists were well versed in the purity of Wahhabism and of the call to salafi jihad. He knew little of their history; only that they were products of KavKaz, created by Baseyev and al-Khattab in 1997 as a special camp where recruited young Chechens were indoctrinated in a manner similar to that of al Qaeda. Fathi Batal al-Shishani and Edris Gaziev were not mercenaries, but Chechens who had suffered as he had suffered. Their families had been butchered by treacherous Russians in much the same way as his own.

The first of these, al-Shishani, with the name assumed of course, had chosen that surname as tribute to a veteran of the Soviet-Afghan war. The real al-Shishani had persuaded Ibn al-Khattab to come to Chechnya. Khattab was an honored guerilla and financier during the first and second Chechen wars. Marek's al-Shishani was made responsible for detonation at Oakville shortly after the train closed its doors ready to embark. Oakville was a significant stop on the Lakeshore West line, so the explosion in the early part of the commuter schedule should create considerable death and destruction. The other cell master Edris Gaziev paid homage with his chosen name to a family forced to flee from Chechnya to save their young children. Gaziev was very bitter that many such families had been forced to flee their homeland and sought to revenge them; that much Marek had gathered from previous conversations. The motive was pure, he had decided.

Marek did not know their real names nor did he need to know. What he did discern was that these leaders appreciated no other way than suicide terrorism, having trained for their mission since a very young age. He expected no trouble from them. Gaziev, on a different train, would explode his device upon arrival at Union Station concurrently with other detonations. Marek had placed these patriots together largely because they were each Chechen, had trained together, and understood fully the value of Wahhabist brotherhood. They would protect each other all the way to whatever end came to them. Dying for the cause was a matter of total commitment.

As the train made its way toward Oakville, Marek considered the second meeting of the day. That would require returning eastbound on the Lakeshore West Go Train to Union Station then transferring to several buses northbound to Aurora. On a weekday he could take the Go train north-bound; however, the Barrie line did not operate on the weekend. The route he had to take was beneficial though, since he would transfer at the Yorkdale Bus Terminal, where he expected to see that the busyness would make it a logical supplementary or alternate detonation point. The crowds of people scurrying from train to bus or bus to bus would be an opportune setting for one or two explosions. He expected to find ranks of buses closely parked side by side at this key transfer point, a situation that certainly would contribute to massive wreckage.

Marek's cell structure for the northern region of the plan involved three captains, Afghanis who had come to Chechnya to support the Wahhabist induced separatism movement. They each had been trained by al Qaeda. Marek was concerned that their attitude was a bit haughty toward Chechens, but was satisfied they were prepared to follow his lead. They had the same kind of passion his Chechen comrades had, their country once having been overrun by the Russians. In the Afghan fashion these leaders claimed only single names, surnames not being part of their tradition, although they used surnames for their Canadian jobs in the fashion of western usage.

Marek neither knew nor cared what these last names were. So he would meet with Daoud, Omid and Gul-Bashra at approximately one PM, as arranged at a chess club. He would eat his gyro sandwich on the train before arriving. Daoud was responsible for detonations planned for the Milton Go Train line, Omid for the Georgetown line and Gul-Bashra for the Barrie line. These three terrorists had unusually good access to the trains, each were employed by the train system as car mechanics. They would know which cars would be in service on the designated day and especially which cars would be at the head of the train's consist/makeup behind the engine. Daoud, in addition to

Ron Stotyn

carrying a package on-board, would attach a charge in the undercarriage of the car next to the engine that would ensure a severe derailment at Erindale, which was a bus transfer location. Omid would do the same for his train on the Georgetown line; detonation would occur upon reaching the Bloor Street Station. That underground location would be exceptionally difficult for emergency responders to contain. Gul-Bashra was responsible for the Barrie line. Marek had decided to detonate explosive devices on two different trains on that line simultaneously. One northbound train would explode when reaching Barrie and the other moving south would explode when arriving at the Yorkdale Go Bus Terminal. Gul-Bashra would have to place his cell members carefully to catch the designated trains in a timely fashion to meet the planned schedule. Even though Marek had not yet closely examined the bus terminal, he believed a location change would reap more devastating results. That southbound train would also be rigged with undercarriage explosives to create a massive derailment underground. Devastation was the key consideration at all times, and the more the better.

For the third meeting and last of the day, Marek was gathering his most trusted captains; both Chechens like himself. The first of these was almost like a real brother, recruited by the Imam Ali Ibn al-Hassan at the same time as Marek. They had nearly grown up together, except for the time while Marek was at Stanstead College in Quebec and at university in Pakistan. During this latter time, Yamadayev went to KavKaz. Muhammad Yamadayev, in his name choice, recognized the tragedy to Chechnya in the murder of Sulim Yamadayev, a former Chechen military commander killed on March 28th of the previous year. Marek entrusted Yamadayev's cell with several detonation points at Union Station, one on the train itself just as it was ready to pull out of the station on the western leg of the twin Lakeshore route and several others inside the station. The exact spots were still pending. Two of Yamadayev's cell members would create the detonations on the Stouffville Line when the train reached Agincourt moving south-west from Markham.

The other leader was Abdul Saidullayev, who had chosen the name of the President who replaced the assassinated Maskhadev and who was himself murdered in 2006, both by Russian forces. Saidullayev would be responsible for detonations on a different train than that of Yamadayev when it reached Scarborough. Once again, Marek was indifferent about the real names of these trusted captains. He only cared that their hearts were pure and that they were prepared to die for the glory of Allah. His plan for Monday morning madness was coming closer to completion. There remained only selection of detonation locations inside the Union Station and several practices over the next two weeks. The plan, which he considered a masterpiece in its expansiveness, would surely cause chaos in the region as well as much retributive death.

Next Sunday the meetings would be used to confirm and finalize the plans. Marek would give out keys to storage lockers to each captain, who would pick up prepared packages of explosives two or three days prior to the set schedule for the explosive plan. He had been able to make duplicate keys without difficulty. His own particular duty would be to take the disguised packages to each pickup location, a task that could be completed over the course of several days in the coming week. There was no danger the selected lockers would be compromised in any way because they did not have keys inserted into the locks. Nobody else, therefore, could use them. His own set of keys gave him the necessary access. The cell leaders would provide explicit instructions to their team members for deployment and detonation. Each captain would give those final instructions to their own cells during scheduled meetings that were already a routine for them.

Late that night Marek returned home, all set for his last prayers of the evening, and ready to give praise to Allah for the good work that would be soon done. Allah would surely return blessings for the manner in which retribution would be delivered. Marek's fury was ripening as the time drew closer to put the plan to its ultimate test. His fury dictated that the intended vengeance occur without any frustration.

Ron Stotyn

{3.3}
Early evening, about 7 PM, Sunday April 2: Hull QC

Pere René Girau sat again in the confessional, for the remainder of the day's schedule, again contemplating his situation, but with the added experience of having met up with former Lt. O'Dwyer-Lariviere. Based on the conversation the two of them had earlier in the day over platters of fries crunchy on the outside and soft on the inside sitting on a lake of wonderfully fragrant beef gravy and ladles of cottage cheese topping the pile; Girau thought that an opportunity had perhaps opened up like a gift from God. *O'Dwyer-Lariviere's new job might well be the chance for the exercise of my own skills and talents toward understanding the mental processes of the human mind, especially when affected by trauma. Sorting out a damaged mind is my stock in trade.*

He'd not said anything to Sean-Guy about that, but the idea was racing in his own mind. *To be involved again with personality analysis would move me back towards satisfying fulfillment in life. But how can I manage a viable connection to what Sean-Guy faces? I have never specifically considered my field of study in terms of terrorists, but I can see the similarities concerning ailments such as PTSD. Severe depression is all too often a major symptom among the soldiers I have counseled. It is often because of things they had been part of on the battlefield, events that had occurred to often to be ignored, or horrors in which they had participated, had actually created, or had closely experienced. These experiences created tortures of the mind.*

René recalled from his academic training that the significance of post-traumatic stress disorder was that of an anxiety disorder related to or caused by serious traumatic events. The symptoms characterized as guilt about surviving or reliving the trauma in dreams or numbness reveal themselves as lack of involvement with reality or recurrent thoughts and images. It was typically debilitating in severe cases.

The priest understood that the typical classification made by mental health professionals identified the condition if the symptoms of stress last for more than a month after a traumatic event. Girau knew also from his own extensive encounters with over-stressed soldiers that a formal diagnosis of PTSD is made only in the wake of a severe trauma. Still, he knew, it is possible to have a mild PTSD-like reaction following less severe stress. He was positive that a study of the behaviors of terrorists would reveal similar patterns of trauma and stress. He made a mental note to do some research on that topic tomorrow. In the meantime he continued to wonder how to broach the idea to Sean-Guy. Sean-Guy was not an individual easy to approach on matters close to his sense of duty. The man typically exercised a high level of possessiveness about his assignments.

That reminded him that there was something else about Sean-Guy that seemed at odds with the man he remembered from many years ago. He cast his thought process backward trying to recall specifics about the then young second lieutenant, fresh from RMC. Sean-Guy had clearly demonstrated his brilliance academically, but he was insecure in his military responsibilities. He had been sent to the 5e Regiment d'artillerie to develop leadership skills. That had not gone so well for Sean-Guy could not seem to understand how to be a team player. He was very much an individualist, inclined more often than not to just go ahead and do a task instead of parceling it out to his subordinates. His talent for understanding how to complete tasks and his skill at undertaking a process was amazing, but that was not the army way. Delegation was expected of its officers.

Today Sean-Guy had demonstrated superb self-confidence and self-control and yet something was not quite right. Pere Dr. René Girau, accomplished psychologist, could not quite put his finger on the issue. It bothered him to reflect that he had no concrete answer. *I need a chance to observe the man at greater depth, soon I hope. Time and proximity is always important when developing diagnosis.*

He chuckled to himself that he was already trying to create a personality profile, something he'd not done since coming to the parish as pastor. And suddenly he realized that was exactly what he could do to assist the work of Sean-Guy and his team at CAS. Doing personality analysis with a goal to creating a profile naturally progressed from the general to the specifics; amending the description as more evidence became available. Surely there is enough general evidence about the

Ron Stotyn

behavior and personalities of terrorists to begin helping this new organization how to more fully understand what they are up against.

He and Sean-Guy could certainly collaborate on that because the new Chief Inspector had talked a bit during their conversation earlier in the day about his own Master's thesis and Doctoral dissertation. Sean-Guy's study of camaraderie and criminal behavior among motorcycle gang members could provide the basis for developing theories about similar behavior and connections among certain kinds of terrorists. The dissertation topic, the priest remembered, involved the idea that criminal behavior was a root cause for the development of home-grown terrorists. There was certainly a lot of evidence about that in Canada's own experience. René remembered being introduced to some of that research in courses such as Abnormal Psychology, Development Psychology, and Social Psychology during his bachelor's degree work in psych. Some research had focused on the FLQ which had perpetrated over 200 bombings and several murders in the name of Quebec sovereignty during the 1960's and early 1970's. If they were not home-grown terrorists, the priest was sure he didn't know of any. *Still, I am not certain that criminal behavior would fit descriptions of modern terrorist behavior of the type described for internationally active terrorists.* That would require some study.

Girau also recalled some research about violence perpetrated by the Doukhobors in British Columbia. They had emigrated from Southern Russia in the late 1800's and in the early 20th century they clashed repeatedly with the Canadian government over noncompliance with land, tax, and education laws. There was some violence involved, their protests got media attention regularly because of their women marching around naked, as well as the burning of and blowing things to smithereens such as houses and power poles. He didn't remember if any death had occurred. *They had been acting out before the term terrorist was part of the modern lexicon, but I think the term can be applied retroactively.*

Then a little light went on in his head. The priest took note about something Sean-Guy had said when asked about his family life. He had mentioned a daughter from his first marriage and seemed sad.

Apparently she was not much in his life. Sean-Guy had not said anything about a second marriage but the use of the term 'first marriage' suggested that was likely. There had also been no discussion of what had happened to the first marriage. The priest surmised, with a high probability of being correct, that there had been a divorce. Perhaps that was what he found disconcerting about Sean-Guy, something that Sean-Guy had not been able to resolve in his life. Certainly it was likely that a divorce would cause some sense of disconnect with the church because of Catholic polity, even though Sean-Guy still attended. The priest wondered if Sean-Guy took communion, or if he came to the confessional. If not that would surely signal an issue with the man. The church did frown on that kind of participation for those who had been divorced in certain circumstances.

In fact, as Pere René reviewed the matter in church law pertaining to divorced members, there were a number of important questions that had to be answered. Was the first marriage made 'in the church'? If so, the sacramental act would endure to death of one of the partners even if a divorce followed. Then one would have to ask about a second marriage in terms of the question: Was there an annulment of the first marriage? If no annulment then a second marriage was purely a civil matter. From the church's point of view the first sacramental marriage was still to be recognized. If there was a church recognized annulment, procedurally correct as directed by a diocesan tribunal, the second marriage would then have to be considered in terms of its sacramental standing. Was the second marriage 'in the church'? If so, the divorced member would not be constrained from participating in the sacraments of the church, but only if the first marriage was properly annulled. If not, then the divorced man, such as his friend Sean-Guy seemed possibly to be, would be excluded from participating in the sacraments including confession and communion. *All of this could be what troubles my friend.*

The priest sighed, concerned for his reunited friend, as he left the confessional and went into the chapel to pray. There was much he had to pray about; for his own sense of faith crisis, his lack of commitment to the pastoral role, and for his re-found fellow soldier.

Ron Stotyn

The future is complex and as usual nearly impossible to comprehend. Tomorrow, he decided, he would need to consider very carefully what God would want him to do about seeking to provide analysis assistance to Sean-Guy and the members of the CAS. But, he knew he was already nearly convinced he was being called. How to make the connection, though, was still a big question.

{4}

"The value of a goal lies in the goal itself; and therefore the goal cannot be attained unless it is pursued for its own sake"
Arnold Toynbee

Early Morning, CAS HQ, Monday April 3: Ottawa ON

Chief Inspector Sean-Guy O'Dwyer-Lariviere expected to arrive early for his first day of duty at the CAS. To do otherwise would mean *I'm not myself, to be ill or gone astray, which would be highly unlikely.* Try as he might, his internal clock just was not receptive to sleeping longer than about 5 AM. So it had been since childhood; he understood it was ingrained habit, as he lingered over his second cup of coffee at Café Slater. But, to be sure, it wasn't necessarily his first preference; a long night on surveillance often meant he very grudgingly arose that early if he had managed at all to get some sleep. Nevertheless, to greet the morning before the sun came up was normal for Sean-Guy.

Up before dawn to do chores and then get ready for classes at Stanstead College, up before dawn on the week-ends to do chores and then get ready for the first Mass of the day. That pattern persisted into university and his military career. The chores changed with the military; calisthenics before classes at the Royal Military College and the same before breakfast in the 5e Regiment d'artillerie légère du Canada. *By the time I returned to the CFIB it was solidified. Rise before dawn; run for a couple of miles, shower and only then, normally, have breakfast prior to beginning a day of duties.* No different today, he reflected, as he prepared to move on toward the CAS offices further up O'Conner Street.

On this second visit to the coffee shop, he appreciated the cheeriness of the wait-staff and the prompt service out of the kitchen. As he got up to pay his bill, he caught a glimpse of himself reflected in the window. He had dressed in a dark brown suit, almost black, with a thin noble blue stripe. Under the suit jacket he had decided to wear a turtle neck sweater, a deep rust color; he did not want to be too formal

Ron Stotyn

on this job, though his wardrobe could accommodate that if needed. And he could dress down; indeed, his ready bag, which he always had with him, contained a change of office clothes and rough wear, jeans and a denim work shirt along with athletic shoes, a cross over design that allowed for brisk walking or running. That bag was being carried today; a smallish duffle bag made of rugged Cordura material.

All his suit jackets and sport coats were tailored to accommodate his service weapon, which he wore in a double shoulder rig. The automatic was a Para PXT P18•9, holstered on his right side because he was left handed and three full clips holstered on the left side in quick release pouches. He continued to use that particular model even though he was no longer active duty at the Surété du Quebec. He would ask to retain it if the CAS used something else; he had grown used to the balance of the weapon and very much liked the idea of the large clip capacity. Altogether, with a round in the pipe, he had 19 ready to fire. It had, in fact, been a bonus when he'd found himself in a gunfight with the motorcycle gang earlier in the year. It made the difference against the murder-for-hire perps. The Para design was a variation on the famous 1911 model Colt. He also carried a compact Para Hawg 9 as a backup tucked in a belt holster at the small of his back, though at the moment it was in the left hand pocket of his topcoat for easy reach when he was all buttoned up. That wasn't often as he usually left the topcoat unbuttoned unless it was really frigid out. Today was cold but not unbearable.

Both weapons were 9 mm and both were Canadian made. The Hawg also had a large capacity, holding 12+1 rounds. He carried two magazines in a belt pouch for the spare gun. His colleagues sometimes had commented that he was overkill with regard to the firepower, but he reminded them that in bad situations time lost reloading was a window for personal disaster. Avoiding personal disaster was a personal credo that he tried his best to uphold, though that had not gone so well in the battle with the murder for hire biker gang. He'd taken a couple to the right shoulder in that gunfight. Fortunately neither hit bone. His luck had always been good. He didn't dwell on it though, that was unlikely to contribute to a good mental state. The biker gang had taken the greater hurt; three top leaders killed and two arrested after they went down.

His clothes were not Saville Row by any stretch of the imagination, nor were they off the rack at Wal-Mart or K-Mart. He went to Big and Tall shops to get the jacket and sleeve length he needed for his 6'3" and 210 pounds frame and for the necessary tailoring adjustments. The stripe in the suit came close to matching the blue-gray color of his eyes, a color that apparently disconcerted suspects when he interviewed them. That color was like slate with similar impenetrable qualities. He had the ability to look at suspects with an unwavering steely gaze when needed. The intensity with such interrogations was always hard focused and probing. On the other hand, women seemed find his eyes charming as if it was a case of them finding some mystery in them. *I'm not often easy to engage on first contacts, not that I've had many of those recently,* he thought ruefully. The second divorce had persuaded him that he was best off if he avoided serious relationships. But casual relationships had been sporadic as well.

As he moved toward the checkout counter, he reflected that his face, as it is sometimes said one that only a mother could love, had aged a bit in recent years. It was to some extent craggy, with more ruggedness as lines around his chin and cheeks had become pronounced. The jaw was still square and there was yet no sag under the chin. He had also developed some lines around his eyes; sometimes called crows-feet he knew, but overall the face remained strong and Irish in appearance, except for the truly Gallic nose, a long rounded hooked beak. That nose, broken twice, was not properly reset either time. The first time was from playing hockey with no helmet at Stanstead College when he was roughly boarded by a player on the other side. The second time occurred with a face plant into the floor, when he had been fouled in a basketball game at RMC. Overall his appearance was of a man who brooked no nonsense. *That is probably an accurate description of my personality. I am a man, once my mind is made up, who holds to strong opinions that are rarely out of bounds. It takes a strong, unassailable factual argument to persuade me differently.*

Ron Stotyn

Leaving the café, he pulled on his tweed overcoat against the chill morning air. Claire Martin, the meteorologist for CBC at its Vancouver weather center had been correct. Arctic air had definitely invaded Ottawa and the Gatineau valley. But no snow yet, despite being forecast. It would likely arrive later in the day. He never wore a scarf since it could impede access to his service automatic. Layered clothing was the better solution against Canadian winter weather. He pulled his Wedge cap down to the top of his ears. Formally called Cap, Man's Winter, Fur, C.F., it was left over from his RMC uniform. It covered black curly hair; quite unruly if he left it to grow too long. People often correctly called him Black Irish, which he was, but as a Canadian Irish-French mix he'd discovered early on that he was not fond of Guinness; in fact he preferred Alexander Keith Stag's Dark Ale.

Walking fairly briskly toward the CAS office now, he turned his mind to the meeting he'd had yesterday with Pere René Girau, an unexpected but fortuitous encounter. Pere René, it turned out, was not particularly happy as a parish pastor. He'd retired from the military chaplaincy but now seemed to regret it. The priest had been an unusual chaplain in that he was as well trained in the military arts as any soldier. He understood soldiers very well. Girau had pursued an advanced education in psychology so that he could work closely with returning soldiers who suffered from their deployment experiences. Sean-Guy believed that René Girau was a unique individual, who could be so much more useful than as a pastoral priest in an urban parish. He was somewhat amazed the priest had accepted such an assignment; indeed, he wondered why the man had left military service, unless only for reasons that he had reached 25 years in uniform. Deep in thought, Sean-Guy considered details from yesterday's several shared hours with Pere René at Bosco Patates over heaping platters of Poutine.

{4.1}
Bosco Patates, yesterday afternoon, April 2: Hull QC

Sean-Guy, in a mood of continuing friendship following the usual pleasantries upon their arrival, had searched for an appropriate comment or query. It was a slightly awkward moment given the amount of time that had resulted from his lack of contact with the shorter bear of a man. "I find it interesting that you have both master's and doctoral degrees in social and cultural psychology."

Pere René had replied, "I am especially interested in and reasonably informed about effects of ethnicity, political oppression, violence induced stress and their potential for developing personality disorders." That point revealed several similarities in their education, especially in psychological topics. "My work," René said, "has frequently involved Forensic Psychology and pathology of the mind such as disturbances in the personality of adults."

Sean-Guy noted "that meshes very well with my own understanding of adult criminal behavior. I have been especially motivated about how criminals develop camaraderie due to shared ideas about behavior against society. This can explain quite a bit about how, for example, motorcycle gangs develop patterns in committing crime." Then he tried to show some boundaries on his studies so the priest would properly understand the thrust. "My research is limited to criminal behavior, and especially to gang culture, with some research into the creation of home-grown terrorists." He also noted, "My research venue has been largely restricted to Quebec, because that is where I grew up. Despite my time in Ottawa with the CFIB, I lived here in Hull, so the foundation of my research thrust continued to be focused toward incidents in Quebec."

The priest responded, "Have you then felt a lack of awareness about what goes on in other provinces, say for example my own, Saskatchewan?"

Sean-Guy had to admit the truth of that observation, as he realized newly that the priest was what some people referred to as Fransaskois, a French speaker born and raised in Saskatchewan. But he did not get the impression that René Girau was Métis, officially recognized by Canada as the same rank as First Nations tribes, but in reality a mix of aboriginal and Caucasian parentage at the earliest lineage.

Ron Stotyn

René confirmed that by informing him, "I was born in Gravelbourg, in the southern end of the province. My parents moved from Quebec with their families when they were quite young. I grew up in a mostly rural environment, speaking French to my family and to many of my neighbors, but English during the day at school with my friends. My French, you must understand, was not perfection. It was a kind of Canadian Patois, a bit of a mixture of country French and English, a sort of slang I suppose you could say. The same for my English I am afraid, that is, not very proper, but that was not so much a problem because all my friends were pretty much rowing the same boat. It was not until university that my English improved." The priest then laughingly said, "My French is, well, still from the provincial I am afraid. My parishioners complain they cannot always understand me."

Sean-Guy, taking into consideration the man's appearance and manner, put the priest's age now as early fifties. René revealed, "I was ordained the same year I graduated from the University of Regina with a BA in Psychology. Most of my seminary training occurred during the same period. It was a very busy time, I can assure you. Later I enlisted with the PPCLI in 1982. I was then 25 years of age." The priest observed that "following a short assignment to the 5e Regiment, I was posted back to Edmonton to my primary assignment in the Chaplaincy of the PPCLI. That occurred after completing my MA in Psych, also at the U of Regina. I did most of the work while functioning as a counselor with the Archdiocese of Regina in the Pastoral Health Care department. "Oh," said René, "that came out a bit confusing. I meant to say the degree was finished already when I joined the PPCLI." The priest added, "I soon found that my psych background, even with limited practical experience at this point, was a boon when I became a chaplain."

Sean-Guy knew very well that The 1st Battalion, Princess Patricia's Canadian Light Infantry was a well decorated unit; with a well deserved reputation for valorous actions. To René he said, "I imagine it was a kind of baptism in fire to engage with soldiers having experience in rather violent actions."

The priest agreed and described his background work as a counselor involved in assisting chaplains in hospitals and other health care centers. "That really was my introduction to the Chaplaincy, and the experience I gained qualified me as a chaplain, especially after the Archbishop provided a letter of certification when I applied to join the military."

Sean-Guy also then discovered that Pere René had completed his PhD dissertation in 1992, shortly after finishing an assignment with 1st Battalion, The Royal Canadian Regiment.

René said, "I was fortunate to be in Edmonton for an extended period of time. I attended the University of Alberta. I was able to do a serious exploration of human conduct in social and cultural situations. I was especially intrigued by ethnic sources of identity that lead to conversations that frame self-perception. I did research into situations that foster psychological defense and imaginative experiences that tend to alter one's sense of self."

At that point the priest confirmed that he had returned to his PPCLI duties the same year, 1992, and after 12 more years had retired from the service two years ago. Along the way he had achieved regular promotions starting with Lieutenant, then Captain and finally to Major.

They then discussed briefly what René was doing at the parish, though he seemed reluctant to say much more than to describe the parish and his pastoral work.

Rene soon asked, "And what have you been doing? When did you leave the military and how did you become a police official?"

Sean-Guy, launching into his own history, said: "Well, since time is short I'll give you a condensed version. You already know I was with the 5e Régiment only a year. That assignment was meant to be training in leadership, but I confess it did not go entirely according to plan. I was, and I reluctantly admit, I remain somewhat an individualist."

René reflected out loud, "I think that I realized that after we had met several times. I had hoped you would not frustrate your career, but I could not intervene as you were not my patient or anything like that. I'm sorry if that caused continuing difficulties for you."

Ron Stotyn

Sean-Guy admitted, "My first promotion was delayed for another year and that put me behind my cohort by two years. After awhile I realized I would never catch up. Then I was advised privately that I was not regarded as senior officer material. At that point I had my minimum years in. I decided to retire from military service."

René asked, "And your education, you had used your service time and opportunities to finish, what?"

"Well," responded Sean-Guy, "my time in Ottawa with CFIB allowed me to go to the University of Ottawa. My schedule was such that I was usually in classes during the day and on duty at night. I was able to do both a masters and a Ph.D. focusing on aspects of criminal behavior inside groups with criminal activities. Like you it was busy times."

"You must have been single, like me, to accomplish such a schedule," suggested the priest.

"Unfortunately," said Sean-Guy, with a momentarily sad tone, almost too brief for the priest to catch, "it did much harm to my family life. I was a father, but not available when needed. I have a daughter who has grown up largely without me."

Pere Girau, his priestly sensitivities aroused, thought to himself, this man is not yet ready to talk freely about this deep hurt. He changed the topic, hoping he would not seem to be prying. "It was your studies about crime I suppose that led you to the police?"

Sean-Guy, as a recent Sergeant of the Sûreté du Quebec, grinned and nodded his assent to that idea. "To this day I am not certain I understand the decision, but yes, that is what prompted me to make application despite having no other particularly relevant qualification other than my academic work. My military experience was, of course, involved with intelligence gathering and the like, thus not exactly what the police would expect." He was silent for a moment, and then stated, "I was very surprised to be accepted. After 15 weeks of intensive training, I was made a sergeant and sent out to serve in the district of Abitibi-Témiscamingue-Nord-du-Québec. That place, as you may know, is near to the back of beyond. I suppose my rank as appointed considered some merit of my military hitch. Of course, as sergeant, I had no supervisory responsibilities. That suited me at that time, but I failed to appreciate I would be expected to participate in actions as a team member. That was and remains a struggle of my temperament. I acknowledge that my tendency to go and do what is needed without team participation causes my superiors to be anxious." He thought to himself that he could not admit the same to a boss. *I was afraid of being dismissed for insubordination.*

{4.2}
CAS Headquarters, O'Conner Street, 7:50 AM, April 3: Ottawa ON

Sean-Guy arriving, in the midst of his recollections, at the CAS building, recalled that their discussion had then shifted to more trivial matters. Soon after, they had broken off, said their goodbyes, promised to meet again soon and went their separate ways. O'Dwyer-Lariviere noted the time as he came to the end of his reflection about yesterday's meeting with Pere Girau. He entered the destination building satisfied he would be earlier than expected.

Upon entering the foyer, he was surprised that no one was on duty at the front desk. He went up to the CAS offices, this time using the elevator, arriving on the fourth floor at 7:55 AM. The office door was unlocked; he entered to find only one other person inside. It was Betty Anne Grabler, he surmised, since she was at the desk that he had noted previously bore a small sign with that name.

"Good Morning," he said, "I have an appointment with the Director at 8 AM."

"Hello, I'm Betty Grabler. The Director has called to say he is slightly delayed. Let me put you into his office. I know that you are the new Chief Investigator. Your picture has been circulated to us." She added, "I have started the coffee pot. You are welcome to help yourself. It's over here in the corner for convenience."

Just then a tallish man entered the room behind him. Sean-Guy turned and recognized Brigadier General Leif Isaksson; fair haired as might be expected for someone of a Nordic heritage, slender with a very erect bearing. Sean-Guy knew enough about the man to recognize that the slenderness should not lead one to assume anything about the

Ron Stotyn

man's physical abilities. The former general had a reputation for toughness from his many years in Special Operations Forces.

Unconsciously coming to an attention stance, but resisting the inclination to salute, Sean-Guy said, "Chief Investigator O'Dwyer-Lariviere reporting for duty sir." The general, he noted, was actually precisely on time.

Isaksson smiled at Sean-Guy's physical attitude, "You need not stand to attention since we both are retired. Welcome. Come with me and sit as soon as you get a coffee. We have important things to discuss right away."

Sean-Guy went to take a cup and followed to the corner office, almost on the director's heals, who had his own mug of steaming coffee. Inside, the director motioned to a comfortable chair, took his own behind the desk and said: "I prefer that we all use given names here. We need to rapidly become comfortable workmates. Again, I welcome you to the team Sean-Guy." He added, before Sean-Guy had a chance to protest about using the director's first name, "My name is Leif, like the Norse explorer."

Leif launched into a run-down of the CAS operations without a pause. "We have only just begun. Most of us have been only a week or so on the job, me included. We are desperately trying to get up to speed. Already there are several things on our situation board. Most of them have little information attached. Your presence is critical to help us discover what we need to be focused on in terms of establishing priorities." Leif switched gears almost as rapidly as he had begun that first topic. "I have read your file and I understand that you have an individualistic bent. That will be fine here up to a point. I need self-directed investigators, but I also need them to be sharing information almost as soon as they obtain it. It is of critical importance that we all be able to function with the same goals in mind. It will be dangerous for each of us, and especially for our country to discover that someone has neglected to keep the rest of us fully informed. Enough said! What do you especially want me to know about you?"

Sean-Guy, slightly taken aback by the high energy comments and the focus on his tendency to go it alone, thought briefly and replied, "I am very glad to have this opportunity to work again for the federal government. I am especially pleased that I can bring my experience and education to bear on such critical elements as terrorism and the possible impact on Canadian life. I have only one request of you. If I am to be an effective chief investigator, I need to have full clearance to see everything that you see. This will help me design the best way to plan for the best possible discovery."

The director replied, "Already done, and in addition, because we are both employed by the DND, I must tell you that we are protected by the Security of Information Act. No one who has not been cleared needs to know what we do here. In fact, we are all designated as persons bound to secrecy. Here is your written notice of that which you will need to sign. In addition everyone in this agency who has had previous military enrollment has been reactivated as reserve officers. We won't be using those ranks here in the office, but in the event we have to deal with regular CF officers we have rank to give us certain credibility. I have brevet rank as Major General, yours is a brevet rank of Major. I insisted on that rank because of your position as chief investigator. If we ever have to investigate the military itself or military personnel we have absolute authority."

Sean-Guy, quite amazed at this turn of events, did not for a moment know what to say. "Well sir, I am flabbergasted. I can only say where do I start?"

Leif, amused at Sean-Guy's consternation, said, "We have about a half hour before I introduce you to the rest of our team, so let me bring you up to date. First, let me say we have a meeting here at 10 AM. The Chairman of the House Committee on Terrorism Control will be arriving to speak to us and officially give us our mandate. Willard Elred, the MP for Grasslands-Cypress in Saskatchewan, is probably more knowledgeable than most of his colleagues about this issue of terrorist threat likelihood in Canada. He has a very good relationship with the DND. He is expected to be our friend and has considerable clout on the hill. As long as the present government remains in power he will try to ensure we have the resources we need."

"About resources, I have had a chance to see some good technology out in the office, but a mix with older stuff. Are we on a short list for upgrades?" asked Sean-Guy. Then, hesitant about

Ron Stotyn

implying some disrespect, he commented, "I'm especially concerned about security. When I entered the building this morning, I was not checked in any way. Surely this must be a problem for our ability to function without concern for interdictions by unwanted intruders? And what do we have for armament and transport?"

Leif laughed and responded; "Well you certainly get started thinking quickly. By the way, we don't yet have a Deputy Director. The Minister is considering some candidates right now that I have proposed. Now, as you see our furniture is older Government Issue. I am not very concerned about that as it is functional. By the way, I expect furniture for your office will be here later today. If you have any special request, I'll try and get the order amended immediately. We will be getting more advanced technology. This is the best we have accomplished in just a week. By week's end we should have two way video links with all our offices across Canada. That is already established with Toronto and Vancouver. We have surveillance gear arriving today as well for our field work. That is also the case for tactical equipment, some of which has already arrived. CFB Petawawa has orders to supply automatic weapons including Heckler & Koch 9 mm MP5 (N) automatic assault rifles, along with some C14 Medium-Range Snipers Weapon System 8.6 mm Lapua rifles. For tactical shotguns we will have 12-gauge, Benelli, Model M3 Super 90. Issue side arms are SIG Sauer 9 mm P226, that's the same as issued to Joint Task Force 2."

Sean-Guy admiringly observed, "That is very nice armament. I'm impressed that you have been able to insist on higher ups taking our tasking seriously. But I have a personal request. I have been using a Para PXT P18•9 for my service weapon and a Para Hawg 9 as a backup for many years now. I am more comfortable now with those than with military issue. I'd like to continue using them."

"Well," said Leif, "we really need to maintain a consistent ammunition style. What caliber are your weapons?"

Sean-Guy said, assuring, "Both are 9 mm. There won't be a problem. But you haven't said anything about building security."

"Oh yes, that is proving to be a bit of a problem," admitted Leif. "We have an obligation as a federal government organization to make use of Canadian Corp of Commissionaires members. As you know, these are mainly retired military and police personnel, but in their role as Commissionaires they don't normally carry weapons. We don't want to put them at undue risk so we have installed them in a room behind the desk, watching all who enter on video. There is a metal detector hidden in the entry door frames as well. If they see someone entering with suspicious behavior or carrying a gun, they have the ability to lock down the foyer completely including the stairwell doors and elevator. In your case, this morning, you were passed because they could identify you from your picture." Then Leif said, "If the person entering appears to be an unarmed ordinary citizen, they'll be approached by a Commissionaire from the back room."

Sean-Guy, still concerned, asked, "Is this 24/7 and what about the side entrance, and through the garage?"

Leif laughed again, "I was wondering if you would bring that up. You were observed when you entered the building twice last week. We have video everywhere. Had you done anything wrong you never would have been able to leave the building."

"I suppose I should be embarrassed, then," said Sean-Guy. "What about the back door that I left open last Friday?"

Again the director laughed, to take the pressure down, "That door was secured as soon as you left the building. We opened it again just moments after you were seen entering the alley when you crossed the street. Our outside cameras can see both across and down the street and alley in both directions. I ordered that special watch because I wanted to see how you work. Yes, you can correctly surmise that your reputation comes in front of you. I came in after I received the report that you had been and gone. A very interesting video it was. "

"Seriously though," said Leif, "we do recognize a need for some armed response if necessary. By this time tomorrow I expect to have a small armed response team in the building at all times. They will be Class C reserve uniformed soldiers assigned to us from The Cameron Highlanders of Ottawa, 33 CBG. You'll recall possibly that Class C soldiers are fulltime paid as if regular soldiers. These teams will be regularly rotated to avoid boredom becoming a problem." Leif stood up and said, "It's time to introduce you to our team and then

Ron Stotyn

gather for our ten o'clock meeting. We'll find time later for more of your questions."

Sean-Guy reflected after the 10 AM meeting that the MP, Chair of the Committee on Terrorism Control, indeed had a handle on the situation facing Canada, that terrorism was on the rise and the country could not afford to be caught napping. The Hon. Willard Elred had a deliberate speaking manner, which Sean-Guy supposed was related to his life as a rancher in southern Saskatchewan. The man was certainly weather-beaten, with a rugged worn face but a clear glint of intelligence in his eyes. The man had been brief and very blunt in telling the team they could not afford mistakes. They were to take any means available short of breaking the law to acquire information leading to arrest of terrorists before any terroristic plans were accomplished. Sean-Guy considered it all very carefully and concluded he could not disagree with anything. Canada definitely needed to step up to its necessary place in the war against terrorism. He was confident, despite a lack of direct experience with foreign nationals meaning to do harm to their considered enemies, that his adversarial relationship with Montreal's murderous and crime ridden biker gangs would serve him as he learned about this increasing threat in the world.

{4.3}
Later that afternoon, about 1:30 PM: Ottawa ON.

Sean-Guy was in his office, closeted with the three critical members of his team, his furniture having arrived a bit earlier. That included a worn leather couch, over-length to accommodate his frame fully stretched out, that he had found on Saturday at a used furniture store in Hull. He'd paid a bit extra to get it delivered ahead of the storekeeper's normal schedule. He had asked Everett Tailfeathers, Betty Anne Grabler, and Ryan McLeod to come in for some preliminary discussion.

Earlier in the day he'd discovered the significance of the shell and eraser on Everett's desk. The shell signified the man's other role. In addition to being a superb sketch artist with paper and pencil and apparently also using computer imaging software, he was a sniper trained while in service with the Queen's Own Rifles of Canada, a Light/Airborne Infantry primary reserves battalion that operated out of Toronto. That, he guessed, explained the man's CAS title of Specialist Investigator. His brevet rank was Chief Warrant Officer, the highest NCO rank of the CF Army, obviously a recognition of his special training. It was clear Everet Tailfeathers was a man not to be dismissed. Sean-Guy was about to discover that the man was also very taciturn. His speaking pattern was brief and very much to the point.

Sean-Guy had also confirmed that Betty Anne Grabler had the title Senior Analyst Investigator, but she was much more accomplished than he'd guessed. She had an exceptional academic background in Statistical Analysis involving Criminal Behavior and Psychology that would compliment his own expertise. They would be able to work comfortably together sharing insights. Her focus on statistics would certainly prove beneficial, he thought. In addition, it became apparent that she was extremely comfortable with computers, with a lightening like facility for finding information. The chunk of abused metal that he'd seen on her desk was her daily reminder that her brother had died, one of 24 Canadians, in the 9/11 attack on the twin towers in New York City. For her it was the up, close, and personal experience with terrorism that helped her to keep focus. Sean-Guy reckoned she would turn out to be a cheerful, talkative colleague. She seemed to him to be the epitome of a favorite Germanic grandmother. He'd just learned however that she had relatively young teenaged children whose pictures had a place of honor on her desk.

The third member of the critical team was Ryan McLeod, a twenty year veteran and retired corporal from the RCMP, as he had expected. Ryan's background did include the Royal Canadian Mounted Police Musical Ride but his particular value was his counter-intelligence experience that came from being loaned as an RCMP liaison officer to CSIS. Throughout his service, Ryan had regularly trained with the RCMP in all of their available programs. Now he was Sean-Guy's Assistant Chief Investigator. Sean-Guy calculated that he was an exceptionally well qualified investigator. It was also clear that the man was enthusiastic about his new assignment.

Ron Stotyn

Earlier in the day the director had mentioned that another critical member, Specialist Investigator Hari Hanoomansingh was delayed in his move from British Columbia. Hari would be very useful as a linguist skilled with Russian, Chinese, Pashto and Urdu as well as his mother tongue Standard Hindi. As a retired member of the Indian Army, he had been given special clearance for a brevet rank of Lieutenant in the Canadian Forces. He was expected to arrive at work the next day.

The group had just begun to talk about priorities when they were interrupted by a shout from the outer office that Toronto CAS was calling on the video link. Sean-Guy heard something about a crisis possibility as he got up with the rest to join that conversation.

The caller was the Senior Lead Investigator in the Toronto office. Stuart McIntyre reported with fitting concern, that his group had heard some chatter about a couple of Afghan men north of Toronto. It was being said on the street and apparently in at least one mosque that the men were part of a cell or cells planning some kind of attack in the Toronto region. McIntyre was worried that the intelligence was still very sketchy, but he said it seemed to involve trains. The Afghans apparently were rail-yard workers of some sort. That was all they had at the moment. Sean-Guy immediately asked if he needed assistance. McIntyre said, "As much as you can send. We think this could be big."

Sean-Guy took a look around his team quickly and, seeing agreement on their faces, told Stuart, "We'll plan to be there late tomorrow."

Immediately following the conclusion of the vid-call, Sean-Guy updated the Director and began to plan the trip. Toronto was about five hours by road and just two hours by air, but Sean-Guy and Leif agreed that taking two vehicles would give them needed flexibility with transport and gear. Sean-Guy appreciated the valuation that his team should not cause a strain for Toronto resources.

Leif told Sean-Guy, "Our transport consists of Tahoe's originally scheduled for delivery to the RCMP. The Department has agreed to order new ones to reimburse the Mounties. They are white, of course, consistent with their paint scheme, but we have removed the blue and yellow decals and replaced their shield with our own. It's a simple design, just the Red Maple leaf from the flag superimposed with the initials of the agency in black block letters. The goal is to keep separate from an obvious government insignia as long as possible."

Betty Anne spoke up, "I'd better remain here to man the computers. With the vid-link you can keep in touch from the Toronto office and we also have good security on our cell-phones. I'll get yours for you right away, boss." She added, "We have Blackberry's specially designed for government agency use by RIM. Ours can be completely encrypted with a single command for voice, text, web, video, and email."

Ryan said, "I'll get Hari on the phone and tell him to be here early in the morning with his away bag. I know he got moved into his place earlier today. What time do you want to get on the road?"

Sean-Guy thought for a moment, "Let's be here at six AM and on the road by seven; that should put us at the Toronto office by early or mid-afternoon." He turned to Everet, "You're with me. Let's go to the garage and check the tactical gear in the two SUV's that we will take." Turning back to Ryan, he said, "I want you and Everet as drivers. I'll ride with you and I want Hari with us as well. Everet will be solo on the drive down for at least part of the way. We need to discuss a distribution of effort. I'll fill Everet in before we arrive."

As he and Everet turned to go down to the basement garage, Betty Anne said, "By the time you get back up here, I'll have hotel accommodations taken care of. You'll be close to the office over there."

With those preparations underway, Sean-Guy felt energized. The game was afoot, and he was fully aware that the day, not yet ended, would feel like a long one when he finally got to bed. As he thought about that he realized he'd have to advise the leasing agent that he would be delayed in making any decisions about getting an apartment for himself. Meanwhile, goose bumps and a shiver convinced him that this situation would be a very bumpy test of the agency's abilities to help keep the country safe. He generally was able to trust his instincts on such matters, but there was certainly a large

Ron Stotyn

element of the unknown at this point. The extent of active terroristic agents in the country was probably not a known number. Indeed, the extent of those lying low as sleepers waiting for instructions was equally an indefinite. There had always been spies, especially Russian in Canada, but terrorism added a new level of danger. Of course Canada had experienced some violent acts of terrorism, home-grown such as the FLQ crisis. Sean-Guy, however, was certain that the country now potentially faced a kind of terrorism that had never before been experienced within the country. Whatever else transpired, Sean-Guy was certain that time would not be as friendly as they might wish.

{5}

"Politics is not a science…but an art." Prince Bismarck, Reichstag, 15 Mar. 1884

Mid Morning, the Olympia Grill, Monday April 3: Mississauga, Ontario.

Angela Maria De Luca was bored. She was in Mississauga sitting in a mostly empty aging restaurant, the Olympia Grill, the morning rush long since over. The cafe was not far from Lester B Pearson International Airport, better known simply as Toronto Pearson. She almost wished she was there jetting to some more exotic locale in pursuit of a 'gimme' story. She was not. Instead she was drinking her third or fourth cup of coffee that morning, maybe the fifth or six; she had lost count. The grill was located in a typical industrial strip mall; shouldered on both sides with merchants who mainly catered to trades people. She'd been there since before 8 AM. Now a couple hours after a breakfast of greasy eggs and bacon with overdone toast, she wondered why she was still watching the building across the street on the 1500 block of Britannia Road East. The waitress had given up on her, no longer expecting she would order anything substantial.

De Luca had yesterday's Toronto Star spread out in front of her open to the employment classifieds. She looked at the page occasionally and scribbled notes on her reporter's pad to make it seem like she had a purpose in life. She did actually and that was to get the story of a lifetime, a career maker….well, at least a career protector. Angela was tenacious and that was why she remained at her chosen post across the street from a building she was certain contained the local offices of a new, supposed secret federal government agency. She was in fact bored as she'd not seen any significant activity for several days now.

She also wondered why the building she was watching had no evidence of a business name attached to the façade or even on the entrance foyer glass. Most buildings in the area, and most of them

Ron Stotyn

expansive with equally outsized flat roofs, a lot of them with brick fronts, displayed the tenant names or business logos and names. This was the third day she had taken up this post, two days last week and now again this morning. Not the weekend, though, since the grill was not open and she couldn't cope with standing outside in the cold. She had almost decided the tip she got about the building and its occupants was bogus. There were two vans, both white, parked by the building; one a Sprinter of a couple years age and the other a step van, maybe ten years old. Both had signs on the side that read ABC Pest Control. There was no phone number, which she thought was odd. In her experience, service oriented businesses relied on making contact information readily available to potential clients. So why not this company; it didn't add up. Paying attention to little things like that made her what she was; a good reporter who usually got the story quickly, but this occasion weighed on her.

De Luca fell into a reverie, recalling that she was here because she was trying to build a solid rep as an investigative journalist, rather than as a general pool reporter. She was a native of southern Ontario, raised up in Guelph, a graduate of the Humber College Print and Broadcasting Journalism program. Her advanced diploma and experience on the college's student newspaper "Humber Et Cetera" coupled with an internship at the "Guelph Mercury" had led her into a print journalism career. Starting at the three-times weekly "Brampton Guardian," she'd been lucky and had moved up to other Torstar papers in the region, including the "Hamilton Spectator" and the "Waterloo Record." Her career so far had been too many community news stories and only a few sturdy politics series: her goal was to write about harder controversies and issues.

Now, finally, she had her first target career job working for the city desk at the "Toronto Star." Her knowledge of regional politics had been the ticket in, but today at 35 years old she felt that her job was probably on the line. *I need a big story to keep the managing editor happy*. That was why she was sitting in the restaurant watching a building across the street with apparently nothing going on.

The tip she'd received seemed solid. It came from a regular politico contact, one of several that she'd cultivated carefully, at the

Ontario Legislature. *She'd sounded very annoyed when she told me the federal government was launching a mysterious agency concerned about terrorism that apparently was ignoring any interests the Ontario Provincial Police (OPP) might have.* Her contact was plugged into the O.P.P. bureaucracy. Her work in the ministry of Community Safety and Correctional Services gave her access to most of the daily information about the O.P.P. on its way to the minister's office. The information she'd received was that the building opposite was supposedly the Ontario regional office for the agency. So far she'd seen little to confirm or deny that theory. There had been no apparent movement in or out of the building while she had been here over the three days. Of course, it was likely that there was another entrance out of her sight line. *Maybe, I should take a walk around the block.*

Her mind made up, she paid her bill and moved onto the street. Dressed in a tee shirt and sweater set, blue jeans and a well-worn duffle coat against the cold weather, she jammed her hands in the coat pockets and trudged down the street, trying to look like she belonged in the mainly light industrial district. She'd bought the coat last week from a Salvation Army Thrift Store just for this expedition. She looked down but not quite out, looking for work. Her hair, long, black and normally silky, was today drawn unwashed into a pony tail with one of those plastic thingies that clasped around the bunched hair. She had no makeup, which made her face look a bit drawn. Normally, with well applied-makeup she could accent her high cheekbones and highlight the unusual blue-brown of her eyes. She was certain she still looked younger than her age when dressed to kill. Her face was a long oval and her skin was a slight olive complexion reflecting her Mediterranean heritage from Southern Italy. She was a third generation Canadian, with Italian parents and grandparents on both sides. Under the best circumstances she could be described as a very good-looking woman, if not exactly beautiful.

Crossing the street to the corner of the building she walked, not really around the block, but along the perimeter of the yard as if heading to a building behind. Walking around the block wouldn't be practical, as most in this area were acres big. When she got to the next building and its entrance, she hesitated as if changing her mind and

Ron Stotyn

then veered off toward her target structure. As she turned the third corner of that building's yard, she suddenly saw a garage door open, a large white SUV exit, and the overhead door close abruptly.

The SUV accelerated rapidly away from the building. She could not make it out clearly but she was certain the vehicle had a government license plate. She also thought she saw some sort of logo or shield red and black on the side of the vehicle's front passenger door. Excited, she reconsidered her earlier thought; now the tip seemed valid once again. But how could she determine what was on the inside of the building, she wondered. There had to be a way of finding out more without revealing her journalistic interest and curiosity.

She decided to go in the front entrance and see if she could talk her way into a job interview. As she moved to the front, she considered the character of the building. Definitely it was an industrial design in a fairly modern appearance with steel frame, concrete panel sections and small horizontal windows high up on the walls. Only the front entrance had any amount of glass down to the floor, and not much at that. As she entered the entrance air lock, she realized the interior doors were blacked out and there was a security keypad for gaining entrance. Looking around, she spotted a call button. She pushed it and waited, and wondered about the security of the entrance. Surely a service company, as suggested by the trucks outside, would be more open to walk-in customers.

{5.1}

A few blocks away, Mid Morning, Monday April 3:
Mississauga ON

Marek was inside an abandoned commercial kitchen near Toronto Pearson. Like the rest of this side of the airport, the 6400 block of Shawson Drive near Courtneypark Dr. E. was a mix of larger light industrial buildings and strip mall retail condominiums. His location was such a condominium, formerly occupied by a commercial food preparation company that had probably disappeared in the worsening economy. He could hear the jets take off and land, coming and going almost directly overhead most of the time. He had rented the kitchen from a landlord who'd seemed overjoyed to get some rent on the otherwise empty space. It apparently had been empty for many months. The lease he'd signed was for a year, but he knew he'd be gone well before that, with rent owing for the balance of the term. He had no intention of staying any longer than absolutely necessary and absolutely no intention of giving notice on his lease. When the landlord would attempt to locate him he would only find a dead end. The papers were signed by an owner, apparently Jewish, of a fake company. He was amused by this deception. Israel was also an automatic enemy and threat to dedicated Wahhabist Muslims like himself. If any Jews succumbed in the destruction being planned, their deaths could be considered a bonus. Any conscience that he might have once had was long since inured to such violence; His conscience did not prick him even momentarily at the thought of the madness that would soon occur on a Monday morning.

The kitchen was ideal for his explosive plan. He had needed a place to mix chemicals in a controlled process and then to assemble the bomb packages. The kitchen was just the thing, being still fully equipped and fully functional. The former tenants had apparently walked away from their investment leaving the equipment for the landlord to deal with in lieu of their financial obligation. It had only been necessary to get water, gas and electric turned on. He'd told the landlord it would be a couple of months before he would be ready to open a catering operation. *By then, of course, the plan will be executed and I will be far away.* He had papered the windows and had hung a blackout curtain on the door into the kitchen area to prevent light leaking out to the street, when he worked into the small hours of the morning preparing PETN, his chosen explosive. He worked only with small batches in order to control the process as safely as possible. That was the normal pattern, coming here after his work at the tea-room and returning home in the morning for prayers and sleep.

Marek was skilled in bomb-making, even more so than some he had trained with at KavKaz, partly because of his Chemical Engineering degree and partly because he was driven by his anger to become the best. Khattab himself had guided part of that training assisted by the Taliban rebel bomb expert, Omar, from Afghanistan. It

Ron Stotyn

had been his second rotation at the camp, the first as a young boy from about age 14, during which time he had learned to think only as a terrorist. The second time at the camp at age 21 had been a revelation to him, to think that he alone could cause such brilliant destruction upon the enemy. He had learned so much more than just the creation of crude buried IED's. His skill now included making shaped charges and decidedly organized devices in small but powerful explosive packages. He was a comfortable user of C4, Penta and a variety of other exotic explosives. He was just as facile with explosive packages laden with destructive shrapnel.

A dedicated suicide terrorist, who mentally accepted the phrase because he was totally committed to freedom in Chechnya, Marek had settled on PETN for his bomb-making enterprise. He had learned during his studies at the University of Engineering and Technology in Peshawar, Pakistan that Penta as sometimes named was one of the most powerful explosives available for his purposes. He was well aware that it was part of the compound that is known as Semtex, which would be an acceptable alternative. But Marek did not have connections to acquire Semtex, so he had to manufacture Penta by himself. That required a detailed and progressive preparation under controlled circumstances.

To be sure of safety, Marek had purchased some non-reactive vessels: he'd bought several large glass carboys. He had then begun by making a nitration of pentaerythritol which required that he obtain nitric and sulfuric acids. Marek had recalled that pentaerythritol is an organic compound prepared by condensation of acetaldehyde and formaldehyde in a basic environment, temperature controlled to below 28°C/86°F. The kitchen temperature could be easily controlled through the air conditioning system. He had discovered that he could obtain both of these chemicals from a company called Alkaloid Inc. in Markham ON, but was able to get a sufficient quantity of pentaerythritol smuggled in from HenenChemco in Zhengzhou, China. It was 98%+ pure which was ideal. He was aware also that he could get pentaerythritol from Alkaloid Inc., but the smuggled compound, he thought, was eminently preferable, as it avoided some of his chemical purchase tracks. *In my line of work anonymity for as long as possible is eminently to be desired, otherwise success could be compromised.*

He had taken very careful steps to isolate his activities. Though he made all the purchases himself, he made every effort to avoid face-to-face contact with suppliers. He had deliveries made to the kitchen, feeling that delivery personnel would not be suspicious. Being at the kitchen to accept deliveries was tiring, coming after a long shift at the tea house, but he accepted the task as a privileged duty in the quest for success against the enemy of Chechnya. He pretended he was merely a watchman over the premises. He'd removed the sign from the previous tenant so there was only the suite number and street address showing on the front door. That meant the delivery people had less to take note of.

Marek was very pleased that the Toronto area was so well populated with chemical supply outlets and so many chemical manufacturers; they never asked why the materials were needed. Besides, by making his purchases in limited variety and quantity from different suppliers, no-one really had any reason to ask. It made his task very easy to bring destructive materials to fruition. The acids needed were purchased under false identity from a local pharmaceutical company near his bomb-making kitchen. By now, false names were routine for him; and by spreading his purchases around to several suppliers using freshly stolen credit cards, he was able again to reduce the trail significantly. That was one useful thing about some of the Russians he knew, Russian Mafia he supposed, they could supply good cards. He'd met them at the Rimouski Laundromat and it was they who'd approached him to buy some cards. The cards were expensive to obtain but effective. So far, his purchases that way had not been denied. He was concerned about the contact with the Russians; he didn't trust them so he took pains to avoid them except at the laundry place.

The preparation process required washing the Penta precipitate, fine white crystals, in cold water then filtering and washing again in a Sodium Carbonate solution until achieving an alkaline reaction. That unassuming compound was easily obtained from another pharmaceutical supply house in Milton ON.

Ron Stotyn

Marek continued reviewing the process he had begun several
weeks ago. He'd purified the Penta. That was accomplished by
precipitating the powder in Acetone obtained from yet another source,
until the acetone vapors were recycled. The result of that stage was
crude wet Penta, which then was combined with small amounts of
sodium carbonate in multiple steps diluted with water and heated to
100°C/212°F. But even after this stage the procedure was not yet
finished. To obtain the result needed for the explosive bundles, he
needed to be able to cast the Penta, which was not possible with
powder. To do that he needed to produce a dangerous supplementary
material, one that could easily go wrong, but he had been able to
accomplish that task because of kitchen ovens and coolers that he
could control precisely enough. His chemistry knowledge included a
recipe for nitration of cellulose, the end product being Nitrocellulose.
That also had required both Nitric and Sulfuric acids, traditionally in
large quantities compared to the amount of fine cotton wool used.

A more modern recipe called for much smaller acid quantities
with twice as much Sulfuric as Nitric acid. A washing process was
wanted to remove the acid residue. The resulting soaked fabric had to
be very carefully dried at a temperature below 100°F or it could
explode spontaneously. He had found a very large dehydration unit in
the food processing facility that was perfect for that stage of the
procedure. The modern recipe demanded washing eight times and a
drying process over 48 hours. The guncotton that he had made was still
not suitable for his final destructive purposes. It needed to be mixed
with the PETN to enable making casts. That had to be accomplished
by soaking the guncotton in Nitroglycerin, perhaps the most unstable
explosive ever invented. The result was a gelatinous material that was
considerably more stable than liquid nitroglycerin which could
explode if merely bumped under certain conditions. This part of the
process was exceedingly stressful and he always suffered painful
headaches for a couple days after undertaking that part of the process.
He thought it was probably due to the fumes, but a necessary thing to
endure if he was to achieve success in his mission. Finally, he mixed
the Penta and glycerinated guncotton together with Diisobutyl

Phthalate to create a plasticized material that he could mold. That gave him a form of PETN that suited his purposes.

All of this contemplation had taken place while assembling the last few of his bombs. When finished over the next couple of days, he would have a total of 37. Three of them were shaped devices that the three Afghan cell leaders would attach, during their car maintenance shifts, to the forward undercarriage of the cars scheduled to be next to the engine in the trains' consists. Most of his bomb packages were and would be disguised within backpacks, attaché cases, computer bags, grocery recycle sacks, and in a couple of cases small inexpensive athletic bags. He'd purchased these over a series of shopping trips in stores near the University of Toronto and in Mirvish Village. The purchases had included boxes of short roofing nails which would be packed around the charges to create shrapnel for added destruction. Where students and the neighborhood poor shopped, he realized, were the places he could get these supplies with little notice and little cash.

With the concealment ideas settled, he needed to complete the bombs and work to complete the detonation devices. That was a troublesome problem that he had only partly resolved. The solution would require more thinking as he prepared to leave the kitchen. He had to get back to his apartment for early afternoon prayers and as much sleep as he could manage before reporting for the late afternoon/evening shift at Samovar House. He breathed a kind of satisfaction grunt as he made sure everything was secured and out of sight of any but a determined infiltrator. He left through the rear as was his habit, thinking he'd be less likely seen.

{5.2}

Toronto CAS, Britannia Road East, about 12:10 PM: Mississauga, ON.

Angela Maria De Luca was now frustrated and frazzled, nearly beyond her comprehension about how a supposedly consumer oriented business could be so cavalier about greeting a potential customer. After all, surely anyone appearing at the front door must be a customer or at the very least a vendor wanting to do some business. But, there

Ron Stotyn

had not been an immediate response. She had stood at the inside entrance to the building she had been observing over the past several days, waiting for some kind of response. Finally after several minutes, a voice came from the speaker above the call button, grumpy at the very least it seemed to her and also demeaning in tone, "What do you want?"

Angela decided it was pretty rude. Still she replied with a question of her own, "Is this ABC Pest Control?"

The voice replied after a few seconds, still off-putting: "Yes. Why do you want to know?"

Again a rude response and even odd considering the name of the company indicated a service orientation. She firmed her resolve to lie and said, "I am certified with most regulated pesticides and I'm looking for a job." She had thought in the moment that such certification would be regarded as good qualifications, as least enough to get her in the door.

The disembodied voice, again pausing several seconds, said abruptly, "Wait there." The loud-speaker went silent and she waited she thought at least ten minutes. She wasn't wearing a wrist watch in keeping with her seeming poor status; it was tucked down in a pocket of her jeans. Finally, a buzzer sounded, signifying the door was being unlocked. Quickly she pushed through the doorway into the foyer.

As she stepped into the foyer, she noted it was relatively small and looked only a little used. There was no bright polish to the few pieces of furniture, though every surface was clean: a desk in front of her with a much worn swivel chair behind it, and two vinyl club chairs against the wall to her left beside an obviously plastic plant meant to simulate an ornamental fig tree. As she entered a uniformed man, came from a door behind the desk and to her right, just as she noticed there was no telephone on the desk, an oddity, she thought. Mistaking for a moment that the uniform was that of a pest company employee, she suddenly realized it was the uniform of a Commissionaire. Puzzled, she sorted out in her mind what she understood about the Canadian Corps of Commissionaires; that it generally hired retired military, police and other security-minded people to handle various kinds of routine work for clients. Still, it did not seem entirely logical for a pest control company to need such services. The man asked her what she wanted, surprising since she'd been asked that just minutes earlier.

Angela replied, as patiently as she could manage, "I'm looking for a job. I have qualifications and certification with most registered pesticides, herbicides and their application procedures," adding to her lie.

The man looked at her as if sizing her up, obviously taking note of her less than put-together attire. "Wait here for a moment. Have a seat and be comfortable, while I find the boss."

That was the first sign of civility De Luca had noted since arriving at the outside door. She sat and waited, again for what seemed like a rather long time. Finally, the Commissionaire returned carrying a sheaf of papers. He held them out and said, "You need to fill these out and return them tomorrow." When she had taken them, he crossed to the airlock door, opened it and held it for her. She rose automatically and was through the door before she realized what she had done.

Angela began to protest, "But it's a long way to come back. Can't I fill them out…" she was going to say "Here right now?"

The man cut her off saying, "Tomorrow at 8 AM sharp!" and closed the door behind her.

Back outside, Angela De Luca, now thoroughly annoyed and even a bit angry, cursed roundly knowing she had absolutely nothing more than she had learned over the three days of observation. She wasn't given to cursing like a longshoreman, but did not consider the occasional hell or damn sinful, certainly not enough to go to confession. But on this occasion the string of expletives she uttered explosively would have probably made a pirate blush. In sum, what she learned was pretty much absolutely nothing. She was, however, more convinced than ever that something strange was going on. She vowed she would get down to the truth of whatever was going on behind those doors. Giving up had never been in her character and she wasn't going to start now. Besides, she had a boss to satisfy and he was a hard man on any who didn't bring the goods when the deadline was approaching. She set off towards where she had parked her car, out of sight of the building, where she planned to think who she could call for

Ron Stotyn

more in depth information about the suspected operation. There must be some favors I can call in.

{5.3}

Inside Toronto CAS, Early Afternoon: Mississauga, ON.

Inside the Toronto regional CAS offices, CAS Senior Lead Investigator Stuart McIntyre, former Edmonton Eskimo defensive end and retired Edmonton City Police staff sergeant, watched the video monitors as Angela Maria De Luca stood for a moment outside visibly unhappy. He waited until she moved away down the block, and turning to his deputy, said, "Collect her fingerprints from the door and the furniture. We need to know who she is. I don't like how she was behaving." The deputy responded, "Sure boss, but maybe she was really just looking for a job."

McIntyre agreed with that possibility but admonished, "You can never be a hundred percent sure, can you? In our business the details matter. Let me know as soon as you can what you find out. And don't forget to wipe down the surfaces after you've got all the possible prints. We don't want the place looking like a crime scene do we?"

The deputy laughed and said, "That surely wouldn't do for a crew like us would it?"

Later that afternoon, McIntyre was in his office where he had been working on a more thorough report so he could be ready for the arrival tomorrow of Joseph Dawson Girard Sean-Guy O'Dwyer-Lariviere, the new Chief Investigator from the Ottawa HQ. What a mouth full of names, he thought, and wondered what he was supposed to call him. He did know the man wanted as many details as were presently known. That much he'd understood from a chat with Betty Anne just minutes after O'Dwyer-Lariviere had signed off from the video conference. She was the recently appointed Senior Analyst Investigator, whom he knew really only by reputation and from the biography that had been circulated. Her reputation was of a woman who knew what she needed to know and was always prepared.

Stuart reflected that they were all new and wondered what O'Dwyer-Lariviere was thinking about him. Grabler had called on the secure phone link to tell him what they would need to prepare for a visit the next day, and that O'Dwyer-Lariviere was bringing Hanoomansingh, Tailfeathers and McLeod. That team would arrive mid-to-late afternoon the next day, probably, according to Grabler. She had also given him a heads up about O'Dwyer-Lariviere. He had a reputation apparently for being individualistic, but also had a strong record with the Suréte du Quebec for solving tough cases. His nickname was Double Dash, but only his closest friends, apparently, could get away with calling him that to his face, and that rarely. Stuart utterly believed O'Dwyer-Lariviere could freeze you out if he thought he was being made fun of. Then he realized the nickname surely meant the man went by Sean-Guy rather than the other given names.

There had been some scuttlebutt the previous week, when he'd been at the Ottawa office; some speculation about the man, but with a backdrop of admiration about O'Dwyer-Lariviere's accomplishments. He was aware of the man's academic background in criminal behavior and that his military career, short though it was, had been a mix of strength and unfortunate independence. That might well be understandable. He'd known several like that on the football field and on the Edmonton PD. They were often brilliant but not always able to fully understand working as part of the team. Only their valuable skills protected them. He had no idea, however, that among the chief investigator's complexities was more than a tinge of self doubt that drove him to be perfection itself. Had he known that, he would be able to commiserate; his own doubts drove him regularly and actually undergirded his desire to be a good team player. His doubts frequently involved imagined inadequacies, so he looked to partner with team mates that he could support and who could support him. That had been a good strategy, leading to several turns as team captain and to promotions in his police career.

Jerking himself back to the task at hand, the report, he reviewed what they knew concerning the Afghan bad-guys, so rumored. They had received a tip from the Go Trains maintenance shop in Georgetown, as thin as it could possibly be, but with a common sense feeling of truth about it. A man named Omid, it seemed, had been heard talking outside the rail yard with some others

Ron Stotyn

with middle-eastern roots that he and a couple of friends were soon going to take great pleasure in punishing the wickedness of the train company's bosses. The tipster wasn't sure of the context of the conversation, he hadn't heard much, but said he thought the men were unhappy about the way they had been ignored on a request for some time off. Something about Islamic holy days, he had thought. McIntyre had debated a long time about passing the information on to Ottawa, but had finally concluded there might be some substance to it after getting back a report from the two investigators he'd sent to do some digging. One of his colleagues, George Brown, the same one now trying to discover the identity of their earlier female visitor, had posed as an immigration officer and had been able to confirm an employee by the name of Omid Faresh worked at the yard.

George was a good investigator generally; as long as he was given unambiguous parameters to follow. A former detective of about 15 years with the Toronto police force, with a total of 25 years on the job, Brown had worked for a private investigation firm in the area for several years before coming to CAS. He had become very familiar with the greater Toronto region. He also had developed a good grasp of security procedures. George had, of his own initiative, tried to trace the man's work record and had found out the man, Omid, had no background in Canada. It seemed as if he had just suddenly appeared.

That information, McIntyre decided, was enough to put a second investigator on the job, literally. He had on his team a Canadian-Iranian, second generation citizen actually; a female officer attached from the Canadian Border Services Agency. Darya Barzaryan was the offspring of a mother of English background and an Iranian father, who had fled Iran with his parents when Shah Mohammad Reza Pahlavi fled his country early in 1979. The parents had been loyalists and under the new regime that took over, were considered suspect and had probably been marked for elimination. Darya spoke English as her everyday language and also handled both Farsi and Turkic believably. As a federal employee, she had also successfully completed French language acquisition courses; she was fairly fluent, enough to pass the tests anyway.

Darya had been placed into a shop office job, which allowed her contact with the car mechanics several times a day. After a couple of days she had been able to chat with the suspect Omid, and after flirting with him had found out he was a rebellious sort of individual. She had confirmed the man was Afghan and fairly traditional, not wanting to respond very readily to a female. He'd done so, Darya thought, to maintain a kind of Canadian immigrant pose. Darya, an attractive dark haired female in her mid-twenties, curvy mused McIntyre to himself, was not worried about the need to flaunt her good looks in order to get information. McIntyre knew he could never think out loud about her figure for fear of being accused of being harassing. *Still, if I was much younger and single….well…. she is VERY attractive.*

There hadn't been enough time yet to get anything significant beyond some whispers about similar conversations overheard at a nearby mosque, the Masjid al-Iman in Mount Pleasant, but Darya reported anyway that Faresh was almost certainly up to no good. How she knew that, McIntyre couldn't guess beyond suspecting a little feminine intuition at work. He put trust in that, being happily married for a long time now. McIntyre decided there was possibly good reason to have the man followed to find out about his movements. He'd put that idea to O'Dwyer-Lariviere as soon as the Ottawa team arrived tomorrow. He'd also suggest that Hari Hanoomansingh might be just the one for that undercover task, coming as he did from that neighborhood of the world. He knew Hari was a linguist and well enough trained in the Indian Army to be able to handle himself.

Stuart McIntyre was just putting the finish to his report and proposal, when George Brown showed up at his door. "Boss," said the man with some fervor, "I've found a match to the fingerprints. I got a really good print from the arm of the chair she was in. You'll never believe it."

Stuart, only slightly amused at the man's attempt to tease out the details, challenged the man to give it up. "No games, ok? What is her identity?"

Ron Stotyn

Brown said, now quite serious: "She's a reporter. I found her because she had to be printed to get credentials at the Legislature. Her name is Angela Maria De Luca. She works for the Toronto Star."

"Oh-shit," McIntyre, now exasperated, exploded, "How in the hell has anyone found out anything about this location so quickly. I was told by the director that we were meant to be a very contained organization with a need to know rating." Brown just looked at him shaking his head. McIntyre, thinking out loud, mused, "I better call Ottawa right away to alert them that this has happened. I imagine this will not make them very happy. We definitely do not need a reporter snooping around when we still have to prove ourselves." Turning back to Brown, he said, "Well George, go see what else you can find out about her. We need to know as much about her as we can find out, to determine if we can somehow brush her off."

Brown hurried off, and before McIntyre could pick up the secure phone to place a call to the Director, it rang startling him.

He picked it up to hear a long time friend greet him.

"Hey Stuart, are you still letting your QB get sacked?" said Colin Fitzgerald, chuckling at an old reference to their days in football, when on an opposing team he had prevented McIntyre from protecting a quarterback play. Colin, a former Offensive Tackle with the Hamilton Tiger Cats had very effectively tackled Stuart, allowing the quarterback to be run out of bounds by the Tiger Cats' linebackers. The game went to overtime as a result, and though the Eskimos ultimately won, Colin never resisted teasing.

Stuart responded with a very sharp, rude retort and asked, "To what do I owe the privilege of hearing from you? It better be worth my while or you'll be buying me a beer."

Colin, still in a teasing mood, said "You'll be the one buying the beer, when you hear this. The squad has just finished investigating a stolen credit card deal." Colin, a Detective Staff Sergeant in the Economic Crime Unit for the Ontario Provincial Police, who ran the Electronic Fraud Squad, told him, "We have evidence that several fresh stolen cards are being used to purchase unusual quantities and varieties of chemicals right in the Mississauga area where Toronto Pearson is. This has been happening in the past couple of months, a matter of maybe five weeks," said Colin. "What's more we have been able to mine the data that we collected and have discovered the materials are being delivered to somewhere adjacent to the airport. We are still trying to nail down the actual location, but I thought you might like the head's up. Our friends in the bomb unit here think the chemicals could be used to make explosives."

Stuart moaned, "Damn and double damn. That's exactly the kind of information we need to hear about and exactly what I don't need on my plate right now. We are still trying to get ourselves organized. I've got brass arriving tomorrow on another deal and this is going to put us in the swamp up to the crotch trying to avoid alligators."

Colin recognized the truth of it from his own experiences, commiserated, and said, "I'll loan you one of my guys if you need someone to track this more precisely. We've got a gal we can spare and she's really good at finding the right pieces in big piles of crap."

Stuart, very pleased with the offer, jumped on it saying, "Hook us up as soon as you can. We cannot afford to take chances that there is some seriously crack kook out there cooking up something nasty. Colin, you're right, I owe you a beer. Let's do that soon. Let me go now, I really have to call my director right away."

"Wait one" said Colin urgently. "You'd better get in touch with our Provincial Anti-Terrorism and Hate Crimes Section. They are going to find out about this and will start an investigation. You guys are federal jurisdiction and you might want to take control first. If you can arrange a coordinated effort, that would be best, I guess."

"You are absolutely right," responded Stuart; "That is a doubly good reason to get onto my Director right now." He hung up the phone and made the call, though he was uncertain about how his new information would be received.

Ron Stotyn

{6}

"Consider what you think justice requires, and decide accordingly. But never give your reasons; for your judgment will probably be right, but your reasons will certainly be wrong."Lord Mansfield, in Campbell 'Lives of the Chief Justices,' ch 40

CAS HQ, Tuesday April 4, 6 AM: Ottawa ON

Chief Investigator Sean-Guy O'Dwyer-Lariviere arrived early at the O'Conner Street location of CAS, driving his own car. It was not especially an object of affection, yet he thought of it warmly as one would a possession that served well. The car was well worn but still powerful; a 1997 Crown Victoria P71 police interceptor, 4.6L V8 4 speed automatic, originally owned by the Surété du Quebec.

No one else had ever driven it since first assigned to the former sergeant of the Surété when he had joined up early in 1998. When the vehicle was retired he bought it at a scrap value price and had it fully restored. Its main exterior difference from new was the paint job, no longer black and white. He'd chosen a deep stealth blue of the shade once used by the RCMP. He'd gotten permission from the Surété to use it for some surveillance and capture work, so he had re-installed flashers for the headlights and back-up lights, and replaced the red and blue ping-pong lights in the front grill and on the back seat deck facing out the back window. They were of a newer design low profile sort that weren't generally noticed unless you were right up close. They were all still in place as was the siren. Under the hood, Sean-Guy had rebuilt the engine by an order so that it was balanced, polished and ported to gain additional horsepower.

By 6 AM he was parked in the CAS basement garage, retro-fitted to the old building, ready for his team to arrive for their trip to Toronto. They were precisely on time as they stepped from the elevator, including Hari Hanoomansingh, all of them carrying winter coats of various styles. Sean-Guy had thought he would recognize Hari from his Sikh turban, the last name being tied to Sikhism according to what he understood. Sikhism advocates the pursuit of salvation by disciplined, personal meditation on the name and message of God. A key distinctive feature of Sikhism is a belief that God can be interpreted as the Universe itself. There was also a fairly strict dress code. Sean-Guy was astonished and within himself embarrassed about his stereotyping. Hari was not wearing the dastar headgear, had no beard and his black hair was cut short in a distinctively western style that framed his slightly round face well. The lack of turban and cut hair was odd, he thought, and might bear a question or two. Upon reflection, Sean-Guy decided it could be a benefit if Hari did not immediately stand out from a crowd, though he was brown skinned like the majority of his ethnic group. In Canada's ethnic diversity, Hari would only rarely be identified as a security enforcement officer. Hari, medium height and weight, was in a stylish gray hound's tooth check sport coat with black trousers and a power blue polo shirt.

As the group approached Sean-Guy, he called out to them to check the tactical gear: "please make sure we have all the weapons and ordnance we might need in each of the two SUV's going to the Toronto CAS office." That request was despite the fact he and Everet had checked last night. He thought out loud, "It never hurts to be doubly sure."

Everet, his graying hair in a long tight pony tail, his exact age difficult to determine, announced immediately, "I've got my Lapua," indicating the case slung across his shoulder.

Sean-Guy noted again what he'd observed last night; that the man was taciturn. He spoke only when necessary but it was precise when he did make remarks. Sean-Guy was not surprised at the comment as he'd expected the sniper to have a personal rifle tuned to his own liking. He noticed again Everet's attire; sleeveless down vest, cowboy styled shirt in stripes, denim jeans, and a heavy belt with a large western motif buckle. Yesterday, the man had worn a western styled grey cord jacket over a similar outfit. And of course, the man's feet were shod in western riding boots, as he stood about six feet tall with tight wiry muscles.

Somehow it all seemed right. Sean-Guy couldn't imagine feeling comfortable in the same kind of clothing; jogging outfits were the more likely attire when he was completely casual. He said back to

Ron Stotyn

Everet, "Good, but will you check to see if there is sufficient ammo." Everet was maybe unconventional, but in reality his attire was consistent with where he grew up. Last night he'd learned that Everet was a Blackfoot of the Kainai Nation from Standoff, Alberta. He suspected but hadn't been able to confirm that Everet was a product, perhaps better to say victim of the Roman Catholic residential schools that had recently provoked a rare apology by the Church. Children had been taken away from their families and put into boarding schools until they reached late teens. It was rare that they were allowed to see their families during that captivity. Sean-Guy didn't pretend to understand why the Church had done such a thing. He'd also learned that Everet didn't drink. He'd developed an alcohol problem while serving in the Queen's Own Rifles and had narrowly avoided a dishonorable discharge because of excessive drinking and alcohol induced violence.

To Ryan he suggested, "Make sure there are flak vests for everyone, including me. I haven't looked yet this morning." He observed Ryan was dressed in comfortable khaki trousers, a white shirt and topped with a brown cord sport jacket. The man was fairly tall, also about six feet and around 200 pounds he estimated. Ryan was clearly muscular, probably strong legs, if he was still a rider. He mentally approved of Ryan's attire. It was suitable for the trip and the job. His own outfit was not so different from Ryan's. The main difference was the Harris Tweed suit and chocolate latte colored turtleneck sweater he was wearing today.

Ryan replied, "There should be, I received the shipment from our supplier last week, so they're all new. They're Type III. I'll inspect them to make sure there is no damage anywhere." Sean-Guy recalled that Type III vests were conditioned armor that could protect against 9.6 g (148 gr) 7.62x51mm NATO M80 ball bullets at a velocity of 847 m/s ± 9.1 m/s (2780 ft/s ± 30 ft/s). Unless they got into firefights with anyone using heavier weapons, they should be safe from significant harm. Getting involved with snipers was an entirely different matter. The vests wouldn't protect against head shots. Everyone was sufficiently aware of that fact to make sure they took cover to ensure they couldn't easily be picked off. Sean-Guy also knew the vests were correct and accounted for, but he wanted to instill a habit for each team member to check everything before leaving on an assignment. He was all for trying to reduce Murphy's Law to as close to zero as possible.

As Ryan and Everet were making their supply tally, Hari stepped forward and making the slightest bow, said, "Good morning sir, I'm Hari Hanoomansingh, reporting for duty. That's pronounced HAH-ri as I'm sure you understand, sir."

Sean-Guy replied, "And good morning to you. Thanks for the tip; I would likely have got it wrong. You'll ride with me. Ryan will drive. I want to have a discussion for awhile about what we think we know about this thing the Toronto team is working on. I'll shift over to Everet's vehicle a bit later to bring him up to speed." He displayed a tight grin trying to be inclusive: "By the way, it's not necessary to be very formal with me. We all need to be on a first name basis. When one says sir to me I tend to try and see if there is a superior officer lurking behind me."

As Hari thought about protesting that it was a matter of his upbringing, both Ryan and Everet stepped up to report. Everet said "One Lapua in each; loaded, one chambered, safeties on, about 200 rounds of 8.6 mm each. Two 12-gauge Benelli M3's in both, full loads of eight rounds, four boxes of shells each."

Sean-Guy recalled that the Benelli M3 is an interesting weapon; it is user switchable from pump action to semi-automatic in a matter of seconds. The ones supplied to CAS by Camp Petawawa were the short version with pistol grip stocks.

Everet added "Good gear 'n weapons storage access where the third seat was."

That was almost the longest speech Sean-Guy had heard from the man so far. He then asked, "What about the MP5s?" The H&K submachine guns were almost a standard for police agencies around the world.

Ryan responded, "One for each of us boss, with six full 30 round clips each. There are about 200 boxed rounds extra in each truck. We each have six spare clips for our Sig Sauer's as well as several boxes of extra 9 mm ammo in each vehicle. The vests are all ready to go."

Ron Stotyn

"Good," said Sean-Guy. "I have three extra clips for my Para PXT and two spares for my Para Hawg, so I'll be fine. I can reload from the spare 9 mm ammo. So if we are ready, let's get in and get rolling. Get your away bags stowed and climb aboard." He added in a matter of fact tone of voice "I like to drive a couple hours and then stop for breakfast. I hope that works for you guys. That's consistent with my particular habit of rising early and going for a run or getting other business out of the way before taking time to eat."

{6.1}
Enroute; Two CAS SUVs on Highway 401 toward Toronto, Early Morning: Southern ON

Ten minutes later they were on route 417 headed for the 416/401 interchange, which would put them on a route straight through Toronto to very near Mississauga. The trip would take a bit more than five hours according to the GPS map. Sean-Guy planned to arrive in not more than five hours total including the planned breakfast stop. He'd told both Ryan and Everet, "Maintain an average 120 KM per hour when we get to the 401. Use the lights but no sirens and tune to the O.P.P. highway patrol frequency to warn any cruisers you might see. Tell them we are on official federal business. I want to be at the Toronto office no later than noon." The goal was to be early so as to have plenty of time to get a thorough briefing from the Toronto office Senior Lead Investigator before the day ran out; besides it would suit Sean-Guy's practice of always being early.

Once they had got underway in convoy spacing, Sean-Guy asked Hari about his tour in the Indian Army. He already knew Hari had been orphaned, had grown up in an orphanage and had joined the army at age 16 to escape certain poverty. He suspected that the age given to the recruiter was likely not a true age, though he didn't know what the policy was for accepting young recruits in the Indian Army. A blind eye was most likely turned. "What was your posting when you were on active duty?"

"I was in the Corps of Signals," responded Hari, "serving with the Electronic Warfare arm. My unit was tasked for anti-insurgency communications along the Pakistan border. It was close to where I grew up in Jammu. My language abilities with Pashto and Urdu were considered good reason to keep me in that region after I joined up."

"Where were you stationed?" asked Sean-Guy, though he was not familiar with Indian geography, he wanted to keep Hari talking freely.

"Our unit was attached to the 8th Mountain Division of the Northern Command headquartered in Dras, Jammu-Kashmir. I rose to an NCO rank of Havildar. That's equivalent to a sergeant in the Canadian army." Sean-Guy knew that like some of the others of the team; Hari had been given a brevet rank in the Canadian Forces Army. It was Lieutenant to recognize his linguistic and communication skills and that had come with a unusual appointment to the Canadian Special Operations Regiment based on his Indian Army service.

Sean-Guy, thinking out loud, "I understand you also speak Russian and Chinese?"

Hari admitted to that but said smiling, "My Chinese is a bit thin. I can order from a Chinese menu though."

The reality was, Sean-Guy knew, that Hari was being quite modest. His HR jacket told a much different story. In fact he fluently spoke at least two different Chinese dialects: Jin or Mandarin and Pinghua or Cantonese. He had genius ability with languages. Sean-Guy had decided he would not be surprised to learn of familiarity with several other dialects.

Sean-Guy, seeking a transition to a discussion about the tip on the Afghans, wanted to know, "Did your unit have any contact with Taliban rebels?"

Hari, thinking briefly replied, "Well probably, but not personal contact of course. My work was a lot of listening to any electronic conversations that we could pick up. Certainly I heard chatter about various insurgency plans and strategies. That let our army take action to prevent a lot of problems in Jammu and Kashmir while I was enrolled. We were basically responsible for maintaining law and order in a very troubled area."

Ron Stotyn

"Ryan" said Sean-Guy, "tell Hari what we have heard from Toronto concerning those Afghans. I want to hear it from your point of view and think a bit about how that compares to what I heard."

Ryan began by summarizing Toronto's video call the day before. "Stuart McIntyre has a couple of investigators, one of them female, on task. The female is Darya Barzaryan, who speaks both Farsi and Turkic; they're both close enough to Dari and Uzbek for her to be fairly fluent with Afghans. People will think she's a Pakistani. She has an undercover gig in a shop office of the Go Train System and has been able to confirm the suspect Afghan is a man named Omid Faresh. The other investigator, George Brown has found out the man has no known background in Canada. He seems to have popped up quite recently. The name is probably bogus, so he could be just an illegal immigrant, but Darya thinks he is up to no good."

"Why is that?" asked Hari.

Sean-Guy chimed in, "That's a very good question. What evidence does she have?"

Ryan continued, looking briefly up into the rear view mirror at Sean-Guy and Hari, "Well, I don't see a good concrete reason for that judgment, but I guess Darya is demonstrating good intuition. After all, she has been trained for quick assessments from border crossing conversations. You don't get much time to try to get a feeling if a person is ok or not."

Hari asked, "What else do we know that makes this Afghan a person of interest?"

Ryan considered for a moment where he was in the story and then replied, "The tip they got at the Toronto office was about a couple of Afghans who were heard discussing some kind of retribution against Go Train management. That part of the story is pretty thin except for the fact that the same sort of conversation was apparently overhead either in or near a mosque in the area of the train yard where this guy works."

After some silence following the end of Ryan's recitation of the details, Sean-Guy finally grunted and said, "I think it's time to find a place for breakfast. I want to think about this some more before taking it any further. Ryan, please notify Everet on two-way that we are going to pull off."

{6.2}

Toronto Star, One Yonge Street, about 8:30 AM: Toronto ON

Angela Maria De Luca was worried. She'd been called, ordered really, to the Managing Editor's suite of offices, where she was now sitting waiting for the meeting. She'd been here since eight o'clock, almost thirty minutes ago. The word around the office had always been that being kept waiting by this man was akin to the blowing of an ill wind. She bet she was in trouble. She hadn't had a good story now for a week. The Managing Editor, Daniel O'Donnell, scared her. He was rough, gruff and demeaning. *Where I want to be seated, is the Olympia Grill opposite that mysterious building, ostensibly the ABC Pest Control. More correctly I want to be inside pursuing my idea of job hunting. I'd been told to be there sharp at eight. There was of course no way now to make that appointment. How will that affect my chances to find out more on a story I am positive is a good one? Will I be able to argue my way inside again when I finally get back there? In the meanwhile, I'll have to talk fast to get my idea for an in-depth investigative story past the Managing Editor.*

As she began to think more about her strategy, her timing was cut short. The secretary looked at her and said, "He's ready for you." Standing quickly, she brushed her hair back behind her ear, tugged on her jacket and checked to see if her skirt was straight. She'd put on makeup hoping to look professional and at her best. She'd even put on hose for this encounter with her critical boss. Taking a deep breath she went to the door, knocked and then entered without waiting for a reply. The office was as elegant as anything she had ever seen; very old boys' club style with oak panels and furniture, dark and burnished to a high polish. Normally she'd seen the man down in the city room working from a desk near the city editor. O'Donnell was standing at the window his back to her. She stopped and waited.

O'Donnell waited at least a full awful minute and then said, "Sit."

Ron Stotyn

She crossed to the front of the desk and was about to pull out one of the straight back chairs. O'Donnell said "OVER HERE!" She turned to see that he'd moved silently across the thick plush carpet to a discussion grouping of leather club chairs. She took another deep breath and wondered if she should feel relieved, but somehow she could not assume she was not still in trouble. O'Donnell was not known to smile often, and he wasn't now. She sat forward, straight backed, while O'Donnell chose the armchair directly opposite, sitting back relaxed. He looked at her for a moment and then launched into what she thought was going to be a tirade about her work or lack of it.

Instead, he barked, "I want to know what you are investigating right now. Don't leave anything out!"

Angela took a deep breath, adopted a brisk tone and started with the tip she had received. "I got a call from an acquaintance on the Ontario legislative staff. She told me about a new Federal secret agency set up quite recently called the Canadian Antiterrorism Service. She said the O.P.P. provincial antiterrorism unit was unhappy that the new organization apparently was not going to work with them on their investigations. I've been told the Toronto area office is located near Toronto Pearson in Mississauga. I've been doing some covert surveillance from across the street for three days now, two days last week and yesterday." She paused to take a deep breath, wondering, though she should probably know better she amended to herself, if he understood the interest value of the story possibility.

O'Donnell, still looking at her with some intensity, said, "What else?"

"Well there's been almost no activity so far. I've seen one vehicle exit the building. It was a white SUV. I'm pretty sure it had federal license plates and some sort of logo on the side, red and black. I wasn't close enough to see it clearly. I decided yesterday to see if I could get inside by posing as a job seeker. There are two vans outside marked with the name ABC Pest Control, so I pretended to have credentials with pesticides and such."

O'Donnell, with what seemed like a slight smirk, asked, "And how did that go over?"

Angela, still anxious and worried about being chastised for the subterfuge, hesitated and said, "I got in, but I didn't get to speak to anyone important. There was only a member of the Commissionaires in the lobby; I thought that was strange, well it was a kind of office space I guess. He came out of a back room and was very terse with me. He went in the back a couple of times, finally handing me a sheaf of papers, application stuff they were. He wouldn't answer any questions and showed me the door rather abruptly. I was supposed to return there at eight this morning."

O'Donnell asked, "Why is a Commissionaire strange?"

Angela replied, "Well, in my experience, they don't normally provide HR services for small businesses, at least I don't think so."

O'Donnell tersely said "Better check that." Then he sat silent for a long moment, not smiling and still focused on Angela as if to take her measure. He spoke abruptly, "I want a memo from you to update me every other day. If you need me to put some pressure on our contacts at the legislature, tell me in the first memo. That needs to be on my desk within the hour. Now get out of here and get back to work. You're wasting time."

Stunned, Angela didn't know exactly how to react, she apparently was not yet in trouble, but given O'Donnell's character that could still come at any moment. If anyone could appreciate what to expect from him, it was that he could bring the hammer down without any forewarning.

Getting up quickly she said "Thank you sir, it'll be a great story, you'll see." She hurried away to her own desk in the city room, in haste, but hoping she didn't seem to be in a hurry. If I'm quick writing up the memo, I can maybe salvage the ruse I'm trying to move forward. She thought she could be at the presumed CAS office in less than two hours if she didn't dally. It was nine o'clock when she got to her desk and began writing. It had to be a short memo, direct and to the point or O'Donnell would toss it unread into the round file. As she finished the memo she added a postscript for emphasis: "I would very much appreciate your help in getting some higher ups at the legislature to respond to my questions." An offer like he'd made could not be ignored.

Ron Stotyn

{6.3}
Near Exit 526, Highway 401 Southbound: About 8:30 AM

The team was ensconced in a booth at one of the country's most popular donut shops, Tim Horton's, finishing off a breakfast of their popular goods. It was standard fare but freshly made and hot. The coffee as usual was excellent and the donuts were absolutely fresh. You could see them coming off the baking line from every seat in the house. The food chain, named for its founder, a former NHL player, was the biggest in Canada with twice as many outlets as McDonalds and had established a presence south of the border with the USA of more than 500 outlets. It had 62% of the coffee market and 76% of the baked goods market in Canada.

Sean-Guy had between bites given Everet a shorthand version of the discussion with the other two members on the way so far. He added, "I'm going to join you for the remainder of the trip and we can talk more. Right now I have a few comments about what I think about this tip so far." He paused for his last bite of breakfast sandwich, took a sip of coffee and reflected. "The tip is valid I think, though I'm not entirely sure why." He paused again and then said "Rien! I do have a sense that something is wrong about the Afghan. If he were a legitimate immigrant, the Toronto team should have been able to come up with some info from Canada Border Service Agency. That there is no apparent background is reason by itself to be suspicious." Turning to Hari, he said, "I think Stuart's undercover people need a third party to do some switch-up tailing of this guy. We need to see where he goes and who he communicates with. You're ideal I think. I'd do it but I'd stick out in his crowd. So would these other two guys."

Leaning back on the bench, relaxing, Sean-Guy suddenly sat upright again, with another thought. "Last night I got a call from the Director. He'd been contacted by Stuart about another deal that the O.P.P. Electronic Fraud unit just wrapped up. It seems they have closed down a stolen credit card rip-off. They found some evidence that some fresh stolen cards have been used to purchase large quantities of chemicals that their bomb squad said could be bomb components. The fraud unit is also going to loan Stuart a guy to do some more digging into the data they have to see if they can discover a delivery point. We need to keep track of that. I have no idea if there could be a connection but I want to know every detail in case it does connect."

Grabbing the bill to put the meals on his agency credit card, Sean-Guy stood and said, "Let's get back on the road. We can make my deadline if we don't waste any time. I'm with Everet for the rest of the trip. No more stops if we can help it, ok? I'll call Betty about this credit card thing and get her started on a search of her own."

{6.4}
Toronto CAS Office, about 12:30 PM: Mississauga

Angela had spent the past 45 minutes having lunch at the Olympia Grill across the street from the building she had already watched over the course of three days and had tried to get into the day before. Now she was going to try and bluff her way in again. She opened the outside door of the air lock entrance and pushed the call button. She waited several minutes, just like the day before. Finally a voice came on the speaker, "What do you want?"

Angela, keeping her voice well controlled for the lie, responded, "I'm Stasi Cabrini. I was here yesterday to apply for a job as a pesticide technician. I was told to fill out the forms and come back today." She carefully avoided the fact she was told to come at 8 AM. She was a firm believer in the idea that information not asked for was not likely to affect the outcome.

The silence seemed excruciating to her but the voice came back and said abruptly, "You were told 8 AM; come back tomorrow at 8 AM."

"But I can't," she said trying to put emotion into her voice as if nearly crying. "I really need to see someone today, I'm running out of money to pay my rent," trying for some sympathy.

The voice replied, "Wait."

Several minutes later, it seemed to Angela, the door buzzer sounded and she was able to push through to the lobby/office. It was

Ron Stotyn

again empty. She went to one of the side chairs and sat down, in her cast off clothing. She had on a well faded denim skirt and a heavy fisherman's knit sweater under the same duffle coat from the day before. She had rushed home from the Toronto Star office to change and wipe off her make-up. Then she had rushed to the mysterious building, stopping first at the Olympia to get calm and organized. The lunch had helped even though it was pretty bland. Again, she did not realize she was being closely observed from behind the lobby.

In the video surveillance room behind the foyer, the Commissionaire had been joined by Stuart McIntyre and George Brown. They watched to see if the woman would get rattled by waiting. In the meantime George recounted what he had discovered about Angela Maria De Luca, including that the name she had used to get in was a well used alias. He ran down her education and work history and added, "She has a pretty good track record as a journalist. She's considered a go-getter, even at the Toronto Star."

Angela would have been glad to hear that last bit, but she was trying her hardest to remain calm and in control. She wasn't sure she could manage that much longer.

Stuart replied to George, "We need to try and get rid of her somehow, but for the life of me I can't see an easy way. We could say we don't need any new hires right now but I suspect that won't stop her." He was about to make a suggestion, when one of the outside monitors caught his attention. It was one that caught views down the street. What he saw was two white SUV's turning the corner and coming toward the building. "Damn it to Hell, I think the team from Ottawa is here early. We'll need to keep her in the foyer until they can get into the building. I'll go and see if I can string her along." He mussed his hair a bit, pulled off his tie, pulled his shirt tail out and with that opened the door to the foyer and stepped through quickly. He was successful; catching their unwanted visitor by surprise.

"There is no-one here to talk to you right now," he said. "You'll have to come back again. I can take your application papers and give them to our manager when he gets back from lunch." Then he said, "You'll have to go. I'm pretty busy right now doing maintenance and I'm the only one here to answer the phones," trying to persuade her there was nothing she could do today.

But she fooled him. Angela reacted quickly to his comment about the manager coming back from lunch. "I can wait until the manager gets here."

"But I don't know when he'll get back." Stuart was hoping now she would give up and go, but she remained seated. So he said "OK, suit yourself, we close at 4 PM today. I've got to get back to work." With that, he turned abruptly and before she could say anything in return he was through the door and gone.

Angela was taken aback. She had thought she would get an interview and then realized her mistake; by coming at noon she had left it open for them to reject her attempt to get in. She was determined to get an interview so she settled in, still being watched. During the interlude she had just experienced, she had no idea that two federally licensed SUV's had entered the building through the garage door without her being aware. George had opened the door as they approached and closed it quickly after the last of the two vehicles got in. On the other side of the wall in the sound proofed surveillance room, Stuart directed the Commissionaire to keep a sharp watch on her. Then he and George went to welcome their expected visitors. He was dismayed that they were a couple hours before he was anticipating them. He'd heard that O'Dwyer-Lariviere was punctual to a fault but arrival this early was downright peculiar.

Stuart arrived in the garage just as the four from Ottawa were getting out of their vehicles. He'd seen pictures of each of them so had no difficulty identifying Sean-Guy. Everet was of course unmistakable as was Hari, leaving the fourth man certain to be Ryan. He and George, who'd joined him, stepped up to make their greetings and welcome.

He said to the group, "Come along this way," leading them into the conference room that was adjacent to office cubicles. "There are the restrooms over in that corner and the kitchenette is beside. The coffee is fresh."

A few minutes later after everyone was settled, he called out to the last cubicle, where George was hunkered over a computer with a

Ron Stotyn

rather young-looking girl. "You guys, come on in here for a bit so we can have a good update on what we know so far on the Afghans and the credit cards."

George and the girl came over without delay. Stuart began by saying "Darya is on her under-cover job so she won't be here this afternoon, but we'll catch up with her tonight. I have reservations for all of us at Samovar House over on Dundas Street West near Roncesvalles Avenue. You've already met George, who has been doing background on the Afghans. Our group has just been joined today by Timothea Green," introducing the young woman.

The female, dressed in an eclectic mix of short purple shorts, black leggings with leg warmers of bright orange and a fuzzy sweater in a multitude of colors, stretched out her hand and said "Hey guys, nice to meet." Then she said, "Call me Thea. I've been loaned from the O.P.P. to help dig more info on the credit card scam."

Stuart hastened to add, "Thea is one of O.P.P.'s Electronic Fraud Squad's undercover detectives. She's a Sergeant and can wrangle a computer better than anyone I've ever met, except maybe Betty Anne in your office."

Sean-Guy, looking at Thea's spiky black hair, shook his head a bit and opined, "I guess that get-up causes the perps to forget everything they ever thought a cop might look like when they meet you. You just blow them away, don't you?"

Thea giggled and agreed.

"Well what can you add to the credit card thing," asked Sean-Guy.

"I've been digging through credit company data on the stolen cards that we have linked up to chemical purchases," responded Thea. "So far, we've indentified a dozen or so used for a variety of chemical and some equipment purchases that make it look like bomb making is a real possibility. The bomb guys at our place suggest that PETN is a real good probability or maybe nitroglycerine or similar stuff. Pretty dangerous, so if that's the case, we've maybe got a real good cook working out there somewhere."

Ryan asked "Can you tell us where this stuff is ending up?"

George and Thea started to talk at the same time, George leaving off when Thea took the lead, "It is still a bit early to tell, we're getting records from the purchase points, but it is starting to look like everything is coming into Mississauga. We're just not sure of the actual address yet. We will likely have to go to each vendor and get their delivery records. That's going to take a day or two."

Sean-Guy asked, "How long has this been going on?

"The cards we have identified have been used only once or twice each over the past couple of months. We have indentified the card theft ring leaders and have arrested them. But they are apparently Russians and so far disinclined to say much. They are being interviewed strenuously now. As soon as we can figure out where they were selling the cards we'll have a better idea who was buying them. Give us another day on that probably." Then she said, "If I can get back to the computer, I'll keep working on narrowing it all down. Maybe later I can give you an update." Thea got up and left as Stuart nodded to her to go back to her task. As she was about to leave the conference room, she turned and said, "Oh, I just remembered, the cards we're talking about were all used on phone call or online purchases. In our squad we always think that means the user is trying real hard not to be seen making purchases."

There was silence in the room after Thea left, as each team member considered the implications. For the next couple of hours they talked about the Afghan situation and came to the logical conclusion that more surveillance was needed. Hari agreed to work on double teaming Omid to see where he was coming and going from. They all hoped they could either eliminate him as a suspect or determine who he was engaged with if he was indeed a bad guy. They certainly needed more information before they could be satisfied that things were good or not.

Finally, Stuart told the Ottawa visitors about the third wrinkle they were facing at the Toronto office. "We have an uninvited guest sitting out in the foyer. George has identified her as Angela Maria De Luca, a reporter for the Toronto Star. She has a reputation as a digger. Yesterday she tried to get in using a ruse that she was a job seeker looking for work at ABC Pest Control. That's probably based on the

Ron Stotyn

signs on the two vans parked out front. We plan to use them for undercover work in the future."

Sean-Guy, with some concern visible on his otherwise composed face, asked, "What's her purpose, do you think?"

George replied, "It's most likely a leak about us somewhere. We know the intent was to set us up as a secretive agency with a need to know classification, but there's no way of knowing where such a leak might be. One possibility we've talked about is the O.P.P. With their responsibility for anti-terrorism here inside the province, they could be unhappy with jurisdiction issues."

Stuart interjected, "But, we have a pretty good relationship already with the Electronic Fraud unit. It was an old friend of mine that hooked us up with the credit card info. He was the one who loaned us Thea."

Sean-Guy asked, "What are you going to do about her?"

Stuart shrugged, "So far we have tried to stall her twice. Yesterday we handed her some phony application papers and said come back this morning at 8 AM. She showed up about 12:30 just before you guys arrived. Today, we told her the manager was out and we didn't know when he would be back. I pretended I was just the janitor. But she settled in. I think she is probably still out there." Turning to George, he said, "Bring up the lobby monitor on this screen, let's see if she is still there."

As the monitor came up everyone could see she was still in the lobby, reading a paperback book, the application papers laying on the end table beside her. Then as they were watching, she suddenly got up, made an obscene gesture and stalked out of the front entrance, leaving the application behind. George quickly switched to the outside view. It was about four o'clock as she headed across the street to the Olympia Grill.

{7}

"Man's capacity for justice makes democracy possible; but man's inclination for injustice makes democracy necessary." Reinhold Niebuhr in 'The Children of Light and the Children of Darkness' 1944

Shawson Drive, Tuesday, April 4, Mid Morning: Mississauga ON

Marek was busy in his bomb making kitchen, nearly finished making the 37 bomb packages he needed to carry out his dark plan to disable the Toronto area Go Train system and kill as many of his country's enemies as possible. He expected that number to be in the thousands. *Praise to Allah* he thought. He was proud and honored indeed to be the chosen one for this exercise in justice. Though he rarely contemplated it now, it was a fact that his training at KavKaz was so thoroughly focused on a militant reaction to oppression that the concept of terrorism had become second nature. It was for him purely the accepted method of resistance in his homeland of Chechnya, and the only way that he could imagine freeing his community of brothers and sisters in the struggle.

He'd given considerable thought to his immediate and indeed practical need about the best way to detonate the bombs. More often than not, he would have elected to provide switches for each chosen suicide terrorist to operate at the appropriate time. But for two reasons Marek determined that would not be a sensible way of setting the explosions off when needed on this project. The first was a continuing concern about his ability to fully trust the three Afghans who were part of his cell structure. *I am not convinced they are wholly committed to the Chechen cause. I know, of course, that they are indeed trained terrorists but I believe their motivations are not correct. My sense of their character is that they have a lack of a firm sense that they are ready to die for the Chechen cause.* For that reason alone he had decided upon dummy switches, at least for the Afghan led cell members.

Ron Stotyn

About his Chechen brothers, Marek had no such reservations. But, the other more important reason for his hesitation was his fixed belief that the explosions needed to be precisely synchronized as to timing. His strategy predicated that simultaneous explosions would create mass confusion in the emergency response system of the region. Part of his goal was to create chaos. Coordinated explosions across the region would force first responders to deal with situations within their own areas of responsibility. There would be no rushing to help beyond their territories. For this reason, he chose cell phone actuators to set off the detonations at the appointed time.

For the final meeting with his cell leaders on Sunday coming up, Marek would tell the Afghans that their switches would activate timers preset to create the detonations at the precise time needed for maximum chaos effect. For veracity he planned to bring a switch joined to a sample timer to show them how it would work. He had picked up the necessary parts at a popular electronic parts store near his apartment. It was a simple positive connection activated with a momentary switch, a push of the button was all that was required. He expected that they would surely understand how easy it would be to contribute to the holy cause.

He planned to spend some time teaching from the sayings of al Wahhib to cement their conviction and commitment. Marek believed that the duty of sacrifice according to Chechen Wahhabism was a powerful motivation. He had engaged a private room at a restaurant for the purpose. He wasn't really worried about the Afghans checking the real bomb packages, but in case he was wrong he had already wrapped those bombs with duct tape with only the wires coming out to the dummy switches. Their instructions would be to activate the timers no more than six minutes before and no less than four minutes before the desired time for detonation. He would claim that would take care of any minor delays in the train schedules. Marek expected, uneasy about their motivation, that should be a short enough time to prevent them getting off the trains and just leaving the packages behind. He did not want some overly alert passenger taking notice of abandoned parcels.

To his Chechen leaders, and, by extension, to their cell members, his instructions would make it clear that their glorious task only required them to carry the bombs to the desired locations and then wait for their transition to Paradise. To his Chechen brothers and well-trusted cell leaders, he would also teach again the Wahhabist principles that all praise possible was owed to Allah, and that personal sacrifice was the only way to express their obedience. Marek was certain all the Chechen Wahhabists would tearfully and joyfully agree that this would be their opportunity for glory.

Marek then reflected that his attempts to configure the detonation triggers had been a bit tricky. He was not as experienced with electronics as he was with chemical engineering. Still, he had figured out how to make a very simple spark generator using a rapid discharge condenser from information gleaned from postings, many by infidels, on the World Wide Web. He had found a low power input, high voltage ceramic capacitor charger and test jig at the electronic parts store. With just the power from the included 12vDC wall-wart he could charge up to 20,000vDC; more than enough for his needs.

A cell phone in the package would be connected to a transistor switch that would cycle the condenser discharge into neo-electric detonators, smuggled from India through Pakistan to him, inserted into the PETN. His design used the headphone circuit of the phones connected to the switch so that the phone ringing would complete the electrical circuit needed even in silent mode. He needed only 0.8 amps over 45 milliseconds to achieve the trigger detonation. Satisfied now that his trigger device would work, he set about getting ready to leave the kitchen for the day. As usual, he made sure everything was safely put away. It was earlier than his normal time but he needed to make the cell phone purchases. That would mean travelling to many different stores. It would not do to purchase more than a couple at a time, to allay any curiosity. He didn't like making such purchases in person, but the lack of time remaining to his deadline for the detonations meant using online acquisition of the phones impractical. That was an oversight on his part. He was annoyed that he had not worked out the trigger mechanism much earlier.

So Marek was frustrated with himself as he set out on this final major shopping trip. His schedule was put back from where he needed to be with final preparations. He felt he'd spent too long

Ron Stotyn

working out the detonation triggers. *It will take the rest of my available time over today and the next to make the purchases. I'll then have to spend many hours on Thursday, Friday and Saturday to construct the trigger devices and add them to each bomb package. I will not be able not get the bomb packages into the storage lockers until early the following week. It would take until Wednesday, even with the van that I have planned to rent, to get everything into place so the cell leaders can make their pickups and distribute the packages to their own teams.* That was a very tight time frame as he then realized to his shame that he was assuming Allah could not or would not arrange for everything to be in order.

Marek sighed and determined that he would pray for forgiveness at the next opportunity. If he hurried, he could get home for afternoon prayers before getting ready for his shift at the Samovar House. Hastening to catch a bus, Marek reviewing the many months of preparation, considered what he now needed to do to leave Toronto after the plan was exercised. While his rent was paid until the end of the month, he would stay only until he could see the results broadcast on the television news stations. Tonight's shift would be one of his last and he was not ready for it to be out of the ordinary. By the weekend following his Saturday shift, he would merely disappear. The employer would likely be angry for a moment only; the turnover of restaurant staff being what it was would cause no lasting reaction.

{7.1}
Wellesley Street West, Tuesday April 4, late afternoon: Toronto, ON

Angela Maria De Luca had had just enough time to finish a cup of coffee at the Olympia Grill, following her abrupt departure from the lobby of the building across the street, when she got a phone call from her city desk editor, Tom Russert. He passed a message from Managing Editor O'Donnell that she was to get her tail over to the legislature. There she would have about ten minutes with the Under Secretary to the Parliamentary Assistant of the Minister of Community Safety and Correctional Services. That individual would answer questions about the stance of the O.P.P toward federal jurisdiction over anti-terrorism affairs. O'Donnell's message also stated, "Don't screw this up. I called in several favors." That was a bonus for her investigation. She expected she would get information confirming what she believed was true about the object of her surveillance.

Angela had left the building across the street in a pique of anger that she had been left sitting for most of the afternoon. She'd wiled away the time with a paperback book she'd had with her, but not really reading it. She'd been trying to sort out in her mind again if the tip she had received the previous week was good or not. She had pretty much concluded again, irrationally, perhaps, she thought, 'That it was too weak to bother with any longer.' Now heartened by the phone call, though a bit fearful about the tone of her employer, she hurried the several blocks to where she had parked her car out of sight of the building she was interested in. It struck her again that she really needed to quit waffling in her mind, and that it was getting in the way of her ability to think logically about things.

Her appointment was in the visitors' gallery at 5:30 PM and she was to meet a Peter Gallaegher. She didn't know him but she did know his boss and the Minister by reputation. Both were generally willing to speak to the media, especially recently because of problems with some bad cops in the province. The O.P.P. had not been involved in those incidents so Angela hoped that would mean Gallaegher would be open to her questions. She guessed the Under-Secretary had been ordered to meet with her; as meant by the favors mentioned by O'Donnell. The timing of the meeting was odd, and then she realized the visitors' gallery would be vacant along with the press room adjacent. They would be as private as possible in the busy building, since the day's sessions would be suspended for the dinner hour. She reached her car and by five o'clock she was hunting for a parking spot as close to the Queen's Park Legislative grounds as she could get. She did not want to be late.

Arriving somewhat out of breath, she'd had to hurry several blocks from the McGill Parkette; at the legislature she caught the elevator up three floors to the visitor's gallery. Entering she found herself alone, grateful that she could have a minute to quiet herself.

Ron Stotyn

She went toward the railing, inspired as she usually was by this site of calm democracy in the formal setting on the floor below. A moment later a mellifluous baritone voice behind her said, "Miss De Luca?" She turned and barely restricted an unconscious gasp as she saw a striking blond man tall and very broad across the shoulders, about her own age, approaching.

His physique was astounding, as she felt a quiver of emotion she'd not experienced before. She had long dreamed of meeting such a perfect man, but her experiences had been disappointing at best over the years and at least once devastating to her confidence with men. This man's face was square, exceedingly handsome, and despite the early time of year had a skin tone color that reminded her of burnished bronze. His hair was a glossy ash brown, wavy and artfully tousled, at least a one hundred dollar cut. She was glad that she'd taken the time to change in her car to an outfit that had a bit more character than what she'd worn earlier in the day. She'd shaken out her hair and given it a quick comb. She had no makeup except a bit of lipstick. God, I hope I don't look like a disaster waiting to happen. Without thinking about it, she dipped her hand into her bag to pull out her reporter's spiral notebook and pen.

She took a characteristic deep breath but still stammered "Ye… ye…yes," and then ventured, "Are you Mr. Gallaegher, I had a message from my boss that you'd agreed to meet me, and I have a hundred questions I want to ask you, can we start right away? I have a story I'm working on that I think relates to your department and I'm sure there is a controversy involved, and…" Immediately she realized she was running her mouth out of control and blushed.

"Slow down," said Gallaegher smiling courteously, "I have instructions to answer your questions. Let's sit down and begin. I understand you are interested in the establishment of a new federal agency called CAS?" He then said, "By the way my first name is Peter; I'm told yours is Angela?" He too was astonished at his interest in her appearance, admiring her figure, profoundly curvaceous. He estimated she was about 110 pounds and maybe 5'8" tall. He could imagine stroking her long silky black hair and cupping her slightly oval light olive face in his hands. He resisted for the moment the idea that he would get his hands on her body and more. He would hope for a succulent kiss maybe even with full tongue if they could get to know each other. He mentally shook his head, knowing it was not wise to get too close to a reporter. *It could mean his job. Still, maybe there is a way....*

Sitting now, Angela, took another deep breath, composing herself and asked, "Mr. Gallaegher, why is the O.P.P. Provincial Anti-Terrorism and Hate Crimes section unhappy about the federal government establishment of a secret agency to investigate terrorism? Why is there an issue of jurisdiction?"

Gallaegher gently told her, "You must call me Peter," and waited until she nodded her assent, then continued. "First of all, it is true that the Department of National Defense has set up such an agency. It is called Canadian Anti-terrorism Service, with headquarters in Ottawa. I don't know where that head office is located but I believe it is quite near the Parliament Buildings. The CAS is rather new, barely two weeks along I think. It is headed by a retired Brigadier General formerly of the Canadian Forces Intelligence Service. We believe that a majority of the investigative staff come from former military positions as well. There may also be some retired RCMP officers and we have just heard the new chief investigator is from the Sûreté du Quebec."

Angela interjected with a sense of her urgent desire for facts, "Do you have any names?"

Peter's eyes crinkled in the hint of a smile as he carried on with his recitation. "Only a very few at this point. The general is Leif Isaksson, a well decorated army man. He has a long career with DND, including being a commander of CF Special Operations Forces Command. The Chief Investigator of CAS was just this past week appointed with the approval of the Minister of Defense, Peter Mackey. That person, as I mentioned is believed to be from the Sûreté and is thought to be a decorated sergeant named Sean-Guy O'Dwyer. Excuse me....that should be O'Dwyer-Lariviere."

"Anyone else?' she asked, again with a pressing tone. "Surely there is more to it than that?"

Ron Stotyn

Peter now laughed out loud. "I have heard that you are a go getter, Angela, but please be patient. I mentioned the RCMP. We are aware of a former Corporal of the RCMP, believed to be now retired, who was attached as a liaison from the RCMP to CSIS. His name is Ryan McLeod. Finally, we have heard through our own O.P.P. sources that the Detective Sergeant in charge of their Electronic Fraud Unit asked for and received permission to loan at least one personnel to the CAS office here in the Toronto area. The Sergeant's name is Colin Fitzgerald. That CAS office was established near Toronto Pearson in Mississauga."

Angela breathed a satisfied sigh, thinking to herself, *I knew it*, and then asked, "Where is it located? Is it on Britannia Road East?" visibly excited now.

Peter, with a small grin, and with solemn face otherwise, "I can neither confirm nor deny that! The DND has yet to issue information about its CAS operations locations."

Angela realized that direction wasn't going to go any further, but saw that there was still some secrecy involved, which provoked her desire for open and free distribution of information. She changed tack repeating her earlier query, "What about the issue of jurisdiction?"

Peter responded, with what Angela thought was a very careful manner, "Officially….there is no problem. The Minister of Defense broached the matter several months ago to the Minister of Provincial Law Enforcement, knowing that the O.P.P. has responsibilities for anti-terrorism within the province. Our Minister has …..ummm….tacitly settled with Ottawa that a federal level of jurisdiction would likely benefit our provincial efforts. There have been discussions within the O.P.P. upper management about how to implement a cooperative arrangement for combined operations. Those discussions are ongoing." Peter stood and said, "Now Angela, I must tell you that the allotted time for this interview has expired. My boss told me I was not to extend it in any official sort of way." He began to move away as Angela startled, stammered, "But there are more questions.…"

Peter, already halfway to the exit of the gallery, turned and looked thoughtfully at Angela. "Perhaps," he paused looking again at her obvious beauty, while trying not to ogle her, and estimating his prospects for later that night, then continued, "….If you would like to come out for a bite to eat, we could continue a casual conversation?"

Angela, not at all thinking about any problematic consequences, said very quickly, "I'd be delighted," and then wondered fleetingly if she was being influenced by a truly gorgeous man.

Peter smiling broadly, now with obvious pleasure and some satisfaction at a rising prospect, said, "Wonderful, come with me, I have a favorite place in mind. Have you ever been to Samovar House?"

He'd already quickly dismissed the idea that he was being foolish to invite this very attractive reporter. Instead he was considering how long it would take to bed her.

{7.2}
Samovar House, Dundas St. West, April 4 about 6 PM: Toronto ON

Marek was an hour into his shift at Samovar house when the party that had reserved the private dining room arrived and were shown to the back room by the maitre d'. He didn't see them come in; he was busy in the kitchen filling his ornate samovar used to decant tea for the customers with as much panache as he could manage, and that was considerable, he believed. For most customers in the front of the house, his task was just wheel the samovar to their tables, draw a pot full to fill their glasses, then pouring from a height often as much as three feet or more. Their tea orders were passed to him by the wait staff assigned to their tables. But for special guests, as management referred to those who booked the private room, Marek would supplement the regular food server who would handle all the food orders. He would take time to recommend various brews to complement the different courses chosen. He would stand in the corner until all the food orders were taken and then would step forward to advise the group of clients. He actually took some pleasure and pride in this task when it came around. His able memory enabled him to unerringly deliver logical tea choices. He was rarely second guessed.

Ron Stotyn

His manner of delivering tea information usually created an atmosphere of total disregard for any other possible choice.

The Ottawa CAS team, along with selected members of the Toronto CAS team, arrived hungry at the Samovar House just after 6 PM. Stuart had recommended the establishment for its variety of splendid quality Eastern European food and a superb tea service. Sean-Guy, Hari, Everct, and Ryan all agreed and so found themselves ready to relax over a good meal with Stuart, George and Darya. They had spent the afternoon discussing the possible terrorist case and had come to the conclusion that Hari would be a good addition to the surveillance already begun by George and Darya. Darya would, as normal, go to the train yard office on a daily basis and continue to try to win over the Afghan. It was to continue as a leading up to a casual seduction with a goal of obtaining tidbits of useful information under the guise of innocence. Hari and George would begin first thing early in the morning, starting at the address they had for Omid. They would spend the day following him to see if his behavior or actions were unusual in any way. Stuart, Ryan and Everet were going to convene with the loaner agent from O.P.P's Electronic Fraud Unit to see where the credit card information might lead. The morning was to be devoted to that task.

Only Sean-Guy had not taken an obvious assignment. Independently, he'd decided to get on the video link to Ottawa first thing in the morning and discuss with the director an idea he had to contract with Pere René about working up a general profile of terrorists and Afghan terrorists in particular. He was convinced there would be profit in such a strategy. The team needed a psychological framework for their investigation that could keep them focused on the possibilities of an active terrorist plan. As he was settling in at the large table in the private room that Stuart had reserved shortly after their arrival earlier in the afternoon; he turned his attention from the conversation he was having with Darya to the two servers who entered the room. One of them stepped forward to the table immediately, the other remaining behind in shadow.

The server, Boris Ottslosky according to his badge, displaying a prodigious menu recited several specialties of the restaurant, handed out the ornate menus and then took a half step back as Stuart added his recommendations. After a few moments, when it became apparent the choices for food had been made to have the set tour-de-force, a four course meal prepared as the Chef's carte du jour, the server stepped forward again and congratulated the group for its wise choice and elaborated on what would come to them.

Boris advised, "Tonight the Chef will prepare four courses for you. He begins with a traditional Russian Borscht of red short rib broth, pickled red beets, and seasonal root vegetables to compliment, dill and braised pirozhki on the side. Your second course is the very popular salad available only on the Chef's carte de jour: Salad Sasha is a divine mix of poached chicken, peas, potatoes, gently boiled eggs, roasted red peppers, and a dressing of sour cream and dill. On the third course, Chef outdoes himself tonight with a tasting of Shashlik: this is herb marinated chicken, beef and lamb skewered and grilled over an open flame in the Turkic manner. It comes accompanied with fried panissa, couscous salad and compote of adjikus which is a red pepper, chili and garlic paste for your taste sensation. Finally I will be pleased to bring you his Pear Tasting for desert: This is a layered saffron-lime pear salad, with caramel mousse, pear sorbet and coffee tuile. Tonight, also just for you, the Samovar House wishes to present an appetizer of the Zakuski platter of smoked meats and fish, pickled vegetables and taramosalata." Finished with his recitation, he bowed and gestured toward the man behind him and said, "And now Marek will advise you on your tea service for tonight. You will be well within his hands, I assure you."

Marek Kafirov, the name on his badge, took his turn, looking around the group taking note of each as he readied himself to pay attention to their interest in his presentation. As he passed his gaze to Sean-Guy, though of course he knew none of their names, he hesitated and then moved on. He was in his mind a bit surprised at the hesitation, he was sure the man was unfamiliar. Thinking no more about it he launched into his advice about six rounds of tea for the four course meal. "To waken your palate prior to the appetizer, I bring to you Rooiboos Chai, the South African red bush leaf tea with Indian spices. The appetizer course will be followed by our own Samovar

Ron Stotyn

Country Tea, a slightly smoky blend of Keemun, Assam, Ceylon, Formosa Oolong and Lapsang Souchong, as a pairing for the soup course. You should sip it along with your soup for the benefit." As he continued, Marek could see that the tall man he had noticed earlier was paying extremely close attention, watching him narrowly. For some reason, Marek felt a bit stressed by that. But he had more to tell the group so he pressed on. "The salad course demands Tung Ting Oolong, which offers fruity notes: coconut, pineapple, the earthy notes of freshly cut wood and nutty notes such as the hinted flavor of peach pits. This complements very well the flavors of the Salad Sasha." Still noticing the gaze of the man at the end of the table, he moved to the main course tea pairing. "The Shashlik tasting from the Chef benefits from the soothing flavors of Moroccan Mint in the manner of Golden Moon tea purveyor: this is green gunpowder combined with peppermint and spearmint. That last presents a natural sweetness which offsets the spice of the main course. Now to presentation of a delightful tea to complement the desert course: I will bring you China Golden Monkey which offers chocolaty hints to go with the caramel flavor within the pear tasting. Finally, while you relax from your meal, I bring you a fine digestive tea: Pu-erh. This will put a very good finish to your evening." Looking around to see if there were any questions, Marek, wanting to escape the stony gaze of the man who had not stopped his attention, made his bow and escaped the room saying as he moved, "I bring to you the Rooiboos Chai directly."

After Marek left, and as the group began chatting with each other again, Sean-Guy thoughtfully resolved to begin a small investigation into the man he had seen from the name tag was Marek Kafirov. He did not consider the logic of his decision; it was just something he did of personal necessity from time to time to satisfy a deep interest when it popped up. *There is something about this person that seems somehow familiar, but surely I have not seen him previously. Still, I must resolve the question in my mind. I'll do this on my own so the team is not distracted.*

He turned his attention back to the conversation he had earlier carried on with Darya, feeling a bit attracted to her, but knowing she was much too young for him. In his mind, he regretted that he was now of an age to be the father of many attractive women he came across. *Perhaps my time is past.* Sean-Guy was not being maudlin, but it was a matter that concerned him. Ordinarily a loner, he was more and more often aware that something was missing in his life.

Outside in the main dining room, Angela and Peter arrived without taking any apparent notice of the patrons, though some of them took note of the attractive couple; some men of course thinking to themselves that they were envious of the man. Angela, in the drive to the restaurant had become quite taken by Peter. He was engaging, clearly interested in her, and a very good conversationalist. She had learned already quite a bit about him; that he played hockey on a local amateur team during the winter and rowed sculls in summer time. She was already considering saying yes to any invitation about a relationship with him. She had talked of her own background and interests and hoped her focus on journalism was not a problem for him. She also hoped that she had successfully signaled she was especially interested in him. After considering previous disappointments, she decided once more into the breach was the thing to do. She wasn't getting any younger and her need for a strong lover and potential life companion was a driving force at the moment.

The time was about 7 PM as they took their seats. Angela took note with great interest, the tea server hurrying by into a private room at the back moving a large ornate bronze samovar. The man carried it off with an air of superiority she thought. She turned her attention to the menu that had been placed before her, scanned the first couple of pages quickly and then asked Peter what he recommended, given this place was his suggestion.

"If you like salmon, then you'll not go wrong with the Kulibiaka, or if you prefer chicken then I suggest the Chicken Tabaka" he replied. "Both are very satisfying culinary experiences."

Angela looked quickly to the menu and saw the chicken dish was composed of porcini and truffle marinated Poussin, with celery root puree, Brussels' sprouts, baby turnips and a reduction of sweet potato, and, of course, the chicken marinated and braised. The salmon included slow cooked onions, mushrooms and vegetables in pastry, braised leeks, roasted squash, caramelized pearl onions and a tarragon

Ron Stotyn

cream sauce. She responded, "This is too hard to choose. What are you having?"

Peter said, "I usually order the Kulibiaka. Why don't you choose the Chicken Tabaka and I will offer you tastings of my dish. I also suggest we begin with the Chestnut soup which is a nice starter." He was pleased to see Angela nodding her assent to that suggestion as the server arrived at their table.

Just then the tea server also arrived and asked what they would like to have for their tea choices. Peter told him they would begin with the Samovar Country and would have Dragonwell with the main courses. Marek nodded and hurried away to the kitchen, taking no special note of this pair of diners. Angela was interested in the server, though she couldn't put her finger on why that would be. She turned her attention to the man opposite, thinking that this one seems to be a very interesting man. I'm looking forward to knowing him much better. She was willing to take this encounter to the next level of relationship whatever that might turn out to be.

An hour or more later, the group in the private dining space behind the main room was breaking up. As the first of the group exited, it happened to be Stuart McIntyre; Angela looked up away from her gaze at Peter, and was startled to see the man that she had spoken with earlier in the day. Now looking well dressed, she recognized the one whom she had been led to believe was just a janitor. This man had the look of much more authority. As he passed, she thought she saw in his brief glance a look of recognition, but she could not be certain. Immediately following him was an extremely rugged and very handsome man, well over six feet tall, with a defined athletic body, a runner surely she thought, and at the very least a very definite competitor to the one opposite her. As he approached, she took note of his steely gray-blue eyes set in a chiseled face. He returned her gaze with self-assured confidence that Angela thought instantly was capable of seeing through any façade that she might try to post. She felt shaken to her core as he moved past her. Astounded at her reaction, she paid no attention to the remainder of the group coming from the private room. She turned slightly to watch the group exit the restaurant and saw to her dismay that the man who had caught her attention so completely, turned just as he left and gave her a very direct gaze, probing her very soul it seemed. She turned away quickly hoping he would not notice her dismay. Now almost completely distracted, she nearly missed Peter saying to her, "Would you like to come to my place for a nightcap?" Flustered she replied without thinking about what that invitation might mean and said rather formally, "I would be delighted. Just let me go powder my nose before we leave." As she rose to go to the restroom, she entertained the thought that she had seen a slice of her future in the man who had gazed upon her with such intensity.

Outside, Sean-Guy told the group he wanted to have a walk-about for awhile, not having had his usual run that morning. He would take a taxi back to the motel where they had registered before coming to the restaurant. They said their goodbyes and as soon as the group had gone, Sean-Guy looked about for a place where he could watch the restaurant. He'd seen that the place was scheduled to close around 11 PM. *I'll not have too long to wait to see where this Marek Kafirov goes when he is finished his shift.* He also considered very carefully the young woman he'd seen with the handsome blond man as he had left the restaurant. *That female is not rightly matched with him. She has special qualities that such a man will not consider to be of value.* He didn't at this point have very useful knowledge of her tangential connection to his business at the CAS, but considered if the circumstances were ever favorable, *she could make a man feel welcomed and well taken care of sexually.*

Inside the Samovar House, in the kitchen, Marek was reflecting about the man with the very probing gaze, wondering why there was seemingly so much interest. It bothered him greatly. *I cannot afford to be spotted as a terrorist plotter at this point. I must be very careful to avoid bring attention to myself; there is too much ready to be undone by any carelessness.* He resolved to give more thought to the possibility that he somehow knew the man.

Ron Stotyn

{8}

"I know that a woman is a dish for the gods, if the devil dress her not." Antony and Cleopatra: Shakespeare

Olympia Grill, Wednesday April 5, Early Morning: Mississauga ON

Sean-Guy had not seen his team since the night before at the Samovar House when he stayed behind ostensibly to take a walk-about. He had not mentioned to any of them about his decision to follow the tea server, nor had he admitted out loud to any particular concerns about the man. He sat now in a back booth at the Olympia Grill in Mississauga contemplating what he knew about Marek Kafirov, which admittedly was not much. *I have dismissed any doubts I might ordinarily have about holding the man in suspicion. I'm sure now that the man is somehow not right. I don't yet know the why of it, but what I do know demands more checking.*

It was still, however, mainly a matter of a gut feeling. He didn't normally subscribe to that, his ordinary attitude was usually to demand of himself some facts before acting, but neither did he ignore a fundamental instinct. When forced to think about his sometimes inclination to respond to an instinctual reaction, he supposed as rationally as possible that it was pragmatic to check. As he sat, he tallied new knowledge.

He checked the time, just about 8 AM, nearly time to go over to the office crosswise the street. This morning, after the previous day without a run, he'd gotten back to his routine of arising before dawn, dressing for running, and was now finishing his breakfast after his loping tour around the larger environs of the Toronto area CAS office. He'd begun his run from the Toronto Airport BestRest Inn in the 5800 block of Dixie near Shawson, running more or less SE along Dixie as far as Highway 410, and then continuing along that highway's verge ultimately NW to the Kings Highway. When he reached Courtneypark Road, he followed it back to Dixie Road and SE toward Shawson. It had been an interesting run visually as he passed by a large variety of light industrial businesses that showed how vibrant the area was.

Following a reasonably priced breakfast, he was now planning to leave the restaurant in a few moments to join the team at the CAS office. His ready bag was in the SUV so he planned to take a shower at the office, change into slacks, a shirt and favorite grey corduroy jacket and then to embark on the rest of the morning. As he sat nursing his coffee, he recalled his rather chilly solitary watch outside the Samovar House, waiting in the shadows for Marek to finish his shift and exit the building. His reasons could very well be regarded as pure whimsy and yet he was certain the man was familiar. The names, first and last, seemed Russian but surely were not; much more likely from one of the former Soviet states, likely one of those considered to be Asian or Asian Border States.

He'd waited for several hours in the chill night's darkness, until just past midnight. Just as he thought he'd somehow missed the man and as the lights of the tea house went out, he saw someone leave from a side door and walk away from the building toward the southeast. As the man passed beneath a street light, Sean-Guy saw it was indeed the one who he wanted to follow. *Now I'll see if he takes me anywhere interesting.*

Sean-Guy, well practiced in the art of surveillance, had kept to the opposite side of the street from Marek, knowing there was a lesser likelihood of the man being concerned about someone walking in the same direction. He'd kept his shoulders hunched to minimize his height and avoided turning his head to watch, just keeping the man in view with mostly side vision. He'd also made sure to stay well behind Marek to further reduce the chance of creating awareness. The traffic, in that early hour of the morning, was light enough to allow him to dart across the road if Marek made a left turn.

After being followed for several blocks, Marek came to an intersection and stood waiting for the change in a traffic light that would allow a crossing. He'd turned to his right. Sean-Guy had paused in a shadow and waited until his quarry had cleared the intersection and was on his way down the cross-street. Picking up his pace, Sean-Guy had crossed at the intersection again to the other side of the street,

Ron Stotyn

trying to make sure he still had Marek in sight. Not immediately seeing him, however, caused an abrupt thought; *Merde, I've lost him* and then Marek passed under another street lamp, paused looking around, and turned into an apartment building. Sean-Guy recalled he'd had to step into shadow very quickly but was lucky that the man didn't seem to see he was being followed. He'd had to hurry then to a spot opposite the apartment, really a sub-divided house it appeared, where he could watch to see where lights might come on. The thought of his action the previous night caused the merest frown, a fleeting internal embarrassment that he'd been following without a shred of useful evidence or good reason.

Sean-Guy then had focused on the front-side room where a light had come on and was lucky to see the man pass in front of a window, step back and look out for a moment. There was enough light to see it was his man. Sean-Guy recalled his concern about being spotted, but knew in reality that the shadowy spot he'd chosen off at an oblique angle made it less likely that anyone looking would actually find him lurking. It seemed a good theory; besides, it did not appear from the man's behavior that he was searching the shadows. He'd not stopped at the window long enough for that. And he hadn't noted any furtive behavior. No, it was clear the man was not alarmed. Sean-Guy did consider it interesting that the man had looked out into the night in that way. Most people would not take the trouble to do that. Sean-Guy's instinctive reaction was that the man had something to hide.

Sean-Guy had waited until the light went out, watching the window carefully for more than fifteen minutes before moving across the street to get the building number and to see if he could verify the man's name on a mail box. But, there were no names on several of the boxes and none of the others matched the name he'd seen on the tea server's badge. Sean-Guy was forced to leave with insufficient information. Walking back to Dundas he managed to flag a rare late running cab and returned to the motel. That was all he had to go on until a chance sighting of Marek this morning near the end of his run.

That unexpected sighting surprised Sean-Guy; the location was many miles away from Marek's lodging space. It came just as he had moved across Dixie Road headed for the Fast-Mart service station to get water, when he saw the man get off a bus and walk toward Courtneypark Drive East. The man's profile as he stepped from the bus was enough to astonish Sean-Guy and to cause him to follow Marek again, this time in the earliest light of dawn, around 6:30 AM, not really even half light. Certain that it was Marek because the man's walk was familiar; a sort of short stepping quick gait that he'd seen the previous night. He had followed at quite a distance, shortening the spacing to keep him in sight when Marek turned onto Shawson Drive. He watched then as Marek paused at the corner of a building near the intersection and looked around. Sean-Guy had ducked into a kneeling position as if to tighten a shoe lace as soon as he'd seen Marek pause, hoping he'd be screened enough by cars in an adjoining parking lot. Again Sean-Guy decided he was lucky. The man didn't seem to be startled, just cautious for some reason. Marek, apparently satisfied, hurried to the back of the building. Sean-Guy was able to move through the parking lot half crouched until he could see along the backside of the building reaching a vantage point just in time to see Marek enter a space about halfway along. Marek had seemed furtive, which certainly added a bit to suspicions. Sean-Guy had then backtracked to the front of the parking lot and having had counted the doors at the rear looked along the front to determine the same number of store fronts.

Only one had no business name at the right location, so he had taken note of the address, making a mental note to find out about ownership, possible lessor and lessee. He had continued away from the space after seeing its front windows were papered over, walking briskly now to stretch his legs after the crouched movements he'd made. It was a good time for breakfast so he headed for Britannia Street East and the restaurant he'd noticed yesterday across from the CAS location. Still with no concrete evidence about any wrongdoing involving Marek Kafirov, Sean-Guy considered what he knew and concluded he could not yet give up any further investigation into the man. It was still a matter of a base instinct.

Sean-Guy had his second surprise of the morning just as he'd started to get up out of his booth, when he noticed the entrance of a young woman. He sank back to his seat when he recognized her as the

Ron Stotyn

dark haired female from the Samovar House last night, the one he'd taken an interest in, who was with the very handsome man he'd decided was a user. He was convinced she had qualities the other man would not be able to see. Just at that moment he was screened by the waitress coming to see if he'd like another coffee. He said yes, settled back into his booth, and watched as the reporter he'd seen on the video screen yesterday took a seat near the front window, sitting so she could look across the street at the CAS office, there being no other building to see from that position. She could not see him. He decided to sit awhile to observe her. She was dressed now in a rather sloppy, street person sort of manner, looking rather down and out.

A half hour or so later, after she'd consumed a cup of coffee and a stack of toast with what looked like a single fried egg, she got up, paid her bill and left. He could see her cross the road and go to the entrance doors of his own destination, the CAS office. As he got up in turn, he observed her entry into the agency's leased quarters. He paid his bill and then pausing at the front door of the restaurant, waited for a moment to see if she would come out right away. She did not so he presumed she had gained entrance to the foyer. As he went to the side door of the building to gain his own entrance he wondered what she was up to. He recalled Stuart telling the team about her being a reporter yesterday. That made her a person of interest for more than one reason, one being a strong personal curiosity. He realized then that the attraction was more than that, it was an appeal connected to her unmistakable sensuality.

{8.1}
Toronto CAS Offices, Shortly after 8 AM: Mississauga ON

Upon entry, through a side door, buzzed in without challenge, he'd been identified by the Commissionaire on duty watching the video surveillance; he went directly to the garaged SUV to pick up his ready bag and on through to the back where he'd seen the shower room. On the way in he was greeted by Stuart who called out, "Can you come to Observation? That reporter is back." Stuart's tone was aggravated, so

Sean-Guy decided it was worthwhile to give Stuart some support in the matter.

He dropped his bag and went to the front room where video screens had been set up to keep tabs on the various security camera views, especially the street and foyer. When he arrived, Stuart motioned to the foyer screen. "This reporter, she's back for the fourth day at least, in here for three days now. You'll remember I mentioned yesterday that we've seen her sitting in the café across the street watching the building and that one day when she took a walk around the building. Lately she's been pulling a pretense of looking for work. We can't seem to get rid of her."

Sean-Guy spoke presumptively, "You said you know who she is right?"

Stuart nodded, realizing he'd covered all that the day before but repeated. "Yup, George ran a fingerprint. She's a reporter for the Toronto Star... name of Angela Maria De Luca. Since then we've found out she's considered to be quite aggressive. She's been pretending that she has credentials as a registered pesticide and herbicide applications technician. That's not true of course."

"Why do you think she is here?" asked Sean-Guy.

"Well George and I both think she must be following a tip about our operation. Yesterday after you guys arrived and we were all getting oriented, she stayed in the foyer until about 4 PM. Then suddenly she got up and cursed, we've got the room bugged of course, and stormed out. She went across to the café but left there pretty quickly."

Sean-Guy said softly and thoughtfully, "Did you know she was at the Samovar House last night when we were leaving?"

Stuart got red in the face and cursed, "God damn It, you can't be serious. She was there? It's got to be a coincidence, don't you think? Shit, was she tailing us maybe?"

Sean-Guy shook his head and told Stuart, "Relax… I doubt she was. She was with a very good-looking guy and seemed to be enjoying him. I looked her over pretty carefully and of course she has no way of knowing who I am. However, as I exited the restaurant I looked back at her and she was looking at me with an expression of

Ron Stotyn

curiosity. She turned back to her date rather suddenly I thought. Not sure if that means anything though."

Stuart asked, "What do you think we should do about her. So far we've put her off. Yesterday I pretended to be the janitor and tried to get her to move on with some guff about the manager being out and not being sure about when he might return. But she wouldn't budge."

Sean-Guy considered the matter for a full minute, all the while watching her very closely in the monitor. She was definitely attractive even dressed way down from what he'd seen the previous night. Finally he said to Stuart, "I need to shower after my run this morning. Let her sit for awhile. When I'm finished cleaning up I'll pretend to be the manager and go out to talk to her. The cover here is the pest control business, right? Keep an eye on her until I can do that."

'OK' said Stuart, "Our Commissionaire can watch and give me a heads up if she looks like she is going to move. We can lock her in if you think it's necessary."

"No, no, don't do that, let her go. If we do a lock in she'll just get more suspicious. My guess is she'll stay put for awhile. Have the commissionaire tell her the manager is expected shortly," said Sean-Guy as he turned to go.

"Done," said Stuart as Sean-Guy departed the room, wondering what he was going to say to her. *It could get interesting.* Stuart left the room also after speaking to their security observer, and went to find Thea, Everet and Ryan to get started on the Credit Card theft info that had been collected. They needed to find a destination for the chemical purchases as soon as possible. He noted mentally that George, Darya and Hari were already in the field and on task keeping up surveillance on Omid Faresh. Checking up on suspected terrorists was definitely a big part of what they had been formed up to do.

Stuart found that Sean-Guy was already speaking with Everet, so he went to gather the others and saw they were already at the desk that Thea had taken over. Ryan and Thea were engrossed with information she'd pulled up on the screens, so Stuart just joined in.

Sean-Guy had beckoned to Everet and said to him: "I need two sketches of that tea service waiter at the Samovar house last night. One with beard as you recollect from his appearance. Then please do one without a beard. I estimate he is in his very early twenties so if you can regress his age even a bit more from his current appearance on the second sketch that would help."

Everet, in his characteristic non-verbal way looked carefully at Sean-Guy and saw he was very serious. "You got something on that guy?" he replied.

Sean-Guy grunted, "Maybe a hunch," as he turned and went back toward the shower. Then he called over his shoulder, "Can you also see if you can Photoshop your sketch, age regressed to early teen years?" Everet went right to a computer and began doing all the sketches in Illustrator, using a Wacom Intuos4 tablet for input.

In less than ten minutes, Sean-Guy re-emerged, looking fresh, now dressed in slacks, shirt and instead of the grey corduroy, a Stanstead Spartans jacket from his ready bag. The jacket had been acquired from the school's gift shop on his recent trip there in his capacity as a member of the Council of Trustees. He'd found a washer and dryer in the shower area, so he chucked his running togs in and left them to wash. Going to a vacant computer he called Ottawa on their secure video link to talk to the Director. "Leif," he said, "Good morning. I have an idea that needs your agreement, please."

Leif responded, "Go ahead, let me hear it. By the way how are things going there?"

Sean-Guy quickly filled him in mentioning especially that they'd put Hari and George together to trail the suspect Afghan, then presented his idea about Pere René as a contractor to provide a general profile on Afghan terrorist behavior. "I have some background with Pere René from my days in military service. I believe he is pretty well qualified to help us even though he does not have direct experience doing this sort of thing. He does have a lot of experience working with personality disorders."

Leif revealed some thoughtfulness over the video-link and suggested to Sean-Guy, "Could he work with Betty Anne here in the office? If he has military experience we can easily get clearance for him to be aware of our operation."

Sean-Guy agreed and said, "Would you contact him right away? I have a feeling the sooner we can get a preliminary profile the

Ron Stotyn

better for our surveillance. We'll have a better idea what behaviors to watch for."

The two said their goodbyes and Sean-Guy turned his attention back to the problem of the woman reporter. As he pondered, he did a name search on the Internet using the name Kafirov as his first input. After a quick result came up suggesting the name was typical of Chechen origins, he then searched for Marek and got the same result. That is interesting he thought as he placed another call to Ottawa: *I need to get Betty to dig up info about Chechnya.* Speaking with Betty briefly on the same installed video link with Ottawa HQ, he outlined his interest and left her to do more research on the names he gave her. He then left the computer and went back to the observation room to see if De Luca was still camped out. As he did so it dawned on him that he had met a Chechen boy a number of years earlier; *about mid-2000 I think it was, at Stanstead College when I made my first visit as a member of the Trustees. He was an exchange student there to learn English as a second language. Now, if I can dig up his name from my memory….*

Arriving at Observation he saw the young woman was still there; the Commissionaire told him she hadn't done much except sit and read a book, or so it seemed to him. Sean-Guy stood watching her in the monitor, remarking to himself in his mind once again, that *she is indeed very good looking; her face is comely and her body is a delight to look at as much as one could with the coverage of the sloppy worn dress she had on this morning, a denim peasant dress I think it would be called.* She'd worn an old duffle coat over top, now lying on the chair beside her.

"Have you spoken to her yet?" he asked.

"Yes," came the Commissionaire's reply. "I guess that's why she seems settled. I told her the Manager would be available shortly."

Sean-Guy nodded at that response, and said, more or less to himself, "I guess I'd better go out and speak to her." He remained in the observation room for awhile longer contemplating her and how he would try to deal with her; thinking at the same time how *I am particularly attracted to the woman, a feeling I've not experienced in*

several years since my second divorce. It is an emotional thing that I
understand and do not understand.

Going to the foyer door and taking one more look at the
monitor, he saw she seemed engrossed in her book, so he opened the
door silently and stood just inside without a sound. He held the door
behind him so it wouldn't close immediately and make a sound. Then
he stepped forward allowing the door to bang, in order to observe her
reaction. She startled but recovered very quickly he thought as he
spoke. "You wanted to see the Manager?"

"Yes," replied the woman, laying her book aside. "I'm looking
for a job as a pesticide technician."

Her face betrayed no guile, as Sean-Guy made a rapid decision
to call her bluff. Fixing her with his patented steely gray-blue stare, he
spoke again, "Miss De Luca, I know that you are a reporter for the
Toronto Star. What is your real purpose here?"

This time when she startled she did not recover composure
nearly as quickly and stammered "How ...Uh...Where did you get such
an idea," desperately trying to maintain her ruse. Then, as she took a
deep breath, she said "Oh hell. Well yes it's true, but how did you
know?"

Now Sean-Guy, making up a quick fib responded, "Our janitor
with whom you spoke yesterday, recalled seeing your picture in the
paper on a story you did recently" hoping the fib would work as he had
absolutely no idea if her picture had ever appeared. He continued,
changing the subject before she could deny, still holding his dark stare,
"You must surely be aware that we are a pest control business. I
honestly cannot believe that we are worthy of a story by someone of
your caliber," thinking to himself a little buttering up couldn't help but
soften her up and perhaps distract her. It failed.

She retorted, "And I know that you are not a pest control
company. In fact I know that you are a federal agency charged with
anti-terrorism investigation. You are called the Canadian Anti-
terrorism Service with headquarters in Ottawa and offices across the
country in all the major cities. I know the name of your director and of
the Chief Investigator. I know most of your investigation staff is made

Ron Stotyn

up of ex-military and ex-RCMP officers and I'd guess with some ex-cops as well."

At that outburst, Sean-Guy's eyebrows went up a little as he realized she had information that was not supposed to be generally known. Abandoning any continuation of the pest-control cover story, he proceeded, "If you're certain of such facts why then are you here? Indeed what is your evidence about your assertion?"

"I want to know why your agency is refusing to work with the O.P.P. Provincial Anti-Terrorism and Hate Crimes section, which already has jurisdiction about that sort of thing here in Ontario," she blurted out, and in a rush also said, "I was told that by a senior official at the legislature," immediately regretting that revelation about a source.

Sean-Guy, thinking she still did not know exactly who he was contemplated his next comment carefully.

After a full minute, all the while staring unblinking at her, but seeing she was unmoved, he spoke with a tone of inexorable authority. "Miss De Luca, by the authority which I hold under the Security of Information Act, I warn you that you are very close to committing several violations of the act, including receiving information which is a danger to the national security of Canada. If you persist in your inquiry you will be subject to arrest, trial and likely conviction. The sentence could be for up to 14 years for specific violations, compounded by however many convictions you end up with." He could see that his brief statement had shocked her. Dismay was written all over her face.

Gulping and thinking furiously about what she knew about the SOIA, Angela responded, "But the Ontario Superior Court has found that action against possession of information obtained in trust is unconstitutional. As a reporter I have a right under the Rights and Freedoms charter to acquire information that's for the public interest."

"That's only partly correct," said Sean-Guy. "The Supreme Court has not taken up the Ontario court decision, so the act remains intact. If you decide to pursue your story you'll have to approach the court on the issue of public interest and demonstrate that disclosure is truly in the public interest, that disclosure is reasonably necessary, that you have pursued reasonable alternatives and that there are exigent circumstances. I presume you have considered all that? Not forgetting of course that if the court rules against you, you would then face the court on the violations I've noted."

Now distressed to the point of tears, with one trickling now down her check, Angela said with a desperate passion, "This is a public interest issue; terrorism always is! The public always has a right to know what dangers it faces!"

Sean-Guy, again holding his stare, thought for awhile, and then said, "As a private citizen I might agree with you, but in my professional capacity I cannot agree that public revelations of your information would protect the people of Canada. It would serve to alert anyone who might be considering action against us."

Then realizing he was entering into a debate with her, he suggested, "We can continue this conversation across the street over a cup of coffee if you like, completely off the record, of course."

Angela replied, brightening somewhat from her earlier turmoil. "I would agree to that only if you tell me who you are," as she recalled her thoughts about the man from the previous evening. She was definitely attracted to him despite his very formidable demeanor. She believed she could persuade him that she was worthy of hearing useful information, and maybe learn more about him as a desirable man. She momentarily forgot about the other man, with whom she'd spent the night, and from whom she had gotten very useful information about CAS as she rose to go to the Olympia with this striking individual.

In the Observation Room behind them Stuart, who'd been watching and listening, amazed at Sean-Guy's conduct, said, "Damn, what the hell is he up to now?" The rumors about Sean-Guy's independent behavior now took on added believability.

{8.2}

Marek's Bomb Kitchen, Wednesday April 5, about 10 AM: Mississauga ON

Marek had begun the process of assembling detonation triggers. He'd been able to purchase several cell phones with

Ron Stotyn

introductory minutes on each, sufficient time for his needs. He still needed to get more, and planned to leave before noon to do some more shopping. Of the ones he already had, he had tested each to be sure they worked, making outgoing calls to the Toronto Time Check number. After making his first detonator trigger, he'd been able to test the discharge of the condensers using the electronic test meter he'd gotten for just a few dollars at the electronics parts store where he'd also purchased the capacitor charging device. That had worked as guaranteed, so he was pleased so far with his progress. There was more than enough discharge to create a necessary ignition spark for the PETN to detonate. Marek knew the success of his plan depended on reliability and instant explosive force.

 Once he had made the first two or three, the task became routine. He was at the same time charging the condensers, one after the other. That was somewhat time-consuming, given the quantity he needed, but it was going to be fine. By tomorrow, or the next day at the latest, he thought he would have the triggers finished and would be able to arm all of the 37 bomb packages that were now completed. His schedule called for putting the wonderfully horrific packages into their various bags and backpacks to make them ready to transport to the storage lockers. He expected to be able to finish that by Monday if he could get at least half distributed on Saturday. As he considered his progress and plan for distribution, Marek made a mental note to rent a van for Friday. He'd need that for transporting the large quantity of explosive devices to selected storage locker destinations across the greater Toronto region.

 As he worked, Marek's thoughts drifted to his experience the previous night at the restaurant. He'd felt disturbed by the tall dark haired man's steely stare every time he entered the private dining room. It was very disconcerting and he couldn't put his finger on the reason for his discomfort. He also recalled his walk home after the tea house had closed for the night. He'd taken his normal route home, but had felt that he was not alone. Recalling some tradecraft taught to him at KavKaz: *I was taught not to look back except in a natural change of direction, in order not to spook any follower. Better that way to see a pursuer without alerting them they had been made.* So he had followed that instruction without attempting to look back until he had reached the traffic-light controlled intersection. But, he had not seen anyone except for another individual hunched over moving along the other side of the street apparently trying to avoid the cold on his way home, though the feeling of being followed continued all the way to his rooms. Even after he entered his front room, after he'd switched on the light, he'd paused at the window to look out, but was unable to see anything. Too late he'd realized a mistake, in the light he was revealed and the light streaming through the window made the darkness outside impenetrable. After turning out the light he went back to the window, not standing too close, but still could not see anyone. After a few minutes, being tired and still needing to make his prayer commitment before retiring to bed, he got his prayer mat and began the ritual obeisance. In doing so he missed the tall dark haired man coming out of the shadows, crossing to the front of his building to read the mail boxes and the address.

Then his thoughts caught up to his activity earlier in the morning. Marek recalled getting off the bus in the barely half light of dawn over on Dixie Drive in order to begin his walk down Courtneypark toward Shawson. He hadn't gotten far when again he felt as if he was being followed. This time he had risked a look back, but he'd only seen a jogger wearing a toque, a couple of blocks back on the other side of the street. When he reached the building where his leased kitchen was located, he'd paused at the corner and looked around. This time he saw the same jogger, kneeling down, partly obscured by cars in the adjacent parking lot, apparently retying his shoe laces. He'd not been able to see the jogger's face and could not tell if the figure was male or female. When he'd reached the door of his space, he'd felt relief, because his quick glance to either side as he entered, did not reveal any follower. Though he did not realize it, he'd failed to see his follower crouched behind a car observing his entry. Despite uncomfortable feelings, Marek decided there was nothing to be concerned about.

An hour later he left the kitchen, as usual by the back door, and went off to continue his purchases of throwaway cell phones. As usual he walked back up to Dixie Road to catch a bus. As he walked

Ron Stotyn

he had a sudden revelation. The dark haired man from the night before was known to him. Nearly nine years earlier when he was barely into his teen years, they had met at Stanstead College. The man had been on the Stanstead College Council of Trustees and had encouraged him in his studies with ESL. Marek no longer recalled the man's name but felt relieved since he would have been identified there only by his real name. Still, there was the matter of the way the man had stared at him every time he entered the private room. That was still a disconcerting whisper in his mind. The thought served at the moment to make him recommit to being very careful.

{8.3}
CAS Headquarters, Wednesday April 5, about 2 PM: Ottawa ON

Father Jean Pierre René Girau, Ph.D., Canadian Forces Major (ret) arrived at the O'Conner Street address he'd been given by Leif Isaksson, who'd called him earlier in the day. Girau was surprised by the call, especially when he realized he recognized the name of his caller as a fairly well known senior officer in CF Intelligence Services and CF Special Operations Forces Command. General Isaksson had asked him about his military background and academic specialty, and had then invited him to come and discuss the possibility of contracting to produce a general profile about Afghan terrorist behavior. He had agreed without hesitation, considering that his discourse with God on the matter and this outcome was surely the fruition of HIS will! He had also been told he would be meeting a CAS operative named Dr. Betty Anne Grabler, an analyst with advanced degrees in Psychology and Criminal Behavior. He was excited about the prospects, and then reminded himself that nothing was yet agreed. The upcoming meeting would, of course, be exploratory he believed. After hanging up the phone, René set about to clear the rest of his day, asking the secretary in the parish office to tell his appointments that he'd been called away urgently.

As he entered the building he was met by a uniformed Commissionaire who escorted him to the elevator and up to the fourth floor and delivered him into the only office suite there. Inside waiting was a tall Nordic male of distinctly military bearing that could only be General Isaksson. Isaksson had been advised of Girau's impending arrival ahead of the commissionaire escort. Beside him was a petite blond woman of apparent Germanic ancestry. Her golden hair, very nicely styled, floated gracefully around her round cheerful face. He could not be certain of her age, so he guessed late forties. In fact, as he later learned, she was 50 and widowed with two nearly grown children. He was struck astonished at her comely appearance, thinking as he had not ever done in his long career as a priest, that she was a very enviable specimen of the feminine form. Oh, it was true that as a man he had often appreciated the beauty of many women that he had met and known casually. But never before, as a priest, had he experienced such an attraction. Shaken, Father Girau tried hard not to stare at her, turning his attention forcibly back to the General who was greeting him and inviting him to come into his corner office. Dr. Grabler followed bringing coffees for everyone.

Following the phone call that morning, René had deliberated about going to the meeting dressed in his priestly garb and had finally decided to dress in mufti, choosing the only grey suit he had from his meager supply of civilian attire and wearing his regimental tie of the PPCLI. Then he'd spent some time outside his parish residential quarters thinking about how he should present himself. Now in the presence of Dr. Grabler, he was feeling a bit out of his league, especially as the Director and the lady began to discuss their needs. He was sensing considerable uncertainty about his expertise despite the fact he was really quite gifted at determining, often from limited information, the direction of a person's personality development.

Betty Anne, sensing his discomfort, paused in the questioning and said, "Please call me Betty Anne and I should like to call you Jean. The Director is Leif. We try to be quite informal here."

Girau responded gratefully. "I am known by most people as René. So please, you can call me by that name. It is true that I am also called Pere René by my parishioners, but here of course I don't have that capacity. I am curious about how I came to your attention."

Ron Stotyn

As Leif responded, René was surprised by his comment, "Your name was presented to us by a former colleague of yours, I believe. It came from our new Chief Investigator Sean-Guy O'Dwyer-Lariviere."

In his innermost thoughts, he said a brief prayer to God *I thank you Father for the blessing of past friends.* Out loud, he almost gasped, he said, " Oh!...but of course...I had not made the connection until just now. Why I saw him for the first time in many years on Sunday when he came to my first Mass of the morning. It was a wonderful surprise to see him after so many years. We had a delightful lunch together later catching up with each other. We spoke of the similarity in our educational background and interests. Is Sean-Guy involved in something right now with your agency? "

The director frowned saying, "Yes, we have learned of the possibility of a significant terrorist threat in the Toronto area, possibly involving Afghans. Sean-Guy is there now, supervising the investigation. His request to call you came very early this morning. I think you will be able to help us if you will come aboard."

René, without any hesitation and with no thought about what his bishop would say, said with alacrity "It would be my pleasure, when do you need me to begin?"

Betty Anne smiled, responding, "I believe we already have the director's clearance to begin immediately."

Leif nodded and added, "We'll discuss remuneration and your contract later. We do need to work on a general profile very quickly."

René suddenly distressed, blurted out loud, "What will I tell my bishop? He will certainly question any neglect of my parish duties."

Leif and Betty both smiled. Leif said with considerable assurance, "No need to be concerned about that, the DND just seconded you to do Security of Information Act work. Your bishop will understand I'm sure. I'll be in touch with him very soon."

With that Betty took him by the arm to lead him out to her desk. Suddenly, both of them startled by the touch, stepped a bit more apart, both wondering what on earth had occurred. René especially was unsure, and wondered how he was supposed to handle these new and unusual emotions, and if he should feel a priestly guilt. Betty, at the same time, felt conflicting emotions, the sudden attraction she felt for the priest and the welling up of sensations as she recalled the love of her husband, deceased now for five years.

Ron Stotyn

"The terrorist and the policeman both come from the same basket" The Secret Agent, Ch. 4: Joseph Conrad, 1907

Early Morning, CAS Headquarters, Thursday, April 6: Ottawa, ON

Sean-Guy approached CAS Ottawa on foot as he reviewed events of the previous afternoon. Reviewing was a constant habit, going over information, sifting hard facts from speculative ideas. Much had taken place in the few hours that followed his conversation with the reporter at the Olympia Grill, where he had accompanied her after the initial encounter in the foyer of the Toronto office. They had spent less than an hour over coffee. Angela, as he now thought of her and surprised at his decision to think of her by her first name, had continued her argument that the public had a right to know about the workings of the CAS. *I explained an issue that anything having to do with Canada's national security could not be revealed without just cause. She has a spirited attitude about her work, and not likely to give up easily. I like that, even though I cannot give in to her demand for information. But I damn sure don't like her no holds barred demands for information that she really has no right to have. National security being what it is, she just doesn't have the clearance.* Despite all that Sean-Guy could not help but appreciate her spirit. *And I like her attitude overall as well, self aware and self confident.*

During the conversation, he had discovered some of her personal background such as where she was from, Guelph, where she had gone to college, Humber, and her journalistic rise through several of Torstar's newspapers to her present position with the Toronto Star. He had also confirmed she was single, never married at age 35. *I am bemused by that last fact, but somehow it seems important to my future. I am damned if I can determine a logical reason for that notion. It perturbs me to think that my now accepted singleness is being made vulnerable by this woman. I have an uncomfortable feeling she is becoming interested in me for reasons other than my position. What have I done to trigger such a reaction in this woman who is essentially still a stranger to me?*

He recalled moreover, to his own amazement, that he had revealed several personal points about his own life. *I have never before told a woman just met, that I am twice divorced or even that I have a grown daughter whom I am rarely able to see.* Thought of his daughter Carole Louise Martine, whose mother his first wife had reverted to her maiden name of Martine, always gave him heart pangs. There were no children from his second marriage. But his little girl had in her early teens followed her mother's lead concerning use of the last name even though under Quebec law her last name remained Martine-Lariviere. *At least as of yet she had not legally changed the name. She is in college now, I know that, but I have no idea what she is studying or what her plans are for the future. Is there any hope for a future where I have a role?*

With a stolid look on his face he heaved a sigh, and broke off that thought, fiercely rejecting any possible display of emotion. He also tried to firmly reject any idea that he would allow any emotions whatsoever to inject into what surely had to remain an adversarial relationship with any reporter. *However, I must admit that I am inwardly pleased that as we left the restaurant, we reached a basic agreement that she could call with further questions under the understanding I might refuse to answer for national security reasons. I believe also we reached an understanding that we can trust each other.... Well I fervently hope so.*

I find myself increasingly desirous of forming a social relationship, but for the life of me I am uncertain of how or if it would be wise to pursue that. I doubt very much if I could ever really fully trust her. She's almost certainly a total hack, interested only in her next big scoop. There was no doubt now in his mind that he was in a serious conflict situation. He knew also the best thing would be to cut it off clean, but, that it might not be possible.

Sean-Guy turned his thoughts to measure his decision to return quickly to Ottawa. Several bits and pieces had collided. He'd learned on his return to the Toronto office from the cafe, that Pere René had indeed been invited to CAS HQ to meet the Director and begin a

Ron Stotyn

working relationship with Betty Anne to develop a broad stroke profile of Afghan terrorists. Then there was the updated report from Stuart about the credit card information research that had revealed that there was still a lot of digging to do. The delivery address information still was not resolving. He had received the requested sketches and computer imaging from Everet of the man Marek Kafirov. The regressed age Photoshop image was the memory trigger he had needed about the boy he'd met nine years earlier at Stanstead College. That boy was Malik Bisliev. The computer rendering that Everet had produced was a dead certain image, as he recalled it, of the young Chechen he'd met then. I'm certain as I can be that the boy and the man Marek Kafirov are one and the same. It cannot be a coincidence. This demands that I do some checking with Canada Border Services Agency. I need arrival information about both Marek and Malik to see if I can determine what he is up to.

Sean-Guy identified that as the moment he decided he needed to be back in Ottawa to work on a general terrorist profile and to track someone who his insight suggested just didn't add up.

A late afternoon flight yesterday from Toronto Pearson to Ottawa's Macdonald-Cartier International Airport put him on the ground in the capitol just after 5 PM. He'd managed a ride on a government Bombardier Challenger 604, operated by CF Air Command, by using his military rank and ID, which avoided the fees at Toronto Pearson, already among the most expensive in the country. The international airport seemed to be under a constant state of construction. That had resulted in significant surcharges on every airline ticket.

He'd taken a cab directly to the Lisgar Extended Stay Suites, where he showered, changed clothes and repacked his ready bag. His other luggage was left for later in the evening after he'd gone out for dinner. When he'd returned to the suite and not certain about how long he'd be in Ottawa, but probably no more than a day, he had reorganized for an extended stay back in Toronto, packing two more suits and some mix and match casual outfits.

This morning his run went through Ottawa's civic government center area and into Confederation Park, then back. After a change from his running togs and a shower, he walked to the office, where he'd left his car. He'd stopped again for the third time at Café Slater, though he realized that he should not create a pattern in order to prevent trouble for himself with anyone who might not consider his work to be innocuous. Now, approaching his destination, he looked around carefully using casual surveillance tactics to ensure he was not being observed before he entered. To be confident, he had first gone down the Sparks Street pedestrian mall browsing in some windows and then around the block to Wellington and O'Connor just to change the direction of his approach. It was seven thirty as he entered the elevator, knowing he'd been identified by the duty Commissionaire even as he approached.

Reaching his office, he stretched out on his leather couch thinking now about what he knew concerning terrorism from his academic studies. *It is likely insufficient*. He decided almost immediately he would have to rely on the added insights that Pere René and Betty Anne could provide. As he waited for Leif and Betty Anne to arrive he also considered what to do about discovering more about Marek/Malik. His definite gut feeling about the man was that he was not kosher. The first step would have to be contact with Canada Border Services. The problem was that he didn't know anyone of sufficient rank over there to get quick results. Just then he heard movement outside in the open bull-pen area of the office. Getting up he saw Leif, followed by Betty Anne. At his door he spoke, "Good morning to you both."

Leif and Betty Anne, both reacting in surprise responded almost simultaneously, "I thought you were in Toronto." Leif added, "I suppose this means you have something unusual going on that brings you here …unannounced!"

Sean-Guy, realizing at that instant that his individualistic manner had caused neglect to tell the director he was coming back before he left Toronto yesterday, replied with just a tinge of chagrin, "Humph…well yes I guess so…I'm thinking that I have something… well I'm feeling a disconnect with some information I got yesterday."

"Okay, I think you'd better come to my office and sit while we talk about your concern," said Leif. "Let's get coffee first though; I'm

Ron Stotyn

guessing we'll need some." Then he added, "Do you need Betty to come in as well?"

Sean-Guy agreed, saying to Betty directly, "you'll be very helpful I think on part of what I have to say."

All three got themselves settled in Leif's corner office while Sean-Guy, with a strained and serious visage, struggled mentally with how to bring up the topic of Marek, which he knew would sound completely bizarre. Finally he began haltingly. "I have encountered a man in Toronto ....that I am sure I met nine years ago in Stanstead. He was just about 13 back then.... an exchange student from Chechnya studying ESL. You know of course I am saddled with an eidetic memory....that I cannot truly forget what I experience. ...When I first met this man...well I have not had exactly a face-to face meeting....what I mean to say, I have experienced the man's presence. I had a sense about that first exposure to the grown man ....that he was familiar and that he was not authentic." Sean-Guy paused for a long moment, lost in thought.

Betty Anne looked at Leif, who nodded imperceptibly for her to go ahead. She said "You think this man is a problem?"

Sean-Guy looked up, startled by her quick grasp of what he was still coming to. "Yes ....you could certainly say I think he is a problem. His name currently...is Marek Kafirov.... Those names are both likely Chechen. The boy that I met those years ago was Malik Bisliev....those names also Chechen. My memory was triggered when I saw sketches and a computer image that Everet prepared for me. The computer image was the man regressed in age back to early teens. It matched perfectly my recollection of the boy's appearance.... It now occurs to me that my experience of disconnect must be the disparity of the two sets of names for the same individual."

Leif interjected, "Why do you perceive a difficulty with the different names?"

Sean-Guy, now with a wry laugh responded, "That is the rest of the disconnect experience I guess, I cannot pin anything down, except to say my gut tells me the man is not right somehow. I need to trace him quickly, I think. But I don't know anyone over at Canada

Border Services. I need a high ranking agent to assist. Leif, have you any contacts over there?"

"Let me call their president right away," said Leif as he reached for his phone. "I'm not at all certain about the value of this but I am willing to trust your instinct." While waiting for the phone on the other end to be answered, he mused out loud not quite to himself, "If this proves to be anything, we'll need to bolster the Toronto team some more."

"Hello, CAS Director Isaksson for President Stephenson." A moment later CBSA President Kevin Stephenson came on the line, "Director Isaksson, good morning, what can I do for you."

Leif, putting the call on speaker, responded "My Chief Investigator Sean-Guy O'Dwyer-Lariviere, who is now listening to our conversation, needs to connect with one of your senior agents to track a person of interest that we have identified. We consider this a matter of some urgency and would appreciate it if we can make this connection this morning."

"That should not be a problem. Just a moment please," said Stephenson. In a moment he was back on the line. "You folks are downtown I think, are you not? If so, I have a senior agent available at nine this morning at the Metcalfe Street office. Will that work for you?"

Leif, looking over at Sean-Guy and seeing him nod, said, 'That will be very good. My thanks for your cooperation."

Stephenson replied, "Not at all, we are all working for the same goals I suspect. Your man will need to ask for Senior Agent Shawna Kennedy. Is there anything else we can do? If not, I need to go, we have a bit of nonsense going on down at Ambassador Bridge, with the First Nations folks as I'm sure you know and their cousins on the American side; we are trying to get a handle on that, so things are busy right now. By the way, I have become aware that your agency has purloined one of my up and coming border agents, one Darya Barzaryan. I think I need to decide if I am miffed or not," laughing.

Leif chuckled and acknowledging the larceny, said his goodbyes and turning to Sean-Guy, asked, "You got all that?"

Ron Stotyn

Sean-Guy nodded and cleared his throat for the next thing he knew the Director would ask about, work started the day before by Betty and Pere René on developing a terrorist profile.

"Now," said Leif with a grin and pre-empting Sean-Guy, "I think I'm beginning to understand your motivations. Are you also here this morning because of the arrangement we have made with Doctor Girau? You are of course aware that he and Betty began a discussion yesterday. He is coming back this afternoon. I believe, and Betty can correct me, that they have set out some preliminary ideas about Afghan terrorists," as he saw a nod of agreement.

Betty responded, "Yes we have established some parameters, but it will be useful to have you in on the discussion. If we can establish the basics, I think we can have a general profile by late today. I'd prefer to chat with you right now for awhile but it looks like you only just have time to get over to CBSA to meet the agent there."

{9.1}

Marek's Kitchen, early morning April 6: Mississauga ON

Marek was uncharacteristically humming to himself with a certain amount of excitement. He had completed the purchases of the quantity of throwaway cell phones that he'd needed for his collection of 37 bombs. He was busy now with a laptop computer loading a software telephone dialer that he'd found on the internet. *If I can get that set up quickly I will be able to dial all the phones sequentially.* He expected he'd be able to test it within the hour. The software called Phone Broadcaster Auto Dialer could handle lists of several hundred numbers, far more than he actually needed. It featured a robotic sequential dialing module and also allowed him to program a trigger signal, a tone that could actuate his sparking device. *This is an added step that I hadn't planned on, but it is a good idea to ensure a deliberate and decisive actuation. All I needed is a simple addition of a tone translation chip to effect the necessary connection when each phone answered.*

That required programming EPROM chips, which had proved to be relatively easy using a cheap tone generator. He set each phone to answer within three rings in order to ensure a quick cycle of all the phones. The software would move on to the next number as soon as the dialed phone answered. He was pleased. It did not occur to him that if a phone did not answer the program would stall.

The software installation proved to be quick and without difficulty. He programmed the numbers into a list the software could read and began the dialing sequence. He watched and listened with considerable interest as each phone on his table rang and answered within the three rings cycle he'd established. It worked as promised, so he reset each phone and repeated the exercise several more time to be sure. Talking to himself out loud he said, "I'll go to a remote location to try it and make sure that distance would not be a problem. That will need to wait, however, until I can rent a van so that I can return to the kitchen without delay. I don't want to unnecessarily use battery power on the phones even though I can recharge them, which I will do before distributing the bomb packages to the storage lockers where my cell leaders can retrieve them." He didn't realize that he was talking to himself aloud, so focused as he was on the task of finishing his explosive plotting.

The van was primarily needed so he could make those deliveries without reliance on public transport where multiple bundles might create suspicion. Satisfied that he was on schedule, he tidied up and left to collect the van that he had arranged to rent from Apex Used Auto Rentals, using a stolen credit card and false identity as usual. He was unaware that the card he'd used had already popped up on a watch list at the O.P.P office of Electronic Fraud. That meant of course that he was also unaware that the net was very slowly coming closer to him. Nor was he aware that the net was being administered very nearby to his rented kitchen space or that he had already been identified and suspected of terrorism. He was blissfully content that everything was progressing as it needed to be.

{9.2}
CAS HQ, approximately 11 AM, April 6th: Ottawa ON

Ron Stotyn

Sean-Guy returned to his own office from Metcalf Street feeling enervated. His meeting with CBSA Senior Agent Shawna Kennedy had produced very interesting information indeed and convinced him that he was right about Marek Kafirov. First the Border Services agent had searched for entry records for the name Marek Kafirov for the previous year. Finding nothing she'd expanded the search for several years back. Still finding nothing and coming to an increasingly certain decision that the man did not exist, she once again modified the search to see if there were similar names in the system, perhaps due to spelling errors. Still nothing. The two of them then turned their attention to Malik Bisliev, the name Sean-Guy knew from nine years earlier. Shawna had entered the name for the year 2000 to see if there was a hit that could be used to verify the child's entry and status at that time. The record that came up verified the boy's entry into Canada on a student visa. Then the surprise, the software search also brought up the same name as entering the country just six months ago on the same student visa. Kennedy was amazed, saying to Sean-Guy with certitude, "That should never have happened. The entry port agent should have discovered the visa was expired. There is no doubt this person entered illegally. We need to find and arrest this person immediately."

Sean-Guy discussed the matter with Shawna urging, "The jurisdiction needs to be ceded to the CAS. I am now pretty much convinced that there are reasonable grounds to justify our involvement as a matter of potential terrorist activity," knowing that his argument was thin. He added, "I'm asking that you trust my judgment on this. I am not often wrong about such things."

Shawna reluctantly agreed, "But, you have to keep me fully informed on this. I need to write a report that will show my boss we'll be called in if needed."

Sean-Guy agreed, shook hands and got up to return to the CAS office. "I'll be in touch again as soon as possible."

Sean-Guy, back at the CAS HQ, was now on the vid-link to Toronto waiting for Stuart to come to his monitor. As Stuart settled into his chair, Sean-Guy told him, "We need some surveillance and tailing teams right away. You need to get the sketches that Everet made for me and make sure that the teams are completely familiar with the face with and without beard. We also need to try and get good sharp photos of the man."

Stuart interrupted, "Whoa, slow down, who are we talking about?"

"Oh, yeah," said Sean-Guy, immediately regretting his do-it-yourself tendency, "I haven't told you about this yet have I. Well, remember our visit to the Samovar place you recommended? One of our waiters is now a person of interest. I thought I recognized the Tea Server."

"The Tea Server!?" said Stuart, not comprehending. "What was special about the tea server?....Oh, I get it, your famous eidetic memory."

"Yeah, that's it. I developed an uncomfortable feeling that I'd seen him somewhere before. I had Everet do sketches and a computer image regressed to teenage features. That triggered my memory. The man's real name is Malik Bisliev, as far as we now know. I met this morning with a senior agent of the CBSA and we have determined that Marek Kafirov, that's the name being used by the Tea Server, has never apparently entered the country anytime in the past several years. But Malik Bisliev is here on an expired student visa, arriving just six months ago. The time he was here on a valid visa, the same one by the way, was nine years ago when he came to study English at Stanstead College. That is when I met him."

Stuart responded, "And how does that make this guy a person of interest? I'm still not following your premise...."

"Well," interrupted Sean-Guy, "That's the rest of the story," as he related the events that led him to follow the man to his rooms and the chance encounter while out on a run the day before early in the morning. "This guy's behavior is just off square, I think. What can we set up for surveillance at the strip mall location on Shawson Drive where I saw him enter? We'd need two units, one for the front and one for the back. I also want teams at his residence and at the restaurant."

Stuart, after a lengthy pause, replied, "I think that's a problem. We don't have enough personnel....I guess we'll need some

Ron Stotyn

supplementary assistance from someone. Maybe the O.P.P. anti-terrorism guys can help, but I don't know anyone there."

"As soon as I'm done with this call, I'll talk to the Director. I'm sure he can get something organized on that front, and I think we can get help from CBSA. Their agent this morning was reluctant to give us the jurisdiction so I'm pretty sure she'll get authorization to help if they can be part of it," said Scan-Guy with confidence.

After some discussion about the planning details, Sean-Guy signed off and went to talk to the director.

On his way into Leif's office, Betty called to him, "Father René is coming here in time for lunch. Will you come with us?"

Sean-Guy nodded agreement and gave Betty a thumbs up as he entered and greeted Leif, getting straight to the point. "We need assistance from O.P.P. anti-terrorism and the CBSA to set up some surveillance in Toronto."

Leif raised his eyebrows and waited for the explanation which he got in Sean-Guy's succinct manner. When the account was complete, Leif reached for his phone and told Sean-Guy he would try to get agreement from the O.P.P. as soon as possible. "They are not entirely our friends yet….still hurting a bit about the way we were set up, but I think we can make points by inviting them in on this. In the meantime, why don't you call Kennedy at CBSA and see what she can do for us."

An hour later, Sean-Guy was able to tell Leif that CBSA was in on the surveillance. They would assign six agents in Toronto initially and could provide a few more as needed. "Kennedy will arrange to have that team meet up with Stuart McIntyre as soon as possible, probably by early afternoon."

Leif, in turn, reported that he'd made contact with Deputy Commissioner Hawker Vince of O.P.P. Investigations and Organized Crime. "Deputy Vince is pleased to be invited into the surveillance task of a potential terrorist in the province. He will supply a six-man team of experienced anti-terrorist agents. They will report to Stuart within the hour for instructions."

As Sean-Guy finished a vid-link conversation with Stuart to apprise him of these developments, Betty Anne called to him that she and Father Girau were ready to go to lunch. "Where are you going?" he asked. "I'll just bring Leif up-to-date, and I'll catch up with you right away."

"We'll be at Sparks Street Club Grill. It's around the corner towards Banks Street," replied Betty as she and Father Girau left the office.

Sean-Guy proceeded toward Leif's office to finish the discussion about the surveillance plans. Entering the corner office, Sean-Guy reported what Stuart had told him. "Stuart is planning to use the O.P.P. team to watch Kafirov with two teams at the strip mall location and one team at the restaurant and a team of our own at the residence. Once they get a fix on his location they'll follow on foot if necessary with backup in vehicles. The CBSA teams will augment Darya's and George's watch on the Afghan for the time being until we see if he is meeting anyone. If that happens, they can follow the contacts made."

Leif nodded at that plan and said, "Keep me up to date on developments, please. Are you meeting with Girau and Betty Anne now? And, what are your plans for tomorrow? Are you going back to Toronto?"

"Yes on both counts, replied Sean-Guy. " I'm hoping that the three of us can come up with a reasonable general profile on Afghan terrorists later today, but now I'm also thinking we have to consider the possibility that we have a Chechen terrorist in the mix as well. That may take more time to flesh out a more specific profile. I'll probably return to Toronto before that aspect is developed." With Leif's nod, Sean-Guy turned and left to meet Betty Anne and René for lunch.

{9.3}
Sparks Street Club Grill, 12:30 PM April 6: Ottawa ON

Sean-Guy arrived at the Sparks Street Club Grill about fifteen minutes after Betty Anne and Pere René. As he approached their table, he could see that Betty Anne was more than professionally interested in René. Sitting opposite, she was laughing and leaning toward him engrossed in what he was saying. René was more reserved, but Sean-

Ron Stotyn

Guy thought there was an attraction there as well. He wondered if Pere René was comfortable in his priestly role less now than he had once been. Both already had a glass of wine each. They looked up and Betty said, "I took the liberty of ordering a pint of Alexander Keith Stag's Dark Ale for you. I understand that is your favorite."

"It is indeed. How did you know?"

"Ahh," said Betty Anne with an air of mysteriousness. "Your tastes are famous."

Sean-Guy, shaking his head at that response, "I'll have to keep my cards more closely to the chest, I think. Nice to see you again, René" He settled into a chair and asked Betty-Anne, "Have you discovered what this place does best for lunch?"

"No. It's my first time here. We'll have to ask the server for a recommendation," she said just as the waitress approached.

With recommendations given and received, Sean-Guy ordered a steak sandwich rare with frites. Betty asked for a salmon salad on baby greens, while René specified pommes frites with gravy and cheese curds, otherwise known as Poutine in a typical Quebec café. Then they settled into a conversation of generalities, saving the main focus of their need to discuss terrorist behavior till after they ate. As they talked, Sean-Guy satisfied himself that there was some electricity between Betty Anne and René. He wondered how that would play out over time.

With all finished lunch, Sean-Guy asked, "Shall we continue our profile development over coffee here or go back to the office conference room?

Pere René, with Betty nodding assent, suggested, "The conference room will perhaps be best considering the sensitive nature of our deliberations."

"Right you are." Sean-Guy added, "I'll get the ticket and will follow you right away. I need to stop at Freemen's Men's Wear for some necessary odds and ends that I'll need when I return to Toronto."

Within ten minutes, Sean-Guy having taken care of his fresh socks and underwear shopping quickly, the three were seated comfortably in the conference room with each ready to begin a discussion. Sean-Guy started by revealing a complication. "This morning I got pretty solid confirmation that a person of interest in Toronto is potentially a subject of extra-special concern in our investigation of possible terrorist activities. I must tell you that there is absolutely no concrete evidence at this point. In fact, I have no reason to connect this man to the Afghan. It is just my feeling that he is up to no good. The man is a Chechen so I would like us to figure Chechen terrorists into our general profile. So where do we begin?"

As it turned out, the beginning immediately took on a distinctly academic tone as the three began to dig into their respective fields of study and expertise.

René in response, "I suggest we need to look at personality disorders that arise from effects of ethnicity and political oppression. That would be logical since we are talking about Afghans and now also about Chechens. Both have been so much in the news recently that we already probably know many broad things about them. In fact, just this morning, there was again news stories about the activity of Black Widow terrorists in Chechnya. We can use the smart white board to list aspects that fit such criteria." (Betty had already been downloading data from the smart board during the previous day's discussions, organizing it in a relational database.)

Sean-Guy, picking up on René's reference, asked, "Black Widows?"

Betty replied, "The Black Widows are a phenomenon almost unheard of outside Chechnya. They literally are widows of Chechen revolutionaries put to death first by the Soviets and then later by the Soviet influenced Chechen government for crimes against the state. Mostly young, they have become violently effective suicide terrorists."

Then she went on with her originally intended addition to René's lead. "Criminal behavior analysis of existing data, especially statistics relating to these areas will aid us in narrowing our focus. I am downloading our smart white board notes on my laptop to keep a running assessment. I can also bring up source materials to display that will support our developing profile."

Sean-Guy reflectively added, "Geographic causes and implications of various domestic issues, and internal conflict focused on political, economic, social and military perspectives, along with

Ron Stotyn

mid-east issues will help me understand the terrain. Also, I think ideas associated with disintegration of political structures, and various kinds of exploitations may help our task."

René, going forward, observed, "It seems to me that an approach from forensic psychology may be a good way to proceed. Let me summarize some ideas. There is some useful material concerning the influence of race and racial bias on perceptions of offenders. Take this with studies of attitudes toward victims by perpetrators, then adding psychological description of mental, emotional and personality characteristics of suspects, we can broadly describe the type of individual most likely to become a terrorist."

"I see some connections to criminal behavior studies, especially the idea that behavior reflects personality," Sean-Guy observed.

Betty Anne interjected quickly, "This is also related to the sociology of deviance and the psychology of behavior looking for forms and causes related to the commission of crime. With deviant behavior, one can see that actions or behaviors which violate cultural norms including formally enacted rules or informal violations create outcasts to some degree. But we should be aware this does not always necessitate negative result, sometimes the result might be for the good of society by preventing stagnation."

"But, here's perhaps a critical question," said Sean-Guy, "What makes the difference between a sheer criminal such as a gang member and a dedicated terrorist? In the case of Afghan terrorists, my sense is they suffer a historical divide that relates to the oppression caused by the Russian overrun of their country in the 1980's. Those associated with mujahedeen efforts to oust the Soviet troops must have developed severe personality and behavior shifts that could be termed disorders, at least so I suppose."

René noted, "I don't disagree; however, in this line of thinking you must also consider the impact of religion being a matter of discord between the mujahedeen and the Soviets. There would certainly have been a struggle to maintain the integrity of Muslim faith and practice. That, I think, is especially the case for Afghanis. They have a more distinct religious focus. Even before the Soviet invasion I believe, based on some hasty research earlier today, the central Afghan government was subjected to rebellion from deeply devout Islamists. Attempts to overthrow the government began as early as 1975, I think. When the Soviets arrived in December of 1979, they participated in extreme violence against those seeking to impose a traditional form of Islamic rule. I believe the mujahedeen became a people dedicated to preservation of a strict form of Islam, a fairly unique kind of nationalism, if you will. The Afghanis as a group are certainly concerned that their culture not be pulled down."

"Well, that certainly seems to tie into ideas of emotional and mental stressors," said Sean-Guy. "Can we then say that Afghan terrorists are singularly focused on establishing and maintaining a particular cultural hard line?"

Betty Anne, shaking her head, "I think that is a bit of a problem…. It avoids the issue of deviance. If that's true, what are Afghan terrorists deviating from? We need to consider ethnic indicators of identity, those things which help an individual frame their self perception and sense of situations that foster a psychological defense against whatever oppression they feel."

René observed, "Remember also that following the exit of the Soviets, the country was severely exploited, especially by Pakistan. The country now is stripped of 98 percent of its forests; the formerly agrarian society is still mostly decimated. And, of course, the rise of the Taliban has effected a serious oppression on the general population, even though Taliban warlords have been beaten back in recent years. Don't forget that the Taliban have trained many terrorists using psychological methods."

"Sean-Guy, your previous question about the difference between criminals and dedicated terrorists can perhaps now be partially answered by considering step number four of the FBI's crime scene analysis procedure, which focuses in part on motives and personality. Similarly, consider step three of the approach known as Behavioral Evidence Analysis, which in part suggests a need to consider the relationship to other crimes in order to posit motives." Betty Anne paused and then continued with her analysis, "Once we

Ron Stotyn

have a list of offender characteristics, we can posit a terrorist profile, I think."

"Let me review some ideas from criminology studies that may also help us do just that," said Sean-Guy. "There's a thought from the classical school that suggests humans have a disposition to seek either pleasure or pain by weighing the cost versus benefits of consequences. But this approach ignores possible irrationality or unconscious drives that might be motive factors. So we then should perhaps consider the positivist approach, which assumes there are internal and external factors beyond a person's control such as biological, psychological and social indicators. I'm not convinced about biological factors, but I do think the other two are valid. There are also the Italian and French views, the first of which proposes physiological traits or criminalistic tendencies. The second rejects the idea of born criminals but asserts direct influence from the social environment. This aspect in particular seems useful to me. Another view which I like is called Sociological Positivism which recognizes societal factors that include poverty, subcultures, low-level education to create predispositions. A more recent approach called the Chicago School that is credible for me, takes a look at what are called zones in transition that are often volatile, subject to disorder. It's a social ecology method that understands how breakdown in social structure creates disorganization which certainly must be regarded as strong stressors. This leads us to ideas such as conflict or structural conflict, poverty and economic deprivation, which lead to difficulty in maintaining social order. I think this leads us to suggest that anyone caught in such turmoil begins to think about, or perhaps, better to say, dreams about opportunity, freedom, prosperity which are powerful cultural and psychological motivators. These individuals are caught in the dichotomy of what society expects and what the individual can achieve."

Betty Anne, reacting to Sean-Guy's last comment, "The inequality that must result for such individuals must surely lead to illegitimate means to achieve…. Many must drop into deviant sub-cultures. It seems then to me that a differential association is likely to occur….a fragmenting from mainstream, adoption of divergent ideas, values and meanings about life."

Sean-Guy said then, "That thought sparks some ideas I have about control theory, which speaks of reasons why people do not become criminals. Attachment to others, belief in a moral validity of ideas, commitment to achievement and involvement in conventional activities....is believed to mean that individuals will ordinarily adhere to the mores of society. But it seems to me that these things can also trigger a negative result if circumstances are different....that little or no self-control in these areas can create attachment to those of criminal aspiration, committed efforts to achieve one's own ends, development of a perverted sense of morality of ideas, and involvement in unconventional activities."

René, as if thinking out loud, "I wonder if we can then posit that such individuals are also stressed by a disparate relationship between themselves,...hmmm... identifying as less powerful,... and the power elite. Perhaps it is this that allows us to bring in the idea of Chechen terrorists, who must certainly have a serious problem with Soviet influenced leadership in their country. It seems to me that Chechens generally can be seen as torn between a desperate need to support and maintain their own culture and a sense that they also belong somehow with the broader Russian society. Their strong fight for independence can probably be compared with the conflict that has endured for so long in Northern Ireland. This is almost certainly an aspect of their sense of oppression that we should not overlook. We must also not lose sight of the religious fanaticism that lies alongside their political motivations that may well be equally fanatic."

Betty Anne, with some enthusiasm about this idea supposed, "If the power elite as a group impose some meaning about the less powerful, especially those who involve themselves in deviance, and then create a label, such as terrorist to describe that less powerful element, then surely they will adopt that meaning, take it on as having value. Taking the label is likely to mean they will adopt the behavior and take pride in it."

Sean-Guy reflecting, "There is some criminology theory that may be a parallel here, I think. It's called Routine Activity or sometimes called Criminal Opportunity. This speaks of motivated

Ron Stotyn

offenders, suitable targets or victims, and a lack of capable guardians. In the case of terrorists, how can we apply these ideas, or can we?"

René immediately responded, "In the case of the Afghans there is a long history going back generations, of motivation to oppose the ruling elite, especially when they are not in line with ideals of traditional Islam. The oppressors, those who put down rebellion violently, certainly make a suitable target for violence in return."

Sean-Guy taking a devil's advocate role for the moment, "What about the capable guardian issue?"

René, without hesitation, proposed, "In the case of Afghanistan, the power elite force the terrorists to make their own, in recent times we see this as the Taliban, radical, but aligned to the idea that the power elite fail to ensure an appropriate Islamic rule and law. Not exactly capable guardians if we structure the argument in negative terms, thus a lack of capable guardians since the word capable seems to engender a positive structure, but a kind of guardian nevertheless. So now we have the presentation of a suitable cause. And I think here we also begin to see the adoption of a radical and often violent stance or way to strike back. Certainly that seems especially true of Chechnya, where survivors of the Soviet genocidal actions, have ample reason to think they need to take retributive actions."

"Indeed, the deviant behavior begins to take on a life of its own," added Betty Anne, as she explored the role of irrationality becoming a norm over time. "Reactive rules of conduct become entrenched as a reflection of the terrorist's inherent biases and particular interests. These are highly selfish and one-sided….that is, the terrorist element begins to make claims and statements that seek to establish their particular sense of right and wrong as immutable. Indoctrination begins to permeate the sub-culture until the members see themselves as inherently justified in preserving the new social system that is developing. But in order for this to work, the members must be radicalized….true believers must be made, so inculcation tactics become the internal strategy."

"René," said Sean-Guy, "Your comment about Chechnya makes me ask these questions: Why have Chechen terrorists taken their fight outside the country into Russia? Why are they not satisfied that the Soviets having pulled back are finished interfering?"

René, hesitating a moment, said, "I think I have not enough information about circumstances there. I would need to do much more study of their situation. But, I do think, part of it remains a sense of unfulfilled redress. The amount of Soviet violence was so heavy."

"I think we may be able to say that terrorism generally and broadly is engendered by a growing sense on the part of oppressed persons that they are without any other means to reject what the elite of society believe ought to be the norms." Betty Anne paused, thinking with her index finger held up to forestall any interruption, and then continued, "The very high degree to which the power elite condemn what they deem deviant behavior gives the deviant person no other choice but to react violently, at least in their own view of that seeming injustice. The elite indeed force a behavior that is highly unintegrated; an extreme egoism results. In addition, because the powerless are forced to be very unregulated, anomie results. This lawlessness in the view of the elite reinforces the decision to label the deviant segment of society as terrorist.

Sean-Guy, now especially alert to the implications, interjected, "I understand then that anomie is a state where social goals of the oppressed and thus legitimate means of achievement do not correspond to their beliefs and concerns. The resulting strain, stress, and frustration necessitate violent reaction. This is an alienation from society that forces illegitimate means to achieve goals. Rejection of normative goals and means results in a seeking to redefine new values for society that do not conform to what the elite require of society. Rebellion is the only way out and because the oppression is severe violent rebellion is the only recourse, at least so believed."

Betty Anne, considering what has been said so far, offered a conclusion of sorts. "The deviance we have been discussing is essentially learned behavior. Interaction with other deviants creates a symbolic structure that enables a meaningful lifestyle. Consider that reality does not define what is meaningful. People must impose meaning by negotiating, manipulating, changing the structure to some degree. I noted earlier that a differential association occurs. Learned

Ron Stotyn

criminality and deviant behavior are not inherently part of individualistic nature. It results from interactions via the communication of symbols and ideas. When manipulators make this more favorable about deviance, the recipients more likely will resort to such behavior."

Sean-Guy asked now, noting his need to return to Toronto shortly, "Can we come to a statement now that will give us a practical profile of Afghan and Chechen terrorism?"

The three of them sat silently for quite awhile thinking about their discussion so far. Finally, René spoke up. "I think we need a bit more discussion about the personality disorder view of the mental disturbances of stressed individuals. In fact, I think you will find, when I explain, that Post Traumatic Stress Disorder (PTSD) is a central theme for why individuals become terrorists. But first, I would like us to take a break. I need to organize my thinking before I can continue." With that he rose and left the room. When Betty and Sean-Guy got to the main office space, they found René standing facing a tall window as if looking out, but he could not, being much too short to see through the tall high windows of the 4th floor. He was lost in thought.

{9.4}
CAS HQ, Nearly 4 PM April 6: Ottawa ON

Twenty minutes later, René, having remained still for all that time, all three made their way back to the conference room. René sat at the head of the table and folded his hands in front of him, cleared his throat and began to speak. "You are aware that my career in the Canadian Forces required me to examine many, many soldiers to determine if their combat or other military experiences caused them to experience personality disorders. It was unfortunately too often the case that I found many, many soldiers who did suffer a variety of disorders; most often a diagnosis of PTSD was possible. This disorder can manifest itself in various degrees of severity ranging from limited effects to extremely severe. The ability to diagnose this problem depends on being able to work with the individual over a period of time, observing them and probing their mental and psychological history. One must also try to determine if there might be medical causes for the symptoms and behaviors being exhibited."

René paused for a long while, gathering his thoughts more tightly and as Sean-Guy made as if to speak, René looked up, smiled sadly and requested, "Please do not interrupt. I ask you to bear with me. This is a difficult topic, because I have seen terrible pain caused by PTSD. First I must tell you that despite my experience mainly with soldiers, the disorder can strike anyone in the entire population. Those who survive severe physical or mental trauma including such as those who experience being beaten severely, being raped, tortured and those who witness gruesome events are subject. They may not experience the symptoms for years, but when it strikes they may begin to re-experience the trauma or the associated anxiety. They may have recurring and distressing recollections, nightmares, and daytime flashbacks. It is possible for many with the more severe symptoms to have dissociative states where they begin to lose touch with reality. It is possible for victims of PTSD to experience psychic numbing, a withdrawal from friends and family, and even strong feelings of isolation. There will often be attempts to avoid situational similarities to attempt to avoid attacks of symptoms. The trauma event memory is one that becomes easily triggered. Some become housebound as a result. And some, I'm sorry to say, may have varying degrees of panic disorder, panic attacks if you will. There is also a risk of depression.

Again René paused, an expression of deep concern on his face. "Now I come to what may be the crux of our need to understand terrorists in general. Frustrations, insults, aggressive behavior toward the victim can raise aggressive tendencies of the victimized people. This can lead to a willingness to join up with groups that are disposed to target such offenders who work against the victims. Such groups may work to amplify aggressive reactions by diffusing responsibility. The victim becomes justified in their retaliatory actions because the guilt has been removed or lessened to manageable levels. These subjects can be seen across national borders, ethnicity, and socioeconomic strata. They can be either male or female, suffering from poor self-image and self-esteem, feeling isolated from their peers."

Ron Stotyn

Rising from his seat now, René began to pace back and forth, pausing occasionally to outline on the white board as he continued parsing PTSD issues. "People experiencing this disorder or similar may be actively recruited by astute leaders, or may join by default, because they are not discouraged by the sacrificial lifestyle demanded. In effect, the terrorist group effectively begins to replace their own lost community. Many issues are factors for joining; no single one can be identified: self-esteem, family issues such as economic loss, peer pressure, respect and promised recognition, protection from fear or threat. Previous family involvement may play a role. Revenge on a common enemy is a common thread."

Suddenly, René ceased his pacing as he took a calmer demeanor, as if more satisfied with the approach of his descriptions. "Diagnosis of personality disorders from the point of view of the American Psychiatric Association requires being able to establish that there are enduring patterns of inner experience and behavior that deviates markedly from the expectations of culture. One must be able to see severe disturbances in the behavioral tendencies of an individual. This is usually observed in several areas of personality, manifested in considerable personal and social disruptions. But I cannot give you any specifics about Afghan terrorists or Chechen terrorists that focus on an individual. I do not have any patients to observe. The only thing I can do is to suggest likelihoods. The profile must be tentative and subjective at best."

As Betty Anne and Sean-Guy looked at each other with some dismay at these last words as René added, "I can therefore say that we must consider that we are looking for the type of individuals who are markedly deviant in terms of cognition, affect, impulse, and relation to others. We need to be aware of any behavior that is inflexible, maladaptive and dysfunctional. These would usually be evident across a broad range of personal and social situations. There may often be personal distress and strong evidence of a stable deviance over long periods. For more than this, I need more time to develop such a general profile, which I suppose must offer you description of the most likely type of terrorist that we may face."

After a lengthy silence, Sean-Guy observed, "You have already created an impressive review, but I think we do need a rather more succinct set of ideas. How long would it take you to give us such a summation?"

René thought for a moment. "I have duties at the parish the rest of the day, but I can return to the task later tonight. Perhaps mid-morning tomorrow?"

"That will have to do," said Sean-Guy. Turning to Betty Anne, he said, "I'm returning to Toronto tonight. I'll be at the office there by at least 7:30 in the morning. I expect to be available by vid-link all morning. As soon as Pere René is able to deliver his profile recommendations, I need you to get it to us by email attachment right away. Please review the findings and work with René to do any fine tuning that you both agree might be needed. Then I would like both of you to continue research toward making updates as new ideas and evidence might come in." With that Sean-Guy excused himself.

Ron Stotyn

{10}

"Sois mon frère, ou je te tue.' (Be my brother, or I kill you), Sébastien-Roch-Nicolas Chamfort (1812). Oeuvres complètes de Chamfort, de l'académie française. 1 (3 ed.). Maradan.

Marek's rooms, Friday April 7, about 1:30 AM: Little Poland, Toronto ON

Marek's front room, sparsely furnished, was dark except for a strong light shining on the wall behind where he sat. The result put him in partial silhouette against a backdrop map of Chechnya. A very small light below his chin directed upward made a ghastly image of his face; he was certain he would not be recognizable. Marek faced a video camera that he set up, connected to his laptop computer, both running, recording a moment that was designed to unnerve the local population in the greater Toronto area. In a page taken from Al Qa'ida Marek recorded an ultimatum, a sort of manifesto intended to create havoc within the Go Train transportation system area.

Marek did not wish to risk discovery at this late date, though discovery was imminent, a matter of which he was not yet aware. The setting in semi-darkness did not reveal his whereabouts; *the timing now is critical.* The silhouette is important; *I need yet to be in public for a few more days in my current appearance.* He remains silent and allows the camera to run a few moments so that the soon-to-be audience can grasp the import of the map. A clock is visible along with its red LED date readout so that viewers will realize time is of the essence. He has prepared his diatribe carefully; it will not take long to complete. When finished, his intent was to load the recording on a flash drive so that later in the day he could go to a cyber-café and distribute the file to all the local papers, radio stations and television outlets including the independents, along with the CBC, CTV and Global. There would also be distribution to several popular web sites, chosen for their appeal to the young and disenchanted in western culture. Marek expected the video to go viral as he has heard happens when something visceral is posted.

This was Marek's statement as later transcribed.

My name means possessor. The actual name does not matter, I will possess revenge that belongs to my brothers; the oppressed in my country and around the world. I will create a chaos in the transportation system here that will kill many of you who are the oppressors of the world. You will be punished for your collaboration. You have chosen to ignore the hurricane of violence done in my country by the Red Army. This will never be forgiven. Allah will be praised and his work will be completed. The dead heroes will be avenged so that their journey to paradise will be completed. Those left behind will have the joy of revenge so that they can praise Allah. Your condemnation will be soon upon you. Allahu Akbar.

With the chilling presentation of his promise completed, he turned out the lights, rose, and replayed the recording to be sure it showed and told what he required. It did exactly that. Satisfied he knelt, bowed facing Mecca, and prayed engulfed in his adoration of Allah thankful for the wisdom Allah has bestowed upon him. As usual, he prayed gratitude to Allah for the honor of killing his enemies. The challenge was nearly complete.

It remained now to do the final test on the phones, the final attachment of the phones and triggers to the bomb packages and delivery over the next several days to the preselected lockers around the region. He has already collected the rented van, now hidden inside the loading dock of his kitchen location. He has also stolen a license plate to reduce chances of it being identified quickly after he abandons it when the task is done. Sunday, Marek will complete his last meetings with the cell leaders, giving them their final instructions. They will be told exactly when to pick up their packages and he would spend considerable time ensuring them that Allah is waiting for them to collect their reward in paradise. *The plan, I am certain, will work well, just as a wound clock creeps inexorably forward second by second.*

He retired to his bed, just a thin mattress on the floor that suits his ascetic manner, glorying in the plan, ready to move forward later in the day, completely unaware that it would soon derail from the track

Ron Stotyn

that he had so carefully planned to date. An unwitting mistake had
already been made and more would be made in the days ahead.

Sleep comes, but he awakened unrested, the first night of
many that he will not sleep well. When he left his residence at mid-
morning to make his way to a cyber-café never before used, he was
followed at a distance, both on foot and by car. He did not notice,
engrossed in his thoughts about the coming days. Those on foot were
skilled agents, well blended into the character and appearance of the
neighborhood, clad in the manner of the everyday residents. Those in
the very ordinary sedan have been carefully warned to pay attention
more to their own comrades and to follow their lead so that the tail can
be vigilantly maintained. When Marek finally arrived at the bus stop,
one agent dropped back and was picked up in the car while his partner
waited alongside Marek. She posed as a dowdy housewife, to whom
Marek pays no attention.

The agents had been prepared for the travel on public
transportation. Marek's habits were known to that extent, so the agents
had been provided with bus passes. When the bus pulled away, the car
leapfrogged ahead to the next stop so the second agent could also
board, maintaining a kind of separation from his partner. The tailing
vehicle would follow the bus after that stop was made. The plan by the
CAS agents was flexible so that whatever the target did they would be
able to react quickly.

The tail went without incident. Marek arrived at his
destination, disembarked and was followed by the agents, one from the
front door and one from the rear exit of the bus. They took up a post
opposite the cyber-café that Marek entered; ready to tail him when he
emerges. They appeared to be a lower class husband and wife
lingering outside a coffee shop for a smoke. An agent from the car,
unrecognizable because they had not appeared within Marek's sight
previously, followed Marek inside and sat at a computer where he
could see Marek's screen. He did not notice that Marek had inserted a
flash drive into the computer's USB slot. What he did see was that the
man appeared to be sending a number of emails, not unusual the agent
thinks. When Marek left, however, the agent decided he would try to

find out where the emails went. He reported to his partner that he would call to get picked up later.

Marek was followed on his bus all the way to Mississauga where he arrived at his kitchen location on Shawson, still unaware that he was being watched. Outside, watching the closing back door, was the team from the O.P.P., while another team was out on the street watching the front. The original CAS team broke off and returned to pick up the member who had remained at the cyber-café. He'd not had any luck finding out where the emails went. There was no obvious evidence any had even been sent. Finally the agents reported to the CAS office. The agent from the cyber café team neglected to tell anyone about his attempt to find the email delivery locations. It didn't occur to him that Marek, the man they'd been watching, might have wiped out the record when he closed down the computer he'd been using. The agents later returned to their post at Marek's residence following a video conference organized by the Director and Sean-Guy.

{10.1}
CAS Offices, Britannia Road, Mid-Morning, April 7: Mississauga ON

The very good Doctor Pere René Girau has been exactly on his word, thought Sean-Guy as he sat reading a printout received just moments before. It was just after 10 AM, the time promised by René for delivery of the general profile. It was quite detailed and he thought he could also see the contribution of Betty Anne in the work. They must have been up a good part of the night doing this. *I'm quite amazed at how much has been put into this report.* As he read, he was waiting for a vid-link connection from Ottawa, where Director Leif Isaksson and Betty Anne Grabler were standing by. He expected René would also be there. He wanted René to make a presentation as soon as possible to the surveillance teams, most of whom he had already called into the office except those directly watching Marek Kafirov and Omid Faresh.

One team had been left at the Shawson Drive location where Marek had been reported to have entered by the back door. The team

Ron Stotyn

watching the back had been called into the meeting on the assumption the front team would be able to observe Marek walking away if he exited. Those agents would be shown a video copy as soon as they became available to view it.

Sean-Guy had approached the office just a bit earlier, driving his own restored Crown Victoria Police Interceptor, parking it in the garage. He'd arrived back in Mississauga late the previous evening. He'd made very good time. His blue and red flashing law enforcement lights had cleared him past several O.P.P. cruisers on the way. He avoided being pulled over by intercepting their radio calls on his radio equipment tuned to their frequency. This morning he did not realize that reporter Angela De Luca had watched him enter the building from her now usual seat across the street at the Olympia Grill. She was still very interested in whatever was going on at the building. And now her curiosity was much increased, having also seen the entrance of at least a half dozen vehicles of various descriptions, none of which fit the character of a supposed pest control business. She was intrigued also by the presence of Toronto and Mississauga police cruisers outside the building along with a marked RCMP SUV.

Within minutes, René was on hand ready to begin, his image on a large monitor in the Toronto area CAS office. Sean-Guy could see Leif and Betty were also ready to make appropriate comments. Grouped around the large screen wall mounted monitor with Sean-Guy were a large crowd of agents including Stuart, Ryan, Everet, Hari, Darya, George of the CAS, and Thea from the O.P.P fraud unit and Shawna Kennedy from CBSA, who had flown in from Ottawa earlier in the day.

Sean-Guy indicated, "All available CAS agents are here in the office, Director, and we also have agents from CBSA, O.P.P. as well as senior officers from the Toronto and Mississauga PDs, and the regional detachment of the RCMP, all of whom we invited as a courtesy. We're anticipating that we will soon need their direct assistance."

Leif addressed the group, providing a bit of background on René and Betty. "I'm very pleased to introduce to those of you unfamiliar with the CAS team Dr. Betty Anne Grabler and Dr. Jean

Pierre René Girau. Betty has advanced degrees in Criminal Behavior and Psychology, focused on Statistical and Psychological Analysis. Betty is our Senior Analyst and Statistician. René has advanced degrees in Forensic Psychology, along with Social and Cultural Psychology. He comes to us as a contracted consultant from a distinguished career as a chaplain and clinical psychologist with the PPCLI, from which he retired with the rank of Major." Director Isaksson had decided René's specific role as an RC priest was irrelevant to the current task. Neither for the moment did he believe it was yet necessary to explain the military ranks that several, including himself, had because of their link with the DND.

"René and Betty have prepared the general profile which you will hear today, with able assistance from our Chief Investigator Sean-Guy O'Dwyer-Lariviere, who holds advanced degrees in Criminology. The profile that you will shortly hear is precipitated by information that we have acquired concerning an Afghan and a Chechen whom we have reason to believe are up to no good. While we have only a slim amount of evidence to date, we are convinced it is worth your involvement to procure more concrete evidence so that we can shut down any possible terrorist preparations. Now, I ask René and Betty to make the presentation for today."

René opened with a brief procedural note and a caution. "You'll all be provided with copies of our statement when I am finished and I'll be able to answer questions at that time as well. It is important first for each of you to understand that I cannot provide a very specific profile on the two individuals you are now watching, because I have not been able to observe them as patients. What I have to tell you are generalizations for Afghan and Chechen terrorists. You will need to try and make applications as you continue to watch Marek Kafirov or Malik Bisliev, of which the latter appears to be his real name, and the Afghan known as Omid Faresh, which is probably an assumed name. Bear in mind that Afghans normally are known by only a single name." René paused and looked down at his notes for a moment before moving into the main essence of the profile.

"Most terrorists can be diagnosed with any of a variety of personality disorders. They may evidence more than one, but perhaps

Ron Stotyn

most typically they suffer from the pathological condition known as Post-Traumatic Stress Disorder. The symptoms of PTSD can range from insignificant to severe. This is not a disorder restricted to military personnel. Anyone who suffers severe physical or mental trauma and survives can be affected. Experience of beatings, rape, torture, witnessing of gruesome events such as mass murders can trigger the disorder, perhaps years away from the original incident. When PTSD strikes, the victim begins to re-experience the traumatic issue, the associated anxiety. Their recollections may put them into distress; give them nightmares, or daytime flashbacks. It can cause dissociative states where they lose touch with reality. Psychic numbing may cause withdrawal from friends and family into isolation where they try to avoid situational similarities. They may develop panic disorder, or panic attacks if you will. They will probably also develop depression, perhaps severely. In the case of terrorists, the disorders are generally well established by early adulthood. They likely will display a profound lack of empathy in various contexts." René checked his notes briefly, taking some water and nodded at Betty to interpolate.

Betty did so, "The traits and behaviors of terrorists can be understood by several criteria. They will often feel grandiose, self-important, superior and they will exaggerate their accomplishments and talents. They will likely exhibit fantasies of unlimited success and brilliance. They probably are convinced they are unique, special and understood only by those who are similar to themselves. They tend to expect, even demand excessive admiration and have unreasonable expectations for special treatment; in short they feel entitled. Interpersonally they are most probably exploitative, at the same time lacking empathy, being unwilling to identify with the feelings or needs of others. Characteristically, they will tend to be envious of others and believe others are envious of them. This suggests they will be seriously conflicted. They will also frequently behave arrogantly or haughtily in the presence of anyone they believe is inferior."

René continued the recitation. "There are several types of terrorists identified in literature; in the case of Afghan and Chechen terrorists and probably any of Middle Eastern connections, the ethno-geographic type of psychopathology is most likely. These terrorists are likely members of a fairly cohesive group that shares the same world-view, in this case a similar history, language or dialect, hopes, folklore, fears, aspirations and, most particularly enemies. In both cases Afghans and Chechens have an enmity toward Soviets due to violent encounters in recent history. Such terrorists have often been traumatized and abused by both internal and external forces that have threatened their self-image, self-identity, sense of self-worth, and indeed, self-esteem. Their trauma probably relates to being subjugated by another nation such as by the Russians; being exiled, enduring genocide, being destitute, being defeated in warfare."

Betty interrupted with a word of warning, "Now please pay careful attention. What we have to say now is of particular importance."

René nodded in agreement. "These traumas cause such groups to become abusive to others, exploitative, detached from reality, bathed in grandiose fantasies, xenophobic, prone to un-controlled rages, over-sensitive, convinced of superiority, entitlement, opportunistic and ruthless. The ethno-geographic terrorist is inspired by religious and/or political forces that are fundamentalist in nature. They will probably adhere to strict and traditional orthodox beliefs and tenets either religious or political. Most likely, individual terrorists of this type will work as part of the group to destroy a common enemy."

Betty underlined this last comment, "The sense of 'to die for the cause is an honor,' is a tightly held belief: all who die for the cause whether volunteer or not will receive their reward in the afterlife. These individuals will often be angry or in rage at any criticism of their performance."

René carried on. "Finally, let me suggest that these terrorists are retributional in their character. They are most likely motivated by the experience of having their homes destroyed along with their community and family as the result of deliberately planned war, crisis, or terror events on innocent and civilian population that they have experienced at close hand. These are the survivors of such events anxious to seek revenge through retaliation or revolt. They have no sense of having anything to lose, since they have already lost all

Ron Stotyn

meaning in life. Suicide … is a fully accepted means of gaining complete retribution."

René paused and then summarized. "You will need to look for tendencies among your subjects to be controlling, to manage or regulate events or objects in their environment. This is a defense mechanism to minimize their anxieties or to resolve inner conflicts. Other defense mechanisms that may present for your observation are rationalization or attempts to justify attitudes, beliefs, behavior that are otherwise unacceptable in society. In addition, you may be able to see acts of anticipation or planning for future acts of aggression. There may also be evidence of intellectualization efforts consisting of excessive abstract thinking with generalizations to avoid creating disturbing feelings for the self. Now we can try to answer your questions."

The silence in both Ottawa and Mississauga was palpable as everyone tried to absorb the implications of the profile just presented. Most had expressions of shock, with some showing dismay, especially the CBSA agents who had not had close encounter experiences with terrorists. Indeed, that could be said mostly true for all of the audience; Canada after all had been relatively free of terroristic events. Even Sean-Guy was somewhat taken aback by the abject ruthless sense presented by René and Betty in their assessment of what Canada might be facing. He asked the first question. "René, are we facing psychopaths?" surely a question others were also thinking.

René replied with an air of thoughtful care, "It is neither likely nor impossible. Psychopathic terrorists do exist. They would display antisocial behavior or a dissocial personality and fail to conform to social norms concerning lawful behavior. This type is typically a gun for hire, who disregards the rights, wishes, and feelings of others. They are deceitful and manipulative for profit and pleasure and are consistently and extremely irresponsible. They evidence megalomania, hallucinations and wish fulfilling delusions. They are generally unconcerned with the welfare of others. They seek only their own benefits thus they kill without remorse. They are extremely individualistic and unlikely to work in concert with others having a similar goal. They are not driven by fundamentalism. My sense is the

Afghans and Chechens are more likely to manifest a religious drive and perhaps political interests."

Stuart raised the question of ties to Muslim faith. "How can we determine if our subjects are acting out of an extreme Islamic belief? And are we likely to find them involved with a local mosque?"

"Well, the Muslim faith in their part of the world has generally developed as Islam dictates, as an all pervasive, missionary focus world view," said René. "Islam permeates all of social cooperation and culture as an organizing principle, narrative, philosophy and value system. But, perhaps more importantly in Chechnya especially and also in Afghanistan, Islam has in part become a radicalized strain that declares itself to be the purest expression of nature. This form, sometimes referred to as Wahhabism, demands unmitigated obedience. It regards all infidels as inferior and as avowed enemies. Wahhabist intellectuals argue effectively that Western civilization and culture is insufficient, morally decadent, degenerate, weak and indeed disintegrating. This type of Muslim dreams of replacing such systems with a rigorous system of Islamic values, a restored social order and a new found glory. Because the West is seen as a bully, it must be replaced by force if necessary. The sword is often considered the only way."

Betty added, "From a terroristic point of view, you should understand that all civilians, that is non-Muslims especially but also Muslims who are not connected to Wahhabism, are regarded as potential aggressors against the faith, thus merit no special treatment or protection. Terrorism is thus an integral part of this kind of Islam; the only way to ensure social mobility, respectability, feelings of omnipotence, omnipresence, and omniscience."

René, answering Stuart's second question responded, "The matter of attending a mosque is a maybe. The issue here is the degree to which the militant Muslim terrorist is able or willing to tolerate what would most probably be a much more conservative attitude in Canadian Mosques, generally. I am not fully familiar with Mosques in this region but my sense is these types of terrorists would not feel comfortable attending. That said, if they do get involved, you may

Ron Stotyn

discover they are vocally critical about the tenor of the preaching by the Imam."

Darya, disturbed by what seemed like an attack on her own partly Muslim heritage, even though not a practicing Islamist, asked, "But the Islamic faith is essentially non-violent. Doesn't the Quran speak of brotherhood?"

René, recognizing her concern and the important observation, replied with some care to explain his earlier point about Wahhabism. "The Islamic form I have identified as existing in Chechnya is considered by many religious and secular Islamists as an aberration. It is a militant growth starting from ideals preached by the 18th century reformist Mohammed Ibn Abd al Wahhib. His original goal was to return Islam to purity through a strict interpretation of the Quran. His focus was on the oneness of God. These goals inside Chechnya and in neighboring regions to some extent were corrupted and used to inform a terrorist ideology as a basis for the establishment of a worldwide salafi jihad. Promotion of this kind of jihad is promotion of terrorism. Outside Chechnya, Wahhabism is generally peaceful and neutral."

George Brown, who had recently been spending much of his time following Omid Faresh, asked, "What about the educational level of the typical terrorist from this part of the world? Are they terrorists because they have no other means to advance?"

Betty took this question, "That is an important concern. When you scratch terrorists from this ethno-geographic region you will find more often than not, individuals who are fairly well educated, often well travelled, and technologically skilled. You may also discover they are fairly well off, sometimes even affluent. Consider Bin Laden for example, well connected to a wealthy family. These terrorists tend to hold strong intellectual feelings about the way their culture, religion, society are being mishandled by the West and its allies. Note that these feelings might well be imaginary but they remain strong enough for these people to feel personal grievances and issues."

Hari, from his considerable experience in the border regions of India next to Pakistan, and well aware of the consequences of terrorism, asked "Why are Chechen terrorists seemingly so willing to give up their own lives for their cause? Even in the past few weeks the news has been full of reports about suicide bombers from there."

René, with a sigh explained, "This brings us right back to Militant Wahhabism. There is a strong possibility that your subjects, if they are connected to each other, are committed to the principle of suicide terrorism. This variety of Wahhabism glorifies martyrdom. It also promotes the idea of brotherhood as more important even than connections to parents and family. Recruits are indoctrinated to the principle of fighting for each other right to the death. Wahhabist instigators use suicide terrorism as an effective strategy to be used as a defense against giving up in despair. Your subjects are quite possibly prepared to go all the way to achieve whatever their goals may be. I don't think I can stress that outcome enough. It is a matter of self-sacrifice as the only effective means to achieve revenge....Ohhh... you should also be aware that suicide is forbidden in Islam, but martyrdom is different. Self-sacrifice is an acceptable means of obtaining forgiveness for sins, to obtain salvation, and instant entry into paradise."

"Historically, my people have understood the principle of revenge," said Everet Tailfeathers, "as one for one. Why do these ones strike at innocents?"

"In terms of Chechnya, the tradition of revenge is generations old. It goes far beyond the original wrongdoer," said Betty. "Traditionally, it is an ideology of rights that puts responsibility on surviving family members.... yes I said that in the plural ....to exact justice. Murder is punishable by murder. Males are first in line for this kind of justice seeking. If there are no males then females adopt the responsibility. The Wahhabists of Chechnya have generalized that response and have expanded revenge to count against any who kill community members or who condone that action. The West is seen as guilty in this respect. In fact, the Chechen terrorists who are committed to these Wahhabist principles and any Afghan or other Islamist terrorists who have joined that cause probably take the position that any nation, who offered condolences to Russia after the Chechen retributions, taken such as the school hostages that were killed, now sees them as equal enemies."

Ron Stotyn

"So Canada is an enemy if they did not condemn Russia for its violence to Chechen people?" asked Ryan.

René responded, "Most probably yes. If there is a terrorist action being planned here that involves the Afghan suspect, and if that is somehow connected to the Chechen person of interest, it might very well be the case that there is a position or belief that Canada is a co-equal enemy."

Hari noted, "In my experience from my border service in India, the terrorists we had to defend against were generally trained by the Taliban rebels. What kind of training are we likely to see if our subjects turn out to be planning terrorist acts?"

Betty answered, "Data that I have considered indicates that Afghan terrorists are frequently Taliban trained. There is also a strong likelihood that Al Qa'ida techniques have been used either in part or in Al Qa'ida training camps completely. The Chechen background is a bit different, but strongly similar. It is known for example,....well.... at least strongly believed.... that a Chechen militant Muslim leader Shamil Baseyev was a co-founder of a terrorist training camp known as KavKaz. The evidence is fairly certain that an imported Saudi named al Khattab led the active recruiting of young Chechens using the influence of Wahhabist mosques and schools. There has been indoctrination that follows pretty closely Al Qa'ida operations manuals and techniques. Kidnapping, beating, and killing of civilians and hostages are justified for achieving so called 'holy ends.' You should also expect that many of them have well developed skills as bomb-makers. They'll be able to turn out fairly sophisticated devices."

"My name is John Anderson; I'm an RCMP Inspector from the Greater Toronto Area District, supervising the Integrated National Security Enforcement Team. Director Isaksson, as I'm sure you are aware, we already coordinate with O.P.P., CSIS and CBSA and other agencies. What can we do to help your investigation?"

Leif replied, "Well, given that we are still early in our investigation.... that is a bit difficult to assess. At the very least right now, we need information. Any intelligence that your unit has acquired in the past year or so about questionable Afghans and Chechens inside the country would certainly be useful. Be assured we are quite prepared to share what we discover. Betty, our senior analyst, will certainly be available for consultations. In the longer term, your assistance in providing tactical squads will almost certainly become important if we are able to confirm terroristic planning and a wider scope of subjects."

"Director," said CBSA Senior Agent Shawna Kennedy, "my division has considerable experience working with Inspector Anderson, so if I can suggest, I am available to assist with liaison and information flow."

Leif, with a diplomatic answer replied, "SA Kennedy, I am grateful for your expression of solidarity, but I'm going to invoke National Security on a high level for this investigation. As you may not be yet aware, CAS is directly responsible to the Department of National Defense. Those of us with military backgrounds have been reactivated. Sean-Guy holds the rank of Major and I'm designating him the lead supervisor and asking all of you from O.P.P., RCMP, CBSA and any other relevant agencies to liaise with him on all matters pertaining to this open file."

Leif, then getting ready to close the profile meeting asked, "Are there any other questions? If not I suggest we should get back to the streets so we don't miss anything."

George Brown noted, "The Afghan subject first came to our attention because apparently he and one or two others were heard to be saying they were going to cause some harsh discipline on the management of the Go Train system. So far, despite the best efforts of Hari and Darya, we don't really have strong confirmation. René, how do you fit such vague threats into your assessment?"

René, silent for a moment, finally offered his conjecture. "It is difficult to be certain that such threats constitute a terrorist activity, but I understand there was a certain amount of braggadocio involved. That at least is consistent with the sense of superiority felt by this kind of terrorist. It also fits with the generalized ideas I have given you about control issues and management of their environment. I think you cannot disregard the possibility that they anticipate an extravagant opportunity sometime in the future."

Ron Stotyn

Leif, stepping forward, said, "Thanks to all of you for your commitment to our national security. It is very important for us to work in concert on this. We hope our investigation will show that nothing is going on, but we can never discount the possibility these subjects are planning great harm. Once again I ask you to stay in touch with Sean-Guy, as we proceed."

Sean-Guy, taking the reins once more, cautioned all the surveillance teams. "Please return to your posts and be vigilant. It is important that we not be noticed…we don't want to alert anyone or scare them off. Keep everyone informed by radio what is happening, especially if anything unusual occurs. Darya and Hari, please continue gaining a trust relationship with Omid, to see what you might be able to learn. That's all for now."

{10.2}
Olympia Café, Noon, April 7: Mississauga ON

Angela Maria De Luca, *reporter not so extraordinaire at the moment* she thought, watched from her position inside the Olympia Café, intrigued by the police cruisers still parked after a couple of hours across the street at the supposed offices of a pest control company. She waited to see if the many cars that had entered earlier would leave in a group just as they had arrived. She did not have very much longer to wait. A stream of cars appeared from the garage entrance and accelerated away from the building, departing in both directions. Uniformed officers climbed into their cruisers parked outside and departed as well. She considered what she knew now. *Not much more, I guess, except that Peter Gallaegher has been able to confirm for me that the CAS and the O.P.P. provincial anti-terrorism unit have begun cooperating on something. But he has no information about the nature of the coordination. He's been unable to discover what was up.*

She thought about her relationship with Peter. *Over the past couple of nights, he's been exciting in bed, but there is something about him that I'm not sure I can deal with over the long term. There is no doubt we make a good-looking couple. He is extremely handsome and I find his athleticism irresistible. The sex is certainly better than any I've had in a long while, not that I have had much opportunity recently. He does not seem to have any interest in furthering the relationship to anything more; certainly I don't seem to fit into his long term plans…. Why do I pick such losers?* Angela came to the conclusion that she was unlikely to get much more information from him and that she was unlikely to find in him a truly compatible life companion. *Have I been a fool once again? Is it already time to move on without him?* she thought disheartened.

As her reverie continued, she gradually became aware she was not alone. Startled she looked up to see Sean-Guy standing by her table, looking down at her, his slate hued eyes fixed upon her as if again probing to see into her soul, his face set in a bemused expression. Angela realized once again, that this man was very different from Peter, indeed from any other man she had ever met. There was a deep mystery to him, even a certain sadness she thought she could detect and at the same time an iron willed reserve about him. Frankly, she thought once more *he is more than a bit frightening. And yet, he intrigues me greatly and I think it is not just about sexual adventure.*

Sean-Guy spoke gravely, "Apparently I forgot we had a luncheon engagement." Only the very slightest hint of a grin, which Angela missed in her confusion, played on his face.

Angela, not usually at a loss for words, stuttered a greeting and a denial she was waiting for him. "Oh!...ah….hello… I'm sorry but you must be mistaken… I'm pretty sure that we had no such agreement…. It's a nice idea though…actually I was…."

Sean-Guy, now teasing a bit more, "You were hoping that I might just show up?"

Angela blushed as she realized that thought had been lurking in the background of her reverie. "Oh damn you…." She retorted, "Sit down if you must, you're embarrassing me….I'm sorry, I didn't mean that curse. It's just that I never know how to react to you. You confuse me," She blurted.

Sean-Guy, taking a seat, continued to gaze at her, his bemused expression still on his face, waiting for her to say more, well aware

Ron Stotyn

that silence often begets a revelation. As he waited he asked himself why he continued to be interested in this woman. *She is a conundrum for me. I find her exceedingly annoying, especially in her single-minded attention to our operation. Yet I cannot help but appreciate her focus. It is in many ways like my own. She is and is not much like me, that is something that I could love....*And that was a surprising thought.

Angela felt compelled for some reason to continue. What spilled out now she thought she would probably regret. "I know about the cooperation with O.P.P. Anti-terrorism that happened yesterday. I know that your group is following someone," she bluffed.

Sean-Guy, with an eyebrow up mentally, stone faced replied, "What do you think you know?" Behind that question he could not help but think she seemed now to be exceedingly arrogant. That was not a trait he admired in any woman.

"But you must be engaged in a surveillance operation. Why else would there be cooperation with the provincial agency tasked with keeping tabs on terrorist possibilities? Why do you constantly deny it?" realizing as she said it Sean-Guy would simply invoke national security once again. But Sean-Guy surprised her, now thinking to himself that she really was rather perceptive and perhaps just as relentless as he was on a case.

"Will you go off the record with me for a moment?" He asked.

"I will, but I want you to promise me the exclusive, if this gets to the point where the story can be told." Angela rummaged in her shoulder bag for her notebook, turning on her recorder as she did so.

"So, okay, off the record then, the answer is that we have mounted a surveillance exercise, using teams from the O.P.P." Sean-Guy omitted, for the moment, that teams from CBSA were also involved. "And, yes the anti-terrorism unit of the O.P.P. is contributing. We are concerned that we be ready in the future if we find that there is a possibility of terrorist activity going on. At the present time it would not be good for the public to be aware that we are ramping up our security awareness." Sean-Guy considered that what he had just told her was close enough to the whole truth, and hoped she would be happy with it. Looking at her face, however, he realized she was not wholly on board.

Just as she was about to respond, her cell phone rang. Grabbing it out of her pocket she noted that it was the managing editor. He face blanched slightly. She still wasn't ready to tell him she had a story all set. She answered with some trepidation. "Mr. O'Donnell, hello, how are you sir?"

O'Donnell, characteristically barked, "Get in here; we've just received an emailed terrorist threat." He hung up before she could say anything.

{10.3}
CAS Office, About Half Past Noon, April 7: Mississauga ON

Sean-Guy had watched her face blanch, recover quickly and then saw shock spread across her face. "What's the matter? Are you all right? Can I help?" He asked with some concern.

Without thinking she responded, "There's been a terrorist threat at the paper" Then, "Oh, I shouldn't have said that," realizing it was already too late.

"Come with me, right now," said Sean-Guy with a voice of authority she'd not heard before, grabbing her by the arm and leading her to the door after tossing some money on the table to cover her coffees.

She struggled, saying, "No, I have to get into the office. That was my boss and he won't be pleased if I am delayed."

"You don't understand, you have just become a witness and I AM going to find out what you know," snapped Sean-Guy, adding, "This is a National Security issue now, and I will detain you for as long as I need to if I don't get cooperation immediately." By this time they were halfway across the street, Angela found she could not break free from his grip. It didn't hurt but it was as tight as any hold she had ever felt. They entered the building she had watched for days, and suddenly she found herself all the way inside, when Sean-Guy released her, indicating a desk and chair. "Sit there, don't move."

"Stuart….you here somewhere?" he hollered. "I need you and anyone else around right now. We've got a new situation."

Ron Stotyn

Stuart and Everet appeared from a back room, looking surprised at his tone.

"Everet, get on the vid-link to the director, tell him there has been a terrorist threat received at the Toronto Star. Ask Betty to get onto finding out if anyone in Ottawa got one too. She needs to check all the media. Everet, I need you looking for the same thing here in the Toronto area, be sure to check the electronic media. If necessary, both you and Betty might need to invoke national security. Let me know as soon as anything turns up. I'll be interviewing this reporter, here." indicating Angela. "I think she has a lot to tell me. Stuart, I want you to sit in on this with me." He motioned to Angela to follow and headed for the conference room. Once inside, he told her to sit once again. "I want to know everything you know or think you know about the CAS and what we are doing. Don't leave anything out."

"But I can't reveal my sources," Angela blustered. "I'm a legitimate reporter and we have rights."

"If I discover that you have received information from anyone in government who is cautioned under the Security of Information Act, I'll cite you and your sources with violations. Wrongful communication of sensitive government information is subject to fines and jail time. The chances of all of you being locked up for a very long time are very good." Sean-Guy's dark visage revealed a fury that truly frightened Angela. His threat was only partly meaningful; he couldn't yet prove anything. *I truly cannot believe the temerity of this woman. How dare she think she can toy with national security interests? Who the hell does she think she is.....God?*

She could see he was serious. She nodded weakly and began to tell about how she had caught the story. "I started watching this building after I got a tip from a contact in the Ontario legislature. I was told the O.P.P. was unhappy about a new federal agency set up to handle terrorism threats. This location was given as the place to watch."

Sean-Guy, speaking abruptly, "Give me the name.... all the names that have had contact with you about this."

"It was Gabrielle Davis first; she's a friend who works as a secretary in the Ontario Community Safety and Correctional Services. Please don't arrest her, she is innocent," urged Angela.

Sean-Guy grunted, "That remains to be seen. Stuart, put her on your list."

Angela, groaned softly as if to herself, "What have I done, Why didn't I drop this when I had the chance?" Then she continued, when she saw Sean-Guy narrow his gaze even more darkly. "I started to watch the building and then after several days I tried to get in. I lied about trying to get a job with the pest control company…that's what I thought it was, but I needed to verify. I was going to give up but…."

Stuart, speaking gently, playing the good cop role, "Don't hold back, it could get you out of trouble."

"My boss, Daniel O'Donnell, he's the Managing Editor at the Star, called me in. I thought he was going to fire me….Oh, I guess that's not what you need. Well… He wanted to know what I was working on so I told him my suspicions. He called in favors at the Legislature. I was put in touch with Peter Gallaegher in the office of the Minister of Community Safety and Correctional Services. Peter gave me information about the CAS."

Sean-Guy, raised his eyebrow at Angela's familiar use of the first name, intuitively making a tentative connection to the man she had been with at the Samovar House. "What exactly did he tell you?" Turning to Stuart he said, "We need to talk with O'Donnell, Davis and Gallaegher right away. Get Gallaegher and Davis in here; keep him alone in an interview room until we are ready. I'll go to the Star myself." Stuart nodded, rose and left the room.

Angela looked up at that last comment and took a deep shaky breath. She could see her career in ruins now rather clearly. "We met at the Visitor's Gallery at the Legislature. It was quiet, everyone was out to supper. Peter already knew I was interested in the CAS. He'd apparently been briefed by someone. He confirmed that DND set up CAS and that it was headquartered in Ottawa. He said he knew the Toronto area offices were in Mississauga, though he didn't actually say the address. He didn't deny it when I said it. He also identified Director

Ron Stotyn

Isaksson and yourself as key figures on the staff along with a Ryan McLeod, formerly of the RCMP."

Stuart re-entered the room, leaning over Sean-Guy's shoulder he whispered, "Betty has confirmed the arrival of the threat at all the media in Ottawa. Everet is still searching in this area but so far the electronic media have confirmed. What do you want to do now?"

"I had better talk to Leif I think." Looking at Angela he said, "You need to think about what else you need to tell me. Don't even think about withholding anything." Then he and Stuart left the room, leaving her to sit agonizing over her fate.

Sean-Guy and Stuart got to the situation room in time to see Leif's image pop up on the Video screen. He didn't look very pleased with life. He spotted Sean-Guy on his return feed and asked, "What do we know for sure at this point? Is there a connection with that reporter?" Sean-Guy filled him in with spare language. "I plan to visit Daniel O'Donnell at the Star right away, but I think we somehow need to have the media hold off on using this threat, at least until we can get a copy and analyze it. Can Betty get right on that? Can you get an official request out to all the media? I know that is going to raise their interest level, but I don't see what else we can do."

Leif nodded, at Sean-Guy's recommendation. "I'll do that as soon as I have apprised the Minister about this situation. Keep in close touch with me so that we can allay the Minister's concerns as soon as possible. What are you going to do with the reporter?"

Sean-Guy responded, "I have already threatened her with violations of the Security of Information Act, which should keep her off-kilter for awhile. I'll keep her here while we pick up Peter Gallaegher, that's the leaker she talked to from Community Safety and Correctional Services here. I might bring her with me when I talk to O'Donnell."

Just then Everet approached rapidly from the desk where he had been trying to actively track who got the video emails. "Bad news. I just found the video posted on You Tube. I'm looking now on other likely social media sites."

Leif, Sean-Guy and Stuart were all dumbfounded. Each of them was rapidly trying to calculate the potential harm of that news.

Mistakes had been made. They had occurred on both sides. Several had yet to be discovered.

Ron Stotyn

{11}

**"We stand on guard so you may enjoy the untroubled
sleep of the innocent." Thomas Harlan "Wasteland of Flint" p.258**

Marek's Kitchen, Shawson Drive Friday April 7, 11 AM:
Mississauga ON

The kitchen-based bomb making was on the verge of
completion. Marek had arrived early in order to spend several hours
packing up; making sure every bomb package was carefully placed
inside an appropriate disguise. He'd purchased various containers over
the course of the past many weeks: backpacks, briefcases, recycle
shopping bags, small duffle bags, and an assortment of inexpensive
travel bags of various shapes and sizes. He'd brought them to the
kitchen location on Shawson Drive one at a time to avoid any curious
eyes. He was convinced that no one would pay any particular attention
to the packages on the appointed day of detonation, now just a bit
more than a week away. Monday after next would be the culmination
of massive explosions set for the Toronto Go Train System.

Marek was deeply satisfied about the calmness he felt. He was
convinced that he was approved by Allah. His plan, very carefully
developed, was soon to be just as carefully executed. Simultaneous
explosions, at least as close together as the phone dialer software could
create, would be the culmination. Thousands of hated enemies,
complacent Canadian citizens, pawns of a dishonest government
would die in a lesson taught to demonstrate the consequences of
supporting Russia for what it had done to his beloved country,
Chechnya. Friends of his enemy must be led to understand they could
not escape retribution. Disruption of the transit system in the region
was merely a bonus. It was death compounded that he was looking
forward to.

The previous day he had done a last test of the cell phone
trigger devices by making calls from various distances away from the
kitchen. His goal was to ensure that distance was not a potential failure
factor. What he had not tested was calls placed from inside tunnels.

The idea that tunnels might impede a signal did not even occur to him as a potential problem. Neither did he suspect that misdirected calls might create a disturbance to the plan that he believed was without flaw. Every other aspect of his preparation had worked according to his expectations.

Marek had planned to use the rented van for the final exercise, but at the last minute had decided against it for a reason he didn't entirely understand. It must be just an uncomfortable uncertainty he finally concluded; he'd used public transport as had been his habit these last few months. Instead of taking the van out onto the streets, he'd simply brought the van to the kitchen and had parked it inside the receiving dock of the space. Once inside he'd decided to create signs for the vehicle that said, On-The-GO Delivery Service. He painted that directly on the doors and now that the signs were dry he'd thought to scuff up the lettering to make the van look more used. He considered that the name he'd chosen with some amusement, given his targeting of the Go Train System, was an appropriate inside joke. The fact he'd defaced a rental vehicle was inconsequential. He planned to abandon it in any event as soon as the need for it was satisfied. The stolen license plate he had put on it would make it harder to trace even if it was quickly found. Marek thought *because I had to pick it up in person, it's important that I not be recognized as the renter before I can leave the area.*

Now after making sure each bomb was correctly attached to the throwaway cell phones and translator chips, he was busy carefully stowing them inside the van. He had the ringers turned up to generate the greatest possible voltage, a quantity sufficient to activate the chips which would trigger the bombs. With the connection to the translator chips from the headphone jack, no one would be able to actually hear the cell phone ringing. He tagged every bag according to the storage location where they needed to be picked up by the team leaders of his cell structure. The carrying bags of various descriptions were planned according to the guise each bomber would be wearing when they boarded the trains. His cell leaders would get the storage locations and detailed instructions about how and when to collect them during his upcoming weekly Sunday meetings with them.

Ron Stotyn

Marek expected to leave the leased kitchen for the last time as soon as the van was fully loaded. The next two days would be spent driving around the region so that he could deposit the bags in the lockers he'd selected at various transportation depots on or near the Go Train lines that would very soon be targeted with destructive force. Duplicate keys to those lockers would be handed to his cell leaders during the Sunday meetings.

With the loading task completed, Marek took one last look around the space he'd rented under an assumed Jewish name several months earlier. It had been a most satisfactory space for his bomb making operation; equipped as a kitchen it had given needed access to large refrigerators for keeping his explosive concoctions appropriately chilled. There had been large cooking units as well for those parts of the procedures that required controlled heating. The whole space was heated and air-conditioned which had allowed overall control of the environment when the explosive mixes were at their most dangerous. Now all was done. He expected it would be at least a month before anyone would be inside so he didn't bother about cleaning up the supplies and containers left over from the bomb construction process. Besides, those materials, mainly glass vessels were so innocuous, most people coming inside wouldn't think twice about their previous use. By the time anyone checked up, it would likely be the lessor wanting back rent, he'd be gone from the country.

Satisfied, with the time just coming up to the noon-hour, Marek climbed into the van, started it, clicked the remote for the loading dock door, and pulled out of the building. Pausing outside, he clicked the remote once more and watched while the door slowly descended. When it was fully down, he tossed the remote on the dash and drove toward the corner of the building and then to the street beyond. As he pulled onto the street and drove away, he didn't notice the surveillance team sitting in their car across the street. It had started to snow lightly, and they were bundled up against the cold trying to stay warm without drawing attention to themselves by letting the car run so they could have heat. They were watching for Marek to leave walking as had been the pattern since the surveillance had begun. They didn't pay any attention to the van leaving the building location. As he expected, Marek believed no one was paying attention to him as he drove away.

Marek planned to begin his drops at the location closest to his Mississauga site where his Lakeshore West cell leader would go to collect the bombs designated for his part of the explosives distribution. That first stop would be the Burlington Transit bus station on John Street in Burlington. His cell leaders, Fathi Batal al-Shishani and Edris Gaziev, would collect several packages each from four traveler lockers at the bus terminal. Everyone would be told to make their pickups over the course of several days during the next week so as to avoid trying to carry too many disparate types of bags all at the same time. This first delivery would account for a half dozen packages.

Al-Shishani's suicidal task would take place at the anointed time during the early morning rush just as the Go Train left the Oakville station on the Lakeshore West Line the following Monday a week away. His cell members would carry packages onto different rail cars for detonation as planned. Gaziev and his cell members, riding an earlier Go Train, would get instructions for detonation to take place simultaneously as that train arrived eastbound at Union Station. Of course, as Marek himself was controlling the explosions, these instructions were just window dressing for the cell leaders. They were all willing to die gloriously for the cause; at least that was what Marek was expecting of them. His desire to ensure the timing of the event meant that he could not rely on his leaders and their crews to detonate on schedule.

From Burlington, Marek needed to drive northeast to Barrie, where a larger quantity of bombs would to be placed for his three Afghan cell leaders: Daoud, Omid and Gul-Bashra. The three worked as Car Mechanics on three Go Train Lines: Milton, Georgetown and Barrie. Each would be particularly responsible for affixing shaped charges onto the first cars behind the locomotives as well as carrying package bombs aboard various passenger cars along with those carried by their cell members. A total of 12 bomb packages were destined for delivery in Barrie at the bus terminal on Maple Avenue. The trip to Barrie would use up most of the afternoon, so Marek had arranged a motel room, following placement of the bomb packages in lockers at

Ron Stotyn

the Maple Street Terminal, for an overnight stay in Bradford on his way to Richmond Hill on Saturday. If it continued to snow, he would certainly need the extra time to complete the round of deliveries he planned.

The Saturday deliveries which would take most of the morning and early afternoon, depending on the weather conditions, would take him first to the Go Train Terminal on Newkirk at Major Mackenzie Drive in Richmond Hill. His two brother-warrior cell leaders, highly trusted Chechens like himself; Muhammad Yamadayev and Abdul Saidullayev had responsibility for the Richmond Hill line as well as the Stouffville and Lakeshore East lines. Yamadayev had the most important task of any of Marek's cell leaders. Yamadayev would arrive early at Union Station in order to place several bombs at selected locations inside Union Station and then would get on the west bound train in time for his suicide bombing detonation as the train left the station. His trusted cell members would take care of carrying packages aboard trains coming south from Stouffville and Richmond Hill.

Saidullayev and his cell members would take care of the planned explosions aboard a west bound train when it reached Scarborough on the Lakeshore East line. Saidullayev's parcels would be delivered in Oshawa at the Bond Street West location for Greyhound's operations. Again, the instructions they would receive were meant to give them an illusion of control in the mission. When these bomb packages were delivered to the customer service lockers the total quantity of 37 packages would be ready for pickup.

Following the completion of the deliveries Marek planned to head west to Oakville for a second night at a motel where he would prepare for his first meeting on Sunday with al-Shishani and Gaziev. From there, after abandoning the van, he would make his way using the bus system to Barrie to meet with the Afghans, finishing off in Eglinton for the last of the three regular Sunday meetings with his most trusted cell leaders Yamadayev and Saidullayev. It would be a rather exhausting three days, but well worth the effort. In just over a week retribution would be carried out

{11.1}
CAS Headquarters, Office of Leif Isaksson, about 1:30 PM, April 7: Ottawa ON

Leif was on the phone, trying to reach the Minister of National Defense, The Honorable Paul Mackey. His call was urgent, following Sean-Guy's report of a terrorist threat by video confirmed as received at all the major Toronto area media outlets both print and electronic and now posted on at least one social network website. Betty had also confirmed the same for the Ottawa/Gatineau region media. The minister's approval was needed for an attempt to shut down the spread of the video until it could be checked out as bona fide. Leif was now watching the You Tube version for the umpteenth time, still amazed at the understated ferocity of the terrorist's claims. Betty was trying to clean up an image of the man's face, a task being worked on simultaneously in Toronto by their skilled artist Everet Tailfeathers. Leif knew that task would not be easy. The lighting in the video was obviously planned to make the face difficult to identify, but he was sure Betty and Everet would succeed. They had both skills and necessary software.

Paul Mackey came on the line, "Leif, how are you? What's the occasion for this call?"

Leif, with a tone of utmost urgency in his voice said, "Minister, we have a national security situation brewing in Toronto and possibly more widespread right now. A videotaped terrorist threat has been delivered to major media here in Ottawa and in the Toronto area. This video has also been posted on You Tube. We are fairly certain that it needs to be considered credible. I think we need the means that will allow us to somehow withhold it from publication and get it taken down by You Tube so that we can work to locate the source without publicity."

Mackey responded without hesitation, "Where can I see it? I'll get back to you as soon as I can."

Leif gave him the web address and filled him in on the media confirmed as having received it before hanging up. He got up and went

Ron Stotyn

out to Betty's desk to see how she was progressing. He found her working on the image and at the same time connected by video link to Toronto with Everet who he could see was also at a computer working on the image. He pulled up a chair and sat in range of the camera "Have either of you made any progress? I have just finished a call to the Minister and he will want to know who this is as soon as we can make an ID. If we can make a positive ID, it will help us decide if this is really a credible threat or not."

Everet responded, "I have remote connection to Betty's work, so I can assist instead of working independently. We are building an image as if conventionally lit. Give us another half hour at least."

"That's good, but I need it sooner than later, okay? Then Leif added, "Is Sean-Guy available to update?"

Stuart appeared on the screen over Everet's shoulder and reported, "He's just left to go to the Managing Director's office at the Toronto Star. He took the reporter with him. He's going to try and get the Star to hold off on any reporting concerning this video. We've also got a team on the way to the main offices of Ontario Community Security and Correctional Services to pick up one Peter Gallaegher, who we think is a key leaker about us to the reporter. We plan to threaten him with violation of the Security of Information act, to see what he knows and what he has revealed." And we have another possible leaker at Ontario Justice. We'll pick her up as well."

"Any possibility these leakers have a connection to the video threat?" asked Leif.

Stuart shrugged, "At this point that seems like a real stretch. It's probably a coincidence that these things are happening at the same time."

Leif, with his tone of authority unmistakable, retorted, "I don't like coincidence. Make sure one way or the other, Okay? Never neglect any potential."

He got up and returned to his office before Stuart could say anything more. He entered in time to hear his phone ringing. Picking up, he heard the voice of his minister, Paul Mackey. "I think you are correct about the possible security situation. Do you have anything on the person in the video yet?"

Leif reported, "My people tell me that they may have a clean image within the next half hour, and then we can try to identify the person in the video. They do think the camera was locked down, so that might mean only one person involved in making the video."

"I think we cannot do much unless and until we can confirm the video is not a hoax. So, it's crucial that a positive ID be made on this person." Paul added, "I know you are very concerned that this should not turn into a public scare, but our laws protect the media for most forms of communication like this. The Emergencies Act has some provisions under the section about Public Order Emergencies. These are meant to cover threat to our security, but we would have to show that the threat is a national emergency. And it requires action by Governor in Council to determine what kind of temporary measures would be needed to handle the situation. As far as media control is concerned, the act does not make anything clear. I doubt that we can invoke any kind of censorship possibility. If it comes down to a solid credibility, we need to work with media to ask them to act selflessly to preserve the stability of the country."

Leif, taken aback by this position from the Minister, realized his experience in controlling information outflow when in command of a military unit no longer pertained. "So, if I understand correctly, we need to co-opt the media as partners in a crusade against Terrorism, but if we are successful in that enterprise doesn't that open our agency up for public scrutiny?"

"Well," said the minister, "That is probably true, but we don't need to have the public informed about our methods necessarily, just about our purposes. In fact, this incident may be just exactly the kind of thing that we need to introduce ourselves to the public, by showing them how quickly we move on potential threats. It's a very good chance for us to demonstrate our readiness. I think I will hold a press conference to introduce you and some of your key personnel just as soon as you have something concrete. Please keep me fully informed as you develop this identification." With that, the Minister wished Leif well and rang off.

Leif sat still for a moment and then, settling back in his chair, expelled a deep breath of air. Some observers might have thought it

Ron Stotyn

was an expression of disgust at the promotional attitude taken by the Minister. Some observers might have been right, but Leif hadn't risen to his rank without recognizing in a pragmatic sort of way that some superiors did understand more than they were given credit for.... unless of course they were total idiots. He didn't think the Hon. Paul Mackey could be described as a total idiot.

Betty Anne popped her head into his office as he was contemplating what their strategy ought to be. She said, "We have a pretty good cleaned up image and Everet has a tentative ID, which is a bit surprising."

Leif rose immediately and followed her to her desk, where he saw both Everet and Stuart on the vid-link monitor. As he settled in front of the camera and microphone, Stuart reported, "Everet and Betty have done a fine job cleaning up the image from the video. It's not perfect because the contrasts are poor, but we do think we have seen this guy recently," he added

"Sean-Guy had Everet do sketches of a man we encountered recently at a Toronto restaurant. We checked him out and it appears he is using an alias for some reason. The man's name is Marek Kafirov, but he's in the country on an expired student visa in the name of Malik Bisliev. The name Kafirov is not in any of our official databases."

Both Betty Anne and Leif recognized these were the names they'd been introduced to by Sean-Guy in the past day or two.

Everet said "I have a side by side of the cleaned image and the sketch I did along with a surveillance photo we got off the guy yesterday. It's on your screen now."

The images popped on the adjacent screen to the view of Stuart and Everet. Leif immediately thought all three images were the same man. He stared and then said, "I would bet we are looking at a genuine terrorist here. Does Sean-Guy know about this yet?

Stuart responded, "Not yet, as he is on the road at the moment, so we thought you ought to see this right away. Everet is going to forward this to Sean-Guy's cell phone now."

Leif responded, "Yes, do that and ask Sean-Guy to get in touch with me just as soon as he can, okay? Good work all."

Just then Timothea Green appeared on screen, motioning to Stuart not to let the Director get away. Stuart introduced her to Leif as the loaned officer from the O.P.P. Electronic Fraud operation who'd been mining data from stolen credit card records. Thea announced with satisfaction, "We have identified a fairly certain location for delivery of chemicals and other supplies that our bomb squad said could be ingredients for bomb-making. In fact it's a location not far from the office here. It's a unit in a strip-mall type of condominium offices or light industrial spaces on Shawson Drive. We found the same address from three different chemical companies and from an industrial container supplier, so we are convinced this is trustworthy information."

Stuart, on hearing the address, noted abruptly, "That's the address we have under surveillance for this guy we have just identified."

Leif, reacting without hesitation, responded, "Stuart, you need to develop a request for a search warrant at that location. Make the request as convincing as possible. I suggest that you get the O.P.P. Explosive Disposal unit on standby immediately and go in very carefully as soon as you can. You had better consider evacuation of the immediate area. Sean-Guy will want to know about this development as well. Better call him without delay. I'm going to alert the Minister about this turn of events just so he is aware."

{11.2}

Sean-Guy's Crown Victoria Police Interceptor, about 1:30 PM, April 7: Toronto ON

Sean-Guy, with Angela De Luca beside him in his restored police interceptor was on the way to see Daniel O'Donnell, Managing Editor at the Toronto Star. He'd called O'Donnell to make sure the man would be available, but had refused to tell him on the phone the reason for the visit. He had said he would have Angela De Luca with him. He'd identified himself as Major O'Dwyer-Lariviere of the Department of National Defense rather than as Chief Investigator of CAS, not yet wanting to make the terrorism factor an issue. The identification was

Ron Stotyn

legitimate even if not exactly to the point. O'Donnell had been abrupt but pleasant enough on the phone, but sounded put off by Sean-Guy's refusal to get into details. Angela had not been present during that call, so still knew only what she thought she knew.

"Angela, tell me again, please, what Gallaegher has presented to you about the CAS," said Sean-Guy, wanting to see if the story would come out the same. Several minutes later, he was satisfied that it was the same and that Angela was still mostly in the dark, though after the meeting with O'Donnell she would be much more enlightened but in a poor position to do anything with the new information that would be revealed. He turned the conversation to safer topics for the remainder of the trip to the Toronto Star offices on Yonge Street, where they arrived after about forty minutes. The snowfall was a complicating factor for an easy trip into the center of Toronto. Too many drivers seemed to think that at this mid-point of the spring it was okay to drive as if they were on dry streets. He'd had to be a diligently careful driver.

Angela had been understandably curious about the cruiser asking, "How is it you have this antique police interceptor?"

Sean-Guy responded with a tone of delight about the topic. "Well, this was the very first police cruiser I ever worked in as a police officer with the Sûrété du Quebec. In fact, we were new together when I first joined the Sûrété. The car was due to be assigned permanently and as the newest Sergeant I was in line to receive a car. No one else has ever driven this vehicle. When it was due to be retired a couple of years ago, I was able to purchase it from the department. I had it fully restored and then received permission to continue using it for follow and arrest situations. It's become a very comfortable vehicle for me."

Angela asked, trying to find out more about the puzzling man, "Have you and the car been involved in any unusual situations over the years?"

Sean-Guy, debating with himself for a moment about how to answer because he was not fond of talking about his exploits, finally responded with some hesitation. "I have been fairly fortunate to escape serious problems during my years as a policeman. Of course, one is not always dealing with members of the public who have been victimized. It is necessary sometimes to confront those doing the victimizing. I have been shot at a few times and on a couple of occasions the car was between me and those doing the shooting. One of those occasions was earlier this year in Montreal. The car sustained several bullet holes in the driver side."

Before Angela could ask any more probing questions, about that they arrived at their destination. Sean-Guy was relieved that he would not have to get into personal details about his also being shot twice in that battle with the motorcycle gang. He thought *not a bad trip, considering the Friday mid-day traffic always seems to be heavier with people breaking off work early if they can to get a jump on the weekend. The snow is fairly light so that wasn't a serious problem. But I am surprised at myself once again. This woman has a way of digging at the truth that makes me uncomfortable in ways I've never before experienced. I need to guard myself. She's a reporter after all and that puts her as an adversary, I think. Still, I seem to be more and more interested in confiding in her. I'm not sure I understand what that is about, but the prospect is intriguing. She has strength and perhaps the ability to be compassionate. I can admire that.*

He found a space for the cruiser right in front of the building, marked loading zone only. Reaching into the glove box he took out a small placard marked Department of National Defense: Official Vehicle and placed it onto the dash. Sean-Guy also turned down both visors so that the DND logo and the words Official Business could be seen. That was the first time he had any occasion to use the signs so blatantly. He chuckled to himself as he asked Angela to get out and wait for him on the sidewalk. As he exited the vehicle, he spotted a Toronto PD car approach. Beckoning to the cruiser, he flipped open his badge wallet when the officer rolled the window down. "I'm with the DND," he said, "as an investigator for the Canada Anti-Terrorism Service. I'll be leaving the car here for awhile while I conduct an interview inside. Please let your watch commander know, okay? Thanks."

Joining Angela on the sidewalk, he took her arm, gently but firmly, and guided her toward the front entrance of the Toronto Star headquarters. Inside, he showed his badge to the desk attendant and

Ron Stotyn

told him who he was visiting. The attendant nodded and indicated the express elevator to the top floor where O'Donnell's office was located. As they entered the elevator, he looked back and saw the attendant had picked up the phone. Sean-Guy grinned and made a reasonable assumption that their impending arrival had just been announced. Inside the elevator, he felt his cell phone vibrate. Getting it out, he saw he had received a text message and an image. The message said, "Check the faces." As he did that, his eyebrows went up in surprise. He was staring at three images of the same person. He was also certain he was looking at Marek Kafirov, more properly known as Malik Bisliev. Then a second message arrived. It said simply, "Call the director." As Sean-Guy prepared to do just that a call came in from Stuart.

Answering the phone, Sean-Guy heard Stuart's voice thick with excitement. "Sean-Guy, we have a strong hit on the delivery of chemicals and other supplies from the stolen credit card operation data. The deliveries were made to that address on Shawson that we have been watching the last couple of days."

Interrupting Stuart, Sean-Guy turned to Angela, "Please wait for me in the reception area. This call is going to take a few minutes." Then, after watching Angela pass through the doors to O'Donnell's suite, Sean-Guy turned his attention back to the phone. "Okay, tell me details about this."

Stuart, now more deliberate, said, "The chemicals that were delivered include some that the O.P.P. bomb guys said could be components for bomb making. The industrial containers that were delivered to that location included carboys and other materials for chemical processing or a production line. It does not seem like a coincidence that we are already watching this place."

"Has the Director been updated?" asked Sean-Guy.

Stuart acknowledged, "Yes, and he wants to talk to you right away. In the meantime he wants me to get a request for a search warrant ready and to get the O.P.P. Explosive Disposal unit put on standby."

Sean-Guy, now in a thoughtful mood, responded, "Okay carry on and get that search warrant organized, but I want you to wait until I can get back before you try to execute it. Make sure the search terms are comprehensive. I'm just getting ready to interview the Star's Managing Editor, but I'll try to get back before three o'clock."

{11.3}

Managing Editor's Office, Toronto Star, about 1:45 PM, April 7: Toronto ON

Hanging up on Stuart, Sean-Guy immediately placed a call to the Director, while watching Angela through the glass. She was perched on a chair looking uncomfortable. Not knowing anything about O'Donnell's character he wondered what she might be concerned about. His attention turned away as the Director came on the line. "Sean-Guy, have you seen the picture produced by Betty and Everet? Can you identify this individual?"

Sean-Guy responded with a note of certainty in his voice. "I believe these three pictures are of the same person, a man claiming to be Marek Kafirov, but more likely the person known to me as Malik Bisliev. At the very least, we have an illegal immigrant, but in light of the new information about chemical and other deliveries to an address on Shawson in Mississauga, we more likely have a potential terrorist. The address is the same one where we have been running surveillance on this person."

Leif replied, "Yes I'm aware of that and have had a discussion with Stuart about getting a search warrant. You are aware I'm sure about the need for us to be completely justified when we enter this place? Our warrant request needs to be certain to show credible cause for entry. Be sure to show reasonable and probable grounds that an offense has been committed and that evidence can be expected to be discovered inside."

"Yes, I understand," said Sean-Guy. "I'll stay in touch with Stuart during this process and I expect to be back at the office before there is any readiness to execute a warrant. If necessary, he'll delay the request until I get back so that I can appear before a judge to make the argument. I'm certain, however, that we have a good justification on this since we have a statement from the O.P.P. about the potential for bomb making using these particular chemicals. Now, Director, please

Ron Stotyn

excuse me, I need to get into my interview with Daniel O'Donnell quickly so I don't antagonize the man. I'll call when I get back to the office."

Leif quickly stalled Sean-Guy's intentions to close the conversation, "You need also to know the Minister is planning to call a press conference to reveal our establishment. He wants to showcase some of us. I don't know exactly when this will happen, but he said as soon as we can show something concrete."

Saying his goodbye without further comments and putting his phone in his pocket, Sean-Guy hurried into the reception area, thinking with amazement about that news. He could see the secretary motioning to Angela. He arrived to hear the secretary say, "He can see you now."

Sean-Guy thought with a mental chastisement *I should have been asking Angela about this man's character. I'll be forced to play this carefully now*. He allowed Angela to enter first so that he could take a quick assessment of how she would be received.

Once Angela had cleared the doorway, he could see a bulky man standing by the window looking out into the city. As the man turned, Sean-Guy amended bulky to well-built with a sort of bulldog physique; stocky yet fairly tall. The man could have been a wrestler in his day.

O'Donnell growled at Angela, "What have you gotten yourself into now?" Then without allowing a response, he faced Sean-Guy full on and barked, "Why is the DND interested in my reporter? Let me see your credentials."

Sean-Guy, wearing a scant smile of amusement, advanced and flipped open his badge case, then put it away with barely enough time for O'Donnell to take it all in. Standing to his tallest, which was an impressive 6'3" 220 pounds of solid musculature, Sean-Guy expressed considerable self confidence. He was dressed in a dark pinstriped suit with a black turtleneck sweater, which though a bit casual for Bay Street's financial wizards, was certainly indicative of power and authority. He was counting on that to sway O'Donnell's overall reaction. Sean-Guy had been able to assess O'Donnell's character in a matter of the few moments that had expired since their entry to his office. O'Donnell was clearly a tough-guy, inclined to be a bit of a bully, used to his own authority and very willing to brook little nonsense. But the man was visibly also interested in gaining information, a factor Sean-Guy was willing to accommodate to a point.

"Mr. O'Donnell," said Sean-Guy, taking charge of the conversation and setting the direction right away, "May I suggest we sit over here," pointing to the group of chairs arranged as a conversation area. Sean-Guy waited until O'Donnell and Angela were seated and then remaining on his feet, he took a position slightly to the left of the man so he could watch Angela at the same time. His position also forced O'Donnell to twist himself in the chair so he could face Sean-Guy, though not comfortably. Angela, with an expression of bemusement on her face, had sat forward on the chair, hands clasped together. Sean-Guy could see she was very nervous and trying hard to control herself.

"Let me begin by answering the question that you just put to Miss De Luca. She has involved herself in a situation that is rapidly becoming a National Security concern. As I told you on the phone earlier, I am a Major in the DND. In addition I am Chief in charge of investigations for the Canada Anti-Terrorism Service. I am here because we understand that the Star has received a video of a possible terrorist making threats against the transportation system in the greater Toronto Area. I am also here because you ordered Miss De Luca to return to the office for that very reason." With that statement, Sean-Guy had made it absolutely impossible for the man to tell him any obfuscating information. "Please tell me how you received the video and what you intend to do with it."

O'Donnell, already several notches into hostility, opened his mouth with intention to bluster, and then suddenly, with an explosive sound like the harrumphing of a grump, taking note of Sean-Guy's uncompromising attitude, replied "We got the video attached to an e-mail addressed to our city desk several hours ago. The city editor followed protocol and sent it up to me. I called Angela in because she has been trying to get a handle on your service. Not that she has produced much that is useful," giving her an offhand glare, "but I suppose much of that is due to your hand on the controls."

Ron Stotyn

"And the plans for your handling of the video," prompted Sean-Guy forcefully, not yet willing to allow the man to relax.

O'Donnell, now suspicious of interference with his right to publish information freely, said, "We intend to run a front page story. That's being prepared right now for the early street edition. That'll roll in an hour or so. It'll take an act of God to change our minds. I want a follow-up story from Miss De Luca for the first home edition due out at 5 PM."

Sean-Guy sighed and relaxed himself mentally, allowing his body to rest imperceptibly, saying, "Mr. O'Donnell, as much I would wish it possible, there is no available authority to prevent you from doing that as I'm sure you are aware. But, there are aspects of Miss De Luca's information that have been obtained, we believe, in contravention of the Security of Information Act. Because of that I must tell you that if information obtained from anyone bound by the act not to reveal sensitive official government information is published, then Miss De Luca and the Toronto Star and of course yourself, could find themselves convicted under the Act's provisions. I will also tell you that we believe this video represents a credible threat and we are concerned that publication has the very high risk potential of causing hysteria among your readers in this region. We ask therefore that you curtail the information for awhile until we can effect some arrests. We are making the same request of all media who have received this material." Sean-Guy moved to a chair and took a seat, waiting with anticipation O'Donnell's reaction.

O'Donnell, silent for a long moment, looked at Angela as if trying to decide what she might have to offer, then at Sean-Guy who had settled comfortably and still obviously confident in his role. "Major O'Dwyer-Lariviere, you present me with quite a quandary.... may I call you by your first names?

Sean-Guy was surprised though not visibly at the man's knowledge of his given names, thinking his eyesight must be very good indeed if he picked them up in the brief presentation of his ID.

Seeing Sean-Guy's nod, O'Donnell proceeded, "Sean-Guy, you're asking a great deal of me....completely aside from the issues of freedom of the press.... you are asking us to disable our readers from protecting themselves. If this threat is credible as you suggest, shouldn't people have the ability to make alternate arrangements until your service can convince them the threat is over and gone?

Sean-Guy, the hint of a frown on his face, sat forward slightly as he responded, "I understand your position and I do not overall disagree, but we are equally concerned about the potential for losing an opportunity to find the terrorist before he can set his intentions into action. We already have several individuals under our watch….there is very good reason to believe they are connected to this threat, but we need a bit more time to confirm these suspicions. If the threat is imminent, there is the very strong possibility the terrorists can accelerate before we can find out necessary details. I'm asking for delay to avoid tipping them off. If this video gets little or no notice, we think the terrorist will be forced to come up with a different means to advertise his intentions. The goal here, we believe, is to create fear. The unknown of such a threat is definitely something that would ignite fear."

Angela unclasped her hands and, making a gesture of uncertainty toward Sean-Guy said, surprising herself at the admission she was about to make, "I think it would be a good idea to suppress the video if we can get agreement to do an in-depth story about the CAS and the reason it was established. We need to prepare profiles of key staff and demonstrate that Canada has taken a serious step toward resolving any threats made against the nation. The story of the video could be held a few days until it would make a great follow-up."

Sean-Guy, forestalling O'Donnell's response, quickly interjected, "I have been told by my Director that the Minister of Defense is considering a public statement about the CAS fairly soon. I have no other details than that. What you do with that information is obviously out of my control."

O'Donnell, again thoughtful and silent, was contemplating what the prospects were for a scoop about the CAS. Here in front of him sat an apparently senior officer of a brand-new agency. His own reporter, again silent beside the man, was, he could see, already connected in ways he wasn't certain he understood. Watching her relate with some high regard unconsciously demonstrated toward

Ron Stotyn

O'Dwyer-Lariviere, she was almost certainly in a position to gain insightful information if she was allowed to go ahead. Never a man to allow any doubts much opportunity to gain ground, he made his decision. Reaching for the phone beside his chair, he dialed the extension for Tom Russert, his city editor. When the man answered his words were characteristically gruff and blunt. "Cancel the video threat story. We'll run it later when I tell you. Angela will be in touch with you soon. She'll be doing an in-depth story about the Canada Anti-Terrorism Service." With that he hung up and looked at Sean-Guy expectantly.

Sean-Guy nodded in a way that might mean approval, though O'Donnell couldn't be certain, then responded. "Angela, I caution you again about the information that you received from Gallaegher and Davis. You should know that they are both being investigated. I'll recommend to Director Isaksson that you be allowed to interview people in our service who can tell you about the service, the reasons it was established and the purposes and goals that it has. I'll also recommend that the Minister be told about your involvement and that it would be reasonable for him to speak to you. After that, it will be a matter of your integrity as to how far you'll be able to proceed."

To O'Donnell, Sean-Guy said, "I appreciate your considerations. I need to get back now to my office to take care of routine matters there. Please excuse me. I'll be happy to take Miss De Luca back to her car, unless you need to speak with her."

O'Donnell looked at Sean-Guy pensively and then, looking at Angela asked her to stay. "I think we need to talk about some strategy for this story, don't you?"

{12}

"Revenge is a kind of wild justice, which the more man's nature runs to, the more ought law to weed it out." Francis Bacon 1561-1626 in Of Revenge

Bradford Slumber Motel, early morning Saturday April 8: Bradford ON

Revenge was very much on Marek's mind, the closer he came to realizing his goal to mete out a special kind of justice for Canadians. It was still dark as he arose from his morning prayers and began to consider once again his nearly completed destructive plan. His memory of a much earlier time kicked in: he recalled, with some difficulty, the loss of his older brother. Marek had been four or five at the time, he supposed. Angry again at the memory, he realized yet again that he couldn't even remember his brother's name. But he knew the event was because of the Russians.

His country was under siege at that time as the Russians did whatever they wanted to the population. At age five his experiences were profoundly disturbing. Any psychiatrist might say they were intense enough to cause pushing them deep into the psyche to prevent continuing devastation to the mental state. Marek had read about defense mechanisms, how they masked memories that if allowed to percolate to the surface could create insanity, but his mentor the Imam had trained him to use such experiences as a source of pride in what he had been taught to accomplish. He knew, indeed, that when he did remember those days, the memories were clearly a just foundation for his rage against the injustice done to his family and Chechnya. Even as early as five, he had known his responsibility to aid his family in finding a solution to that outrage. His father, though, had told him gently to wait until the time was right. So as a good and obedient child, he did wait.

Until age 13 he waited.

After the Russians had come a second time to wage war against his people, he sustained another crushing reason to hate. In

Ron Stotyn

1999 during the so-called Second Chechen War, some debauched
Russian troops went on a drunken rampage though his town of Shali.
When it was over, his parents were dead. He'd seen every shameful
deed happen from the hiding place his mother had hurried him into.
His father was brutally dispatched with repeated rifle butt blows to the
head when he had tried to prevent the soldiers from raping his wife.
His mother took much longer to die as drunken Russian after drunken
Russian had their way with her. Finally, she had been discarded like a
broken doll. When the Russians left her and went on their way to find
other victims, he went to her but she was unresponsive. She died with
him holding her head up away from the blood on the floor. He had no
recollection of how long he remained with his mother's head on his
lap. At last, hunger drove him out of the home he had known as a place
of refuge into the streets where he soon discovered that he was utterly
alone.

After days of wandering and scrounging, he was forced to
understand that there was no longer any Bisliev family left in Shali.
He'd found the remains of his grandparents and several uncles and
aunts and their children. Others of the family had just disappeared. He
could not discover what had happened to them. More days passed, then
weeks, till finally several months. Marek lost track of the days, but
became increasingly street savvy, learning to avoid Russians on patrol
during the day and Russians out of control at night. Then one day he
met his savior, when he slipped into a building seeking food to steal. It
was the mosque overseen by Imam Ali Ibn al-Hassan, who grabbed his
cloak as he tried to run away. The Imam was very tall, it seemed to
Malik Bisliev, a formidable figure to a child of nearly 13 still with
only a stripling's physique. What Marek mostly recalled though, were
the eyes, the darkest brown pools of mystery that made him at once
fearful and at peace. Surprisingly, there had been no punishment for
what he had done; the stealing of food from a holy place.

Punishment came later and for different reasons; for the
moment he had been treated as well as a lost lamb, taken in, clothed,
fed, and given a soft mattress on which to sleep. He was taught to
respect the Qur'an and to learn it by rote memory. That was when the
punishments began; whippings when he failed to recite the passages

correctly, especially those passages that he was told spoke to his responsibilities to take the task of revenge upon himself. Slowly he realized that was what his father had meant about the time being right. The time for his responsibility had arrived. Nearly a year passed until one day the Imam announced he would be sent away to learn better English. His protest gained him excruciating pain as he was forced to endure more punishment for rejecting the will of the Imam.

At almost the age of 13, Malik Bisliev began a journey to Canada alone, indeed, completely on his own, shipped as if unaccompanied baggage to a preparatory school in Stanstead Quebec. As a Muslim child with unskilled efforts in English to be understood, Marek recalled lonely days and nights, struggling and slowly succeeding until one day he met a tall stranger who greeted him gently and encouraged his studies. He had revealed he was a policeman and a member of the school's governing board. That man's eyes he also remembered; slate gray-blue that seemed to probe his center being. He was not frightened by that gaze; rather he was disconcerted, wondering why the man was so deeply interested in him. They exchanged names and then saw each other no more, until last week when Marek encountered those probing eyes again at the Samovar House, his erstwhile place of employment.

Marek's momentary recall of that recent event shocked him back to the present as he realized he needed to have some breakfast and get on the road to continue the task of bomb delivery. But his recollection of the stranger's eyes continued to be a disturbing thought. They had been again probing, but surely, thought Marek, I could not have been recognized. Many years have passed and I have grown to manhood. I am different. Besides there is no reason for that man to be interested in me, even if he is still a policeman. Nothing in that brief encounter makes me a suspect for any reason whatever. Marek tried to focus on the task of the moment, his distribution of the bomb packages, about half left still to place in lockers. But he continued to be perturbed about the man, whose name was, as he remembered, Sergeant O'Dwyer-Lariviere. The first name he seemed to recollect was Sean-Guy. Those eyes not only probed but they also seemed to reflect sadness as if the man understood Malik's own difficulties. How

Ron Stotyn

could that be? The man had not inquired directly nor had he commented about his situation back then. He had only said a few encouraging words.

As Marek gathered up his few things and left the motel room, he could not escape a realization that where revenge was concerned, it was completely absent in connection with the man O'Dwyer-Lariviere. He was struck by another realization. No one else in his life as an orphan, not even his mentor Imam al-Hassan, had ever expressed any form of compassion. The Imam, while portraying a front of compassion, really was an intolerant individual who brooked no slacking when it came to training for revenge and for having a complete recall of relevant passages of the Qur'an. Marek had quickly learned that the deep brown pools of the Imam's eyes merely masked evil intent. He had, as a result, learned out of a need to survive, to emulate that same intent. The outcome was that he was completely without remorse. *If I have to for some reason deal violently with O'Dwyer-Lariviere I will do so. I might perhaps experience some regret but it shall be done without remorse.* With that thought centered, Marek put O'Dwyer-Lariviere to the back of his mind as best he could and went on his way toward a glorious moment of destruction for Canadians who had committed the sin of befriending the Russian nation.

{12.1}

Toronto CAS Office, 7 AM, Saturday April 8: Mississauga ON

Sean-Guy arrived at the Toronto CAS with an armload of Tim-bits and donuts from Tim Horton's, expecting that his team members would already be present. He'd said as much to them late yesterday afternoon after he got back from his discussion with Daniel O'Donnell at the Toronto Star's HQ. He was satisfied with that conversation. O'Donnell had agreed to hold off on any story about the terrorist video. Sean-Guy had promised to encourage the Director to grant the Star first opportunity for a story about the agency. In all,

Sean-Guy was pleased that his current investigation would escape notice for the moment.

But, the search warrant request was still being processed at 4 PM the day before so Sean-Guy had decided it would be better to call an expanded team together for first thing in the morning so they could make sure the search went without incident. This morning, Sean-Guy knew pretty much what they would find. He'd already made a first foray late the night before without telling anyone. That move of course, typically according to his propensity to act alone, was certainly against protocol as laid down to him by the Director when they'd first met in his office a little less than two weeks earlier. Leif had been very specific: no going off the reservation without clearing it first.

It was characteristic of his bent to go off and act independently whenever he felt a need for new information to add to his knowledge. The fact that the building was under surveillance both front and back was a small problem but he'd found a solution. The far end of the building afforded roof access by scaling the heavy duty power conduit he'd spotted when the building was first identified as one of the locations Marek went to regularly. He'd inspected the exterior soon after assigning his teams of watchers. The power conduit was out of his agents' view; he had only to be careful approaching the building from the opposite end of the street from the surveillance locations. He'd approached in jogger's mode, running easily. Those watching the building were focused on the front and rear exits of the space used by Marek, so he wasn't observed accessing the roof. The space he wanted to know more about had been easy to identify by the ventilation units that every location with stoves and ovens had to have. Moving across the roof in a crouch dressed in a SWAT-like black jogging outfit along the building's center line allowed him to ensure he wouldn't be spotted by any observers.

Once at his rooftop destination, he found a hatchway into the suite. Surprisingly, though the thought passed quickly out of mind, it wasn't secured so he had very carefully and quietly opened it and crept down the ladder inside a storage closet. Inside the closet space he had waited for a long while, his Para Ordnance P18•9 automatic in hand, listening for any sound of activity, then had opened the door a crack to

Ron Stotyn

see if there were any lights on. That had been risky. He had no idea if there was any form of security inside the former food preparation kitchen, but had thought it most unlikely. Still where a possible terrorist was involved, caution was dictated. Everything had been clear; no lights, no sounds, and no other evidence that anyone was about. That was consistent with the last reports he'd had from the surveillance teams before leaving the Toronto Office of CAS shortly after 6 PM.

The surveillance on the suspected bomb making facility had been increased along with that for the restaurant and residence locations associated with Marek Kafirov as a result of the realization that Marek and Malik were one and the same. The man had not been seen at any of these locations for more than 24 hours now. Sean-Guy was perturbed, better to say furious that they may have lost track of this person, he thought.

This morning, on his way into the office from the Tim Horton's, he'd reviewed what he'd seen inside the space, sans warrant, in a quick survey. Using a small penlight as he moved carefully through the former bakery, being careful not to touch anything; he'd observed large glass vessels. He knew they were called Carboys and were typical of large scale chemical processes. There was other evidence that someone had been working at what certainly was not a food enterprise. There had been a pair of wire cutters on one bench and duct tape on another. He couldn't determine exactly what had been going on; that would take experts' attention from the O.P.P. Explosive Disposal team to determine if Thea's data mining information about chemical deliveries was realistic. He'd been satisfied that they definitely needed to conduct a very thorough examination of the entire inside of the building. He did not think there was any danger to other lessees of the remainder of the building but he would order an evacuation in any event.

He had left the same way he'd gotten in without being spotted by the surveillance agents, continuing his run until he got back to the motel. That he had not been observed probably demanded comment about the scope of attention from the surveillance teams, except for the fact it would draw attention to two problems for himself. *The first, of course, is the fact I would have to admit to doing what I am not to be doing, and the second of my neglect about ordering a wider range of surveillance. Silence will have to be the better part of valor here.*

As he entered CAS's main office area, he noted with satisfaction that Everet, Ryan, Stuart, Darya, George and Hari were present along with selected members from the O.P.P. surveillance teams and the CBSA agents on loan for the same purposes. In the back of the room he also spotted Thea, again dressed in an oddly attractive but out of the ordinary brightly colored attire akin to a hippy from the 60s. There were also three individuals in black coveralls that he'd not met before lounging against a wall. He saw also on the video monitors that Leif, Betty and René were available for consultation at the Ottawa HQ office. He made a mental note to ask about the three strangers.

Depositing his load of breakfast items, such as they were, on a desk he went to get a coffee without any greetings to the group, indicating they should help themselves. Returning to the group he ignored courtesy and got right down to business as he saw it. "Our primary person of interest is missing. That does not please me nearly to the point of being both frustrated and angry. If I find out he slipped away because we let our guard down, there will be hell to pay! The fact that he is out of our sight makes our task this morning the more dangerous."

Thea tentatively asked, "Why is that? I don't understand the concern."

Sean-Guy looked to the vid-link camera and said, "René, care to comment?"

René, who'd been in a mood of introspection with his head down, was startled at the request.

Betty interjected to give him extra time to compose himself, "We have been trying to discover information about Malik Bisliev, known these days as Marek Kafirov. It's confirmed that name is fictitious. There is not much available so far about Bisliev. We know he was here in Canada about 9 years ago studying English in Stanstead Quebec. We know that he was sponsored by an Imam al-Hassan, a radical Muslim Cleric in Shali, Chechnya, which by the way appears to be where Malik was born and grew up. There is no information

Ron Stotyn

available at this point about Bisliev's family. We've drawn a blank and that might mean the family are all deceased, a distinct possibility given the activities of the Russians during the Second Chechen War in the late 90's. If that's true then we need to consider that maybe this man has an incurable rage against his enemies. Oh…I should also say that Imam al-Hassan is believed to be well connected to terrorist training in Chechnya."

Stuart asked, "Does that mean Bisliev is a particularly dangerous individual? After all, we apparently don't know if he is a terrorist."

René began to respond but Sean-Guy cut him off sharply, saying, "Before you answer, René, I want everyone to put out of their minds right now any doubts about the possibility of his being a terrorist. We have information that leads to a reasonable hypothesis about bomb making components being delivered to a location where we know he has been going. We know that his name is phony and we now know he is connected apparently very closely with a radical cleric known to be connected with terrorists' interests. None of us needs to be distracted by lesser possibilities." Nodding to René to continue, Sean-Guy fell silent.

René carefully responded, "I have of course not been able to do a thorough analysis of this individual, but I am prepared to say he fits fairly well a profile of a young distraught personality shaped by violent events in his life. His apparent age means that he likely experienced the events of both Chechen Wars and doubtless experienced…. at a very close and personal level…. destruction. That makes it very probable that this person suffers from severe PTSD, which could very well make him retributive in terms of behavior, especially if he is trained as a terrorist. In a worst case scenario, I would have to say there is every likelihood that this person has a single minded goal to cause destruction as a means of gaining satisfaction against his enemies…or even perceived enemies….I cannot tell you if he is armed and dangerous….but….I would not be surprised to discover that he is prepared to do whatever is necessary to carry out whatever plans he may have."

Leif spoke up, "I cannot help but be very concerned about the safety issues that now face us. I urge everyone to understand very carefully all the ramifications of undertaking this search warrant exercise. But my concerns go beyond your safety, we must also be very aware of the safety of all civilians in the vicinity."

Sean-Guy resumed the lead in the discussion. "I want the advance team to ensure a quiet and orderly evacuation of the entire building and the buildings to the rear, the sides and across the street before the main force moves in. It is imperative that movement of the evacuees be such that it cannot be seen or at least not be especially obvious from the target location. We need two or three individuals on the roof in place before we hit the entrances."

Everett asked quietly, "Sharpshooters?"

Sean-Guy, surprised and realizing he had been vague about an important point, looked carefully at Everet before replying. "Yes, we will need you and at least one other to cover the front and rear entrances. You'll need to find access to the rooftops on the buildings to the rear and across the street. Do you have a suggestion about a second rifle?"

Everet responded, looking at Ryan sharply, "Ryan has suitable training from the RCMP."

Sean-Guy decisively finalized that aspect of their plan. "OK, take care of it. Everyone else make sure you check your body armor and weapons carefully for safety reasons. Upon entry you must assume you will be in darkness as all the windows appear to be covered. Instead of using lighting let's use night site goggles. But that still means you must be very cautious as two teams will be merging toward each other from the front and the back. Make sure all your radios are working properly and review all the standard communication cues. Any questions? Be ready to move out in 20 minutes. Stuart, any comments?"

Stuart nodded and reminded everyone, "We don't want any cowboys. Have your weapons in hand but absolutely no shooting unless fired upon. Aim to incapacitate. We need this guy available to spill the beans. Right?"

Hari spoke up, "How are we getting to the target?"

Ron Stotyn

Stuart responded as transportation coordinator. "The advance teams and the sharpshooters will leave immediately in the SUVs. They need to be parked well away from direct line of sight. Evacuation agents will wait until Everet and Ryan confirm they are in position and will then move out on foot to guide people away from the site. The rest of us will ride over in the ABC Pest Control Vans. They are both set up for Swat Team use and the Sprinter has command center capability as well. We'll approach the building from either end of the street and park so we have a short charge from the rear doors directly to the entrance points. Hari will be in charge of communications coordination, if that's okay with you, Sean-Guy?"

Sean-Guy nodded, satisfied that Stuart had read the situation appropriately. He intended to be one of the first through the doors at the front of the building when they made the strike. As everyone began to organize themselves, Hari stepped forward followed by the three strangers Sean-Guy had observed earlier. "These gentlemen are Explosives Disposal personnel who've been supplied by the O.P.P. They have advice about who should enter first."

Sean-Guy looked carefully at the three, fixing his gaze on one whose stature and grizzled appearance suggested he might be the leader. He waited, his face signaling a question.

"My name is Lt. Art Romanowski, in command of ONE Squad of the Explosives Disposal unit of the O.P.P. Do you have any Intel on the interior of the building and about possible explosive traps?"

Sean-Guy hesitated, realizing the question was valid, and that his answer would reveal what Leif probably did not want to know. As he answered, he saw Hari's face tighten with interest. "I've been inside, last night in fact. I found no evidence of trip wires or any kind of rigged devices. Your expertise, however, is certainly needed to tell us what has been going on inside if our information about chemical deliveries are what they seem to be." He looked at Hari, his eyebrow twitched slightly. Hari nodded back imperceptibly. Sean-Guy hoped that meant he would keep silent.

Romanowski looked carefully at Sean-Guy, as he rubbed his jaw. His next words showed considerable insight and made a lot of sense. "If you have been inside and your people did not see you, it must have been through the roof. The fact you saw nothing does not mean the front and rear entrances are safe. We should go in the same way as you did and verify before your people enter at ground level. We could, … make that should… insert robotic cameras for an infrared look-see before risking forced entry."

"Okay," said Sean-Guy "There is an unsecured roof hatch. I scaled the power conduit at the end of the building. The hatch gives access to a ladder inside a storage closet. I'll go with you," he decided instantly.

Looking at Hari he said, "Tell Stuart I'm going in with these guys before anything else happens. No entry until I give the all clear, okay?" Hari nodded and turned to go. "Wait, on second thought I better talk to Stuart directly myself," said Sean-Guy, moving to catch up to Hari. Calling back over his shoulder to Art he said, "I'll be ready in five."

As he moved away he heard Pere René say softly, "God go with you all." Sean-Guy had almost forgotten with all René's expertise poured into the work of profiling that the man was still a priest. Even though his own connection with the church had been diminished, deep down he was grateful for the prayer uttered by his friend.

Outside the CAS offices and across the street at the Olympia Grill, Angela De Luca was back at her usual spot just inside the front door, watching the building. She noted with considerable interest two men emerge, go to the ABC Pest Control vans, start them and head around the corner to the building's garage entrance. She'd not seen those vehicles move previously. But she was even more interested in the unmistakable vehicle of the O.P.P.'s Explosive Disposal Unit parked right outside the main entrance. That has got to mean something is ready to pop, she thought with excitement. Then in the length of less than a minute, she saw several CAS SUV's emerge from the garage and even more interesting a group of four men coming from the front entrance. One of them was Sean-Guy, his height and manner of movement distinctive. The group climbed into the bomb unit vehicle. She immediately got up, dropped some money on the table to cover her coffees and moved quickly toward her car, now parked out in the restaurant's lot. No reason to hide any longer since Sean-Guy

Ron Stotyn

knew about her interest. Her reportorial instincts told her she'd better follow or miss a story. She started her car and waited until the O.P.P. armored truck moved further down the block. She pulled out and followed at a half block distance.

{12.2}
Shawson Drive & Courtneypark Drive E., about 7:46 AM, April 8: Mississauga ON

Angela didn't think she'd been seen since she'd been careful to hang back quite a distance as she followed the Bomb Squad truck. Ahead of that truck she could see the CAS vehicles turn the corner onto Shawson Drive and immediately pull over, though one had proceeded up the road further before it stopped. The Bomb Squad truck also pulled over as soon as it turned the corner. She decided to move to the curb on Courtneypark Drive E. before reaching the corner, but edged forward until she could see down Shawson. Turning off her car she turned and began to rummage in the back seat looking for her binoculars. She grabbed them from the floor and looked back around to see two men get out of the lead SUV. They went to the back of the vehicle, opened the back door and began to unpack something. Through the binoculars she could see long gun cases being lifted and slung across the back of each man. A chill ran though her as she guessed these two were very possibly snipers getting ready to set up somewhere. She wished she could get closer, but could not. There was no cover and dawn had already brightened the day. She settled in to watch what was coming.

Up ahead, Sean-Guy and Art Romanowski were conferring. He and Art would wait until Everet and Ryan were in place across the street and to the rear of the target location. It could take them as much as twenty minutes to gain roof access and find suitable sniper positions. Then Art and Sean-Guy would move to gain access to the roof using a lightweight extension ladder to prepare for their foray inside with robotic cameras. Once on the roof they would signal to the evacuation team to begin removal of any innocents in adjacent suites and buildings. The bomb squad truck would be moved out of sight to avoid causing a panic among the evacuees. What they couldn't see would be to their benefit. Sean-Guy was stimulated by the tension, but knew that great care had to be exercised. Any failure to conduct the exercise according to a strict protocol could be disastrous.

Fifteen minutes later, Sean-Guy heard in his earpiece a confirmation that Everet and Ryan were both in place. He and Art began their movement toward the roof.

Hari announced, "Evac Squad Leader, confirm ready." Darya confirmed.

Sean-Guy placed the ladder and held it while Art swarmed up carrying his bag of robotic cameras and a small video screen. He followed up the ladder and hauled it up to the roof right away, confirming by radio that they were in place on the roof, saying also, "Next phase ready to go?"

Hari replied, "Proceed with Evac operation. Confirm when complete." Everyone settled into a waiting game until the buildings adjacent were cleared for safety. Everet and Ryan both sharpened their focus on the doors they were covering, ready for any sudden exit of anyone with a weapon. Art and Sean-Guy reached the hatch and opened it carefully. Art peered over the edge and satisfied himself the room below was clear. He hung a small mic over the edge and carefully closed the hatch again to prevent any daylight from being visible in case anyone came into the room. He prepared to lower his bag by a thin rope to the floor. Then they waited.

Down on the street, Darya and her Evac team went methodically from door to door dressed in dark overalls with no weapons visible; clearing the building suites. Some were still closed, being Saturday and still early in the day. Those were entered with a bit of skilled lock picking followed by a swift sweep to ensure they were clear. The suite was then relocked and they moved on. There was no expectation anyone would show up trying to get in. All streets in the area had been barricaded. Where they found people inside, instructions were given about the evacuation on the premise a gas leak had been discovered. Managers were asked to ensure the premises were clear and then locked after the last employee had departed. The entire evacuation enterprise took about half an hour without incident. When

Ron Stotyn

all the suites had been approached and secured, Darya reported that all was clear.

Hari radioed Art and Sean-Guy saying, "Ready for insertion?" Art confirmed, having had no pick up of occupation sounds from the microphone inserted earlier, and opened the hatch quietly, peered over and then lowered his bag, following down the ladder quickly. By the time Sean-Guy reached the floor, two robotic cameras were out of the bag and ready to go. Sean-Guy, his Para P18•9 in hand, eased the door of the closet open, listening carefully. Satisfied that there was no-one around, he motioned to Art to deploy the first robotic camera. The second one followed, both operated by a dual joy-stick unit, while Art peered at a small double monitor. The robots moved slowly both advancing toward the front and rear entrance points respectively, with Art swiveling the camera lenses from side to side looking for possible traps. Caution dictated by Art meant the whole process would take some time, but finally he announced quietly that the entrances were clear. Another quarter hour had passed by. He reversed the robots and brought them back through the bakery watching for other possibilities within the prep areas of the large room. "OK," he said on his radio, "Next phase can begin."

Sean-Guy placed the actual order to Hari "commence entry" and under his breath "loose the dogs." Not actual dogs of course, but his private reference to the dogs of hell which he hoped would soon be ready to devour the terrorists he suspected were already well advanced in their plans. He also announced to Hari "advise all; no lights available." That meant the entry teams needed to exercise extreme caution.

Hari responded, notifying all entry team agents. "Extreme Caution. No light inside, Commence entry operation. Night sights must be live. Sweep till clear. Touch nothing."

Outside, the entry teams swarmed out of their vans, carrying a collection of weapons: Sig Sauers, Glocks and some H&K MP5s, depending on which service they were from. The lead agent in each team carried a massive pry bar typical of what fire fighters use to get through a door quickly. In a matter of seconds they had the doors open; the first agents through were Art's companions with eyes searching for whatever the robot cameras might have missed. In a matter of minutes the teams had met each other and had declared clear all the spaces inside the food prep kitchen. Sean-Guy and Art emerged from their closet. Art gathered his team together and gave quick instructions about making analysis of any chemicals found.

Sean-Guy organized Darya, who had come in on the all-clear signal, along with George and Stuart to begin looking for general evidence of their suspect. They immediately began looking for fingerprints on all surfaces where Marek might have been working. He told Everet and Ryan to stand down and join them as soon as possible. The O.P.P. and CBSA agents were released and reassigned to relieve the surveillance details at Marek's place of employment and residence. Some were sent to tell the evacuees they could return to their places of business. That part of the overall exercise was delayed until all weapons could be stowed out of sight, again so the civilians would not be alarmed. Overall, the entire operation had taken nearly an hour and a half. Sean-Guy expected they would need several more hours inside before they could return to the office to consider what they had found.

Darya soon called Sean-Guy over to one worktable, pointing to a box of vinyl gloves, saying "I don't think we are going to find many prints if he has been wearing these." Sean-Guy grimaced with agreement but said, "We'll look for any discarded ones. We'll need to check the insides for prints and the outsides for residues."

Meanwhile down the block, just around the corner on Courtneypark Drive East, Angela was nearly beside herself with excitement. She had witnessed the most amazing sight in her entire career, she thought. She'd had the presence of mind to get her camera out and had attached a telephoto lens in time to grab some shots of the teams swarming out of the two ABC Pest Control Vans. One team disappeared around to the back and the second team hit the front entrance weapons up and ready. They had moved into the building with surprising speed and efficiency. Now checking the digital display on the back of the Nikon, she considered the results spectacular. Front Page for sure, she exulted. Throwing caution to the wind, she decided to leave her car and move toward the action. She needed to get some quotes from somebody. Almost running, she arrived at the back of the

Ron Stotyn

Sprinter, where she could see though the open door that there was someone at a communications console, she thought it was. Suddenly, the man swung around surprised to see a civilian climbing inside. Angela froze as he pointed an automatic pistol at her and demanded identification. "I..ah..I... need to speak with Sean-Guy," she stammered. "He can vouch for me."

Hari blinked, and then realized it was the reporter that had been dogging them. He activated his link with Sean-Guy "We have a problem here boss" he said, "That reporter has just climbed into Command with me. I have my gun aimed at her, what do you want me to do?"

Sean-Guy cursed out loud, thinking at the same time *just what we don't need right now*, then without considering his remark barked, "Shoot her in the foot, that will slow her down." Angela blanched at hearing those words on the loud speaker and then sank to the floor with relief when he said, "Belay that, I'm coming out."

{12.3}
Toronto CAS Office, Saturday April 8, Early Afternoon: Mississauga ON

Sean-Guy was aggravated and knew there was nothing much that he could do about the cause. *I'm furious that she keeps getting under my skin. She's like a bad penny, always there when you least expect it and there when she shouldn't be interfering.*

The cause of his aggravation was sitting opposite from him at the desk he was using at the Toronto CAS offices. He had escorted her personally from the bomb Investigation site directly to the CAS office, not permitting her to return to her vehicle. She had protested that mightily, and had then fearfully lapsed into silence when he told her the other option was an immediate arrest for interfering with a legal police action. She was Angela De Luca, who had shown up at the site of the search warrant execution earlier in the day. The reporter, who he was forced to admit had merely followed her instincts; *There is no doubt she is good at her job. I just wish she was doing it somewhere else, where I am not.* The search operation had been exercised in public and there was nothing to do but accept the circumstances, as much as he would like to tell her she had no story. She had apparently entered the area before they got a perimeter up and sealed.

His aggravation was deepened by the certain knowledge that she had been promised the overall story in exchange for holding off on publication of the video sent out by the terrorist that they were now actively hunting. Publication of Marek's identity, which Angela did not yet know, would almost certainly mean he would go to ground. That meant a very strong likelihood of an escalation of his terroristic plans whatever they were. And whatever they were was almost certainly a plan involving bombs. That much was clear from preliminary reports from the Explosives Disposal guys from the O.P.P.

The bomb squad had confirmed that there were chemicals on site that could certainly form the components for a bomb making enterprise. They had also found residues of what they thought would be demonstrated to be Nitroglycerine and Penta. There was also a suspicion that Nitrocellulose had been produced at one point. A chemical analysis would be required but Art Romanowski was sure the result would bear out the guess. The analysis, he suggested, would also tell them about the relative purity of the explosives and thus the potency of the materials manufactured by the supposed terrorist. Their best projection at the moment was that the bombs would be strong. What was still unknown and might not be known even after the entire site was fully examined was the quantity that might have been produced.

All of this was gripping Sean-Guy's mind as he sat staring at Angela, part of his thoughts debating what he could allow her to know in the short term. Neglecting some information flow was certainly something he could consider even if not strictly kosher given the relationship that had been created following the meeting with O'Donnell. *This relationship is taking unexpected turns. I'm certain, I think, that I cannot trust her discretion and yet I definitely like her ability to stay tightly focused. I know that is a trait I value in myself. I never thought I would meet a woman so compatible.* His long term intent was becoming clearer even as he angrily pushed it to the back of his mind.

Ron Stotyn

Another part of Sean-Guy's thinking process was engaged with the fact that Peter Gallaegher and Gabrielle Davis were still in custody, sitting in interview rooms where they had been brought late yesterday afternoon. That also aggravated him, because they had not been entirely cooperative; one reason why they were still present. He hoped the uncomfortable overnight stay would loosen their tongues. Sean-Guy had learned in a preliminary interview that Davis was a secretary at the Ontario Justice Department. He thought she probably knew and had told very little. Still he couldn't afford to be lenient unless she was truly naive. That seemed like a possibility.

Gallaegher, on the other hand, seemed like a truly guilty individual, arrogant about his role as an Undersecretary to the Parliamentary Assistant to a very important minister of the province of Ontario. That of course was the Minister of Community Safety and Correctional Services, to whom the O.P.P. ultimately reported. That at the very least created a very awkward circumstance, since at least three divisions of the O.P.P. were now completely engaged in the anti-terrorism situation in which CAS now found itself. Gallaegher had been especially reticent, denying that he had revealed anything to anyone. Sean-Guy was considering the possibility of putting Angela in a situation that would make Gallaegher think his cover up was blown. Somehow he needed to break the man's bravado.

Angela, in the meantime, was demonstrating considerable attitude about her position. She had seen an elaborate operation involving a bomb squad unit, heavily armed officers and an extensive evacuation of several buildings surrounding the target location. She had seen two men armed with long arms, certainly rifles, perhaps even sniper rifles she thought. She had the address, but since there was no sign on the suite, did not know what was supposed to be inside. She was nearly completely confident that Sean-Guy was in charge of the whole thing. Now she wanted a statement from him, but wasn't sure how to begin her questioning. She was still a bit frightened of his demeanor which at the moment appeared to be fierce rage, if the expression on his face could be accounted for anything.

As she cleared her throat and made a characteristic deep breath, Sean-Guy held up his hand open palm forward while thinking.

It is her attitude that aggravates me, she is so arrogantly certain that she has a right to know every damn detail. Angela took the hand motion to mean don't speak right now. She closed her mouth but leaned forward as a challenge. Sean-Guy sighed mentally *I cannot fault her for her self-confidence.*

"I need to have you wait for me in the conference room. I must have a private moment with my Director," he said pointing towards the room. He waited while she got up and moved away, looking behind as she went. When she was inside the conference room with the door closed, he signaled though his computer link to Ottawa that he needed to speak with the Director. In a moment Leif came on screen. "Leif, I have a situation with the reporter Angela De Luca. She showed up this morning at our search operation on Shawson Drive. She clearly knows something, though at the moment I don't know how much. My question is how much shall we confirm about the operation?"

Leif was a bit surprised by the question, expecting that Sean-Guy would be more likely to tell him what he had already said rather than ask for advice, if that is what he was doing. He hesitated as he thought about what best to say. "You'll recall what I was told by the minister a while ago about the freedom of information rights held by Canadian media, so I cannot tell you outright that we have the right to withhold information. That said, I suggest you consider the prospect of confirming only what she does know." Leif considered that statement would throw the ball back into Sean-Guy's court. It was an expression of trust.

"Thanks Leif; that is more or less what I was considering. I'd be concerned about volunteering information that might make our suspect escalate or disappear completely." Sean-Guy then discussed the preliminary report from the O.P.P. Explosive Disposal unit's findings so far. He confirmed with Leif that they seemed to have a full blown terrorist threat ongoing now.

The Director responded, "I'll call the minister at home and let him know. Do you need any more resources?"

"That's a bit difficult to call at the moment. With our main suspect missing, we are concentrating our surveillance efforts on the other two known locations where he has been seen. But my best guess

Ron Stotyn

is he won't be back to those places. I think I need to do a search of the man's residence to see if we can find some clues as to his whereabouts. If he has actually moved to a new phase of his planning he has probably cleaned up after his last time there. When we have finished examining the bomb factory location we might have a better idea, but it's pretty vague so far." Sean-Guy did not mention that he still had some surveillance going on the Afghan suspect. He wasn't really thinking yet about any probable concrete connection to Marek and the nearly certain fact of his making bombs at Shawson Drive.

He took his leave from Leif and turned his attention back toward Angela. Before he went to speak with her, he went to find Stuart who had been interviewing Peter Gallaegher. Taking him aside so Gallaegher could not overhear, Sean-Guy told Stuart to take the man out for a rest room break in about 15 minutes, parading him past the Conference Room. He wanted the man to catch a look at Angela and perhaps think she also was being grilled. That might provoke a break in the man's flow of information, or rather lack of it.

Then he went to the Conference Room and entered, carefully arranging his face to what he hoped was a neutral expression. He was not entirely successful as his eyes betrayed some anger that Angela had penetrated the raid. "I'm now available to you for about 15 minutes" he said in a soft tone of voice, seating himself opposite her across the table so as to create a distance. The time limit he hoped would force her to avoid any small talk. He sat still and waited for her opening, his steel blue-gray eyes fixed upon her as he reflected how striking she actually was, especially with her expression of passion strongly exhibited. *I like this woman, but I can't take a risk with her until somehow I know her better. But how do I know her better unless I take some risk?*

{13}

"All truths are easy to understand once they are discovered; the point is to discover them." Galileo Galilei

CAS Offices, Mid-afternoon Saturday, April 8: Mississauga ON

Angela had used her time alone in the CAS Conference Room to compose herself and get organized with questions that demanded answers. Sean-Guy, when he came into the conference room, just sat still without saying anything to her. There was still some anger showing in his eyes, she thought. She put that out of her mind; not wanting to be cowed by his reaction to her presence at the strip mall site where she had observed the insert operation. She just launched into the first question she wanted an answer for. "Why did you evacuate several buildings on and near Shawson Drive this morning?" That was an incontrovertible fact and Angela believed the public certainly had a right to know why a Saturday morning's calm had been disrupted .

Sean-Guy replied with the planned cover story. "There was a report of a significant gas leak in the area. It was thought expedient to clear the buildings until that could be checked." Immediately on saying that he realized it wouldn't fly. She had almost certainly seen the bomb squad truck, which wouldn't normally respond to such an issue. He was proved right on his assessment as she came back with a challenging question.

"Then why on earth was the O.P.P. Explosive Disposal unit called out?"

With a slightly embarrassed tone of voice unsuccessfully hidden, Sean-Guy responded carefully by trying to reveal as little as possible. "We recently received information about extremely volatile chemicals inside the suite that we entered." He hoped that reply would disarm her suspicion and doubted at the same time that it would. *I keep failing to recall how sharp she is to see through cracks.*

Ron Stotyn

"Are you suggesting that those chemicals were volatile on their own or that there was actually a bomb-making factory inside?" she demanded with considerable insight displayed.

Sean-Guy knew he had to make a choice between the alternatives presented. "Yes," replied Sean-Guy reluctantly. *I am forced,* he thought, *to provide more specific detail and perhaps also now it was time to trust her, at least somewhat.* "Because of that possibility we would like to have you keep the address a secret to avoid the possibility of tipping off any involved person that the location has been found. We do need to find any possible suspect quickly."

She fired back without acknowledging the request and without hesitation. "What kind of chemicals and what kind of bombs did you find?"

Ah, she has made a fundamental mistake in her questioning. Two questions, a double barreled attack that I can defuse with a single vague answer. "I am unable to tell you. I haven't had a definitive report yet." That answer was only partly true since he did know what the explosives experts were pretty certain was the case.

Angela looked at Sean-Guy with an expectant expression, thinking he would add something more if she kept silent. After a very long moment, she decided it wasn't going to work. She decided to change course. "Why did you place snipers on the roofs opposite your target location?" Her question was speculative as she hadn't actually been able to see the rifles end up on any roof.

Not knowing exactly where she had been during their swat-like entry exercise, Sean-Guy could not be sure of what she had or had not seen. He decided she must know that particular truth. He thought, however, *the truth can be spin-controlled slightly.* "When we are in an uncertain situation, we try to place sharpshooters in a position to protect against unexpected dangerous confrontations involving weapons." He deliberately avoided confirming the concept of snipers, thinking *that word was a very negative concept for most civilians.*

Angela could not think of a retort question. His answer seemed entirely logical and yet she wasn't completely satisfied that he had told her exactly the truth. She moved to a question about the manner of entry that she had observed. "I saw the Bomb Squad enter first completely attired in protective gear. Why was that?"

"That was the call of Explosives Disposal Unit Leader Lt. Art Romanowski. His team is trained to spot potential problems when explosive materials are even a remote possibility." Sean-Guy added, "I consider it quite reasonable to follow the advice of experts." *That statement of course,* he realized, *belied my own inclinations; after all,* he reflected, *I planned to be one of the first through the door disregarding personal safety, a habit that has aggravated more than one superior officer.*

Changing direction again, Angela quickly asked what she hoped would be a disarming question. "Was this search conducted with a duly authorized warrant?" She observed what appeared to be the slightest grin on Sean-Guy's face.

"But of course. It would be illegal to proceed without one. My agency has a responsibility to remain within the law just as any other law enforcement group." Sean-Guy thought it unnecessary to admit they had not found anyone on which to serve the warrant.

Angela thought now she had him boxed in. Her next question, she expected, would force him to tell her about the CAS. "How is it that the CAS, an agency tasked with investigating terrorists would be conducting a search warrant entry on a building here in Mississauga?" Just then she was startled by the sight of Peter Gallaegher, her erstwhile lover and informant, being escorted past the window of the Conference Room. Dismay rushed over her face as she wondered why he was in the building. The officer escorting him looked rather grim. In a moment, they were out of her sight. As she turned back to Sean-Guy, she thought she saw a fleeting expression of satisfaction as if he knew that something important had just occurred. Then his expression was just as quickly back to a neutral state. She forgot what she had just asked him.

"Please excuse me," he said as he rose from his seat, thankful that her distraction allowed him to ignore the question. "I have duties I must take care of; may I see you to the exit?" That was important. He did not want any reporter around to possibly see what would happen next with Peter Gallaegher. He led her into the foyer and held the door

Ron Stotyn

open for her, waiting until she stepped through to follow her. "Oh, by the way, you didn't confirm that you would keep the address out of your story. That would be a big help to us. Okay?"

Angela, rather distracted by the condition of the last few moments, nodded and said, "Sure, that won't harm my story."

{13.1}

CAS Interrogation Rooms, Mid Afternoon Saturday April 8: Mississauga ON

As Angela left the building, Sean-Guy sighed and hoped he had defused what could be a bad situation. He wouldn't know if he had succeeded until he could see the story in the paper. *I suspect, however, that her tenacity and single-minded focus will result in something that might very well hurt us.* He remained frustrated by the situation she had created as he turned and went down the hall to the interview room where he would confront Peter Gallaegher once again. This time, he thought he had a wedge into the man's blustering attitude. Entering the room, he observed that Gallaegher was uncomfortable, no longer lounging in his chair. Stuart was standing in the corner, looking expectant. Catching Sean-Guy's eye, he nodded just the slightest degree. The ruse had apparently had a beneficial effect on Gallaegher's demeanor.

"Mr. Gallaegher, nice to see you again…. I hope our hospitality has been adequate. Was your breakfast acceptable?" Sean-Guy knew they had arranged for bacon, eggs and hash browns to be brought in from the Olympia Grill across the street. He could also see the remains of a roast beef sandwich from the same place, supplied for the man's lunch. Coffee, of course, came from the bottomless well of a coffee machine in the CAS's own kitchenette.

Gallaegher's reply was filled with unhappiness and a tinge of anger. "I have been here overnight. I had to try and sleep on the table. I haven't had a shower and I am being watched even when I need a bathroom break. I haven't done anything wrong. Why am I being held?"

Sean-Guy responded with all the charm he could muster, which several people could attest was never very much, especially at the moment, given the anger that was reflected in his steely gaze. "Peter....may I call you Peter....you have been terribly naughty with us. I know everything." Sean-Guy thought *I just cannot be positive until I hear it from him.* "What I need from you just now is for you to confirm to us what you told Angela, leaving nothing out please. By the way, we have just as much time as we need....to hear everything from you." *That should suggest he is in for a longer stay if he does not cooperate*, thought Sean-Guy as he looked at Stuart and saw him smile briefly at the comments. Gallaegher's shoulders slumped; a sign Sean-Guy took to be recognition that there was now no longer any point in withholding his story. With a sigh, Peter began to talk. Sean-Guy looked at the digital video recorder; it was on and running.

Twenty minutes later, Gallaegher finished his recitation of all the information he'd provided to Angela De Luca over the course of several meetings, which apparently had included time spent at his apartment and at hers. Sean-Guy noted that clearly included pillow talk. He had told Angela the circumstances surrounding the establishment of the CAS and who its principal staff was, including the names of the Director, Sean-Guy and Ryan, as well as several others in both the Ottawa and Mississauga offices. He had revealed details about the awkward relationship at the beginning with the O.P.P. He had provided information about the close links to the Department of National Defense and the fact that key personnel with previous military experience had been reappointed with various brevet ranks. There was financial information that provided the reporter with details about budget and supplementary fiscal resources from the ministry. There was even information about a possible threat by his own minister to try and undermine the task of the CAS in favor of an expansion of anti-terrorism duties of the O.P.P. within the province of Ontario. That last, an effort of sorts to make that sort of security a provincial responsibility instead of federal. Sean-Guy made a mental note to advise the Director of that fact right away.

"Mr. Gallaegher," said Sean-Guy changing the tone of the interview with his use of the last name. "I'm very glad that you decided

Ron Stotyn

to play nice with us, but I must tell you that you are not completely off the hook by coming clean. So I tell you again that this investigation of your activities will be ongoing under terms of the Security of Information Act. We will be questioning your superiors, so do not discuss any of this with them, or it may go very difficult for you. A decision about charging you with violations of the act may be forthcoming. Please do not attempt to leave the Toronto area without checking with us. Do you understand?"

With a somewhat sullen expression mixed with perhaps relief, Peter Gallaegher nodded and said with a stress-pitched voice. "I don't like what you have done to me, but yes, I do understand."

Sean-Guy looked penetratingly at Gallaegher for a long moment, his blue-gray eyes narrowed with a certain amount of disdain for the man's attitude, still tinged with arrogance even after there should have been stronger apprehension of being deeply in trouble. Then, looking over at Stuart, raising his eyebrow suggesting a chance to pose questions; Sean-Guy saw Stuart shrug and shake his head in the negative, so he turned back and said, "You are now free to return to your home. Please keep yourself ready for us in the near future; we'll be in touch again soon." He went to the door and held it open. "We will provide a ride for you to return to wherever you wish." As Gallaegher rose to leave Sean-Guy said casually, "Oh, one last question if you don't mind. Do you know Gabrielle Davis?" He wanted to check to see if there might be a connection between the two leakers.

Gallaegher reacted with a note of confusion. "Davis…Gabrielle Davis…who is she?"

Sean-Guy dismissed the thread; "Never mind, just someone I thought you might have heard of." He was now satisfied that Ms. Davis was essentially innocent of wrongdoing, but perhaps not innocent of being a gossip.

Sean-Guy motioned to Stuart to arrange the ride, pointing at an apparently unoccupied CAS agent and then turned to go to speak with Gabrielle Davis in the next interview room. He had not previously spoken with her but had watched a brief interview with her conducted by Stuart the day before. His recollection was that she was a mousey older woman, who was probably an effective secretary but clueless about the need for being circumspect about information she heard. He paused for a look at her again before entering the room. He was correct in his assessment, he thought. She looked haggard now after spending a night alone in an uncomfortable room. But, as he entered, he noted with interest the ordeal had not seemed to affect her appetite. The luncheon plate was cleaned off.

"Ms Davis," he said, in a soft tone, trying to set a scene of apology, "Please excuse this intrusion on your personal life. My name is Chief Inspector Sean-Guy O'Dwyer-Lariviere. I have oversight of this particular investigation," alluding to the interviewing process she had already been subjected to. "I have just one or two questions for you and then I think we can arrange to get a cab for you and let you go home." He hoped his smile was genuine and that his eyes reflected concern for her well-being. He took a seat at the end of the table more or less beside her. She looked at him and smiled weakly in return, which he took to be a good sign. "I'm sorry that this has been an ordeal for you, but we received information that you might have knowledge about a national security situation that is happening right now. We don't believe that you are involved, so please don't distress yourself any more. Before I continue with my questions though, I must tell you that this situation is a matter of national security and thus is covered by the Security of Information Act. Everything that you have experienced in the past day and the information that we think you might have for us is to be considered secret. You must not share this with anyone, even if one of your superiors asks about it. Is that understood?"

Gabrielle Davis sniffed and sat up straighter, looking now more in control. "Yes, I do and I do want to be helpful."

"Thank you," said Sean-Guy. "Now, I know some of this may have been asked and answered already, but please tell me again in any event, for my personal understanding. First, do you know a man by the name of Peter Gallaegher?"

"Yes," she responded, "That is, I know the name. I have seen it signed to some memos that came into our department."

"Do you recall anything about the content of those memos?

Ron Stotyn

"No, of course not," she replied with a somewhat haughty tone of voice. "I don't read materials that are marked personal for my employer."

Sean-Guy grinned mentally at that denial and asked in a manner intended to appeal to her ego, "But Ms Davis, I know that every superb secretary keeps close track of everything her boss is involved in so that she can keep him or her on track. Surely you do the same?"

"Well, since you put it that way," she admitted: "I do try to maintain a certain level of awareness. There have been some memos recently from Mr. Gallaegher that were asking about a new federal agency concerned with terrorism."

Sean-Guy, his interest now heightened asked, "And what happened to those memos?"

She responded, "I believe my boss passed them forward to our provincial Minister of Justice. What happened to them after that I couldn't possibly know!"

"Your boss never responded to Mr. Gallaegher?" Sean-Guy especially wanted to establish any links that the man might have created.

"Nothing came across my desk to be sent to Mr. Gallaegher. I'm certain about that."

Sean-Guy contemplated that information for a moment, then rose and offered his hand to Ms Davis. "Thank you very much for your cooperation. If you will wait just a bit, I'll arrange to have a cab come and take you home. We'll cover the cost of the trip for you. Thanks again for your important contribution to the safety of our country." He left her looking much more self-assured and perhaps even a bit puffed up from the praise he'd just offered.

Back at his desk, Sean-Guy sat for a moment contemplating what he'd learned from his two interviews. As Stuart came into the room, he beckoned and said, "Stuart, we need to assign a couple of investigators to follow up on Gallaegher's access to information. Ms. Davis is a dead end I think, but we need to discover what the Ontario Minister of Justice might have told Gallaegher. Some memos from Gallaegher were forwarded to that minister's office. We also need to interview the Parliamentary Assistant and the Minister in charge of the O.P.P., that would be Community Safety and Correctional Services I think. Find someone who is able to be very diplomatic. It won't do to have these people get unhappy with our inquiry."

With that bit of important business taken care of, Sean-Guy turned to his computer and opened the video link to Ottawa. He needed to alert the Director to the fresh news that the Provincial Minister of Community Safety and Correctional Services might still be thinking of ways to undermine the authority of CAS related to counter-terrorism activities inside Ontario.

{13.2}

Marek's residence, near Dundas Street West, about 9 PM, April 8th: Toronto ON

For the second time in just four days, Sean-Guy stood in deep shadow, across from Marek's apartment in Little Poland. Except for the change of days, it was almost like déjà vu. He'd decided he had to be again autonomous, telling no one of his intentions to break and enter; he knew also that intention would not gain approval from the Director, should he be found out. Leif had been very specific that the CAS could not act in any way that broke the law. But to enter without a justification....well, he felt he must; time was getting away from their now critical search for the suspect terrorist.

Technically, a search warrant was indicated for what Sean-Guy planned; the entering of Marek's apartment to try and discover something about the man's movements. But the circumstances lacked sufficient legal grounds. Only the fact that Marek had been seen at both the bomb making location and the apartment was relevant. There was no direct connection between the apartment and the bomb making that could be demonstrated as probable cause. He had nothing that would create likelihood to persuade a judge to sign a warrant. It would be considered a fishing trip. The alternative, not entering the apartment, wasn't at all satisfactory for Sean-Guy. To do nothing was to admit failure. So it became necessary to consider the third alternative, an act that defied everything he knew was proper under the

Ron Stotyn

law; an illegal search formed the basis for Sean-Guy's intentions now. *If I'm caught it will be the end of my very short career at CAS; therefore I must not get caught.*

The risk was more severe this time. Now there was by his direct order a doubled surveillance on the apartment. It would not do to be seen entering by his men, but he had to get in, he told himself: *It is critical to what we need to know about this man and his potential movements.*

He had carefully approached nearly the same location where he had waited earlier in the week to observe Marek enter. That turned out to be the front second floor flat of the converted house in Little Poland, not far from the Samovar House where he had first noticed Marek during the man's shift at work. Tonight he'd spotted both surveillance vehicles, one at either end of the block. Dressed as he was in a black running outfit and a dark duffle coat against the chill air, he didn't think he had yet been noticed, but he would have to move along very soon before one or the other observed that he'd stopped in the shadow.

He looked through the dark at the house and decided he would have to try and get into the back yard from the next block. He moved off toward the second agency car parked on the other side of the street just away from the corner of the block. Reaching the corner he strode briskly as if he was out for a nightly constitutional, passing behind the car and moving toward an alleyway. As he passed behind, he saw no movement to indicate any interest in a pedestrian passing by. A moment later and a hundred feet further on, he paused to look around and then made an abrupt right turn into the alley, suddenly deep in a stygian darkness. Picking his way carefully, he moved to the rear of the apartment building taking his position based on the large tree across from the front where he had watched earlier. He was at the edge of a small parking area at the rear of the apartment house. He wondered why they....no....he hadn't thought to put surveillance at the back of the house. It was another point to discuss at a meeting when post-mortem time came.

Now the question was how to get into the house without being seen. He couldn't go to the front where he would be seen by his surveillance teams in the light from a street lamp outside the front entrance. As Sean-Guy surveyed the situation, he could see a dim light through the door of what appeared to be a rear entrance. There was also a light from the second floor, a corner window, possibly a rear facing flat. A moment later that light went out, and an instant after that a shadow, came between the light and the back door. The back door opened as Sean-Guy moved deeper into the shadow of the yard next door. A figure went to the only car parked in the rear area of the house he was interested in. As the car backed out, Sean-Guy was suddenly caught in the glare of the headlights: he froze and wondered if he'd been seen. Apparently not, as he could see that the driver was looking behind as the car reversed into the alley and then pulled away, heading past and away from where he was standing near the corner of the parking area.

Sean-Guy still frozen, slowly realized his heart rate had gone up, and he had been holding his breath. *A close call,* as he took several deep breaths to get control of himself. *Clearly I'm not cut out to be a thief. I'll be old before my time if I'm not very careful. I have to decide, though, if what I just saw means there is a hallway from the back entrance to a central staircase. It seems very likely.* He decided not to hurry with his personal mission to explore Marek's apartment. *Better to wait and see if the driver might return after just a short errand. Of course, if I wait too long I run the risk of the person returning in any event.*

After what seemed to be an interminable time, Sean-Guy checked his watch and saw it was just a half hour since he'd arrived at the front of the residence. It crossed his mind: time to go in or time to leave altogether. In the next instant he moved with authority toward the door. Reaching it, his gloved hand on the knob, he twisted and was not much surprised to see it was not locked, a good sign that it opened into a common hallway. Entering he moved forward, quickly and as silently as possible, staying to the side of the hall where floorboards might be less likely to squeak. He wasn't keen on announcing his presence to any resident busybody, of which many apartment houses often had at least one. At the end of the hallway he was glad to see a set of stairs going up.

Ron Stotyn

He moved up the stairs, stepping at the outside edges in the hope of avoiding a squeaky tread. The stairwell came to a landing and then bent a 180 the remainder of the way to the second floor. He paused and listened, but heard nothing, again a good sign he hoped. At the top of the stairs he saw a small landing with two doors. He mentally oriented himself to be sure of getting into the correct apartment. The door he saw was secured by an old fashion lock set. There was no separate deadbolt, a fact that gave him a bit of relief. It would take too much time to break in had there been one. Moving closer, he bent and observed a significant gap between the lock and the door jamb. A credit card would be sufficient to open the door, so he set about to accomplish the task. In less than ten seconds he was inside, where he closed the door carefully and silently, all the while listening for any sign of anyone else being inside. Now, feeling surprisingly calm, he took out a small slim flashlight and began a careful study of the interior. He was in a kitchen. His sweep of light revealed a porcelain sink with one set of dishes piled, still dirty. The counter was empty, except for a small coffee machine and a toaster. He opened the fridge to find it was empty. The freezer section held a small package of what appeared to be lamb sausage. Opening the doors of the two small wall cabinets he found the remnants of western breakfast cereal and a box of muesli. Under the sink, in an open garbage can, were several take out boxes, including some unfinished rice and what was perhaps a lamb curry. None of it told him about the whereabouts of the tenant he was interested in. What he did learn was the tenant had not been gone much longer than the point at which his surveillance teams had lost him. But the trail of course was still cold.

Sean-Guy moved into the next room keeping his flashlight shielded and aimed low to prevent light being seen through the window. He moved directly to the windows and looked out to see an empty street, not able to see the parked surveillance vehicles from that vantage point. Turning his back to the window he played his light carefully on the walls. To his left he could see a table and on the wall behind a large scale map pinned to the wall. It was of Chechnya: that satisfied him he was in the right apartment. The map corresponded perfectly with what he'd seen in the terrorist's video. More interesting was a map that hadn't been seen in the video. Opened on the table surface was what turned out on close inspection to be a map of the entire Go Train system. Sean-Guy moved closer and lifting one corner carefully bent to see if there was anything underneath. He saw nothing.

Moving around to the wall side of the table he focused his light on the Go Train system map and found that several stations had been circled. There seemed to be no other written or printed notes anywhere on the map face. The marked stations included Oakville, Union, Scarborough, Oshawa, Agincourt, Stouffville, Oriole, Richmond Hill, Barrie, Aurora, York University, Georgetown, Bloor, Milton, and Erindale. Sean-Guy considered the list as he memorized the locations. It had no recognizable context, thus seemed to be meaningless. Knowing he would not forget what he had seen, he left the table and moving his light around the room at floor level, spotted three indentations in the worn out carpet, the kind that a tripod might well make. As he swung his light he was a bit surprised not to find any kind of furniture that would normally occupy a living space. That made his visual inspection easier, but still the lack of comfort was unusual, well at least not the ordinary expectation for a residence space.

Opposite the table was an open doorway. Surmising a bedroom, Sean-Guy moved toward it and looked through. Again, there was a lack of furniture. A mattress was in the corner directly on the floor, a small night table had a manual alarm clock. Bending to look at it, he saw the alarm was set for 4 AM, rather early for a person who worked a late shift at a restaurant, he thought. Beside the clock was a small table lamp. Turning toward the closet, Sean-Guy carefully opened the door, his hand on his automatic in case someone might be hiding inside. The closet was empty, completely and utterly. In fact it really didn't appear as if anything had been there anytime recently. At his full height Sean-Guy could easily see the shelf space. It was dusty.

Turning away, ready to leave the room, he swept the light around one more time, bent over and picked up the mattress and saw nothing. Letting the mattress go, it settled back to the floor slightly askew of its original position. In the gap left beside the wall, Sean-Guy saw a slip of paper. Picking it up by a corner he unfolded it and read a

Ron Stotyn

list of names, first names only it seemed. Several had checks and three had question marks. The names were: Fathi, Edris, Daoud, Omid, Gul-Bashra, Muhammad, and Abdul. The middle three names had the question marks. Looking at it a moment longer for it to be fixed in his memory, he carefully refolded it and replaced the slip where he had spotted it, then pushed the mattress back against the wall. *Again, I have something with no context, though there is something about those names that I should understand.*

Sean-Guy left the apartment as he had come, quietly and carefully, keeping to the side of the stairs to avoid creaky treads. As he went out the back door, it popped into his mind, that the name Omid was the same as the name of one Omid Faresh, currently under surveillance because of statements made about creating discipline of administrators at the Go Train System. Now, though the link was as tenuous as it could be, he was certain there was a connection with Marek Kafirov. That link was as likely as not to be serious indeed, and dangerous. The Go Train System map suddenly had context and he didn't like the implications.

{13.3}

Toronto Airport BestRest Inn, about 11 PM, April 8: Mississauga ON

The ride in Sean-Guy's restored police cruiser from Little Poland to the BestRest Inn near Pearson International Airport hadn't taken long following his break-in at Marek's apartment. He had parked several blocks away and walked to his immoral goal. He had returned to it without being seen by his surveillance teams. The hour was now late and the traffic was light. Sean-Guy was bothered, not about the break-in, but about the information found. It necessitated involving his team because of its critical nature. He had made a cell phone call to his assistant investigator. As he pulled up to the BestRest Inn, he saw that his phone call to Ryan had been swiftly acted upon. Ryan, Everet and Hari were waiting. They each had large coffees from Tim Horton's, which he hoped was helping keep them warm against the much colder temperature from earlier in the day. Snow was a distinct possibility again this night.

He hurried to invite them into his room, asking them to find a seat wherever they could. Shedding his coat, he took a position against the wall separating the sitting area from the bedroom. Hesitating, still unsure of how to involve the team members without implicating them in his improper search, he finally said, "Hari, if I were to give you a short list of names, would you be able to identify their likely ethnic origin?"

Everybody looked surprised at that question, unsure of what Sean-Guy was leading up to.

Hari responded with some uncertainty. "It depends on what corner of the world they come from, I suppose. But, yes maybe."

Sean-Guy, still trying to figure a way to protect his team announced, "First, I have to tell you that I cannot tell you where I got these names. In fact, it is probably best if you don't know that information."

Hari suddenly understood and cast a look toward his boss with a raised eyebrow. Everet, at almost the same moment, and Ryan, just a beat behind nodded their understanding; with Everet saying ironically in a low voice, "Been off the reservation, huh?"

Sean-Guy, realizing at that moment his reputation was no secret, gave a slightly embarrassed grin. "Okay, well, you just don't want to be implicated in that. So ask me no questions and I'll tell you no lies. Okay then, tonight just an hour or so ago I found a list of what appears to be first names. Hari, tell me what you can about these," as he recited them slowly, "Fathi, Edris, Daoud, Omid, Gul-Bashra, Muhammad, and Abdul. Oh….it's probably best if you don't write these down just yet." At a query from a thoughtful Hari, he repeated the list.

"The first one and last two names sound like typical male names from an Islamic segment of society. I cannot be certain about the second on the list, but I'd hazard a guess that it comes from one of the countries whose names end in 'stan' of the former Soviet Union. The middle three names do not seem to be quite the same as the other Islamic names, but there is certainly likelihood they have an Arabic connection. I'd guess they are Afghans. Oh....wait a minute....Omid is the same as the first name of the Afghan we've been watching at the Go Train yards in Barrie."

Sean-Guy nodded and replied, "Yes, I think that is a logical conclusion, given where I found the list. Let me tell you about the other piece I found. There was a Go Train System Map with about a dozen of the station locations circled: Oakville, Union, Scarborough, Oshawa, Agincourt, Stouffville, Oriole, Richmond Hill, Barrie, Aurora, York University, Georgetown, Bloor, Milton, and Erindale. I think we need to consider a possible context for these two separate pieces of information."

There was silence for quite awhile as the three chewed on what Sean-Guy had just told them. Ryan finally broke the silence with a terse statement. "It's a lead to Marek's crew and plans."

Hari added with a solemn tone, "This has just become a very big problem."

Everet said, implying a big verbal question mark, "We need a search warrant for Marek's apartment?"

Ryan responded, "Our grounds are thin though, don't you think? We need maybe to sleep on this."

"Please think very carefully about whatever grounds we have for seeking a warrant. I agree with Ryan but Everet is on target. We need to get this warrant and get it as quickly as we can. Shall we meet for breakfast at the Olympia Grill? "It was a question that Sean-Guy's team took as a strong suggestion not to be ignored.

{13.4}
Olympia Café, 6 AM, Sunday April 9: Mississauga ON

Sean-Guy hadn't had a good sleep following the meeting with his team the night before at the motel. After tossing and turning, then falling into a fitful sleep, he'd awakened at 4 AM. No more sleep seemed to be forthcoming so he got up and went for a run. It had snowed only very lightly, so his circuit around the light industrial district and back, out towards the King's Highway, which bordered the south side of the area, and north along the 410, was safe enough.

Returning first to get a quick shower at his room, he arrived at the Olympia Grill just as it was opening for the day's business at 5:30 AM. His breakfast finished and the dishes pushed aside, he was reading the headline story on the front page of the Sunday edition of the Toronto Star. That paper was not his favorite and thus not a normal read. He preferred the Globe and Mail, but this morning the Globe and Mail did not have the story about the CAS raid the day before. The Toronto Star did. The byline on the story was Angela De Luca. Seeing that name caused an unfamiliar reaction, partly disdain, partly admiration and certainly at the moment anger at feeling betrayed. That last he reluctantly acknowledged was unjustified. He read the article with a view to try and formulate a recovery of the high ground they needed to prevent a potential tragedy that he now believed was real and imminent.

The article was disturbing on several levels. The first was the full page width picture of agents entering the building on Shawson. Fortunately, the picture had been taken from a fairly oblique angle. It was difficult, probably impossible for most people to identify the building as any particular condo-strip mall anywhere in the Toronto area. The big question, however, was the degree of familiarity possessed by Marek. Would he be able to recognize his rented space?

The second worry was about the details of the raid, somewhat vague but accurate enough to cause concern about public reaction. A public panic about the real possibility of a terrorist attack close to home would create unimaginable control problems for the Canadian government.

The third issue was that the biographical detail about himself and some key members of the team was also accurate, if vague. It was publicity he did not care for. He didn't like being an open book and though the detail was very brief he felt exposed. Exposure was contrary to his need to keep the team safe from scrutiny by any possible terrorists. Sean-Guy's reaction was based on a new belief that to perform counter-terrorism well, he and his team had to be essentially as unknown as those they were searching for. This was a very basic notion that Sean-Guy had formulated out of a grudging respect for the ability of some terrorists to blend well with their locale

Ron Stotyn

as they plotted against the people living within it. He understood at the most fundamental level that most terrorists did not want public exposure, preferring to work from the shadows of society, popping in and out as quickly as possible to wreak their havoc. *I recall the exploits of the terrorist assassin known as The Jackal. That man's effectiveness had been chillingly efficient for years. For a terrorist to be exposed would mean a much higher likelihood of being caught before the terror plan could be executed.*

For Sean-Guy's team, the corollary meant that public knowledge of their existence could mean their investigational efficiency might very well decrease. Or it could mean a failure completely if the terrorist could more easily stay a step or two ahead in carrying out whatever attack was being planned. The bottom line was that the CAS effectiveness was now jeopardized. Sean-Guy recognized that some of his control had been purloined.

{14}

"Comment is free but facts are sacred" C. P. Scott in the Manchester Guardian, 6 May 1926

Olympia Café, 6:30 AM, Sunday April 9: Mississauga ON

Sean-Guy, having finished breakfast and with a second cup of coffee growing cold in front of him, was carefully rereading Angela De Luca's first article about the CAS. He had discovered, from nearly the first moment they met, that she had a real talent for getting under his skin. She was proving to be all her reputation said she was: smart, curious, and highly motivated to dig for the facts tenaciously. Not only that, but she was intrusive with nearly every part of her behavior. But, he somewhat grudgingly and increasingly with admiration admitted, *she is beautiful and highly desirable. Every time I see her, I have to concede I want a personal, indeed if I'm honest with myself, a more than social relationship with her.*

New Federal Agency Busts Suspected Terrorist Lab
Angela De Luca: Toronto Star Political Reporter

Normally quiet on the weekends, a light industrial district a few blocks from Dixie Road and the King's Highway in Mississauga close to Toronto Pearson was the scene of a highly contained but vigorous building invasion Saturday morning. Agents and supporting players of the Canadian Anti-Terrorist Service were active at the scene.

The target was an apparently empty industrial condominium, formerly a bakery, thought to be vacant for many months. It was not unoccupied in recent weeks according to the Director of the CAS Leif Isaksson, Brig Gen (ret). Isaksson confirmed that the site is believed to have been a location visited frequently by a person of interest. Isaksson declined to identify the individual.

The sweep of the building was conducted by the CAS under the supervision of CAS Chief Investigator Sean-Guy O'Dwyer-Lariviere, formerly a Detective Sergeant of the Sûreté de Quebec, recently based in Montreal.

Ron Stotyn

CAS agents were accompanied by members of the O.P.P., RCMP, and the Canada Border Services Agency (CBSA) as identified by jackets each was wearing. All were heavily armed with automatic weapons, assault rifles and shotguns. This reporter, present nearby, observed an O.P.P. Explosives Disposal truck outside the target suite. Attendant bomb squad technicians entered the building first, fully protected in heavily padded bomb disposal armor.

Chief Investigator O'Dwyer-Lariviere has yet to confirm the finding of any possible bomb-making components inside the building, saying only, "We need to wait for results of some testing of chemicals found inside to determine if they are related to possible explosive compounds." The O.P.P. Explosives Disposal Unit is known to be well equipped to provide such analysis.

At least two agents were observed carrying long rifles, one going behind the building target and one proceeding to a building across the street. At that building the agent was seen to take a position on the roof, much as a sniper would. O'Dwyer-Lariviere would not confirm that the riflemen were snipers, saying only that, "Whenever acting in a situation of danger, rifles are posted to protect the agents on the ground making entry."

The assault on a former bakery was swift, taking only a matter of moments to achieve an entry to the condo suite. In less than half an hour most of the agents were back outside packing up and gone shortly after. O'Dwyer-Lariviere confirmed that prior to the armed entry adjacent buildings and suites had been evacuated as a precaution. "It's protocol to protect civilians in the area as best we can. Evacuation to a safe distance is the best way to accomplish that. We also blocked off streets in the immediate area to prevent accidental infiltration of innocent individuals."

One agent, in charge of the command operations and communications vehicle, held this reporter at gunpoint for several minutes until getting a stand-down order after credentials were verified. He refused to answer any questions about the operation.

O'Dwyer-Lariviere, who consented to an interview at the scene, offered no apologies, saying that, "Presence of a reporter on the scene created added risk to the agents involved in the operation." He declined to explain why the operation included O.P.P. and CBSA agents. He said RCMP officers are routinely asked to provide assistance to the CAS as both are federal agencies.

The Chief Investigator is a no-nonsense individual, blunt and at times almost disrespectful in his responses. His team of agents, however, appear to regard him with fierce loyalty, amazing given that they have been a team for only a few weeks.

A highly placed source in the Ontario Government first revealed, just days ago, the creation of the CAS. The source was unable to say where the agency is headquartered, but it is believed the head office is located in the Parliamentary District of Ottawa. A Toronto Branch is located in a light industrial district of Mississauga not far from the location of the raid.

The Ontario Minister of Community Safety and Correctional Services, Douglas Angus Stewart, is known to have opposed the creation of CAS, having put it about in the inner circles of the Ontario Cabinet that his own O.P.P. through its Provincial Anti-terrorism and Hate Crimes division should have sole responsibility for combating terrorists within the province.

But with the actions taken yesterday, it is apparent that the CAS and the O.P.P. are getting along in a very cooperative fashion. Background information confirmed by the CAS reveals that the O.P.P. Anti-Terrorism and Hate Crimes Division, the Explosives Disposal unit and the Electronic Fraud Division have all been part of the investigation leading up to the raid.

The CAS has had a short existence so far, formally established just about three weeks ago by Federal Minister of Defense, Paul Mackey. His office told the Toronto Star that the Minister won't be available to make any statements about CAS until Monday, but did confirm that the new agency reported directly to the Minister. The new agency is responsible for combating terrorism within Canada as a mandate of the Department of National Defense.

The new Director of CAS is Leif Isaksson, retired recently as a Brigadier General commanding officer of CF Intelligence Services. Prior to that assignment, he led the CF Special Operations Forces Command rising to command position through the ranks. General Isaksson was born and grew up in Gimli MB. He is regarded as an officer of unusual intelligence who had a driven commitment to the work of the SOFC.

Chief Investigator Sean-Guy O'Dwyer-Lariviere is a native of Stanstead QC, and a retired Lieutenant in the CF Intelligence Branch. He is a graduate of the Royal Military College in Kingston with a degree in Political Science and Economics. He also has graduate

Ron Stotyn

degrees in Criminology from the University of Ottawa including a PhD earned in 1998. Following his retirement from the military he joined the Suréte de Quebec as a Detective grade Sergeant where he earned several awards, including the Croix de Bravouredes Policiers just last year for an act of heroism under exceptionally dangerous circumstances.

There are several additional individuals identified as employed at the CAS; however, neither Isaksson nor O'Dwyer-Lariviere were forthcoming about any other staff members, which apparently include the following.

Assistant Chief Investigator of the CAS in Ottawa is identified as Ryan McLeod, a retired Corporal after 20 years with the RCMP. McLeod served several terms with the RCMP Musical Ride but spent most of his career as a Liaison with the Canadian Security Intelligence Service (CSIS).

The Lead Investigator of the Toronto area branch office in Mississauga is Stuart McIntyre. Formerly a Staff Sergeant with the Edmonton City Police, McIntyre (retired) was a defensive end for a dozen years with the Edmonton Eskimos in the early 1980s.

The agent apparently in charge of Communications and Operations is one Hari Hanoomansingh. Little is known about this man except that it appears that he had a lengthy service with the Army of India, retiring with the rank of Havildar (Sergeant).

Considerable secrecy surrounds the CAS at this point. It is evident, however, from the event of yesterday that this agency has hit the ground running with considerable expertise and savvy.

(Editor's note: Ms De Luca was present at the site of the CAS action yesterday.)

Sean-Guy finished reading the article for the second time and looked up to see Ryan, Hari and Everet approaching his table. He greeted them without rising, motioning for them to take seats. Ryan signaled the waitress and asked for menus and coffee all around. The three did not look like they'd had much more sleep than Sean-Guy

"Have you seen this?" said Sean-Guy, pushing the paper toward Ryan.

Ryan looked, seeing the full page width picture of their raid at Marek's kitchen location and shook his head ruefully, knowing no good could come of it. Looking up into Sean-Guy's face he could see fury. "Who?" he asked, anticipating the identity of the author.

Everet muttered, "Seen it. It's trouble."

Sean-Guy looked at Hari, who shook his head. He pushed the paper further toward them and said, "Read it as soon as possible. It's written by Angela De Luca." Turning to Everet, he raised his eyebrow, signaling a query about his take.

"Publicity is too early. Our man might disappear or accelerate."

Sean-Guy, with an exasperated explosion of air agreed. "That damn reporter can't keep her nose out of things. She has broken a promise made with me. I'd like to throttle…," then, breaking off as he suddenly realized she had not broken the promise. The article had carefully avoided any mention of the video made by Marek Kafirov. "Actually," he said thoughtfully, "She did not really break the promise."

"What promise," asked Ryan with an expression of confusion on his face.

Sean-Guy, with more than just a tinge of embarrassment in his voice, realized he hadn't filled them in on the meeting with the Managing Editor of the Toronto Star with Angela present. He began a brief explanation, venting as he proceeded. "I went the other day to interview Daniel O'Donnell, the managing editor of the Star. I took Angela with me and extracted a promise they wouldn't publish anything about the videotape threat in exchange for allowing opportunity to write about the CAS generally. It's my own damned fault I didn't insist on a promise that covered the scope of our current activities. That god-damned woman slipped through the crack I left," he finished shaking his head in quieting anger at himself.

Hari, having skimmed through the article while Sean-Guy was speaking, looked up and observed tentatively, "It might give us a wedge for the search warrant."

Sean-Guy, startled by the observation, looked at Hari and snapped, "How so?"

Hari carefully considered his response, hesitated and then said, "A tough minded judge might consider this reasonable probable cause if we carefully show the physical connection between Marek's movement between the apartment and the bakery. After all, we have unbroken surveillance of this happening, expert witnesses if you will. And, of course, finding evidence of and confirming the presence of bomb-making components could only help our cause."

Sean-Guy mused out loud, saying in a low voice, "Okay, I see the point. We'll need Stuart to get on this right away. I'd better call him and get him to come into the office as soon as possible. We'll need sworn affidavits from the surveillance teams. Ryan, please call the bomb squad guys and see if they can push their analysis. And we need to find a judge who'll work with us on a Sunday. Merde, we have to turn this into a break for our side."

Everet, shaking his head, reiterated, "Still trouble. The picture confirms the location. Our presence makes a terrorist inference."

Sean-Guy, forced to agree added, "Yes and the story places the location within a relatively small area of Mississauga. Fairly easy for Marek to realize he has been exposed. We also have public reaction to be concerned about." Then thinking out loud he asked, "Is there any way to deflate the possibility of panic? Don't forget that video is still up on You Tube. We couldn't get them to take it down. And even though the rest of the regular media agreed not to do anything with the video story, I'd be a pitiable cop if I didn't believe they'll break that aspect of the whole story now that the Star has published this."

Hari thoughtfully suggested, "We need some disinformation I think. That was one of the ways we tried to combat terrorist communication when I was on the border with Pakistan during my army days."

Ryan observed, "The video might be the most damaging. If the news people go with it that creates a credible link to the search we did. But maybe we can spin the Star's story by reporting that we found nothing in the way of explosives on the inside of the bakery. That's the most of the truth. That way the public reaction would likely be diminished. We can only hope the terrorist doesn't see the story or isn't concerned about possible harm to his plot."

"The video has its own credibility gap, that we can leverage," said Sean-Guy. "Marek does not identify a location for his plot. He says nothing about where his action will take place, not even a country name. We can get the Director to do a press conference right away, maybe even with the Minister to push the video into the realm of the implausible. Make it out to be a hoax as best we can. And, using Ryan's idea, they can be devious about the findings from the raid. That might give us the time we need to find the bastard."

Hari asked "Is there a way that we can get Angela De Luca up to Ottawa without her suspecting anything? Appeal to her ego maybe?"

Sean-Guy responded, "I'll bet a call to her Managing Editor tipping him about the press conference, especially if the Minister is on board, will get her on a plane. We could get Betty Anne to make that call as if on behalf of the Director. I'll go over to the office now and get a hold of the director to get this stuff started. Finish your breakfast and get over there as soon as you can. We have a lot more 'what-if' planning to do today."

{14.1}
Marek's Kitchen, about 9 AM, Sunday April 9: Mississauga ON

Sean-Guy with Everet close behind, approached the rear door of the location they had broken into yesterday, their previously obtained search warrant in hand. Surveillance was still in place on the off-chance Marek might return, though Sean-Guy suspected he was done with the place. He'd alerted his surveillance teams that they were coming over. The location was deliberately devoid of any obvious evidence of yesterday's events in and around the building. Normal crime scene tape had not been put up since they didn't want to tip off the terrorist if that was what Marek actually was. A light snow overnight had somewhat obscured the many tracks made by the team that had entered the building on the sweep search.

Sean-Guy was acting again on an independent streak sparked by intuition rather than firm or concrete evidence, looking for something, anything, which might have been missed the day before.

Ron Stotyn

He had, contrary to his initial instinct to act alone, brought Everet along thinking the First Nations member might see more than he could by himself. Sean-Guy knew that his thought was probably racially motivated and stereotyping, but he put some stock in the unique heritage of Native Americans who had eons of experience dealing with sometimes minute changes in their environment. The reality was that he had absolutely no idea if Everet knew anything at all about tracking. He'd called Everet to his side following a brief conversation earlier in the morning with the Director. They left Hari, Ryan and Stuart to construct an argument for obtaining a search warrant on the other two locations where Marek had been observed. It now seemed imperative that they get into the apartment and his place of employment before much more time passed. They needed to find clues as to his possible whereabouts, if such clues existed. It could prove very bad indeed to let the man stay out in the general public for very long.

Upon his arrival at the CAS Toronto office across from the Olympic Grill prior to 7 AM, Sean-Guy had immediately placed a call, using his encrypted Blackberry, to the Director's home. He was confident that the early hour would not upset Leif, especially given the sensitive nature of the probable terrorist situation, now exposed by the Toronto Sun's front page story. He assumed the story was not yet read by his commander, so he suggested that Leif call up the story at the Sun's website and had almost patiently waited for the director to read it. Their ensuing discussion led to an inevitable decision that the Minister had to be engaged without delay. Leif was willing to be persuaded that a search warrant was needed to get into Marek's apartment over in Toronto's Little Poland district realizing, with Sean-Guy's team, that their grounds were rather stretched far from any kind of gravitas. He also agreed to discuss with Defense Minister Paul Mackey the need to find a tough-minded but friendly judge in Mississauga so that Stuart could argue for a broad search warrant. Though their minister was not directly connected with the Department of Justice, it was expected that he would be able to ask a favor of the Justice Minister to find an appropriate Federal judge. It seemed probable that the Defense Minister could ask his colleague to identify such a judge.

Leif and Sean-Guy, during the course of the discussion about that issue, had also come to the conclusion that Marek's place of work, the Samovar House should be included in case Marek had a locker or some kind of cubby that might contain details or items of interest. As soon as they could get a search warrant executed, Stuart would lead a team of forensic specialists from the O.P.P. to Marek's apartment while Ryan and Hari would go to the restaurant.

Sean-Guy's discussion with Leif concerning the Defense Minister's involvement prompted Leif to decide he would make a strong representation for adding to the planned Monday press conference by forwarding a brief statement to the media as soon as possible. His sentiment was to ask the Minister to come to the Ottawa CAS office to forge an appropriate message. Alternatively, Leif was prepared to go to the Minister's Parliamentary Office. The particular goal, stage-managed by both Leif and Sean-Guy, was designed to urge the Minister to focus on the idea that the video threat might be a hoax without actually saying that. They were banking on the Minister's ability to put a political spin on the matter. They would also ask for some diversion of the question of possible bomb-making materials found during the entry of the suspect location the day before. Deflecting that piece of information would mean, they hoped, that the suspected terrorist would be persuaded he was still safe and still in the wind.

The truth of the matter, that Sean-Guy was forced to admit to Leif, was that they had absolutely no idea where Marek was at the moment. Success of that overall plan depended on whether or not the Minister was even in Ottawa, given the fact it was a weekend day and most MPs and Cabinet members typically went to their home constituencies if there was nothing significant requiring their presence near Parliament.

As the conversation concluded, Sean-Guy suggested that Betty Anne be given the task of calling the Managing Editor, Daniel O'Donnell, of the Toronto Star to plant the thought that Angela De Luca should come up to Ottawa for the press conference planned for Monday morning. Leif agreed to call Betty to make that request and to have her arrange for René Girau to be available at the press conference

Ron Stotyn

in case any questions arose about terrorism in Canada. The three would put their heads together to arrange a response that was truthful in the broadest possible terms while deflecting or dismissing the possibility the Toronto affair was a full-blown problem.

With the conversation complete, Sean-Guy and Everet had headed out in Sean-Guy's antique police cruiser bound for the lab located in the abandoned bakery. The cruiser was parked down the block away from the building in case any possible and curious terrorist might happen along. The surveillance teams were ready to alert the pair in the event Marek showed up.

As he approached Sean-Guy, suddenly halted a full ten feet away from the rear entrance door and stared down at the base of the overhead door that was a vehicle entrance into the bakery. Everet immediately focused his attention to the same place and then got down on hands and knees putting his head close to the ground. It was light enough to see any shadows that might exist, even though the sunshine was weak because of an overcast sky. He shortly announced, "A vehicle left this door sometime before that last snowfall overnight."

"How on earth do you see that?" Sean-Guy asked, though he did think he knew. Then he breathed out slowly, carefully trying to understand the implication. "That would possibly suggest why the surveillance never saw anyone leaving from here. We're damn lucky that there was no snow removal this weekend. Anything else you can tell me?" he asked optimistically.

Everet grunted, "Maybe a truck or a van. Not the kind of tires from a car."

Sean-Guy got down on his hands and knees to see if he could see what Everet saw. He could see the hint of a long indentation, actually two tracks, but could not determine any detail. Shaking his head mentally he got up and stood looking down in contemplation. "Probably, I should call Stuart to launch some kind of search, but for what exactly?" Motioning to Everet he said, "Let's see what's behind door number two." He removed a lock pick from his pocket and opened the standard access door that was beside the overhead doorway.

Once inside he said to Everet, "Apply your skills please to the loading dock area and then work your way into the bakery area. You haven't been inside before so you have fresh eyes. I need to know the slightest unusual detail." He turned to go forward, deeper into the building and then noticed that Everet was already squatting with a flashlight held obliquely to the floor. "What is it?"

Everet replied, "Fairly fresh paint spots here and some dripping about five feet over. If a van or truck was backed in, the doors would be parallel to this spot."

Sean-Guy musing, asked, "Are you thinking a paint job on the vehicle?"

Everet shook his head, "My hunch is a sign on the doors."

"OK, please keep on looking," said Sean-Guy as he moved away.

Sean-Guy took out his own flashlight, switched it on and went into the area where they had seen evidence of chemical use. He was not at all certain he could or would find anything as he was confident the O.P.P. Bomb Squad and his own agents had been thorough, but he could not psychically avoid doing his own search. His method of searching was to stand in the center of a space and methodically turn in a circle slowly, looking sharply at everything within his range of sight. Then he repeated the move squatting or kneeling as needed to see lower levels. Finally he usually then moved close to the walls or furnishings, bending near to examine surfaces. He never touched anything.

On this occasion following his second turning, he spotted an odd shadow below a bench. It was just inside the far left side leg. Moving as close as he could and directing the flashlight's beam of light across the floor, he found a thin cylindrical object with a bit of wire protruding from one end. He took out a pair of tweezers and a small Ziploc bag. Reaching out, he captured the wire end and lifted the object carefully and placed it into the bag. Holding the bag up in front of his flashlight beam; he decided he was looking at a very sophisticated detonator. That, he was certain, was the icing on the cake. Looking up he saw that Everet had come in and apparently had been watching his silent scrutiny.

Ron Stotyn

"You saw me get this?" He asked. A witness for the chain of evidence would be a good thing.

Everet grunted, "Sure. A detonator, huh!"

Sean-Guy looked expectantly at Everet. "Find anything out there?"

"Pile of paint cans. Small black paint recently opened. Paint brush with paint matching the spots." Then he produced a set of license plates from behind his back. "Found these pushed down behind some flat bread boxes."

Sean-Guy looked close at them and then with pleasure said, "I'll bet those are plates issued to a rental company for a truck or a van. Truck plates here have four numbers and two letters, black on white, just like those. This gives us a possible lead. We can trace the plates and find out what kind of vehicle they were on. If they are rental plates that might help us look for the driver. We need to check for fingerprints." Then, as some reality invaded, "Could we be so lucky?"

Everet just gave an expressive shrug.

"Well," said Sean-Guy "Take a look around in here. See if you can spot anything we might have missed yesterday."

About 30 minutes later as they left to go back to the cruiser and then to the office they had found nothing else. Still Sean-Guy felt their search had been productive. They had two items that seemed to add possibilities to their investigation. Once back at the office Sean-Guy determined that it would make sense to have Thea run a data search for stolen credit cards used at vehicle rental agencies. It was a long-shot but if they could match the plates to a rental vehicle and a stolen credit card that might bring them a step closer to Marek's activities. The problem with that idea was that the plates were no longer attached to a vehicle. Actually finding a rental vehicle that belonged to the plates would be very difficult indeed. Sean-Guy amended his thought about tracing the vehicle. Unless the vehicle turned up identified as abandoned, they would have little or no success on that score, he thought. They would have to find out about stolen license plates in the greater Toronto area as well. Discarded plates more than likely meant a different set had been put on the missing vehicle.

Tracing the detonator would probably be a hard task as well, but it did look like conclusive evidence that bomb making was a strong likelihood at the former bakery. The O.P.P. Explosives Disposal Unit leader Art Romanowski would be needed to help identify the make and likely source of the detonator as soon as possible.

{14.2}

Lakeshore East Line, Sunday April 9, approximately 9 PM: Scarborough ON

Marek was satisfied that all was well with his Go Train System suicide bombing plan. Not his own suicide of course, his time was not yet dictated, but those of a seriously committed group of terrorists comprised of Chechen and Afghan Muslims. Their reward in Paradise was now just days away.

The past three days had been grueling. His expertise with driving a van on snowy streets and roads had been extremely limited. The result was rather harrowing due to his inexperience with the kind of winter weather that Toronto was enduring of late. His ordinary practice of using buses and trains was interrupted by his need to carefully distribute his 37 bombs to secure pickup locations without drawing any undue attention. It meant using the rented van to navigate through a large regional area to the extremes of central Ontario, including destinations in Burlington, Barrie, Richmond Hill and Oshawa. His habitual use of public transportation also meant he was completely unfamiliar with the best road routes to get his packages to where they needed to be for his cell leaders to pick up. He had, however, tried to plan thoughtfully, despite a lack of actual route experience. By using a well marked road map of the region and by paying close attention to road and street signs he had not gotten off track. Still, because of the weather, his best estimate of the time needed to drop off the disguised bombs had been inordinately off the mark.

His last packages were deposited in passenger storage lockers in the Oshawa Train Station well past midnight; many hours past his goal. The lateness of the hour meant that he had missed the last train

Ron Stotyn

headed west. That meant his plan to reach a motel destination in Oakville had to be abandoned. The reservation for that place was with a stolen credit card so it didn't matter that he would never show up. By the time the motel realized they had been ripped off, he'd be long gone anyway. He was also forced as a result to change his plan to abandon the van in Oshawa, though his afterthought was that taking the van to Scarborough might turn out to be a useful decision. Distance between the last place the van was possibly seen in the vicinity of a train station and its place of abandonment would surely be for the best. Scarborough was a large enough destination to find an alternate form of lodging for the night. He had been lucky, finding a place to stay just above flophouse standards not far from the Go Train Station in Scarborough. Cash was the expected form of payment and the sleepy night clerk would be unlikely to remember him, despite the fact he'd not checked in until almost three AM. It was an independent weekly rates residence hotel, frequented, it seemed, by the very poor whenever they could gather enough money to afford indoor accommodations for awhile. His revised plan to stay at the hotel for a week or more would not be complicated by the night clerk, whom he never expected to see again. He would not be outside his small studio suite during the hours of that person's shift.

He'd managed to get just four hours sleep before getting up to rush to the Go Train Station for a west-bound trip. He'd scheduled his first cell leaders meeting in Oakville. The van had remained parked on a side street a few blocks away from the weekly rate hotel, where it would likely be unnoticed for days, if not stolen before then. Now, more than 12 hours later, Marek was ready to disembark the train from Oshawa, having completed his current and indeed last cycle of informational and spiritual support meetings with the three groups of cell leaders. His own spiritual situation was presently at odds with his habitual religious practice of obeying the call to prayer five times daily. Being on the road and in public to and from the meetings meant he'd been unable to pray facing Mecca at the appointed times. He did not suppose he would be punished by Allah for carrying out a sacred task instead of being at prayer as required. To be certain of staying in Allah's favor, however, he resolved to spend additional time in prayer for the coming days at each of the times for prayer beginning immediately with ISHE, the nighttime prayer, as soon as he reached the residence hotel.

{14.3}

The Manor House Suites, Brimley Road, 9:30 PM, April 9: Scarborough ON

Marek left the westbound train and headed for the Manor House Suites, where he would wait patiently for the anointed hour of the explosion schedule on Monday a week from tomorrow. The poorly appointed studio-style suite was satisfactory. It had a basic kitchenette and a working color television set where he could tune in both the CTV and CBC television channels along with a few other stations. He was interested only in those where he could get the news of the expected aftermath of the explosions. As soon as that was complete, he would leave for his next assignment, using a new set of false documents and a new beardless appearance.

For the moment, he thought about his instructions delivered earlier in the day, at three different locations, to his three groups of cell leaders, and his exhortations to reinforce their resolve to die gloriously for the cause. Never had he spoken to them of suicide, for that of course, was forbidden in Islam. His advice and exhortation was always about the right to accept martyrdom in a jihad against their enemies.

As normal, he'd begun with the cell leaders in the Oakville area. They had met for breakfast and then had moved to a private room in an Islamic social club where one of the leaders was a semi regular visitor. Giving instructions for picking up the bomb packages was straightforward as was handing out keys to the storage lockers. Each key was carefully tagged in Chechen with locations specified for placement of the bombs. Though each cell leader would decide which of his own cell members should go to the specified locations, Marek had directed which of the bomb packages in their carry-on disguises should be used by the selected terrorist. He had wanted to be sure that there was a variety rather than a similarity of packages. Each cell was told in absolute terms to follow a strict schedule for pickup and

Ron Stotyn

placement. Early morning times were preferred on the assumption
fewer curious witnesses might be around. Marek insisted they must
complete the pickups by Wednesday.

This first group could be relied on to follow that mandate, for
they were fellow Chechens; Fathi Batal al-Shishani and Edris Gaziev.
Marek was aware that each had been carefully chosen many months
ago, had passed many tests of loyalty, and had accepted into their
deepest being the tenet of their Wahhabist trainers that martyrdom was
the key to Paradise. Still, he entered into a strenuous discourse with
them with the intent to strengthen their resolve. He was confident that
they would do the same with their cell members.

He began by reminding them that their task was not just an
intention any longer, but rather a sacred act ready for fruition. That
they were called suicide terrorists by the foreign media should not, he
had said, "make them think they had abandoned Islam. They were
indeed, each of them Islamic heroes....Jihadists....carefully prepared
to take revenge to heart in a way calculated to bring sudden and
terrible violence to their enemies." He reminded each leader of the
violent attacks they and their families had endured. It was a vengeance
bound truth that many of their kin had not survived the rapes and
murders committed by the Russians. It was also true that their beloved
homeland had been severely torn nearly to the breaking point and that
politically, culturally, and spiritually their goal was completely
justified by Allah to restore what had been stripped.

Concerning their mission in Canada, Marek reminded them
that the Qur'an at 22:39 gave them explicit permission to fight non-
believers and that Allah was eminently able to give the victory. Indeed,
said Marek, 4:76 made it clear that their enemies were in fact friends
of Satan who deserved no compassion. "We fight because we were and
are attacked on every front." He made it clear that any friend of an
enemy was equally an enemy. "Any nation that permits acts of
immorality is an enemy," he declared with the utmost belief. It was of
course entirely a matter of his own interpretation. He did not think of
the possibility that he might be wrong.

There was no doubt in Marek's mind, and so he told his cell
leaders that Allah was the ultimate legislator of permission and option

to take revenge. He declared with absolute confidence in that wisdom of Allah, "Thus, whenever attacked, we are obligated in return to attack our enemies. Whenever our villages and towns are destroyed, we are obligated to destroy the towns and villages of our enemies. When our wealth and property are taken unjustly from us, we are obligated to take the economy away from our enemies. When our civilians are decimated, we are obligated to kill the civilians of our enemies."

Marek believed that Islam was a nation of martyrdom, that martyrdom was not only permitted but was in current circumstances a demand of the faith. "Martyrdom," he said "desires death more than you can desire life." Again he quoted the Qur'an, wherein 3:169-171 revealed that, "The dead are alive in their Lord and are being provided for and are rejoicing in grace and beauty, with all that comes from Allah." Again he pointed out that this passage promised the faithful that Allah will not waste any "reward of the believers." Marek reiterated that 58:21 promised that Allah's messengers shall be victorious. He did not comment about the widely held belief by the majority of Muslims worldwide that peace was an abiding tenet of the faith. That was not a theme of Wahhabism; which he believed was the correct view of Islamic life.

Then he joined in prayer with his brothers of the cause. Even though it was still well before ZUHR, the noon-time prayer, Marek believed that extra prayer was desirable to cement the resolve of his cell leaders. He finally embraced his Chechen brothers in arms, confident that they would not see each other again except in Paradise. Indeed, he told them they should make no future attempt to either contact him or accept any contact from him. Leaving without any other ceremony, he hurried to catch the first bus and several more that would take him to Barrie to meet with the three Afghan cell leaders.

It was more than two hours later before Marek arrived at the rendezvous with his Afghan leaders; Daoud, Omid and Gul-Bashra. They met for a noon-time meal, as he had done for breakfast earlier in the day with the first group of the Chechen cell leaders. It was especially important to do that, he thought, to build upon a sense of camaraderie and brotherhood with his Afghan compatriots. These men,

Ron Stotyn

he understood, would likely value that greatly, the concept of brotherhood being heavily stressed in Wahhabist training. As he had also done earlier he moved the meeting, after the meal, to a more private location, this time to a back room at a chess club used several weeks earlier for a meeting. Sufficient time had passed that Marek was comfortable to reuse the facility without any notice from anyone. Again, following the delivery of instructions about pickup and placement of the bombs, Marek handed out the locker keys. The key tag labels had been printed using Dari, the language which he knew his Afghan cohorts understood being Tajiki and of which he was sufficiently familiar to create the location instructions. Again, he expected that these leaders would make logical assignments and would follow his directions about which disguised packages should be distributed to the carriers.

His discourse approach differed somewhat to that which he had delivered at his morning meeting. He began with an approach intended to appeal to the Afghani sense of manhood. From his own terrorist training he realized that it would be beneficial to have the Afghans appreciate that their training could make them truly invisible and thus well able to carry out their task without fear. It was important to reinforce the terrorist training and indoctrination of the idea that terrorism was their new occupation, one that calls men forth to define themselves as manly. He knew from his own training that the Taliban way included teaching young boys that the only way to be a real man is to prepare for death in the service of the cause. A key support for their sense of being men would be to assure them that becoming a martyr can only mean they would become dominant men. He wanted them also to adopt the idea that in becoming a dominant male they would in fact be defining their own terrorism, and that they were in control.

Knowing also that they would probably hold Bin Laden in greater regard than his own Chechen countrymen, he added words from that man's teachings. He especially included the idea Bin Laden had used based on Surat Al-Ahzab 33:70-71 of the Qur'an, "That He may make your conduct whole and sound and forgive you your sins: He that obeys Allah and His Messenger, has already attained the highest achievement." Bin Laden, of course, was focused on the idea that by making every deed right Allah would achieve a mighty success. Marek, thinking that both a carrot and stick were useful, added a thinly veiled threat used by Bin Laden: One can expect punishment if one fails to see an oppressor and then also fails to restrain that oppressor.

Marek reminded the Afghan cell leaders that Bin Laden had spoken about injustice, the impact on industry and agriculture, on both rural and urban areas committed by the oppressors of Afghanistan. Marek had no doubt but that that would strike a chord with the three, in the full knowledge that their country was a mere shadow of its former self. Marek assured them it was also true that western media in particular was guilty of misdirecting the truth, that it acted essentially as an agent of the enemy, and functioned largely to spread scandal among believers. He then stressed the idea that there is no more important duty than to push the enemy out of the Holy Land, another theme from Bin Laden's messages.

Marek also quoted Ibn Taymiyyah, "To fight in defense of religion and Belief is a collective duty; there is no other duty after Belief (more important) than fighting the enemy who is corrupting the life and the religion." Marek understood that as a reinforcing call to sacred brotherhood, a matter that he had always been concerned about with regard to the Afghan component of his planned retribution to Canada. Brotherhood felt and acted upon in concert with the Chechen cause was critical in this situation. He'd closed his exhortation with a reiteration that enemies should be fought with one's best abilities, in this case the expertise for placing bombs where they would do the most effective work of revenge.

The last thought shared was that there was no exemption from the duty of Jihad against the enemy. As Marek left to go to the third meeting of the day he encouraged them to spend the day's late afternoon ASR prayer seeking to accept the blessing of Allah's reward soon to be placed upon them.

Another round of bus travel was required to get from Barrie to Union Station where he could finally get on an east bound Go Train to Oshawa. That was due to a weekend reduction by the Go Train System

Ron Stotyn

that eliminated trains to and from Barrie. The train eastbound from Union Station was lightly used at that mid-afternoon period of the day, which satisfied Marek. He had spent the travel time meditating on the rightness of his masterful plan, as he tended to characterize what he had rendered. He also had looked forward to one last meeting with the two Chechen leaders, Muhammad Yamadayev and Abdul Saidullayev, in the eastern zone of his organization's bomb distribution area.

He really considered them true brothers, both Chechens from the same area in which he had grown up. Both of them recruited about the same time. He did not know their real names, theirs had been changed before their first meeting, but knowing the names was not important. What was important was his certainty they were as diligent in their Wahhabist acceptance of their proper fate as was he. He knew they had completely accepted the soon to be awarded reception into Paradise where they would enjoy sexual favors forever. His own time for that reward was still sometime in the future, but he waited expectantly for the same outcome when his usefulness would finally be complete.

Once again, he had amended his discourse to meet the needs of his friends. The emphasis on pickup and placement of the bomb packages had been presented as before, in confidence that there would be no errors. As to spiritual support he was more encouraging than demanding, sensing that these two leaders were confident in their faith. He'd simply reminded them theirs was a just cause because of the misery each had endured at the hands of the Russians. He spoke of what all of the three, himself included, already knew that by taking a martyr's approach to revenge they would be glorified. He recalled for them that the Qur'an Sura 9:29 calls for submission to Allah and that their basic task was to subdue everyone to full submission under Islamic rule. Part of that meant, of course, that they had a duty to fight any who would not believe. Marek understood, with his brothers that Jihad was the best method of earning temporal and spiritual readiness for entry into everlasting Paradise. He had reminded them of the Qur'an 4:74 which promised, "For the fallen and victorious alike, the rewards are instant and plentiful; for whoever fights in God's path, whether he is killed or triumphs, we will give him a handsome reward." The ultimate goal, he said to this last meeting of leaders was simple and clear: The Verse of the Sword 9:5 states directly, he assured them, kill the unbelievers. The importance of the mission he added meant they did not need to be concerned about civilian casualties. They were part of the enemy forces.

With Marek's discourse completed, he joined his friends in prayer for it was time for the late afternoon prayer of ASR. When it was done, he and his two strongest cell leaders came together for a meal before he left them to fulfill their duties.

Now well after 10 PM, secure in his room at the residence hotel, Marek came to what for him was an inescapable conclusion: Canada would face a dangerous future. In a week its calm, self-assured attitude would be broken by the decimation of an important transportation system. Soon the citizens would understand that their country had followed the wrong path and that chastising the Russians could have saved the recourse that was being visited upon them. Marek was sure that he would not be able to count how many would be killed as justification for their grievous error. It was long past time for this revenge to be engaged. In the morning he would shave his beard as he prepared to see the consequences and then disappear until reassigned.

Ron Stotyn

{15}

"My house and yours, your bus terminal and my train station, our children's schools—all of them and all of us are on a terrorist's hit list." Jacob Perry, Former Director: Israeli SHABAK, 2009

CAS Toronto, Sunday April 9, about 8:30 PM: Mississauga ON

Sean-Guy was working late at the office, not that unusual in the midst of a case, writing by hand a daily journal of events in his characteristic and uniquely personal shorthand. It was a highly adapted, one might say bastardized, version of Gregg Shorthand he'd learned from a high school course at Stanstead College. Sean-Guy knew that Gregg Shorthand was hardly ever taught anymore so he supposed that very few people would be able to read his journal, not that it would matter much if they could. He only wrote the most important elements of the case as an exercise to verify his eidetic memory. He connected with the basic Gregg form because he enjoyed its compact style and the way he could make it flow.

He wrote first of the Minister of Defense, the Right Honorable Paul Mackey, who had acted decisively following a call to his Ottawa residence by Leif Isaksson, Major General and CAS Director. Sean-Guy had been included in a conference call. His notes recorded that both Leif and Sean-Guy had been relieved that Mackey was not away from Ottawa at the time. Mackey had reacted quickly and positively to Isaksson's explanation of a provable link between the site of the former bakery based on confirmation of bomb residues found and the suspected terrorist Marek Kafirov. Sean-Guy's brief report from the O.P.P. Explosives Disposal team leader Art Romanowski sealed the obvious decision. The O.P.P. explosives technicians reported that both Penta and Nitrocellulose had been produced at the site they had helped to raid. They also concluded, with some tests yet to be completed, there was a likelihood some other materials such as nitroglycerine had been cooked at the location. Mackey promised to call a federal judge in the Mississauga area and ask for an immediate appointment. That appointment had occurred at 10 AM earlier that same day.

Madam Justice the Honorable Allies Nicholson, a federal judge of the Superior Court of Justice of Ontario, had made herself available on the understanding that her time not be wasted. Sean-Guy and Stuart had hurried to her chambers where the Justice and a court reporter arrived precisely at 10 AM to find them waiting. Justice Nicholson was well known as a vigorous privacy rights advocate. Already in her short time as a federally appointed judge, she had ruled against numerous police searches and their results on grounds that privacy rights had been violated. Several key police cases had been overturned as a result. Her decisions prompted the media to begin a series of stories about possible crimes committed by police officers. The ensuing controversy had embarrassed officials at nearly all levels of government from Ontario's legislature right down to some of the smaller towns in the province. The O.P.P. had eventually been cleared of wrongdoing but investigations into several local police departments were ongoing.

Her questions demonstrated the privacy rights attitude to be true as she insisted that Sean-Guy exhibit satisfactorily that Marek Kafirov was beyond ordinary protections. Sean-Guy had shown the results of their search of Marek's identity; that he was in fact Malik Bisliev, who had been legally in the country when he was a young teen travelling on an educational visa, and that he reentered the country illegally earlier the current year on that same visa now expired. Sean-Guy omitted that the search had sprung from his intuition that Marek and Malik were one and the same, based solely on his eidetic memory of the boy and a suspicion that the boy grown was the suspect. He was concerned the intuition and eidetic memory would be hard for the Justice to grasp and believe. Madam Justice Nicholson had then asked for evidence of connection between the bomb-making site, the apartment, and the restaurant locations. Stuart was able to produce sworn affidavits from his surveillance officers who had followed Marek from the Samovar House to his apartment and then to the former bakery, with a stop at a cyber-café.

Ron Stotyn

Sean-Guy was surprised at that last bit of information and made a mental note to ask sharp questions about that particular destination as soon as he could.

The collection of sworn affidavits had been a close thing. They had found a local Crown Attorney who had agreed to take the statements, the same typed by a court stenographer and then validated by the attorney just a half hour before the appointment with the Justice. Finally, the Justice had asked if there was any concrete evidence such as fingerprints. Sean-Guy was forced to admit there were no fingerprints that could be matched because no criminal record existed in Canada for Malik Bisliev. He had not been fingerprinted when he first entered the country to go to Stanstead College. Justice Nicholson was silent for a long while as she considered the implications of issuing a search warrant based on what seemed to her to be thin reasons at best. Finally, she had concluded that the existence of bomb residues was sufficient to grant the request. The whole process had taken only 15 minutes. Justice Nicholson warned Sean-Guy and Stuart as they were leaving that the search must be properly executed, especially at the restaurant where the scope of their authorization was only for any space used by the suspect for the storage or keeping of personal articles.

Sean-Guy, instead of Stuart, went immediately to Marek's apartment accompanied by two forensic investigators from the O.P.P. who had been standing by. Ryan and Hari went to the restaurant after finding the manager, who reluctantly agreed to come and open the place for them. Stuart in Mississauga with Betty and Leif in Ottawa connected by secure video link worked to develop a brief statement that would seek to disarm the media prior to the Monday press conference scheduled for 2 PM in the Ottawa office of the Defense Minister. Paul Mackey had refused to move the press conference forward but had agreed to have a statement come from the CAS Director, and that it should spin down the character of the video threat delivered to the media outlets some days earlier. The Minister had decided it unnecessary to be directly involved in the preparation of that message. Sean-Guy cynically thought it a political cover that might allow the Minister to distance himself if anything went wrong.

The finished statement dismissed the video threat as a prank committed by some unknown person, and pointed out that its considerable vagueness made it difficult to categorize it as significant; this not very close to the truth of course. In fact, said the Director's statement, it was believed possible the video had been posted from somewhere outside the country; also not true as they already knew from the IP addresses tracked to a Toronto area cyber-café. Also dismissed was the idea that any bombs had been discovered in Mississauga, essentially true, with the Director saying that some spilled industrial chemicals, close enough to the truth, had been discovered and cleaned up. Finally, the message confirmed that the Minister of Defense would hold a press conference about the CAS the following day at 2 PM at his ministerial office in Ottawa.

Completely missing from the statement was any mention that the CAS was interested in a person of Chechen extraction sought in connection with terroristic activities. The Minister had already approved sending the message to the media; so it was with a copy specifically addressed to Angela De Luca of the Toronto Star. The version sent to Managing Editor O'Donnell showed that De Luca had been copied. Stuart and Betty were confident that would prompt either O'Donnell or De Luca or both to make sure De Luca was in Ottawa for the press conference. The Director was prepared to agree to an exclusive interview with De Luca, if necessary, to clinch the maneuver. As it turned out, given that it was Sunday, neither O'Donnell nor De Luca had received their copies of the statement until early in the morning the following day. At that point O'Donnell did the unusual; he put De Luca on the company's private jet so she could get to the press conference in ample time.

Sean-Guy, at 10 AM, did not know that the surveillance crew assigned to watch Omid Faresh was following that man from Georgetown across Barrie, ending up at a restaurant where he was joined by two other men of a similar ethnic appearance. A couple of the CAS agents entered the restaurant and surreptitiously snapped cell phone pictures of the three and sent them via their Blackberry phones to Darya Barzaryan. She was at the Georgetown Line Go Train yard office in case she was needed. The agents, after a quick cup of coffee, then took up positions outside watching the various exits and did not pay attention when the fourth man entered. They did not see that he joined their target suspects just before 11 AM. They were focused on seeing who would come out. In the meantime, Darya went into the Go Train System's HR database which had been previously hacked by Thea with a backdoor added for Darya's use. Loading a special search program she went through the records looking for possible matches to the faces in the pictures. She already knew that Omid was employed at the same yard where she was at the moment. It was the other two men she was interested in, but of course it was a long shot they were employed by the Go Train System.

As the search was progressing she called Stuart and advised that additional agents were required to follow each of the three men if they split up when they left the restaurant. Stuart promised more agents would be there as soon as possible. Darya sat back to wait as her software chewed through the HR files when suddenly she got a match on one of the men and almost as quickly a match for the other. She was amazed that her long-shot had paid off. The first man was identified as Daoud Tariq who was a car mechanic at the Milton Line yard. The second also turned out to be a car mechanic, but located at the Barrie Line yard. He was Gul-Bashra Muhammad. Darya, familiar with the tradition of Afghanis identifying themselves only with double first names, was sure the last names that appeared in the records were probably not correct, though Daoud-Tariq made some sense. The 'Muhammad' of Gul-Bashra was probably just tacked on, she thought. Nevertheless she immediately placed a call to George Brown who was supervising the current surveillance, to tell him what she had caught. George said he would call Sean-Guy, but later reported he was unable to reach him.

Sean-Guy realized later that that was because he had silenced his phone while in chambers with the federal Justice. However, as soon as he had received the surveillance report of the new persons of interest, he had immediately hoped that something might come of that new information. There was no real evidence of any significant connections of these three Afghans to his principle suspect, Marek Kafirov. Still each man was followed carefully upon leaving the restaurant by additional agents as requested. The three had left in a group and were followed to a chess club, where the agents again waited to see what would happen next. The fourth man left the restaurant after the agents and their targets had already moved on. He arrived at the chess club and, tagging along with a small group of other patrons, entered the building again unnoticed by the surveillance team members. Knowledge, had it been available, of the fourth man would have set up a very different set of circumstances. Later, when Sean-Guy realized what had happened, he knew he had made an error by not advising his surveillance teams to also watch for Marek, seeking to identify him using the three picture versions they already had. In hindsight that would have shortened their search considerably.

{15.1}
Manor House Residence Hotel, Sunday April 9 about 8 PM: Scarborough ON

Marek was, at approximately 8 PM, engaged in changing his appearance. His beard, part of his physiognomy for the past five years or so, a traditional symbol of manhood, had to come off if he was to successfully escape the area following the explosions on the Go Train lines. With a cheap pair of scissors, he cut it close to the skin so that his razor could finish the task. He left his sideburns fairly long. As he looked into the mirror, he decided a haircut was called for as well, in order to tame the dark curls. That could be done the next morning, as well as getting some clothing to effect a change of attire and overall appearance. He needed to look a bit more like a well appointed young business person who would be unnoticed on any street in Canada. He might have changed his hair color had he had any sense that his pictures were already being circulated among the CAS searchers. If he had thought about such possibilities, which he had not, being inexperienced as a terrorist leader, he would have been in some fear of discovery.

A bit later he settled onto the cheap couch in the sitting area of his studio suite and turned the television to the CBC channel. He was not expecting any unusual news but wanted to see if all was quiet. He

Ron Stotyn

was shocked and then very dismayed at the first story about a statement issued by the CAS on behalf of the Department of Defense. The statement referred to what surely must be his kitchen lab where it was confirmed volatile industrial chemicals had been identified, though there was no inference about bombs having been constructed. The statement also debunked his video....his carefully prepared video....saying it was probably a meaningless prank distributed possibly from outside the country. Marek felt betrayed and was angered that the agency had not considered it genuine. Still, though uncertain, he did not suppose that the media had been persuaded otherwise for he was sure that Canada's media was conspicuously independent from government influence. The story finally told him the Minister of Defense would do a press conference the following afternoon. On that bit of information he feared that his plan might soon be in danger.

He turned the television off as his mind raced to come to a decision if he needed to try and take some kind of corrective action. But, the more he thought about it, the more he came to what for him was the obvious conclusion, that everything would be fine. The bombs were where they needed to be; ready to be picked up and doled out to the members of each of his cells. He was confident his plan was well laid out and that he was in total control of the time for detonation because only he could activate the triggers. The only flex factor was the final distribution of the bombs onto trains and the other specified locations, such as the construction areas of Union Station. His cells were now completely reliable; they would perform their tasks exactly as directed. Marek was certain of that. Ultimately he decided there was nothing to do but wait, indeed he knew that was all he could do because he had told the cell leaders he would not try to contact then again, that any type of contact purporting to be from him would be a ploy. They would not be able to contact him directly. They had never been given phone numbers to use. They could not use e-mail because his email to them had always been seen via an anonymizer.

Still, as he prepared for his night prayers, Marek was uneasy for reasons that he could not express. He prayed that Allah would grant success; He was sure that would be the case. It was promised in the

Qur'an, after all. Still, he remained uneasy as he retired to the bed and
continued to be uneasy through a restless sleep.

{15.2}
Toronto Area CAS Office, Sunday April 9 about 9 PM:
Mississauga ON

Sean-Guy continued with the creation of his journal notes,
knowing with clarity that the first names found by Darya had appeared
on the slip of paper he had found inside Marek's apartment during his
illegal entry. That same slip of paper had been found by the O.P.P.
forensic investigators without any prompting by Sean-Guy. He had
carefully remained a silent observer during the forensic examination of
the apartment rooms executed under the federal search warrant. He
now knew that they had not just one but three Afghans possibly up to
no good. That still suggested a very thin connection to Marek. How
could he be certain that Marek was involved in their plans? It was
crucial that the three Afghans be closely watched over the next few
days. There needed to be a more definitive link.

There was no such link found from the search at the Samovar
House conducted by Ryan and Hari. In truth, absolutely nothing
relating to Marek had been located. The desired key link would come
if Marek could be seen in the company of the three Afghans. That
would be conclusive but no-one had seen that. Sean-Guy did not know
nor did his surveillance team know they had missed the opportunity in
Barrie that same day. When the three supposed terrorists left the chess
club, they were each followed individually: Omid Faresh back to
Georgetown, Daoud-Tariq to Milton and Gul-Bashra Muhammad to
elsewhere in Barrie. An overnight surveillance had been established
for each of them at what seemed to be their residences. Backup
surveillance teams were called for duty in the morning to take over
following the men if they emerged. There were now several dozen
surveillance members engaged across the Toronto region; with help
provided by the CBSA, the RCMP and the O.P.P. With all those
agents in place no-one had seen Marek emerge from the chess club.
The agents had already left following their specified suspects. Sean-

Ron Stotyn

Guy knew that the reputation of CAS was now very much on the line. Expenses had taken a sharp rise upward.

What Sean-Guy had done upon getting the report of their identities was to get in touch with CBSA Senior Agent Shawna Kennedy to request an urgent tracing of Daoud Tariq and Gul-Bashra Muhammad. There was no confidence that the two would show up in the CBSA database. Sean-Guy was pretty sure the names would prove to be assumed. Indeed, the resulting search of the Border Services database turned up no evidence the pair had ever entered Canada and yet they were inside the county and being watched. Senior Agent Kennedy assured Sean-Guy that her agency would continue to seek information. Sean-Guy asked her to be circumspect: He didn't want to spook the suspects in any way.

Sean-Guy paused from his journal writing in a distracted moment as an issue began to plague his mind. It was something about cyber-cafes. That was an unfortunate thing about having an eidetic memory. There was so much information that he couldn't always make an immediate connection between bits and pieces. Then it coupled. There had been a remark from the sworn statements about having followed Marek from his home to the bakery with a stop at a cyber-café. But nowhere in his memory could he find any detailed information from a report about what had transpired inside that cyber-café. The surveillance report had said nothing about any investigation into Marek's activity inside. He also made a connection to the Director's statement of the video hoax. Everyone associated with the current situation knew that the video had been posted from a Toronto area cyber-café. Had there been any attempt to determine if the cyber-café where Marek was observed was the same as the one for which they had IP addresses? He guessed there had not been.

Sean-Guy decided that a call to both Thea and Betty was in order. He made the calls and connected both in a conference link along with the surveillance team member who had reported the stop, who had been inside, and who failed to report his attempt to find the e-mail targets. Under some questioning he admitted to that failure. Sean-Guy told him there would have to be some recompense for the error. Sean-Guy told Thea, Betty and the agent what he had understood about the cyber-café issue. He wanted a search of the cyber-café computers to find the one used by Marek. Betty recommended the computer identified as used by Marek be seized immediately and that Thea hook it up to the CAS network so that both of them could sift through its contents. Betty assured Sean-Guy, who expressed doubt, that anything erased was not really gone unless the cyber-café used some kind of deep cleaning software on a regular basis. She doubted that was the case because it would take the computer out of service for too long a time. Sean-Guy dispatched his agent, the one who had been inside, to go back to the cyber-café and get the computer without delay. He was to take a declaration of national security authorization to make the seizure. If the Café management made any fuss about that, the agent was to threaten to take every computer and shut the place down. It would not be an idle threat. If necessary, Sean-Guy had the CAS authority to invoke a little known national security proviso and effect the seizure.

Sean-Guy turned his attention to making a note about the two discoveries he and Everet had made at the bomb-making location. Once again, he felt they'd gotten lucky that there had not been any snow removal behind the building. Sean-Guy had been predisposed to have Everet take special notice of anything unusual inside the garage/loading dock area inside the former bakery. That had produced a set of vehicle tags hidden behind some broken-down boxes. The other discovery was his own spotting of what he was sure was a detonator cap. It was small, metallic and pencil-like, with a bit of wire coming out from one end.

After returning to the office from that search he had set Everet to starting a search for the tag's registration record. Thea had arrived and began to help with that search. It hadn't been very long before they found that the plates belonged to a van rented from a low-cost rental agency near the airport. It was a Ford Econoline, sometimes called a Club Wagon, near the end of its useful life as a rental. It was described by the agency as a cargo version, meaning there were neither side windows nor any in the rear doors. It had been rented by credit card. The manager, worried that his vehicle might have been stolen, very readily turned over a copy of the rental agreement. He was unable to

Ron Stotyn

tell Thea anything about the person who rented the vehicle. His desk clerk, who had taken the order, was away for the weekend skiing in the Laurentians. But, the manager revealed that the van had a built-in GPS for which he provided a computer link. Thea immediately logged into the GPS to see if she could download its history. She also ran the card number against her database of stolen cards and to no particular surprise reported it was one of the groups of stolen cards that they had become interested in. That was an interesting fact, but there was no provable connection to Marek. Sean-Guy asked Thea to arrange a grilling of the Russians who had been arrested to see if they recognized Marek's pictures. Then, as a matter of routine, they put out a Toronto region-wide APB on the vehicle with no real expectation it would be found soon if it had stolen plates on it. As far as the GPS was concerned, Thea told Sean-Guy success would depend on finding the GPS still powered up. Later she reported it was not and that they would have to depend on the van being physically found by police.

The device Sean-Guy had found indeed turned out to be a detonator. Art Romanowski, O.P.P. Explosives Unit team leader, who seemed to have an encyclopedic knowledge of bomb components, took one look at it and identified it as an import. He was positive the device was of Indian manufacture. He told Sean-Guy that as far as he knew the only commercial user of that particular detonator was a Gold Mine in the Northwest Territories. There was no report of any ever having been stolen. Art suggested the only way it could have shown up in Mississauga was by means of smuggling. The typical route was from India through Pakistan.

Sean-Guy had reacted with some annoyance, for which he immediately apologized; Art was in no way responsible for a connection to Marek that was so thin as to be nearly non-existent. There was simply no way to be sure Marek had imported it; but the sense of certainty weighed on Sean-Guy still.

{15.3}
Parliamentary Office of the Defense Minister, Monday April
10 nearing 2 PM: Ottawa ON

The night before, Sean-Guy had taken a call at the Mississauga
office of CAS from Leif Isaksson, his director, asking what time he
would arrive in Ottawa to attend the press conference. Sean-Guy, who
had not expected to attend, had to scramble to heed what was certainly
a request not to be refused. The call had come late at night, too late to
drive up to Ottawa, even at high speed with all the flashers going on
his police cruiser to clear the way. The alternatives were a late night
commercial flight paying the full cost of a last-minute ticket or an
attempt to get a CF executive jet flight. The latter had proved to be the
effective solution. A call placed to the Canadian Forces air base at
Toronto Pearson, and the exercise of his military authority gained him
an early morning flight to Ottawa. He arrived early enough to go to his
Lisgar Extended Stay suite and get into a double breasted charcoal
pinstripe suit. He'd also worn a white shirt with an expertly knotted
bow tie bearing the regimental stripes of the 5th Artillery Regiment of
Canada. Then he went to into his headquarters office to find out what
Leif wanted of him.

Sean-Guy had hoped it was just to be window dressing. That
was not to be, as he discovered to his chagrin. The Director was
expecting Sean-Guy to participate in the conference by describing in
some authoritative manner that they had discovered only chemicals
and no actual bombs in the Saturday raid in Mississauga. That much
would be the exact truth.

Shortly after 2 PM, as Sean-Guy was being introduced by
Minister of Defense Paul Mackey, identified as a Major in the
Canadian Forces rather than Chief Investigator of the CAS, he was
puzzled by the misdirection and wondered if he should have been in
uniform. He noted that Angela De Luca was front and center in the
audience of media reporters, seated right beside Terry Milewski, senior
political correspondent of the CBC and Craig Oliver, chief
parliamentary correspondent of the CTV network. Most of the other

Ron Stotyn

reporters present were recognizable as the key political reporters and columnists of Canada's major newspapers. Just as he was getting ready to make his statement he also noticed Rex Murphy, a frequent commentary contributor to CBC's The National night-time television news show and sometimes participant in that program's weekly At Issue panel. Murphy, he was sure, would be a voluble critic of the CAS if he spotted anything out of line. Scan-Guy resolved to present a minimalist version of the truth.

Sean-Guy began by observing that CAS had no demonstrable evidence of any terrorist activity in Canada at the present time and that all activities to date were designed to discover if there was any cause to suspect any problems whatsoever. "Watchfulness is the order of the day at all times," he asserted. He then launched into a concise review of the previous Saturday's search of the former food preparation establishment space in Mississauga, specifying that the full on Swat Team approach, based on tips received, was designed to ensure no innocent could possibly be put at risk. "The entire exercise has been treated as a high-level test of our response abilities." Finally, he reported, honestly if not fully sanguine, that traces of industrial chemicals had been found and had been carefully cleaned up to be sure no danger could crop up.

As he finished and invited questions, Defense Minister Paul Mackey stepped back beside him and immediately recognized Angela De Luca. Sean-Guy took a half step back, preparing to let the Minister answer the first question. It came in the form he suspected it would when Angela asked pointedly about his rank in the Canadian Forces. "Why is a man, previously separated from the Intelligence Branch, being identified as a Major, when he is in fact the Chief Investigator of the CAS? Isn't that indicative of a subterfuge by the government, and why hasn't your office revealed the true nature of the CAS long before this?" demanded Angela.

Paul Mackey stepped up to the podium and grinned at Angela, thanking her for an important question. He then very skillfully redirected Angela's attention, "Major O'Dwyer-Lariviere has never formally been separated from the Military, he has in fact continued as a member of the CF Reserves. His appointment to the position of CAS

Chief Investigator has resulted from a very welcome suggestion by his superintendent at the Sûreté du Quebec, where he served with great distinction as a Sergeant of Detectives, recently wounded and awarded a Police Bravery Medal for actions taken in a gunfight where he saved the lives of two fellow officers."

Mackey continued by addressing somewhat obliquely Angela's insinuation that his office had been neglectful in announcing the formation of the CAS. "The CAS came into being as the result of careful study about the best approach Canada might take to increase our watchfulness on the subject of terrorist interests in our country. That study was very ably conducted by the House Committee on Terrorism Control under the direction of Chairman Willard Elred, MP for Grasslands-Cypress in Saskatchewan. Mr. Elred also contributed to the development of the CAS mandate and is with us here today. My government has previously enhanced counter-intelligence procedures with the RCMP and our own military resources. The ramping up of terrorist activities in and toward Western Europe and the United States have made it clear that Canada would benefit from a senior agency that could help to coordinate all known issues and information about terrorist activities and interests directed toward Canada. The CAS was formed very recently. In fact it became operational barely two weeks ago after the necessary time was taken to assemble the foundation of investigations teams for major cities across Canada. We put the major city teams into operation, that is, Ottawa, Vancouver and Toronto just two weeks ago, with other major city teams becoming effective today."

"This news conference was scheduled mainly for the purpose of announcing the operational status of CAS formally. We anticipate the expansion of CAS to second tier cities, especially near the border or with international airport access such as Gander, Labrador-Newfoundland, over the next few weeks as we get teams assembled and oriented to our procedures. The events of this past weekend in the Toronto area gave us the welcome opportunity to demonstrate that we have a strong force available well and truly able to find and put down any terrorist plots against our country before they can become violent. Though what our teams found in the Toronto area cannot be identified as a terrorist plot, we are very satisfied that our procedures are well

Ron Stotyn

designed for identifying any potential threat. The strong force that is CAS is being led by a well qualified leader, Major General Leif Isaksson, formerly commander of Canadian Special Operations Force Command. I am very pleased that General Isaksson agreed to come out of retirement. Please give your questions about CAS now to General Isaksson."

As General Isaksson stepped forward, Angela was suddenly well aware that she had been expertly sidelined by the Defense Minister. She looked over toward Sean-Guy as both Craig Oliver and Terry Milewski sought to get the attention of the General for their questions. Sean-Guy looked back at her with an impassive expression. She imagined that she could see a glimmer of satisfaction in his slate grey eyes. She resolved to ask some tough questions in the private interview with General Isaksson, as had been promised, though she was certainly not sure what more she would glean after the press conference was finished. She turned her attention to the responses being made by the General.

Oliver asked Isaksson about Sean-Guy's credentials for his position as Chief Investigator. Isaksson detailed a career in the Canadian Forces Intelligence Branch, saying Sean-Guy had shown a talent for making apparently unconnected data fit together into logical assertions about counter-intelligence issues facing Canada at various times. "Major O'Dwyer-Lariviere has a finely tuned memory which he is able to use to develop carefully thought out theories about what people, who might be described as unfriendly toward Canada and her policies, are likely to be plotting. Coupled with his advanced degrees in Criminal Behavior, this leads to a kind of profiling that is very useful for developing counter-strategies." The General also characterized Sean-Guy as a thoroughly motivated investigator with many years of well developed detective skills from his service with the Sûreté du Quebec. "Sean-Guy has a stellar record in Quebec for resolving many very complex and difficult cases including bringing to justice, very recently, violent offenders connected to motorcycle gangs in that province."

Then Terry Milewski asked for details of the swat team search of the former food company establishment in Mississauga. General

Isaksson patiently reviewed what Sean-Guy had already presented, adding only that the operation came about as a result of valuable cooperation between the CAS and the O.P.P. Electronic Fraud Unit which had identified that stolen credit cards from a now closed investigation had indicated that chemicals had been delivered to that location. "Major O'Dwyer-Lariviere acted as the coordinator of a combined task force exercise that included members of the CAS investigation team in Ottawa and Mississauga as well as RCMP and O.P.P. members. This exercise has given us a lot of useful ideas about how we can work together in the event of a real terrorist incident in Canada. We count the exercise as a very successful test of our readiness."

By the time the media briefing drew to a close, Angela had taken copious notes; she decided it was also important that she try to get Sean-Guy pinned down as well. In the surge of reporters trying to get out of the room to file their stories, she realized that she could not spot Sean-Guy. It appeared that Major/Chief Investigator Sean-Guy O'Dwyer-Lariviere of the CAS had slipped out a back door and was once more distant to her in more ways than one.

{15.4}
Toronto Area CAS Offices, approximately 5:30 PM Monday April 10: Mississauga ON

Sean-Guy, having left the news conference as soon as he could via a rear entrance of the Defense Minister's committee room, went directly to the airport to catch a CF executive jet, held on standby on the Minister's orders. Before climbing aboard, he'd checked in with Stuart and discovered that the three Afghans had each been followed to their jobs early in the morning and that when they'd gotten off work, each had gone to bus depot storage lockers at the Barrie Bus Terminal on Maple Avenue. The surveillance teams reported that each had acted as if they did not know the others, even though they arrived at the terminal locker area more or less at the same time. The three had been observed collecting various pieces of luggage in the form of duffle bags and back packs. Stuart commented that though only a few such

Ron Stotyn

bags had been collected, a total of three pieces each, it seemed rather odd that these bags had each been stored separately in nine different lockers. "What do you make of it?" he asked Sean-Guy. Sean-Guy's response was succinct. "I don't like it. Where are they now?"

Stuart had said they all had returned independently to their places of residence and had not gone out elsewhere since.

On his return to Mississauga and during the supper hour at the Toronto Region CAS offices, as Sean-Guy met with George Brown, Ryan, and Stuart, with Everet quietly listening in, the group considered what they should do. Legally, their hands were tied. There was no opportunity to obtain search warrants, no apparent probable cause to ask a judge for permission to search the premises of the three Afghans. In fact, there was absolutely no visible connect to Marek and no logical reason to assume the contents of the baggage were anything but innocuous. George reported that as far as work histories were concerned, the three men were basically competent and had never caused any problems on the shop floor at the three Go Train maintenance yards. Ryan and Stuart both shrugged their shoulders and suggested there was nothing to go forward on. Sean-Guy didn't like that outlook but kept control of a rising frustration. Silence reigned as the four men sifted vague ideas, sometimes starting to speak and then trailing off as they realized the thought was going nowhere.

As the silence was becoming burdensome, Everet spoke uttering just three words, "Bomb Sniffing Dogs." All four men, startled, turned towards Everet with surprise. Everet added with a shrug, "Long shot. Worth a try."

Sean-Guy breathed out slowly. "Of course. If there were any bombs involved there would have to be contamination of those bags..."

Ryan cut in, "But how will we get close to the bags with dogs or chemical sniffer equipment for that matter? We have no grounds for a warrant."

Sean-Guy chuckled, "We don't need to get close. We take the dogs to where the bags were picked up, check the lockers and see what might pop... traces of bomb chemicals would be in the lockers I suppose. Stuart, call Art Romanowski right away and get something organized for immediate response. In the meantime, don't let these guys out of sight for even a second. If we do, who knows what we might fail to prevent."

Stuart got up from the table and began to head toward his desk outside the conference room where they had been sitting. As Stuart reached the door, Sean-Guy suddenly smacked his hand to the table. "Stuart, wait a moment. There is something maybe I overlooked. Our surveillance has these three in three different communities, right? I think we have to consider the possibility they are cell leaders for a bigger operation. They each work for Go Train in three different maintenance yard shops. What are the odds that Go Trains are the target for a terrorist strike? If these guys are cell leaders, we have to try and discover if they have others standing by to carry bombs or weapons onboard trains sometime soon. How many more surveillance team members are we going to need?"

"How many dogs we need?" asked Everet who then added, "Lots of lockers to check in this area."

George reminded the group, "These three work at three different maintenance shops: Barrie, Georgetown and Milton. Why were they picking up stored luggage in Barrie? Georgetown and Milton are quite a distance away from Barrie. So I'm thinking… if I were a terrorist, I would probably pick a central location for pickup of bomb packages, but if that is the case, does that mean that I would be planning to plant the bombs in all three communities? That's a real possibility, and I think Sean-Guy has the right idea to suggest that Go Trains are the target. That would make the task huge for bomb sniffer dogs if we have to look for explosives aboard trains. I'm not even sure that there are that many trained available in this area."

"I think George is right," interjected Ryan. "When I was active in the RCMP, there were less than a hundred RCMP dog handler teams across the country… a few more now I think. Not very many are handling bomb sniffer dogs. As a liaison-officer with CSIS, I was aware that both Transport Canada and Canadian Border Services Agency had dog teams, but I think maybe only Transport Canada has a small number trained to locate explosives. I might be wrong about that."

Ron Stotyn

      Sean-Guy turned back to Stuart and suggested that he ask Art if they have any sniffer dogs available close by. He then turned back to the group and said, "Sniffer dogs might be a bit of a legal problem for us. The Supreme Court of Canada ruled awhile back that sniffer dogs could not be used on board trains, buses and planes where passengers were present. I'm guessing that if we try to use them in the area of lockers at terminals, someone might argue that constitutes a violation of that ruling. I'll have to ask the Director about that, I think. Meanwhile, I think it's time for some grub. I'll call across the street for some sandwiches. A long night is ahead of us." Deep in his thoughts, Sean-Guy mused about the idea of neglecting to ask the Director. Tempting just to ask forgiveness later.

      An hour or so later, with the remains of hot beef sandwiches from the Olympia Grill littering the table, George, Stuart, Everet, Sean-Guy and Ryan were again discussing what needed to be done. Art Romanowski had reported that the O.P.P. had one dog trained for explosives detection stationed at Pearson International and that Transport Canada also had a couple. The O.P.P dog was off duty at the moment, but he could get it up to Barrie in about two hours. Sean-Guy estimated that would mean sometime shortly before 9 PM. Looking toward Everet he said, "Let's you and I go for a ride, okay? Stuart, will you call Art back and let him know we'll join his dog handler at that Maple Street bus terminal. I think we might avoid a confrontation if we invoke national security to anyone who might complain." I'll call the Director later to fill him in on what I have done.

      It was just coming up to 7 PM as Everet and Sean-Guy left the CAS office garage bound for Barrie. Sean-Guy had gotten direction from George Brown, a long-time resident of the region, about the fastest way to get up there. Using lights and siren on routes 410 north, 407 east, and then 400 north, George thought it should take only about an hour and a half. They were about 20 minutes into their drive when Stuart called to tell them they'd had a lucky break. The APB had produced a result. Scarborough PD had towed a van that was impeding snow removal a few blocks from the Go Train station. It had been parked on a street that was subject to snow bans. The snowfall over the past few days was enough to activate the parking ban. When the

Scarborough traffic division booked it into their impound, they discovered that it had a stolen license plate affixed and that its VIN number matched the APB put out by CAS. They wanted to know what CAS wanted to do with it. Sean-Guy asked Stuart to patch him through to the impound yard sergeant in Scarborough on a conference connection. When the man came on the phone, he was told that under no circumstances should anyone be allowed to touch or search the vehicle. "Wrap the van in plastic film….get your forensic guys to do that if necessary and then arrange to have it loaded on a flat deck tow truck and transported to the O.P.P's nearest forensic garage for a thorough going over. Stuart, stay connected with this guy and pull any necessary strings to make sure it all happens. Sergeant, we owe you guys a debt of gratitude. Stuart, get Art Romanowski involved and check very carefully for chemical residues and fingerprints. Any other stuff that might connect the van to Marek is also very important, yeah? I'll check back with you later."

Back to focusing on the drive to Barrie, Sean-Guy muttered under his breath, "That was lucky."

Everet responded "Luck of Naapi."

"Huh!?" exclaimed Sean-Guy.

Everet explained, as usual, with few words, "Our trickster God, but helps my people sometimes."

Sean-Guy had no response, but reflected that there was a lot to learn about Everet. He now thought Everet must be a spiritually connected individual in some way true to his First Nations heritage. Sean-Guy decided he was curious to know much more about the man but wondered if the taciturn individual would willingly give up any personal information. *In fact, Everet more and more seems like the ideal investigative partner that I have never managed to hook up with.* He switched the subject back to what was needed when they reached the Maple Street Bus terminal. "We'll need to work the dog at every locker in the place. By this time at night, I'm hoping that we'll not have too many passengers to worry about, but if there are and if any give us grief, I think we need to explain that we are just trying to protect the public based on a tip we've received. I am concerned about deflecting the issue of the Supreme Court ban on using dogs in connection with

Ron Stotyn

Buses, Trains, and Planes. I don't know if the ruling affects passenger areas of stations and terminals. Maybe we can get around it by getting the station manager to close the area temporarily for cleaning or something. We also need to be careful if there are any obvious Muslims inside. They consider dogs unclean and I don't want to raise a fuss about that."

The remainder of the trip northbound to Barrie was made in silence, but made quickly. In less than an hour later, just over an hour and a half in total from leaving Mississauga, Sean-Guy with the help of his GPS pulled up in front of the bus terminal parking behind an O.P.P. cruiser marked as a K-9 unit. The officer got out as they climbed out of their own cruiser. He greeted the pair, introduced himself as Corporal James Montgomery, and got right down to business. "What are we looking for?"

Everet, in a rare burst of visible enthusiasm responded without a pause. "Baggage containing bomb packages, probably PETN or something similar. Suspicious luggage was taken out of here within the past 24 hours. Can your dog track anything that old?"

Corporal Montgomery nodded his head and said referring to his basset hound, "Sparks has a pretty good hit record, about 90% confirmed detections. I have already spoken to the station master who agreed to come down here to help us secure the area. We can start right away. The last train out of here is due to leave about 11 PM and the current scheduled train is due to leave in about five minutes, so the place should be pretty empty in just a bit for a couple of hours."

Sean-Guy said, "James, where is the Station Master? I want to find out what his position is on opening the lockers if we find something that bears a closer look. I'd like to avoid hunting for a search warrant at this time of night if possible."

"You'll find him in his office just over there. I'll join you in a moment after I have Sparks out of the car and prepped. I've got a PETN scent cue to freshen his nose."

Sean-Guy and Everet stepped over to the office and knocked. The door opened right away and a small wiry man looked out, dressed in a typical bus company uniform. "You must be the gentlemen from the government," he said. "My name is Warren Grady. What can I do to assist? I assume since you've a dog standing by, you must have suspicions of finding something hidden here?"

Sean-Guy agreed but decided to be a bit vague in his response. "We have some reason to believe that your locker area may have been used as temporary storage of contraband. The dog is a trained sniffer dog. We need to work the dog at each locker in the building. If we find anything suspicious I plan to invoke probable cause for a search and seizure. Do you have any reason to be unhappy with that course of action?"

Grady thoughtfully looked at Sean-Guy and at Everet, taking note of their serious-looking expressions, shook his head slightly, and pointing to a prominent sign at the entrance to the terminal said, "We have the entire building posted with notice that any dangerous or illegal objects or substances are banned and subject to seizure with referral to legal authorities if found. That has been company policy ever since 911. We don't believe that our policy in any way infringes on passenger expectation of privacy."

Sean-Guy, slightly surprised at that kind of cooperation, said, "Excellent. We'll try to be as quick as possible so that you can return home soon. Thank you. Please stand by here in your office. If we need a locker open we'll come and get you and your master key."

About an hour later Corporal Montgomery and Sparks had covered all the lockers. Sparks signaled on six lockers, the ones already identified as those opened previously by the three Afghans, as well as three more. Sean-Guy took down the locker numbers, while Everet went to fetch the Station Master, who came and opened them. Gingerly, Everet lifted the bags found inside three of the lockers and placed them on the floor. He did not attempt to open the bags as he could not be sure of what was inside, or if they were in fact bombs, how they might be wired. As he stepped back and Montgomery brought Sparks forward again, the dog once again signaled hits. Satisfied, Officer Montgomery rewarded his friend with treats and took his leave.

Everet turned to Sean-Guy and said, "Those guys prob'ly comin' back here soon."

Sean-Guy silently agreed and before taking out his phone, closed the doors on the lockers having replaced the bags they found inside. He approached Warren Grady, who was hovering in the background, to thank him, shaking his hand and to say he could go home. "Please do not approach the lockers, these ones especially in the next few days. We are going to be watching them to see who comes to open them." Sean-Guy watched as the man departed and then placed a call to George Brown, who was supervising the surveillance operation in Barrie, Georgetown and Milton, to tell him what they had found and what needed to be the action now. "I want an absolute secure attitude on watching these three. They are now suspects in a terrorist action. Follow them carefully and if they come here to the bus station to open the lockers I want them arrested without delay. If they open the lockers, let them claim the contents but do not let them remove the contents from the building. Secure the area and get the bomb disposal guys here as quickly as they can arrive." Giving George the locker numbers, Sean–Guy said goodnight. He and Everet climbed back into the antique police Crown Vic for the ride back to Mississauga. As they rode, both silent, Sean-Guy was deciding it was time to release Marek's pictures to Interpol and the US Homeland Security connections that CAS had established. That was his first priority in the morning. He would also conference with the Director about releasing the pictures to the Canadian Media.

{16}

"Any man's death diminishes me, because I am involved in Mankind; and therefore never send to know for whom the bell tolls; it tolls for thee" John Donne in LXXX Sermons 1640

Downtown Terminal, just at dawn, Tuesday April 11: Burlington ON

As the sun began to bring light to an almost spring-like morning, the day began with a bang; literally, at least, in Burlington at the Downtown Terminal on John Street. At that location shortly before 5:30 AM, as the night sky changed slowly to the predawn grey of still chilly morning, an early commuter planning to catch the first train of the day into Union Station was standing on the sidewalk adjacent to the Terminal waiting for a shuttle to the Go Train Station at Fairview Street East. John Mathison took out his smart phone to call his wife who was just getting off shift at the Joseph Brant Memorial Hospital. He dialed but the phone rang just twice when there was a massive explosion from the building behind him. Thrown hard to the ground, Mathison tried to roll over and sit up and then collapsed again as his sense of dawn faded rapidly to blackness. He did not notice as he slipped into unconsciousness that there were actually several explosions in rapid succession. Neither did he realize that his phone call to his wife had not gone through. Later, it would be determined that he had dialed just one digit wrong, probably because his fingers were cold. His wife was using a loaner no-contract phone until hers could be repaired; He had yet to enter her current number to his speed dial.

Inside the terminal at the locus of the explosions there was no longer any semblance of normalcy. The passenger storage lockers were dispersed in wreckage that defied the imagination. The devastation was monstrous. Gone were, as later estimated, ten early morning passengers who had been passing though the locker area to await buses that would take them to their final destinations of the morning. Gone also were two individuals who had just opened several lockers to collect a miscellany of bags placed there by Marek Kafirov

Ron Stotyn

just days before. John Mathison would turn out to be the thirteenth victim and the only survivor.

In moments the sound of the explosion had died away leaving only the roaring sound of rushing waves of flame. That sound also quickly died away as most of the consumables in the concrete and brick building were used up. John Mathison mentally floundered in a barely conscious state, unable to fathom what had happened, hearing sirens coming ever closer. They arrived in time to save his life. He had suffered a collapsed lung from colliding with a fire hydrant, massive blunt force trauma to his head from impacting the sidewalk as well as deep lacerations to his back from flying glass as the doors to the terminal blew out. The first responders could barely comprehend what they were seeing when they entered the building looking for other survivors, of which none could be found. Police located only a couple of shocked and astounded witnesses, who could tell them very little of value. Still, they were held for treatment of stress and asked to remain for the arrival of senior investigators.

{16.1}
A few blocks from CAS Toronto, an hour before dawn, Tuesday April 11: Mississauga ON

Sean-Guy was close to completing his morning run, a circuit of the industrial zone surrounding the Toronto area CAS Office. Those runs typically early morning long distance efforts rarely missed; this morning a pass in front of the former bakery establishment, now abandoned for the second time in its history, recently used for a short while as a bomb-making lab. Two surveillance teams were still on the job at the location, though Sean-Guy now doubted Marek would ever return. As he moved past it Sean-Guy could not help but mull over the probable outcome if they failed to bring a supposed bombing situation to a satisfactory close. Marek, if he was in fact the terrorist Sean-Guy suspected he was, must be brought in quickly. The country and this heavily populated region simply could not afford any lapse of effort to curtail a probable terrorist plot. For Sean-Guy, the matter was becoming a single-minded focus, given the tangible if tenuous connection he had with Marek.

Sean-Guy was sure that the location had been a bomb making kitchen, given the results of tests conducted by the Explosives Disposal Unit of the O.P.P. He was just as convinced, though perhaps not sufficiently conclusive for testimony at a trial, that the bomb maker was Marek Kafirov, real name Malik Bisliev. Kafirov/Bisliev was still unaccounted for, Sean-Guy supposed at large somewhere in the greater Toronto area. Sean-Guy didn't like that at all. *A suspected terrorist at large potentially meant that a volatile event was being planned and was just as potentially drawing towards a violent conclusion. Indeed, there was the reality to be considered, based on the names on the list found in Marek's apartment, that there were at least four more unknown associates somewhere in the area. Time, it is often said, is of the essence,* thought Sean-Guy. That seemed certain to be the situation now. With three known persons of interest almost certainly in possession of weapons of destruction and more still in storage lockers, Sean-Guy anticipated a collision course with potential devastation.

Unaccounted for terrorists was a huge concern. Certainly the three suspects connected with the explosives traces found inside passenger storage lockers in Barrie were a concern. Their employment at the Go Train Yards in Barrie, Milton and Georgetown suggested that it would be folly not to assume that Go Trains were among possible targets. The potential destruction of explosions aboard passenger trains at rush hour was almost more than a mind can comprehend The extent of damage could cripple the regional transportation system for months.

The three of Marek's supposed accomplices, Afghans whose names matched three found on the list in Marek's apartment, were under close scrutiny in Barrie, Georgetown and Milton, as was a bank of storage lockers at the Maple Street Bus Terminal in Barrie. His own observation with Everet had, aided by a small Bassett Hound named Sparks, established that several bags believed to contain explosives were in three lockers at that passenger location. By his independent decision there had been no physical examination of the contents.

Ron Stotyn

Sean-Guy had not wanted to bring explosives disposal experts to the scene at that time to avoid any public exposure and thus to create the potential for panic. Besides, if they had opened the bags and had found confirmed bombs, they would then be bound to carry them away and explode them safely. That would alleviate part of a threat but would reduce considerably the ability to arrest and hold anyone opening the lockers. Leaving the bags untouched and then replacing them into the lockers could mean a possible arrest for possession of explosive materials, soon he hoped. That was, of course, an immense risk that he considered as a necessary action.

Anyone opening the suspect lockers and removing the bags would be immediately detained. The station would be closed and innocents removed from the area. The bomb squad would be brought to the location to conduct a very careful examination. Only then could bombs be confirmed and only then could the style of manufacture be known. Those arrested would be charged with suspicion of transporting illegal substances, possession of bombs and/or bomb-making materials, and upon verification of the contents of the bags, of intention to carry out terrorist acts. But as it turned out, not looking inside the bags failed to reveal an important clue. An event unfolding a few miles away, of which Sean-Guy was not yet aware, would soon give him pause and perhaps force reconsideration of some actions taken so far that he had recommended.

As Sean-Guy approached his motel accommodations on Dixie Road he considered just what had to be accomplished as soon as he could get in touch with H.Q. in Ottawa. Top of the list was to get pictures of Marek distributed to Interpol and US Homeland Security and, he thought, probably to all Canadian Media. No telling where Marek might be. Best to get the pictures out and hope for a sighting. Sean-Guy also considered if pictures of the three Afghans should be distributed after they were arrested. *Will that bring any valuable information to light he wondered?*

Upon entering his room at the Best Rest Motel, Sean-Guy was anticipating the arrest of the three Afghans. Sean-Guy could not imagine that they would delay going back to the Maple Street Bus Station lockers to pick up the rest of the explosive packages. Then *we should be able to get some solid tie-in evidence.* After a quick shower and a change of clothes, he headed to the Olympic Grill opposite the Toronto CAS office for some breakfast and to check the newspapers for stories on yesterday's media conference held by the Minister of Defense. He was especially interested to see what Angela De Luca would have to say; then on to the office to effect some necessary actions and play the waiting game. But none of that was going to happen quite the way he hoped.

At 6 AM sharp, Sean-Guy entered the Olympia Grill, carrying copies of the Globe and Mail, the National Post and the Toronto Star from last night. Heading for his preferred booth near the back of the café, he spread the Star onto the table first; ordering coffee, toast and a couple of eggs over easy from the waitress who had followed him. The Star's headline was bold and direct The byline was exactly what Sean-Guy expected to find. The story thrust was not far from his expectations as well.

Terrorist Bomb-Making Denied

Angela De Luca, Ottawa.

Today at a short notice media briefing, Canada's Minister of Defense Paul Mackey denied that there was any evidence of bomb making when agents of the Canadian government entered an abandoned premises in Mississauga over the weekend.

Mackey introduced the chief investigator for the Canadian Anti-terrorist Agency, Major Sean-Guy O'Dwyer-Lariviere, who reported his agency, acting upon tips, had entered the building to find some spilled industrial chemicals, which were carefully cleaned up.

O'Dwyer-Lariviere said the entire exercise was being treated as a test of the new agency's readiness to thwart any real terrorist threat that might come in the future

The Star has previously reported that this 'exercise' was attended by explosives disposal experts of the O.P.P., RCMP members, O.P.P officers, and agents of the Canadian Border Services Agency as well as the CAS.

None of the senior officials present at the media briefing, which included besides the Minister of Defense the recently appointed Director of CAS, Major General Leif Isaksson, would confirm that real terrorists were suspected to have a connection to the location of the swat team-like attack on the facility. Previously the Star was told an exercise such as this was always a cooperative effort with other law enforcement agencies.

Mackey spent very little time explaining why a former sergeant of the Surété de Quebec was now a Major of the Canadian Forces and leading the senior investigation team of the CAS. "The major was a well respected detective sergeant recommended for the new post," said Mackey. Mackey indeed spent only a few minutes outlining the goal to establish additional CAS offices beyond Ottawa, Toronto, Montreal and Vancouver.

Secrecy was evidently the order of the day as Major General Leif Erickson, a retired commander of the CF Special Operations Force Command, had very little to say about O'Dwyer-Lariviere or the CAS except that his new Chief Investigator had acted as coordinator in the exercise that took place late last week....

Sean-Guy, distracted by two things, looked up to see first: Ryan, Everet and Hari entering the café, with Stuart hurrying from across the street to catch up, and second; the buzzing of his Blackberry. Looking at the phone, he decided it needed to be the priority of the moment. It was Art Romanowski of the O.P.P. Explosives Disposal Unit. Art began speaking as soon as the phone was answered, not waiting for any pleasantries. "My team has been called out to a major fire in Burlington, specifically the Burlington Bus Terminal." Art kept on speaking in a rush not giving Sean-Guy any time to interject. "Reports are it happened within the last half hour. First responders are telling us that it appears to be an explosion of some sort, but they don't think natural gas was a factor. I think you better get yourself over there just as soon as you can. This looks to me like something you'll want to keep the media noses out of as much as possible." With that he hung up leaving Sean-Guy with an amazed look on his face.

Getting up from his table and gathering his newspapers, Sean-Guy dropped some money to cover his tab and moved to the front door of the café. Pulling up short, his team turned to follow, surprised at the move and at Sean-Guy's failure to greet them as he normally did. As they all got outside, meeting up with Stuart, Sean-Guy said, "Back to the office. There has been a suspicious fire, a probable explosion, at the Burlington Bus Terminal. Art Romanowski's unit is on the way. He thinks I ought to be there as well. Ryan, I think you'd better come with me. Everet, Hari…. I want you to be in close contact with George Brown and Darya. As soon as those Afghans are in custody, I want you involved in their interrogations. Everet, take the lead in that please. We need focused information as soon as possible. Get it any legal way you can. Hari, you need to be ready to listen to anything they might say in their own language, Farsi is it? Have Darya listen as well. Use that against them. You might also consider using Darya as part of the interrogation team, though that might shut them up or make them angry, which would be good, I guess. They certainly won't like talking to a woman. Ohhh…It might be useful to pit them one against the other. You know how to do that, I know."

Sean-Guy, entering the front door of their headquarters, turned his attention to Stuart. "Stuart, sorry about this but I think you'll be best staying here for the moment. I need you to call Ottawa and talk to Leif or Betty. We need to circulate pictures of Marek to Interpol and US Homeland Security and of course, to all our normal official channels. Make sure Border Services, especially, gets the pictures out all across our border control system. Please get the Director's input on the possibility of releasing Marek's pictures to the media. I'm not sure that is necessarily a good idea right now but it might flush him out if it doesn't make him escalate or run for it. Ask also about circulating pictures of the Afghans after they are arrested. It might produce tips about their connections. Then I need you to get in touch with Father René. He can maybe give us a handle on how to tweak the interrogation of the Afghans. Any insights he has need to get to Hari, Everet, and Darya. Probably best if he can hook up directly with one of them when the interrogations begin."

Sean-Guy then said to the group, "Ok, what have I missed?"

Everet responded. "We need to know where that van has been."

Stuart jumped on that. "I'll get in touch with O.P.P. and see if they have been able to access the GPS on the truck. If they did we

Ron Stotyn

should be able to get a stop by stop report. They should be able to rush that for us. I'll ask for a download so that Thea can help."

Sean-Guy observed, "Any of that information might be useful to break the Afghans. Everet, you can probably intimate pretty strongly without saying any name that we know who their controller is and that we have him in custody. They might get the idea that they have no more options and spill what they know. We especially need to try and clean up any other members of their organization."

Hari asked, "How much can we make them uncomfortable? Can we manipulate their environment during the questioning, their physical comfort, challenge their emotional stability? That would help us break them more quickly."

Sean-Guy, slowly and thoughtfully said, "I understand what you are asking and what you would like to do. But I have to caution you that we are subject to the laws of Canada. If we cross any lines that could be a serious problem….if there is any 'visible' evidence…. that we have done a wrong against them."

Hari gave Sean-Guy a long hard look to try and evaluate what he had just heard. Then he gave Sean-Guy a slight bow as if accepting what was given in instruction.

Sean-Guy looked around the group waiting for any last inquiries. When he glanced again at Everet, the First Nations constituent seemed to straighten and get even taller. He spoke slowly. "Why me to lead the grilling?"

Sean-Guy, looking at Everet eye to eye spoke so softly that only Everet seemed likely able to hear; "You have a powerful spirit. The Shaman in you that you deny will have a beneficial consequence. The Afghans will respond to spiritual power." Sean-Guy laid his hands upon Everet's shoulders. "I think it is time for you to express yourself fully."

Later in a CAS Tahoe on the way to Burlington with Ryan riding in the shotgun seat, Sean-Guy thought, bemused, *I have no idea why I said that to Everet. But I know I'm right and that Everet is the right person for this particular job.*

{16.2}
Manor House Suites, about 6 AM, Tuesday April 11:
Scarborough ON

Marek completed his morning prayers, having confessed his worry to Allah that the plan was not as secure as he needed it to be. He had asked, and he believed had received complete forgiveness for any inadequacies that he might have brought to the planning of the retribution Canadians needed to experience. His worry stemmed from the news reports he'd seen on television and in the newspapers about the media briefing conducted by the Canadian Minister of Defense yesterday afternoon.

Marek wasn't really quite able to put his finger on the why of his discomfort. Those who spoke at the media conference had been very polished, not hesitant in any way about what they had to say, but there was something inherently not complete, he thought, about the topic and the thrust of the comments. He thought the article written by the woman Angela De Luca exposed that lack of completeness without actually revealing that something was not said. He wasn't sure, of course, that any woman not trained as he was could be trusted to speak truthfully, but the De Luca woman had defined a theme of an overly smooth discussion concerning the Chief Investigator of CAS and the so called exercise at the former secret bomb-making workplace. Marek thought long and hard about that location, which he had thought of as abandoned. He was certain he had left nothing behind that could be connected in any way to his enterprise.

Marek knew fundamentally that his scheme was always at risk of being discovered if it were not already. Of course, he had no means of knowing that his three Afghan cell leaders were already compromised. Even if he had known there would be little he could do about it except hope they had already placed their allotment of bombs. Given what knowledge he had of the circumstances, he was still comfortable that the placement of the bombs would proceed without difficulty. So at the same time, based on the De Luca story overall and the other reports he could, if he ignored his worry, believe that everything was still on track. He wondered, though, in the midst of his continuing fury, as he prepared to leave his motel room, whether he should reconsider his resolve to remain close to the scene of his momentous action, to stay nearby so he could see up close the results of many bombs being exploded simultaneously. *Should I move on to begin preparation to launch another plan somewhere else?* Then, recognizing that his telephone sequencer software program could start the detonations from any distance away, Marek decided that it might well be time to put his exit planning into motion. There was no particularly good reason to remain close to the scene of the explosive scenario. His fury would be satisfied wherever he might be.

He was certain as he could be at that moment that he was not under observation and therefore free to make contact with his transportation coordinator. He could easily go out and find a place for some breakfast, preferably a café that could provide good yogurts and traditional items such as siskal and churychay. He knew of such a place not far away that he had been at before. He was not concerned about making a return visit since it was a place that attracted travelers. Then he would find a cyber café so that he could begin arrangements for his extraction. With a fresh haircut and a smoothly shaven face he confidently left his rooms surely to be unnoticed among those moving about this early in the morning. In fact, in Scarborough there was as yet no one looking for him.

Following a satisfying morning repast, which included some freshly made kurzanesh and excellent yogurt, along with some nearly syrupy Turkish coffee that he especially enjoyed, Marek went to a cyber café just down the street. There he sent, using coded text, a short message containing the number of a new never yet used disposable phone to his transportation organizer. That person, of course had never met Marek, nor had any knowledge of Marek of any consequence. The coordinator's task was only to arrange a pick-up at a location that Marek would specify when contact was established. The conversation would be brief and disguised as ordinary conversation. Certain code words would direct the coordinator to plan the pickup for designated days. The contact would be told to have a car waiting on a street in Derby Line VT adjacent to the Canada/US border. It would wait for three successive days for just 10 or 15 minutes each time. Marek would have to be quick in his crossing of the border. When the single phone call was complete, Marek would dispose of the phone. After that call he would receive confirmation via an email address he'd established for the purpose and had not used to date.

Marek had decided that Stanstead, QC would be a quite reasonable place to cross the border. He recalled from his days as a visiting ESL student at Stanstead College that the community was contiguous with Derby Line VT. It amused him to choose this location since it was there he had first met Sergeant O'Dwyer-Lariviere. He knew also there were numerous places where citizens had habitually crossed between the two villages without checking in at the border crossing stations. But, some time spent browsing on the Internet though had revealed that crossing was now less easy. There was now a steel gate across Maple Street opened only by first responders when emergency vehicles needed to cross. Still, the bars of the gate were widely spaced so that a slim adult could get through. A dark of night crossing might be possible. Another of the streets had a permanent barrier in the form of a wall so that would not permit an easy crossing, dark or otherwise. Church Street had an official border station under constant watch with cameras. It did have the advantage of being very near the Haskell Free Library, which one entered from the U.S. side of the border. That could work, as I can wait in comfort inside the library until the car arrives. He had an unused Canadian passport, very well forged, that he could use to enter the U.S. at the Church Street location. The only difficulty was that his picture showed him at a somewhat younger age. The good thing was that it did not show him with a beard.

It would not be unusual for a Canadian to cross in order to return books to the library, an innocuous errand undertaken by many every day. Border guards would hardly take any notice of him, especially if he approached the border when several others were also checking in. He would be able to get into the library and meet the car at closing time when all the patrons were leaving, US citizens walking to their cars parked along Church Avenue or on Caswell and Canadian patrons going back through the control point. No one would notice a

Ron Stotyn

Canadian patron who failed to return until he was well away from the area. Marek decided that plan would be fine, a low risk way to exit Canada before the damage to Canada's ego was effected. As Marek left the cyber café, he strolled along a street that would take him back towards his low-rent weekly suite at the Manor House. His phone call came shortly after, a good thing because it allowed him to speak without fear of being overheard.

"Hello. This is Stanstead Derby. Go ahead please," he said. (This name indicated to the caller, his transportation coordinator, where he wanted a pickup.) The phone number was known only to the transportation coordinator so Marek was confident the recipient of information being passed would be especially attentive. "Oh cousin Haskell, it's very good to hear your voice. I'm so glad you called. I have wanted to get together with you to catch up with you. Can we meet on Thursday? I have to take 5 books back to the library this week before closing." (Marek used the name of the library and the number of books to indicate the specific location and time. Five books meant he would be ready no later than 5 PM. 'This week' meant the upcoming Thursday. Marek knew that was a bit of short notice, but was certain it could be accomplished. His indication of closing time instructed for a 6 PM pickup.) "Of course if Thursday is not so good, I can delay my errand until the next day, when I could go to the library at 4 PM before closing. Or even Saturday at 1 o'clock if necessary. As you know I am able to be quite flexible. I have no obligations until Monday morning early." (That last comment would get passed on to his mentor as confirmation of the date and time for the bombing event.) "By the way, I plan to cross into Church before I go to the library." (Marek's wording indicated his plan to make the border crossing on Rue Church in order to go to the Library entrance on the US side of the border.) "Yes indeed, it's the church on Caswell." (That finalized the pickup request by confirming the U.S. street the library faced). "I'm looking forward to hearing you soon." Marek hung up his call and looked for a waste receptacle to dispose of the phone right away. Spotting one just ahead at the corner he stripped out the SIM card and chucked the now disabled phone in. He twisted the SIM card until it broke and put the pieces in his pocket for disposal elsewhere.

Marek turned the corner to proceed to his motel rooms just ahead and suddenly realized that the street he had just left was where he had abandoned the van. He had not seen it, focused on his phone communication as he had been. He looked back to confirm what he felt that it was not there. It was not. *I guess it has been stolen, not such a bad thing to happen to it* he thought as he turned back toward the motel. In a few more steps he had already dismissed the importance of the missing van. Now he needed to get out of Scarborough and off to Stanstead QC to be in place by Thursday morning. He had few possessions at this point. Everything was in a medium-sized back-pack. He could collect that in minutes and be off to catch a bus to Montreal and then a transfer to a bus south-bound for Stanstead. His part of the deadly detonation plan would soon be completed. His immediate travel plans caused him to miss the news of a deadly explosion in Burlington a few hours earlier.

{16.3}

Downtown Bus Terminal at John Street, about 9 AM, Tuesday April 11: Burlington ON

Sean-Guy and Ryan arrived at the Burlington Downtown Terminal just before 9 AM to find the area was cordoned off for several blocks around, the closest streets still jammed with emergency vehicles and a police command center RV parked close to the terminal building. Sean-Guy flashed his Military ID at the patrol officer on the barricade and was allowed to park behind the command vehicle. He and Ryan went toward the scene looking for Art Romanowski, finding him leaning against the O.P.P. explosive disposal unit truck adjacent to the building. The man was dirty, smudged with what appeared to be black greasy smoke particles. He looked both tired and perturbed as he held a two-way radio to his ear. He turned away from the vehicle and took several steps back toward the explosion site when he saw Sean-Guy. Pausing, he motioned for the pair to follow him.

As Sean-Guy and Ryan caught up, he said, "There is absolutely no evidence that this was caused by a natural gas event. The building doesn't have any gas furnaces. It was heated by electric forced

Ron Stotyn

air blowers hung, or used to be hung from the ceiling. Pretty standard for these bus stations. Everything has been blown away. The explosion nexus is....was....the storage locker passageway. All passengers for buses had to pass through to the loading platforms. We found body parts....the coroner....just arrived. His people think they can count at least a dozen....bodies that is. There is apparently a single survivor. Poor bastard was outside on the sidewalk at the time. He's been taken to Joseph Brant Memorial Hospital on North Shore Boulevard East right here in Burlington. No idea of his condition. The Commander of the local police response might know. I'll introduce you, but I think you need to see the blast scene first. You have to see it to fully appreciate what happened, though we are still making our assessment. You'll maybe want to take over the scene to control it from media interference. Our O.P.P. Anti-terrorism guys will be here soon, so you'll no doubt need to discuss jurisdiction with them....not my business really but my gut feeling is this is a federal deal."

Art led them inside through the now broken, glassless, and off kilter hanging double doors that were the main entrance. As they entered and their eyes adjusted to the dim still smoky interior, Sean-Guy could see that the lockers on both sides of the wide hallway were more or less flattened against the walls. Looking closer he was able to discern that a set of lockers on one side appeared to be more destroyed than on the other side. There was also a substantial crater in the floor at that position. Ryan muttered, "My God…"

Art raised his hand in a signal to stop where they were. "The coroner's people are still processing the area, but I think they have found everything they are going to with regards to bodies. If you look closely just above the crater you'll see two heads jammed into the lighting grid. The damage is pretty severe but I'll give you odds they do not belong to westerners. I also think the coroner's people will not find any other body parts to match."

Sean-Guy asked, suspecting he already knew the answer, "Why do you say that?"

Art sighed with a hint of melancholy and explained, "When a blast is somewhat disorganized....as this one seems to be....that is not contained or shaped....its force expands rapidly in all directions.

Anything that is very close to the center pretty much gets dissolved. When we get a chance to look at the debris, my guess is that we'll find evidence of shrapnel packed with the bombs. It seems likely that heads were sheared away by the shrapnel and the force of the blast launched the heads up there."

Ryan, who had been looking at the destroyed lockers, suggested an alternative that made Art startle and then grin crookedly with approval of the thought. "There is one locker over here that doesn't have a door. All the others around it are collapsed against the wall doors and all. What's the possibility that door acted like a scythe when a bomb inside the locker went off cutting the heads off as other bombs exploded maybe already in the hands of these dead guys?"

Art started to reply, saying, "That's a good concept…" but Sean-Guy cut him off. "I need to speak to the Police Commander and the Coroner or whoever is in charge from that office. Ryan, call the nearest local CF base on my authority and get a bunch of active duty soldiers out here to take over the perimeter guard so the police can get back to their regular duties. I'll tell the police commander that his people can stand down as soon as the soldiers get here. On the double for that, okay? Art, I need your people to determine as quickly as possible to confirm a bomb, how many....if possible....and of what kind of manufacture if there are enough residues to make a determination. I especially want to know if there is any chance these were made over in Mississauga."

A few minutes later Sean-Guy informed the assigned on-site Police Commander that he was taking over the crime scene as a possible federal terrorist action site, thanking him and his force for a job well done. Sean-Guy advised that the police perimeter guard could be released as soon as the military guard arrived and asked that all media inquiries be referred to him. The Police Commander was glad to have the chance to reassign his perimeter guard back to normal duties as soon as possible. Morning rush hour made him nervous without enough squad cars on the road. Then, because the local police were well equipped to handle next of kin enquires, Sean-Guy asked that police continue to work on that aspect of the situation. "Have your people found anything outside the building that might have anything at all to do with what happened here."

The Commander said they were still conducting a ground search but had found nothing of consequence, except for a cell phone located just a couple of feet from where the survivor had been thrown. Sean-Guy immediately asked to see it. When it was brought to him, he checked both outgoing and incoming calls, finding one call outgoing at the same time as what had been reported for the blast. He noted it and called Stuart to have that number traced. Thanking the commander again for his cooperation and assistance, Sean-Guy turned to the Coroner's Assistant who had just stepped over. "When you retrieve the two heads that are lodged in the lighting grid, I'd very much like to have you focus your post on them first. Please obtain DNA from each and see if you can determine ethnic background. This site is being declared a terrorist action location so I need to know as quickly as possible." The Coroner's man nodded and hurried off to tell one of his death investigators of the request.

Sean-Guy beckoned to Ryan and said, "I'm going to Joseph Brant Memorial. I have been given the name of the survivor…It's a John Mathison. If he is awake perhaps he can tell us something. In the meantime, please work with the police commander. I've declared the site a federal Terrorist Crime Scene. The police will stand down from perimeter duty when the CF soldiers arrive. Any command issues can be referred to me as I'll be the ranking officer in charge under DOD procedures." Ryan nodded and asked, "What about the media? I see several already camped out at the barricades and I think I just saw Angela De Luca arrive."

Sean-Guy, seeming to ignore the information about Angela, looked toward the barriers and said, "See if the Police Command vehicle has a media officer inside….they probably do. Get them to put out a statement that I will hold a preliminary briefing here at noon. That should keep the reporters on-site waiting. In the meantime, you can also say that the investigation is still at early stages and a determination is being made that a terrorist action may have taken place here, so the site is being declared a Federal crime scene. I expect to be back in an hour or so…. Oh, and better call Ottawa and update the Director."

On his way over to the hospital, just a few minutes away, Sean-Guy took a call from Thea. She had a report about the GPS database that the O.P.P. lab had stripped from the van found in Scarborough. The list of stops made showed it had been stopped for about 20 minutes on John Street on the previous Friday. It had then proceeded to Barrie where it stopped outside the same Barrie terminal where the explosives indicators had been found by Sparks, the O.P.P. sniffer Bassett Hound. There had been a somewhat shorter stop outside the Richmond Hill Go Train Terminal on Mackenzie Avenue. Before a final stop in Scarborough it had been stopped for about half an hour outside the Oshawa Greyhound Bus Terminal on Bond Street West.

Sean-Guy asked Thea to put Stuart on the line. When Stuart answered, Sean-Guy said, "I think it is not possible to call this coincidence. We need to get sniffer dogs into the Richmond Hill and Oshawa locations immediately....I mean right now....Get Sparks and his handler moving and co-opt a dog from one of those stationed at Pearson out to Oshawa without delay. Based on what we are seeing here I'd say it's a slam dunk bet there are or have been bombs stored at those two locations."

Stuart said in response to the unspecified instruction, "I'll arrange for surveillance to be set up at both locations as well. Pending any discovery of bomb indications in some of the lockers, we'll open them, check, reclose and then watch to see who comes calling."

Sean-Guy closed the conversation with an emphatic comment, "I hope to God you find bombs waiting to be picked up," as he pulled up to the Emergency Department of Joseph Brant Memorial Hospital. Leaving his lights flashing, he got out and hurried inside where he found that the survivor John Mathison was still comatose. He called Ryan to arrange for an O.P.P. detective from the anti-terrorism unit, to come to the hospital ready to ask Mathison for any details the man could recall, as soon as he was conscious and stable. After checking on Mathison's vital signs with ER staff, Sean-Guy returned to the blast zone to do some poking around on his own.

Ron Stotyn

On his way back, Sean-Guy took calls from Stuart and Everet. Stuart reported the outgoing phone call went to a no-contract phone, user unidentifiable; a dead end. Everet reported that the three Afghans had been arrested moments before and that he and Hari were en route to take over the interrogation with Darya already on scene where the three were being held. George Brown was expected to arrive there momentarily. An O.P.P. explosives disposal crew confirmed bombs were inside the packages of luggage and that the firing mechanism included cell phones and detonator caps. Pictures had been taken, the mechanisms dismantled and the explosive portion safely exploded. The same would occur as soon as the living quarters of the three terrorists were confirmed and could be entered with search warrants. In the meantime, a safe zone around each location was being evacuated.

Sean-Guy hung up and muttered out loud, "That explains the no-contract phone here." and made a mental note to tell Art what had been found. He called Stuart then to warn him about the likelihood of bomb packages armed the same way at the two other sites where the van had stopped briefly. As he arrived back at the terrorist crime scene, Sean-Guy suddenly realized that no-contract phones were a clue that needed checking against the stolen credit cards purchases. He called Thea to have her begin hunting for another possible tie-in to Marek. When he had finished his instructions, she reported that the Russians had denied knowing the man in the pictures of Marek they had been shown. Sean-Guy filed that information and thought it probably meant they were being dishonest.

He found that military personnel were on-site and had taken over perimeter duties. He showed his military ID to get though the barricade, pulling up again to a spot behind the Police Command RV. There he found a cluster of media people being briefed. He was spotted by Angela as he tried to walk past. She hurried to catch up with him, so he stopped and made a point of motioning her back to the briefing, saying he would add his own comments at noon, now less than two hours hence. As usual, Angela tried to press him with questions. He was forced to glare fiercely at her, which gave him some discomfort given his growing feelings for her; it was enough to cause her to falter and return to the media scrum.

More than two hours later Sean-Guy made ready to leave the scene, having turned the bomb-site over to Stuart and Ryan; Stuart having come to the site at Sean-Guy's order for that purpose. Sean-Guy had, as promised, made a statement to the media about the investigation. He confirmed an explosion by man-made devices. He confirmed that the scene was being examined for further evidence of terrorist activity. He advised that the coroner was estimating that as many as 12 were dead, but did not say that two were thought to be the terrorists themselves. He referred to John Mathison as an unnamed survivor, still comatose, who was expected to provide useful information when sufficiently recovered. There was no reference to the arrest of the three Afghans in the northern area of the Toronto region, nor of any belief that other bombs were expected to be found in the eastern region.

{16.4}

Queen Elizabeth Way toward Toronto, About 1 PM, Tuesday April 11: Burlington ON

Sean-Guy was on his way to Stanstead QC, having told no one where he was going. He'd made an abrupt decision to go purely on his gut level intuition about where Marek would most probably turn up. As he took the interchange north of Burlington's downtown onto the QEW named for the Queen Mother, he trod on the accelerator and brought his speed up to 120 KPH; his lights and siren on. He glanced at the passenger to his right, making sure she was properly belted in. Angela De Luca looked back at him, an expression on her face that told him she was partly afraid and partly excited to be where she was. Her presence in that seat was still a surprise to him. She had climbed in just as he had finished making a u-turn reverse back at the Burlington Downtown Terminal. She climbed in as he put the CAS Tahoe into forward gear and was already rolling.

As she had settled into the seat and tossed her duffle into the back seat, she gasped, "I need to go with you, it's important for both of us. I want to be with you."

Ron Stotyn

He'd growled at her that she couldn't, that her presence in a federal vehicle was not authorized, though of course he could authorize it. He'd added there was no story, though of course there was as he well knew and so did she. He argued with a tone of finality that she had no sense of the danger, though he knew she put herself into danger regularly without compunction to get her stories.

She had repeated her claim, "I must be with you." And had added to his very great dismay, "I think we are both are learning to love each other."

He'd fallen into a stunned silence as he navigated Burlington's downtown streets to get to the on-ramp. His thoughts ran wild: *was that a possibility...even a probability?* "That's unwise," he blurted out and then wished he'd deliberated more carefully about such a statement. Now he could see dismay cross Angela's face. "I mean, our work is a conflict of interest for us both. It creates all kinds of problems. Surely such a relationship…"

Another glance at Angela now revealed that a ferocious determined expression had taken over her face."Don't you dare suggest that this cannot work. It can and it will. I know it and so do you!"

Sean-Guy was now sure his own expression was one of uncertainty, maybe even of disbelief that what was happening was....well....happening. Sean-Guy fell back into silence as he chewed on all the possible outcomes, repercussion potentials, complications for his job, and changes to his now long-settled solitary lifestyle following his second divorce. *Is it possible that this woman could possibly be the one with whom I might spend the rest of my life? For so long now I have believed that I was destined to be a single man.*

Angela leaned her seat back, slipped off her shoes, smiled a soft smile at him and then after turning sideways placed her foot against his thigh, closed her eyes and went to sleep. That was about an hour into a six-hour trip at the present speed, which Sean-Guy expected to maintain. It was just over 748 kilometers to Stanstead. He knew there was much to think about during the remainder of the road-trip and that much of it had very little to do with the hope of finding Marek still on this side of the border.

Two and a half hours later, well past Toronto, heading towards Montreal, Sean-Guy's Black-berry buzzed. He took it out and saw that it was Stuart calling. He plugged in a headset and answered quietly, hoping not to awaken Angela. Glancing quickly toward her he saw that she had apparently been awake for awhile and was gazing at him with a pleased expression. Holding a finger to his lips, signaling that she should not speak, he turned his attention to Stuart.

"We have arrested two individuals, one in Richmond Hill and one in Oshawa, both after they took possession of bags from lockers the sniffer dogs signaled on for explosives. Explosives Disposal teams have confirmed bombs inside all the bags, pictures have been taken; the bombs are disarmed and safely detonated. Cell phones as expected for the triggering devices. But of course, we have no way of knowing if these are all the bombs accounted for. Neither of the individuals will talk to us. I only know they do not appear to be Afghans. They are not carrying any identification and we don't know yet how they got to the terminals."

Sean-Guy considered the news briefly and suggested, "I think it's best to transport them both independently to Mississauga and put them into separate interview rooms. Don't let them see each other in case they are connected. Have George Brown and Darya break away from the interrogation of the Afghans and come back to the office to begin questioning of the new suspects. Charge them, of course with the usual terrorist related charges and detain them for as long as needed. Get search warrants as soon as you can get information about their places of residence. Try and get them to break in the same way Everet and Hari are working." Sean-Guy listened as Stuart made a couple of suggestions about the pending interviews and then said, "I'll trust you to push appropriate buttons just as long as Darya is able to try and listen to whatever they might say in another language. Hopefully, it will be in her repertoire. I might be gone a couple of days so please keep me and the Director updated." Sean-Guy ended the conversation before Stuart could ask where he was or what he was up to. Glancing at the dash, Sean-Guy saw a need for gasoline soon. It was also a good time to stop for a short meal break, short because he was anxious to get

Ron Stotyn

to Stanstead as soon as possible. His GPS indicated a ramp ahead leading into Cornwall, where he was sure to find what was needed.

Looking at Angela, he could see considerable curiosity welling up. He tried to put a damper on that by saying, "You didn't hear any of that, Okay? Secrecy is a part of my life always. Some things I cannot reveal to you ever and some things maybe not until they have played out." Angela blinked, though not indicating surprise but rather just a hint of disappointment and perhaps, Sean-Guy thought, *a willingness to understand.* Still, he could not yet be certain she would comply. He thought, *She is a consummate investigative reporter, and unfortunately for me, rather good at it. I am unable to fault her for that.*

An hour later, back on the road after just a 20-minute break for freshening, a bite to eat and a fuel-up, Sean-Guy switched his radio frequency to that of the Highway Division of the Quebec Provincial Police to request a couple of cruisers to clear a path for him through Montreal. He needed to maintain a high rate of speed as safely as possible through the city so he could bear south toward Stanstead. He estimated they would arrive in Stanstead about 7:30 PM. Where he had come from and where he was soon to arrive was in the same time zone. There had been no time to arrange any accommodation for him and Angela at a motel or hotel, so he decided reluctantly to impose upon his parent's hospitality. He knew anyway that his mother would be disappointed if he didn't stay in his own former bedroom. She would be surprised and then welcoming to Angela, and he was sure, ready to make some assumptions. And so it was.

Shortly past 7:30 PM Sean-Guy pulled the Tahoe up to the front of the modest Quebec style farmhouse, a home in his family tree now over 100 years old, just down the street from their parish church, Presbytere Sacré Coeur on Rte Maple. As Sean-Guy waited for Angela to pull herself together, he had said he was going to stop at his parents, he saw a familiar movement at the front window as his mother looked to see who had arrived. He knew it would be only moments for her to appear at the open front door. He and Angela walked up the front steps and arrived just as the front door opened. He decided not to delay the inevitable so he said a bit haltingly for his normal character

"Maman…This is Angela…We have discovered each other." His father appeared behind, looked at him and murmured "So…"

{16.5}
Rue Church, south of Rue Phelps, approaching 6 PM, Thursday April 13: Rock Island QC

The previous day, Wednesday, had been spent with Sean-Guy showing Angela around his home town and environs. Tuesday night had been spent in separate rooms; one absolutely did not sleep with an unmarried woman in his Maman's house. The truth at the moment was, of course, that his attention was rather distracted, something he could not hide from Angela, due to his focus on Marek. She did not ask, but knew something connected to his work was forcing a deep center of attention that was not her. She had watched as Sean-Guy's eyes kept shifting as they drove and walked; observing every detail around. Surprisingly, Angela had decided fairly quickly that she was not upset to be partly ignored; she understood at some level that her relationship with Sean-Guy had the potential to be tumultuous. That would be a difficulty but she resolved to avoid letting that interfere with her growing affection, love really, for this enigmatic man.

As the day had progressed, she had allowed her thoughts to entertain the idea that she might one day become Madame O'Dwyer-Lariviere, the younger. Sean-Guy's mother was a wonderful woman she had quickly realized, a mother who loved her son unreservedly, a mother who could not but want the best for him. At the same time, she was a spirited Irish woman, quick to say her mind, demanding to know why Angela had decided she loved her son. That had not occurred the night of their arrival, but she could see in the eyes of Sean-Guy's mother that she was waiting a bit only out of a sense of propriety. The question came before breakfast while Sean-Guy was showering after an early morning run. She had poured out her heart and was immediately enveloped in the arms of her to be hoped future mother-in-law. It was a warm welcome for Angela, who outside her own mother had never felt included despite several earlier attempted and failed relationships, none of which had led to marriage.

Ron Stotyn

Now this afternoon, Thursday, Angela, had contentedly walked with Sean-Guy, first along Rue Phelps and then south on Rue Church toward the Canadian Border Crossing Station. For the past hour they had been sitting on a bench nearby, with a clear view of the Haskell Library, which she now knew from Sean-Guy's commentary the previous day, straddled the border with the U.S. Sean-Guy appeared to have totally forgotten that she was present. His gaze was that of an active and alert sentry. Every person passing by was getting careful scrutiny. Every person entering or leaving the library from its US side, the front entry, was the subject of an obdurate inspection. When Angela attempted a question about what was concerning him, Sean-Guy had grunted in a distracted manner, "Nothing for your concern." She knew instinctively that something important was at the core of Sean-Guy's tightly controlled behavior.

As the time approached 6 PM, she could feel Sean-Guy's body take on a steel spring-like quality. He was coiled as a snake might be coiled ready to strike. He was fixed on a small group of people who had just exited the library opposite. As the group split up, some going to the U.S. border station and others proceeding along Church Street in Derby Line, Sean-Guy rose and stepped quickly toward the Canadian barrier, where he stopped unchallenged by the CBSA officers, who had already seen his military identification and those that designated him as Chief Investigator of the CAS. He was unable to cross; his jurisdiction ended at that line.

Across the line mere yards away, Sean-Guy could see the subject of his investigation. Now clean-shaven and well groomed, Marek Kafirov, was moving toward a parked car beyond the American barrier. Then, without apparent explanation, Marek stopped, impelled by an unusual sensation that he was being watched, stood still for a moment and then turned to look behind. His eyes met the slate gray eyes belonging to Sean-Guy; he immediately recognized that he had barely escaped arrest by the man he'd met only twice before. Breaking the gaze, Marek made a very slight sardonic nod, turned back to the car, got in and was driven off. Sean-Guy remained fixed for a moment; his only thought, *You and I are destined to meet one more time.*

{Postscript}

Post-Event Evaluation Report

Prepared for: Canadian Anti-Terrorist Agency; Leif Isaksson, Director

Prepared by: Jean Pierre René Girau, Ph.D., Major (Ret)

Date: May 1, 20xx

Security Classification: Secret

Overview :

In April of the current year, agents of the CAS became involved in a hunt for a suspected terrorist of Chechen origin, known variously as Malik Bisliev (birth name), Marek Kafirov (assumed name) and Borz (nickname). This individual has been linked to the making and distribution of bombs and to the development of a plot to target various trains and stations within the Go Train System serving Toronto and surrounding region. It is believed this individual was responsible for bombs planted in the Downtown Transit Station on John Street in Burlington ON which exploded on April 11 and which caused the deaths of 10 innocents and 2 presumed terrorists.

This individual came to the attention of the CAS from information developed by CAS Chief Investigator Joseph Dawson Girard Sean-Guy O'Dwyer-Lariviere, Major CFIB. Major O'Dwyer-Lariviere reported that he had met Bisliev when Bisliev was a young teen studying English as a Second Language at Stanstead College, Stanstead QC approximately ten years ago on a student visa. Major O'Dwyer-Lariviere subsequently saw the individual recently, while attending a dinner at the subject's place of employment, Samovar House, Toronto ON. O'Dwyer-Lariviere and his CAS Ottawa team, accompanied by agents of the CAS Toronto Office, were at that point

Ron Stotyn

engaged in surveillance of an Afghani, known as Omid Faresh, suspected as a potential terrorist.

The combined teams augmented by loaned agents of the O.P.P., RCMP, and the CBSA using surveillance techniques developed information that led to scrutiny of two additional Afghanis known as Gul-Bashra Mohamed and Daoud Tariq. On several occasions, Bisliev/Kafirov was followed to a former food preparation plant located in Mississauga near Toronto Pearson International Airport. That location was subsequently identified as a place of interest when an O.P.P. Electronic Fraud Unit investigation revealed it was the delivery point for a variety of chemicals and supplies believed useful for bomb making.

The subject Bisliev/Kafirov made and delivered a video threat to media within the province of Ontario. The person in the video was identified as the subject of interest following use of facial recognition software. Warrants were obtained and searches were made of the subject's place of employment, residence and of the light industrial condo space in Mississauga. Evidence was collected that confirmed explosive residues at the latter location. A list of names discovered at the subject's residence connected him to the three Afghani suspects. Maps discovered at the residence led to the reasonable conclusion that the Go Train System was the target of a terrorist plot involving explosive devices.

Following the search of the former industrial food location, CAS determined that their suspect had successfully escaped the surveillance efforts. With the suspect missing, a closer watch was placed on the three Afghani suspects. They were observed removing a variety of bags and containers from storage lockers in Barrie ON. A bomb sniffing dog, brought to that location revealed additional bags believed to contain explosive devices. The three Afghanis were subsequently arrested when they returned to remove the additional bags from the storage lockers. Warrant executed search found that the originally collected bags also contained explosive devices.

A Saturday morning explosion April 11 in Burlington ON at the Downtown Terminal, determined by the O.P.P. Explosives Removal Unit to be the result of several explosive devises, led the Chief Investigator to order the use of Bomb Sniffer dogs to search storage lockers at several additional terminals within the Go Train System. Locations to be searched were identified from GPS records from a rental van discovered abandoned in Scarborough ON. The GPS database was opened after evidence of explosive residues were found in the van. The records showed the van made stops at the Downtown Terminal in Burlington, the Barrie Terminal, The Richmond Hill Go Train Terminal and the Oshawa Greyhound Bus Terminal. Surveillance at these locations resulted in the arrest of two Chechens at the Oshawa Greyhound Bus Terminal. Seized packages revealed explosive devices inside each. These individuals known as Muhammad Yamadayev and Abdul Saidullayev were arrested and held for questioning.

Two other names from the list found at the Bisliev/Kafirov residence; Fathi, and Edris, last names unknown, may possibly be the names of human remains found at the Burlington explosion site. DNA tests revealed that two of a total of 12 dead were likely from Chechnya. The two were conclusively put at the center of the explosion adjacent to lockers that sustained the most damage, thus likely used for storage of explosive devices. The site was declared a place of terrorist action.

CAS Chief Investigator O'Dwyer-Lariviere declared at the end of the active investigation that Malik Bisliev aka Marek Kafirov is a wanted Terrorist, presumed at large and dangerous. Five individuals as named above are charged with possession of weapons of terror and destruction, plotting to commit acts of terrorism, and murder. Other charges may be forthcoming.

Goals and objectives:
The CAS is charged with national responsibility for investigation of any and all indication of terrorist activity within the borders of Canada, bringing any and all suspected terrorists to justice, and providing the justice system with solid evidence of terrorist crimes committed against the sovereign nation of Canada. The agency is further charged with taking action as required within the purview of all relevant laws of Canada.

In the case which is the subject of the current review, The CAS sought the cooperation of several law enforcement agencies of Ontario and of Canada: O.P.P., Toronto Department of Public Safety, RCMP, and CBSA. CAS took the lead and supervised all aspects of the investigation of Malik Bisliev/Marek Kafirov aka Borz. The CAS charged itself with discovering the extent and participation in a scheme believed to target the Go Train System serving the population of the Toronto Region. The critical goal was to frustrate the attempt to do terroristic harm to the system and its customers.

Analysis of outcomes:
Despite that 12 persons died in an explosion at the Downtown Terminal in Burlington ON and that 10 were likely innocent victims, it may well be said that the CAS was instrumental in preventing an event of considerable violence against Canadians. It is estimated that the quantity of explosive devices recovered and safely disposed of, was sufficient to create havoc and unimaginable destruction had they been successfully deployed and activated by the terrorists arrested in connection with the plot.

The details of the plot are largely unknown. Questioning of the five persons arrested revealed only the specifics of the participation by each of the individuals. A tightly organized cell system meant that only each individual knew requirements of their own participation. None of the five individuals admitted to knowing the name of their coordinator. None admit to having any means of contacting their coordinator. Communication was, as far as can be determined, one way from the coordinator to each individual. Face to face meetings were limited to cell leaders only with the coordinator, and then only two or three at each meeting. None of the individuals admitted to knowing any cell leader beyond those at the same meetings. None revealed any other participants beyond themselves.

The CAS Chief Investigator declares that the case remains unresolved and, thus, ongoing.

Analysis of the performance shown on critical tasks:

Agents assigned to the Toronto Region of the CAS all carried out tasks related to this case with expediency.

Stuart McIntyre, Lead Investigator of the Toronto Region Office demonstrated appropriate leadership qualities and conducted critical investigational tasks efficiently.

George Brown, Assistant Investigator and Darya Barzaryan, Investigator conducted surveillance and observational tasks expertly, maintaining their cover appropriately. Ms. Barzaryan's linguistic abilities were valuable during the surveillance of the three Afghani suspects.

Agents assigned to the Ottawa HQ office of the CAS all carried out tasks associated with the case appropriately with one or two exceptions.

Major General Leif Isaksson, Director of the CAS, carried out supervisory tasks associated with the case expertly, in particular keeping the Minister of Defense appropriately informed at every critical stage.

Ron Stotyn

Major Sean-Guy O'Dwyer-Lariviere carried out supervisory tasks on his team members as should be expected, delegating responsibilities as appropriate to the skills of each agent. His activities in the ongoing investigation of the case sometimes left something to be desired. (See Recommendations below.)

Ryan McLeod, Assistant Chief Investigator, performed his duties very well, accepting delegated responsibilities expertly and without complaint.

Everet Tailfeathers, Specialist Investigator, demonstrated exceptional observational ability and insight when required.

Hari Hanoomansingh, Specialist Investigator, demonstrated exceptional command of several languages used by terrorist suspects in this case. His ability to translate proved valuable as the case developed.

Betty-Anne Grabler, Senior Analyst of the CAS, was instrumental in preparing summaries of crucial information derived from Internet and other searches. (Note: The present reviewer was contracted to work with Mrs. Grabler in the preparation of general psychological profiles of Afghan and Chechen terrorists.)

Summary:
The case is essentially concluded, based on the amount and quality of information developed. Five individuals were arrested and charged with crimes against Canada including the murder of Canadian Citizens in a terrorist action. The terrorist plot, believed created by Malik Bisliev/Marek Kafirov, was in most respects successfully prevented by the actions taken by both sets of agents from Ottawa and Mississauga. The explosion at the Downtown Terminal in Burlington, though obviously the result of terrorist made bombs, was apparently an accident of a bizarre character rather than a direct detonation of any of the

terrorist, under arrest. The misdialing of a phone number by the lone survivor of the Burlington explosion caused the detonation of a device attached to one of the bomb packages placed in a storage locker at that location. Nevertheless, the resulting explosion is part and parcel of the intent of the terrorist plot, thus the charges of murder. That the principal suspect remains at large is good reason to consider that the case remains open and ongoing.

Recommendations:

All the agents, save the Chief Investigator should be commended for their professional attention to the demands of the case. Chief Investigator O'Dwyer-Lariviere should be commended for achieving critical results as a result of the application of his well-known and phenomenal memory; however, he must at the same time be reminded that any propensity to act independently is not conducive to the best outcomes of any investigation.

###

Ron Stotyn

{<u>Author's Notes</u>}

Beginning this first novel was intimidating. I have been both a broadcast journalist and a communications professor. I began in Canadian radio in 1970 as a part-time stringer getting paid per story used. Later I wrote news for radio and television. Still later I began teaching broadcasting, mass media, and broadcast news, etc. at colleges based in the Midwest and South of the USA. At the same time I provided management oversight and guidance to volunteers at a variety of college radio stations in the USA.

Writing was a big part of both my professions. For perhaps twenty years or more, I thought I had a book or two in me; however it was hard to imagine writing fiction. Everyday duties got in the way. But my successful large historical PhD dissertation prompted me to give it a try. That dissertation maybe ought to be published but first I think Sean-Guy needs another appearance. I like Sean-Guy and I can see more troubles for him working against terrorists.

The idea for this novel was partly inspired by the Canadian Broadcasting Corporation (CBC) series 'The Border'. I liked the idea of an agency tasked for special Canadian defense system responsibility. My creation, the Canadian Anti-terrorism Service is entirely imagined, meant to be seen as part of the Canadian Department of National Defense network that includes such units as the Canadian Forces Intelligence Branch, the Canadian Special Operations Regiment, and the Canadian Special Operations Forces Command, each of which have as part of their mandate the responsibility to protect Canada, its friends and allies against those who would threaten our democratic lifestyle.

I was further inspired when I learned that the very distinguished Canadian inventor, entrepreneur, soldier, and renowned spymaster Sir William Stephenson CC, MC, DFC, was appointed the first commander of the Canadian Forces Intelligence Branch. Stephenson known as Intrepid during WW2, was instrumental in setting up under the aegis of British Security Coordination (BSC) Camp X in Whitby, ON which ultimately trained members of ISO, OSS, FBI, RCMP, USN, U.S. Military Intelligence services, and the United States Office of War Information, among them five future directors of what would eventually become the American Central Intelligence Agency. That suggested a rich background for a fictionalized anti-terrorism organization in Canada.

I have shamelessly borrowed from reality, sometimes parts of real names, and personal histories for molding my characters. Essentially all my characters are made up. I have mentioned some real individuals where they provide realistic background. Along with some real geographic location names, and church names; I do not intend to demean in any way. I did invent the name of a mosque in Mount Pleasant ON but it does not exist in the real world. Names of hotels, restaurants and other businesses used are a mix of real and imagined. The real ones are all known to be fine establishments. Those imagined were made to create a particular scenario. All weapons mentioned in the story are the real thing. Most are available in the Canadian Forces armament supplies and the pistols mentioned can be purchased in Canada, though for many years under very strict registration laws.

In the preface that begins the novel I provide a fictitious Order in Council, an example of how such an agency might come into force under the parliamentary style of Canada. Any error in the style and wording of this example is the fault of the author.

Sean-Guy, portrayed as a graduate of Stanstead College, Stanstead QC, Royal Military College (RMC), Kingston ON, and The University of Ottawa, in Ottawa ON is not based on any one identifiable person. His name, Joseph Dawson Girard Sean-Guy O'Dwyer-Lariviere, defines him as a hybrid Irish-French Quebecois. I hope the following will not be too confusing. To comprehend his mouthful of names; the pattern represents partly Quebecois tradition and partly modern Quebec's Bill 101 language law requirements. His first given name does comport with the Quebec Roman Catholic custom for naming male children. His given second name is the middle name of my own maternal grandfather, who was not Irish. This small personal arrogance uses the Quebecois tradition representing the godfather of the child. The third given name in Quebec culture is typically that of the Father. Then according to custom the child is finally given his own common name, by which he or she is normally called. In this case I bow to the idea of an Irish mother (first part) and a Quebecois father (last part) seen in the hyphenated name of Sean-Guy and of course in the hyphenated surname.

Ron Stotyn

The last hyphenated name is not realistic because the character is too old to be subject to Quebec's language law. There is evidence of Irish families in the Stanstead QC area, where my character was born and raised. For example, cemetery records from the Beebe Plain cemetery reveal the names: O'Donnell, O'Dowd and O'Leary. Beebe is one of three towns that merged to create Stanstead. Names such as McClary are seen at the Cassville Cemetery near Stanstead. Fitzgerald and Dwyer are seen in the Crystal Lake Cemetery at Stanstead. By the way, the mother's last name O'Dwyer has the meaning "Black" which implies the Black Irish physiognomy that I gave the character. As far as I know there is no-one by this particular name in Quebec.

The terrorist cell leader Malik Bisliev, aka Marek Kafirov, aka Borz is named from my possibly inadequate research of Chechen naming conventions. The name Malik means 'possessor', which is significant if thought of in terms of Chechen Wahhabist ideology. The aka Marek Kafirov and the birth name are entirely imaginary and do not specifically represent any individual living or dead The last name in the form Kafirov, however, is how the Chechen Mujahedeen referred to assassinated former president Ahmad Kadirov (Kadyrov). Kadirov was hated for being a collaborationist of the Russians. The nickname Borz means 'wolf' which may also be significant in terms of the long history of Chechen conflict.

I made Marek a chemical engineer and graduate of the University of Engineering and Technology, located in Peshawar, Pakistan. I urge that no one should think that this fine institution is knowingly, or in any way deliberately engaged in the training of terrorists. I merely imagined an educational track to round out my character. Similarly his one year of ESL training at Stanstead College is not meant to impugn the very fine reputation of that preparatory institution in Stanstead QC.

I have identified Canada's renowned Royal Military College (RMC), the University of Ottawa, Winnipeg Bible College, The University of Winnipeg, The University of Manitoba in Winnipeg MB, The University of Regina, Lethbridge Community College, University of Calgary, Banff School of Fine Arts/Banff Centre, and the University of Alberta in Edmonton, AB as institutions where some of my good guy characters achieved various educational degrees. No-one should believe that these institutions would be satisfied to claim alumni with the shortcomings I have given to my characters. Each academic institution does their best very successfully to turn out worthy individuals.

Similarly I associated characters with various Canadian Forces Regiments and Battalions: such as CF Intelligence Branch, Canadian Special Operations Forces Command, 5e Régiment d'artillerie légère du Canada, Royal Canadian Horse Artillery, 1st Battalion Princess Patricia Canadian Light Infantry (PPCLI), 1st Battalion The Royal Canadian Regiment, The Cameron Highlanders of Ottawa, and the Queen's Own Rifles of Canada to add background. There are also mentions of various Police organizations: École nationale de police du Quebec, Surété du Quebec, Ontario Provincial Police, Canadian Security Intelligence Service, Canada Border Services Agency and the RCMP. All have their own deserved reputation in Canadian history. My characters of military or police backgrounds, with various foibles should not be considered a real product of these fine military and police agencies.

I have been influenced by names and places from my own growing up in Canada for some characters. I recall learning about Gimli MB as a key population of Icelandic heritage in Canada. From that came the naming of Leif Isaksson, Brig. Gen (ret.) commander of the CAS. His names are typical of the patrimony of the Icelandic culture as far as I know. I hope I got it right.

I worked in Lethbridge AB many, many years ago at one of the older pharmacies there. I became acquainted with two very fine artists of First Nation bands in the area. Both were customers at the pharmacy. Everett Soop, journalist, activist, satirist and very witty cartoonist, a Blackfoot tribe member in the Kainai Nation and Gerald Tailfeathers, painter and sculptor, a Blood tribe member of the Kainai Nation from Standoff AB, achieved considerable renown as artists. Both died much too young. I am richer for having known these men. I was especially saddened to learn that Everett died after nearly forty years a victim of muscular dystrophy. From those memories I produced the name of Everet Tailfeathers, CAS team-member, former cowboy, artist and sharpshooter.

As a broadcast journalist later in Lethbridge I became quite familiar with the McIntyre Ranch at Magrath AB. That ranch has been

Ron Stotyn

owned by the Thrall family of Lethbridge since 1947; I have some familiarity and acquaintance with that family. My character Stuart McIntyre, lead investigator for the Toronto unit of the CAS is named from that connection. He is otherwise not connected with the ranch; one of Canada's largest; encompassing some 87 sections of land. A section is a mile square made up of 640 acres. That means nearly 56 thousand acres or nearly 23 thousand hectares. Almost all the land is preserved in native condition suitable for grazing.

There is another connection to Southern Alberta. Fort MacLeod is a historic site where the North West Mounted Police, forerunners of the RCMP, built a fort. The town is named in honor of Col. James MacLeod, founding commander of the NWMP. My character Ryan McLeod and his RCMP connection is named, with a slight spelling change for the fort and town.

My journalistic career led me to mention a real individual formerly employed by the Canadian Broadcasting Corporation (CBC). Claire Martin, a meteorologist for CBC at its Vancouver weather center and later Toronto, was once a colleague of one of my news room mentors, Bill Matheson of CJOC Lethbridge, later the senior weather anchor at CITV-TV in Edmonton AB. I had the pleasure of meeting Claire on at least two occasions. The CBC figures in one other character. My CAS Linguist, a character named Hari Hanoomansingh, is inspired by a man I have never met but whom I think is a very fine and accomplished television journalist working for the CBC. Ian Hanomansing was born in Trinidad and Tobago, but grew up in New Brunswick. My character was born in India's northern state of Jammu and Kashmir, which is bordered on the North and East by the Peoples Republic of China and on the west and Northwest by the Pakistani administered territories of Azad Kashmir and Gilgit-Baltistan. His last name ending in 'singh' conveys a Sikh heritage which is consistent with the history of the state of Jammu and Kashmir, which currently is mostly Muslim and disputed by Pakistan, India, and China.

My mother-in-law was born into a Canadian Mennonite family in a very small southern Manitoba community. Her maiden name was Unger. So, as homage, that's the maiden name of my character Betty Anne (Unger) Grabler, the CAS Senior Analyst and Statistician for the

CAS in Ottawa. I have placed her birth location in Rosenort MB, a real largely Mennonite community about 65 Km south of Winnipeg.

My research into the conflicts between Russia and Chechnya, led me to an excellent academic study about the adoption of suicide terrorism by very militant Wahhabist Muslims of Chechnya. I am indebted to the study conducted by Anne Speckhard and Khapta Akhmedova (2006) The New Chechen Jihad: Militant Wahhabism as a Radical Movement and a Source of Suicide Terrorism in Post-War Chechen Society, Democracy and Security, 2:1, 103-155. It should be noted that outside Chechnya, Wahhabism is not generally a militant or even violent form of Islam. These authors show very clearly how conditions in war torn Chechnya contributed to the evolution of Wahhabism to violence and militant behavior in that country mainly. Their study also reveals much about how suicide terrorism became a means of taking revenge on perceived enemies. My understanding of terrorism from a psychopathological perspective was enabled by the following papers. Adrian Feeney (2003) Dangerous Severe Personality Disorder, Advances in Psychiatric Treatment 9:349-358; Sam Vakin (2001) Narcissists, Group Behavior, and Terrorism in The Idler: 19 December; and Raymond H. Hamden, Psychology of Terrorists: 4 Types. Terrorist Types and Psychological Characteristics. www.all-about-psychology.com/support-files/psychology-of-terrorists.pdf accessed April 6, 2010. If I have misunderstood any of this information it is probably because I have insufficient background in the field.

In Chapter 5, Marek reflecting about the construction of his bombs includes the preparation of PETN aka Penta. I have deliberately tried to obfuscate the description of the process, but I have to note that any student of chemistry can figure out the exact process based on information gleaned from the Internet. I do not in any way recommend that anyone attempt to do so. The results could easily be disastrous and very likely highly illegal.

My thanks are paid to Fr. John G. Feltz, Psy.D., D.Min.; pastor of St. Ann Parish in Milton VT and St. Luke's in Fairfax VT. Fr. John, who is also a Colonel Chaplain in the VT National Guard, very kindly advised me on matters of RC Church Polity regarding Divorce and the Sacraments as well as critique of sections where several of my characters

Ron Stotyn

discussed relevant background of certain personality disorders preparatory to their creation of a general profile about Chechen and Afghan terrorists.

Thanks is due as well to Elizabeth Ann Gillespie, retired technical writer and technical editor, who painstakingly read every jot and tittle of the novel, pointing out many grammatical and punctuation errors that I created. Without her careful work, the quality of the writing would be much less believable.

Finally I need to acknowledge the contributions of my son Shaun, who contributed the graphics work on the front cover, and who read multiple drafts of my manuscript offering very useful criticism.

When all is said and done, the end result and any problems contained within are my responsibility.

Connect with Ron Stotyn online:
Twitter: http://twitter.com/conquistadoc
Facebook: http://www.facebook.com/ron.stotyn
Smashwords author page:
http://www.smashwords.com/profile/view/conquistadoc
LinkedIn: http://www.linkedin.com/in/ronstotyn
Blog: http://northof49blog.com

{Glossary}

al Qae'da: alternatively spelled Al-Qaida or Al-Qaeda and sometimes Al-Qa'ida; an Islamist group founded between August 1988 and late 1989/early 1990. It operates as a network: both a multinational, stateless arm and a fundamentalist Sunni movement calling for global jihad. Activities may involve members of the movement who have taken a pledge of loyalty to Osama bin Laden, or more numerous "al-Qaeda-linked" individuals trained in Afghanistan or Sudan, but not having taken any pledge. In recent years with the killing of key leaders including bin Laden, its effectiveness may be in doubt.

Baseyev: Shamil Salmanovich Baseyev, considered one of the most important Chechen terrorist leaders, mastermind of some of the most infamous terrorist acts such as the Beslan School hostage taking. AKA Emir Abdallah Shamil Abu-Idris.

BMOQ: Canadian Forces Basic Military Officer Qualification program.

CEGEP: Collège d'enseignement général et professionnel, "College of General and Vocational Education".

CFB: Canadian Forces Base as in CFB Petawawa.

CFIB: Canadian Forces Intelligence Branch

Croix de Bravouredes Policiers: loosely translated as Police Bravery Cross.

CSIS: Canadian Security Intelligence Service, the internal security agency of the Canadian government responsible for collecting, analyzing, reporting and disseminating intelligence on threats to Canada's national security, and conducting operations, covert and overt, within Canada and abroad. This role was formerly conducted by the RCMP Security Service.

CSOFC: Canadian Special Operations Forces Command

DND: Canada's Department of National Defense.

École nationale de police du Quebec: Quebec National Police Academy.

ESL: English as a Second Language.

FLQ: Front de libération du Québec, a violent Marxist group, responsible for over 160 violent incidents which killed eight people and

Ron Stotyn

injured many more, including the bombing of the Montreal Stock Exchange in 1969. These attacks culminated in 1970 with what is known as the October Crisis, in which British Trade Commissioner James Cross was kidnapped and Quebec Labour Minister Pierre Laporte was murdered. Founded in the early 1960s, it supported the Quebec sovereignty movement.

Gendarmerie Royale Du Canada: the RCMP or Royal Canadian Mounted Police.

IIPB: Islamist International Brigade established by Baseyev and al-Khattab

Jahilayya: An Islamic concept of ignorance of divine guidance, or the state of ignorance of the guidance from God, or Days of Ignorance referring to the condition Arabs found themselves in pre-Islamic Arabia: by extension those who do not follow Islam or the Qur'an.

KavKaz: This name appears as an identification of a training center in an article published by Speckhard, Anne & Akhmedova, Khapta "The New Chechen Jihad: Militant Wahhabism as a Radical Movement and a Source of Suicide Terrorism in Post-War Chechen Society" Democracy & Security 2:1-53, 2006. The founder of the camp is not identified though the leader of the camp is, as Al-Khattab. Baseyev, Ibn Al-Khattab, and others are sometimes reputed to have set up terrorist training camps of this nature. Another real organization known as The KavKaz Center (KC, literally Caucasus center) exists as a private Internet publication claiming to be a Chechen internet agency which is independent, international and Islamic that does not represent any state structures or viewpoints. The mission is to report events related to Chechnya and provide international news agencies with newsletters, background information and assistance in making independent journalistic work in Caucasus.

Kainai Nation: Káínawa, or Blood Tribe, a First Nation of Southern Alberta.

Métis: The Métis people came about from marriages of Cree, Ojibway, Algonquin, Saulteaux, Menominee, Mi'kmaq, Maliseet, and other First Nations to Europeans, mainly French. Along with the First

Nations and Inuit, the Métis are one of three officially recognized Aboriginal peoples in Canada.

Mirvish Village: an area of Toronto bordering on Bloor Street, named for "Honest" Ed Mirvish, Entrepreneur and Impresario.

OPP: Ontario Provincial Police, largest deployed force in Ontario and believed to be the second largest in Canada. The service provides policing services throughout the province in areas lacking local police forces. It also provides specialized support to smaller municipal police forces, investigates province-wide and cross-jurisdictional crimes, patrols provincial highways (including Ontario's 400-Series Highways) and is responsible for many of the waterways in the province.

Paroisse Notre-Dame-De-L'Isle: Our Lady of the Island Parish, a real Roman Catholic church in Hull, QC.

PETN: Pentaerythritol tetranitrate.

Poutine: A popular Quebecois food confection consisting of French Fries on a bed of savory beef gravy, topped with cottage cheese, often with more gravy over the top.

PPCLI: Princess Patricia Canadian Light Infantry.

Presbytere Sacre-Coeur De Stanstead: Presbytery of the Sacred Heart of Stanstead, a real Roman Catholic church in Stanstead QC.

PTSD: Post Traumatic Stress Disorder.

RCMP/GRC: Royal Canadian Mounted Police, Canada's national police agency.

RMC: Royal Military College.

RSM: Regimental Sergeant Major, an appointment position in the Canadian Forces, normally held by a non-commissioned officer at the rank of Warrant Officer or above.

Salafi jihad: a school of thought of Salafi Muslims who support violent jihad.

Saskatoon Jelly: made of a fruit from a shrub native to the southern Yukon and Northwest Territories, the Canadian prairies and the northern plains of the United States, member of the rose family with the common names serviceberry, saskatoon, Juneberry, shadberry, sugar pear and Indian pear. They look like Blueberries but are not related.

Ron Stotyn

Surété du Quebec: Sometimes regarded as the Quebec Provincial Police, but more properly understood as Quebec Security or Quebec Safety.

TD Bank: Formerly the Toronto-Dominion Bank, formed by a merger of the Dominion Bank of Canada and the Bank of Toronto.

Wahhabism: Founded by Islamic reformist Shaykh al-Islam Muhammad ibn 'Abd Al-Wahhab ibn Sulayman ibn 'Ali ibn Muhammad ibn Ahmad ibn Rashid al-Tamimi, during the 1700's. His goal was to return Islam to purity with a strict interpretation of the Quran. In Chechnya, this form of Islam turned to violence and terrorism.